GEOFFREY CHAUCER was born c. 1343 in London. The son of a prosperous and well-connected vintner, he was in the service of the King's court from youth. He was probably educated at the Inns of Court in law and finance, as well as letters. Widely read, he was one of the most learned men of his time, and as soldier, public official, and court poet, he came in contact with many important figures. Chaucer was sent on diplomatic missions to Italy at least twice, where he was influenced by the works of Dante, Petrarch, and Boccaccio. His *Troilus and Criseyde*, completed c. 1386, is an adaptation of Boccaccio's romance *Il Filostrato*. Chaucer worked on *The Canterbury Tales* during the last fifteen years of his life. He died in 1400 and was buried in Westminster Abbey; about his grave grew "the Poets' Corner."

DONALD R. HOWARD is Donovan Professor of English at The Johns Hopkins University. He was a Fulbright fellow to Italy in 1959–60, an American Counsel of Learned Societies fellow in 1963–64, and a Guggenheim fellow in 1969–70. He is author of *The Three Temptations: Medieval Man in Search of the World* (1966), and editor of the Signet Classic edition of *The Canterbury Tales*. His most recent book is *The Idea of the Canterbury Tales* (1976).

JAMES DEAN was born in 1943 and received his Ph.D. from The Johns Hopkins University in 1971. Since 1972, he has been Assistant Professor of English at Colgate University. He previously assisted Donald R. Howard with the Signet Classic edition of *The Canterbury Tales: A Selection*.

Geoffrey Chaucer

Troilus and Criseyde
and Selected Short Poems

EDITED BY
Donald R. Howard
AND
James Dean

The Signet Classic Poetry Series

A SIGNET CLASSIC
NEW AMERICAN LIBRARY
TIMES MIRROR
NEW YORK AND SCARBOROUGH, ONTARIO
THE NEW ENGLISH LIBRARY LIMITED, LONDON

For E. T. Donaldson

PR
1895
176

74784

NAL BOOKS ARE ALSO AVAILABLE AT DISCOUNTS IN BULK QUANTITY
FOR INDUSTRIAL OR SALES-PROMOTIONAL USE. FOR DETAILS,
WRITE TO PREMIUM MARKETING DIVISION, NEW AMERICAN LIBRARY, INC.,
1301 AVENUE OF THE AMERICAS, NEW YORK, NEW YORK 10019.

Copyright © 1976 by Donald R. Howard and James Dean

Library of Congress Catalog Card Number: 76—14707

SIGNET CLASSIC TRADEMARK REG. U.S. PAT. OFF. AND FOREIGN COUNTRIES
REGISTERED TRADEMARK—MARCA REGISTRADA
HECHO EN CHICAGO, U.S.A.

SIGNET, SIGNET CLASSICS, MENTOR, PLUME
and MERIDIAN BOOKS
are published *in the United States* by The New American Library, Inc.,
1301 Avenue of the Americas, New York, New York 10019,
in Canada by The New American Library of Canada Limited,
81 Mack Avenue, Scarborough, 704, Ontario,
in the United Kingdom by The New English Library Limited,
Barnard's Inn, Holborn, London, E.C. 1, England

First Signet Printing, July, 1976

1 2 3 4 5 6 7 8 9

PRINTED IN THE UNITED STATES OF AMERICA

Contents

Introduction

Chaucer's *Troilus and Criseyde* is a medieval romance with a dramatic structure. It is often compared with a psychological novel or play, and the comparison, though anachronistic, is justified. The poem gives us the kind of experience which novels and plays give us—we seem to see episodes happen before our eyes, hear the characters talk, understand their thoughts, inner motives, and conflicts, feel the atmosphere of a war-torn city, a "smoky rain," a secret chamber, an emergency in the parliament. And it is the first experience of its kind—the first at least of such scope—in English literature. It was not to be rivaled until the drama of Shakespeare's day and the novels of the eighteenth and nineteenth centuries. From this point of view Chaucer *invented* those literary qualities which we now call "novelistic" or "dramatic." The *Troilus* is the first English work in which these qualities appear fully developed; its influence on later works is incalculable. "No one will ever gauge or measure English poetry," said Ezra Pound, "until they know how much of it, how full a gamut of its qualities, is already *there on the page* of Chaucer."

Although we know little about Chaucer's personal life or his habits of composition, we know a great deal about this "invention" of the *Troilus*.[1]

Chaucer was by profession a trained civil servant and diplomat. He was a child of about five when the Black Death

---

[1] It was an "invention," not a discovery—discoveries are lucky accidents or happenings which often seem to make no sense; inventions are the result of thought and planning, and once accomplished, they make all the sense in the world. "Invention" was the term medieval rhetoricians used to describe what we would call "getting an idea" and planning how to get that idea on paper. The rhetorician Geoffrey of Vinsauf compared the process to a builder's measuring out a house and planning its construction step by step; Chaucer embedded Geoffrey of Vinsauf's famous description in the *Troilus*, I.1065–1069.

—the great plague which depopulated England by more than a third—hit London in 1348–49; the memory of that, plus periodic recurrences of the plague, cast a shadow over his life, and over the life of his times—a shadow we can see in the gloomy, tragic side of *Troilus and Criseyde*. He probably knew French from childhood, and he was steeped in the courtly French poetry of his time, an influence we can see in the *Troilus* and in his short poems (those presented below on pp. 283–298 are nearly all based on French forms). In his twenties he evidently studied at the Inns of Court, where he would have been educated in law and commerce, as well as in rhetoric and letters. The rest of his public life was a series of government posts in England and diplomatic missions (some of them secret ones) abroad. He was under the patronage of John of Gaunt, third son to King Edward III and the most powerful baron of the realm, and he served three kings in his lifetime—Edward III, Richard II, and Henry IV. He therefore knew the life of the ruling class, which the *Troilus* depicts.

But the most important fact bearing on the *Troilus* is that in his capacity as a public official Chaucer was sent twice, possibly three times, to Italy, and so became acquainted with Italian literature. He was sent to Genoa at about the age of thirty, probably to negotiate with the powerful Genoese merchants for the use of an English port; during this trip he visited Florence. Five years later, in 1378, he was sent to Lombardy, probably on matters touching the English war with France. From these trips he returned, so it is usually assumed, with books by Dante, Boccaccio, possibly Petrarch. Among these must have been a copy of Boccaccio's *Il Filostrato*, written some forty years earlier; he seems also to have known a French translation of it. *Troilus and Criseyde* is an adaptation of the *Filostrato*. This fact is what enables us to understand Chaucer's conception of his poem: we can compare it with its original and see what he omitted, added, and changed.[2]

The big, important change, the one that dominates all others, is that he turned the book into a tragedy—even called it (in V.1786) a tragedy. Boccaccio's poem was not a tragedy but only a romance with an unhappy ending, a love story in

---

[2] The student who wishes to compare passages can find a table of correspondences between the *Filostrato* and the *Troilus* in F. N. Robinson (ed.), *The Works of Geoffrey Chaucer* (1957), p. 813. The translation of the *Filostrato* by Griffin and Myrick gives numbers of parts and stanzas as cited in this table.

which the lady admits the lover to her bed and then jilts him for another. (Boccaccio took his plot from some short sections of a twelfth-century French romance, the *Roman de Troie* by Benoit de Sainte-Maure, and from a Latin prose translation of it made over a hundred years later by a Sicilian, Guido delle Colonne.) In a preface, Boccaccio identified himself with Troilo and the lady with his own "poetical mistress," Maria d'Aquino: he intended his poem as a plea and admonition to his lady-love. Chaucer removed this personal element and made Troilus a romance hero: his fate—as his name suggests —is linked with the downfall of Troy, with his role as a

The Wheel of Fortune (adapted from a fifteenth-century manuscript painting)

warrior in one of history's decisive battles. Chaucer's stated subject was the "double sorrow of Troilus"—Troilus's initial sorrow in unrequited love, and his later sorrow when he has been betrayed. Chaucer viewed the unhappy ending not, as Boccaccio had, from a self-absorbed viewpoint but from a philosophical and religious one. At the end of Chaucer's poem Troilus seeks out death on the battlefield, and we see his soul rise to the edge of the universe, look down upon this "litel spot of erth," and laugh at the emptiness of human loves.

The tragedy is a particular kind of medieval tragedy, *de casibus* tragedy. The name comes from another work by Boccaccio, the *De casibus virorum illustrum* ("On the Falls of Famous Men"). Such tragedies compare the course of human life to the figure of the Wheel of Fortune (see p. viii). When men strive for such worldly things as fame, riches, power, or human love, they were said to climb upon the wheel of the "goddess" Fortune, a symbol of blind chance. As she turns the wheel, those who have climbed on it go up to prosperity, then fall into misery, defeat, or death. There is no reason behind this—it is not (as it became in later times) a punishment for faults, but just the way things are in this world, unpredictable and unfair. The image of Fortune's Wheel, often found in medieval art, teaches one lesson only: if you climb on the wheel you must be prepared for a disappointment. The only remedy against Fortune is not to *care* about the worldly gifts which Fortune offers.

This tragic, religio-philosophic conception is barely hinted at in Boccaccio's version; in Chaucer's it is developed into a philosophical search after the meaning of life. The characters themselves all discuss at various times Fortune, "false felicity," destiny. Much of their discourse is drawn from Boethius's *Consolation of Philosophy* (sixth century A.D.), one of the great books of the Middle Ages, which Chaucer himself translated into English about the time he was writing the *Troilus*. Although Boethius was a Christian, he was writing about the consolation which philosophy, as opposed to prayer or faith or mysticism, can offer to one who is miserable. His book is an imaginary dialogue between himself, in political exile, and "Dame Philosophy." His conclusion is that in the harmony of the universe all that happens, even when it seems a misfortune, is for the best; all events are overseen by God as if in a timeless present, and so from man's viewpoint God foreknows and predestines all. But one part of God's plan is that He has given to human beings free will in the moral sphere. We cannot choose what happens to us, which is in the hands of Fortune and part of universal necessity, but we *can* choose between right and wrong. Hence we can choose to "accept philosophically" the misfortunes which befall us—to make a virtue of necessity by exercising patience.

Chaucer introduces these concepts piecemeal in his poem, as if the characters, living before the time of Christ, were struggling and wrangling with ideas too difficult for them—ideas whose true meaning will only be clear after Christ's revelation. Thus he has Troilus reason about necessity in IV.953–1085: the passage is taken straight out of Boethius. Troilus concludes that all things are predestined, that man is not free. Chaucer does not have Troilus get the point—which Boethius goes on to develop—that man is free in his own mind. While his tragedy commends this view of life, in the end Chaucer permits it to rise above the level of philosophical speculation. The final moral, addressed to "younge, freshe folkes, he or she," is a spiritual rather than a philosophical one:

> . . . of your herte up casteth the visage
> To thilke God that after his image
> You made, and thinketh all nis but a faire,
> This world, that passeth soon as flowers faire. (V.1838–41)

Although Chaucer raises the story to such a philosophical and spiritual level in the end, he makes us, in the body of the work, believe in the love affair itself. It is an intense and beautiful and excruciating experience which lasted only a little while and is now only a sad memory or story. This poignancy can be understood from the viewpoint of philosophy or moral theology, but we would be reading the poem the wrong way if we did not *feel* it.

That feeling is what has drawn generations of readers to the poem, and Chaucer meant us to be drawn to it that way. We know he meant this because we know he introduced into the poem *an ideal and a myth of love which was not there before*. It was most certainly not in Boccaccio. In his version, Troilo's motives were frankly sexual. So was the interest he wakened in Criseida: she, a widow, had tasted sexual pleasure in marriage and was hesitant only about her reputation. Chaucer pushed this physical element into the background, letting it emerge now and again as the fundamental animal desire which it is. In its place he offered the elaborate rituals of courtship which seem to have been a custom among the nobility since the twelfth century—not just in France (where they originated) but in England, Germany, Italy. He restored to the poem a tradition which Boccaccio had cast aside.

This tradition is what we call "courtly love." The term itself was coined in the nineteenth century; in the Middle Ages it was simply called "love." We know it existed because it crops up in literature—in songs, lyric poems, romances, allegories, dream-visions, even a few prose treatises—from the end of the eleventh century through and past Chaucer's time as late as Shakespeare's *Romeo and Juliet*, in a transmuted version later still. We do not know exactly what it was because it was different things to different people at different times and places. But in its basic *literary* form it expressed the experience of falling in love *from the man's point of view*. The lover views the lady as an object of idealized and spiritualized adoration, so high in his estimation that she seems unattainable; she is unaware of his existence, and he dare not approach her. Hence he experiences alienation and a loss of self-esteem; he remains by himself, sighs, weeps, cannot eat or sleep. Yet this devotion, akin to religious devotion, has an ennobling effect on his character: he is more courtly, has more "gentilesse," is braver as a warrior, more generous and outgoing to others. His hope is to gain contact with the lady somehow, through a go-between, a letter, a song he sings or a poem he writes. He must attract her attention and make her aware of his "sorrow," gain her "pity" and ultimately her "grace." He is prepared to act as a servant to her, in hopes that she will take notice of him and respond to his love. The goal is not necessarily marriage; it is instead some kind of union, if only the prize of a friendly look or a kiss or "love of friendship." But the most satisfactory prize for all but the most idealistic lovers was a sexual union which would bring the lover into "heaven's bliss."

This tradition, which seems to have appealed to women, must have had some effect on men's actual behavior, if only on their fantasies. Seen one way, the lover is passion's slave and from any Christian viewpoint a sinner; seen another way, he is following an ideal which tends toward the spiritual—lovers may take secret vows (as Troilus and Criseyde do) or have a secret marriage (as Romeo and Juliet do). The many-sidedness and extravagance of the tradition was what gave it its appeal. Poets presented love as a pseudo-religion with Venus and Cupid for its gods. Because of such extravagancies, it lent itself to comedy and parody, and we see this in the

Troilus: Pandarus can make Criseyde and her ladies roar with laughter by joking about his own love. Love was appropriate to young folk, so it was incongruous and comic in older people, as it would. be in lower-class people, such as those in the Miller's Tale. Like all comedy it has its dark underside: Pandarus *is* unsuccessful in love—life has cheated him in this respect, and he is resigned enough to make a joke of it, though we see him anguished too, just once, at the beginning of Book II. At the other end of the spectrum was idealism. Once Troilus is "converted" to the religion of Love, his idealism is very intense—it is the only appeal which succeeds when Pandarus tries to make him say whom he loves: many a lover, Pandarus observes (I.810ff.), has suffered in love for twenty years, even when his lady knew of his love, but never kissed his lady's mouth. Should he fall into despair? No, he should serve his heart's queen and know that love is its own reward. "Of *that* word," we are told, "took heede Troilus."

Chaucer took this medieval ideal and myth of love—a pseudo-religion devoted to pagan gods—and made it part of the story's "historical" background. The love affair takes place in ancient Troy during the last days before its fall. At the beginning Criseyde's father, Calkas, a seer or soothsayer, deserts Troy and goes over to the Greeks who are besieging the city. He has foreseen the city's downfall, and we know by hindsight that he is correct. But he does a shocking thing: he goes off by himself, deserting his daughter. We first see her enlisting the protection of the prince, Hector; we next see her in a pagan temple during the feast of Palladion, where the Trojans are worshipping the statue or "relic" of Pallas Athena. Chaucer makes the atmosphere starkly pagan: the gods they worship are false gods. We the audience know that Troy will fall, that Aeneas will escape and found Rome, that the West will be settled as far as Britain, that Christ will be born and Christianity spread through Europe. And Chaucer, in his role as narrator, addresses us directly with a clear understanding that we *do* know all this. We, his audience, are Christians; they, the characters in the story, are pagans. It is therefore completely natural for them to believe in a "religion of Love," to invoke Venus and vow service to Cupid.

Chaucer presents this historical background in a wonderfully convincing way. You can almost believe you've been picked up and set down in ancient Troy. How does he do it? In part, by making himself seem real. He creates a narrator who calls himself "I," who tells us at the outset that he is like a priest or bishop in the religion of Love, that he is going to tell us a sorrowful love story—how Troilus went "fro woe to wele, and after out of joye." He asks us to pray to the God of Love for all lovers. As the story progresses, he shows appropriate emotions—excitement, joy, envy, depression, pity. In the end he concludes that all earthly loves are disappointing, that only the love of God can endure. This narrator who learns from his own story the Christian lesson of renunciation is obviously not Chaucer himself in any literal or biographical sense, but a masquerade figure that Chaucer "puts on" and plays. Yet we sense Chaucer's own presence behind the role-playing. When, for example, the narrator speaks of the lovers' blissful first night, he says

> Why n'ad *I* swich one with *my* soul y-bought—
> Yea, or the leeste joye that was there?
> Away, thou foule Daunger and thou Feere,
> And let hem in this hevene blisse dwelle,
> That is so high that all ne can I telle. (III.1319–23)

The narrator is carried away with enthusiasm to the point of being ready to sell his soul for such bliss. It is a curious utterance—shocking if taken literally, comic if you think of its extravagance, perhaps sad if you remember the narrator's "unlikeliness," his feeling that love's joys are not for him. By having the narrator talk this way Chaucer shows us how intense the lovers' pleasure is—intense enough to make the narrator lose his head. At the same time, by reminding us of our immortal souls, Chaucer reminds us that this intense pleasure is temporary and mutable, and the narrator's (or our) desire for it questionable. We become aware of Chaucer himself precisely because we are aware that the narrator behaves and talks as Chaucer could not possibly have done.

This poet-narrator is, like us, a reader, poring over an "old book," responding with various and conflicting emotions, sometimes deeply involved with the story, sometimes drawing away from it to comment or to think. He claims that his "old book" is by an author named Lollius. This is not a mere code-name for Boccaccio but a deliberate fiction: there seems to have been a legend during the Middle Ages of a lost writer named Lollius, the greatest of those who wrote about the

Trojan War.[3] Chaucer has his narrator claim to be in posses-
sion of this lost book. It is the kind of fiction we are often
asked to accept in a storyteller's "truth-claim"—that it is a
true history, is based on an authentic record, has authority
behind it. In these moments when the narrator stops to
comment (III.1191–97 is a good example) or mentions his
"old book" or "mine auctor," he draws us away from the
story. We are alone with him at his desk in fourteenth-century
England. These moments "distance" us, give us a chance to
catch our breath. But no sooner do we get such interruptions
than we are pushed back into the world of ancient Troy. The
narrator steps aside, as if to sit down in the audience and
watch with us. Actions are described directly and without
comment; we hear the characters talking to each other; we are
even told sometimes what they are thinking.

This world we are observing seems real and familiar, and
Chaucer made it so by deliberate anachronisms. As often as
he reminds us of the strangeness and paganness of the ancient
world, he depicts it as the world familiar to his audience.
Pandarus's house, described in detail, is a typical upper-class
London house of the period.[4] The characters use colloquial
English of the fourteenth century—"Ey! which way been ye
comen, ben'dic'te!" cries Criseyde when Pandarus enters her
room unexpectedly at night. The image in the temple of
Palladion is called a "relic," though the word suggests medieval
Christian worship. And the characters follow the medieval

---

[3] The idea was based on a misunderstanding which came about
through a single misspelling in a line from Horace, *Epist.* I, 2, 1.
Horace was addressing an actor named Maximus Lollius who
evidently gave public recitations from Homer: "While you, Maxi-
mus Lollius, are in Rome reciting the writer of the Trojan War . . ."
Medieval readers didn't realize that Maximus was Lollius's first
name, but took it for an adjective ("greatest"). And in some
manuscripts *scriptorem* ("writer") was incorrectly copied *scrip-
torum* ("of the writers"). Hence they thought it meant "You,
Lollius, the greatest of the writers of the Trojan War . . ." Pro-
fessor Robert Pratt discovered a manuscript in which the line was
written this way, and another manuscript where in the margin the
scribe commented (in French), "For he says that Lollius was the
principal writer of the battle of Troy." See *Modern Language
Notes*, 65: 183ff.

[4] See H. M. Smyser, "The Domestic Background of *Troilus and
Criseyde*," *Speculum*, 31(1956), 297–315. An adaptation of Smy-
ser's diagram of Pandarus's house is printed on p. xv.

"religion of Love." This is the sort of anachronism which any writer must use to make the long ago and far away believable. So in Book IV, when the Trojans discuss an exchange of prisoners with the Greeks, Chaucer speaks of a "parliament" and lets his audience conjure up their own notion of a fourteenth-century meeting of the English Parliament. (He got the hint from Boccaccio's word *parlamento*, which only meant a discussion.) Even in our time, though we have accurate historical information and have a taste for "historical accuracy" (as Chaucer's age did not), the real problem for the artist is to make historical events understandable to his audience. Chaucer comments on this necessity at the beginning of Book II, suggesting that he has "translated" ancient and foreign usages into familiar ones and asking us to make an effort to understand the Trojans' ways:

> Ye know eek that in form of speech is chaunge
> Within a thousand yeer, and wordes tho
> That hadden pris now wonder nice and straunge
> Us thinketh hem, and yet they spake hem so,
> And sped as well in love as men now do:
> Eek for to winnen love in sundry ages,
> In sundry landes sundry been usages. (II.22–28)

But what most draws us into the ancient world of the story is the sheer power of Chaucer's language. There is an early fifteenth-century manuscript painting of Chaucer reading the *Troilus* aloud to the court of King Richard II, and it is generally believed that he did read his poems to the court. It is easy to imagine that he was a skillful reader—a born actor with flawless timing, with *presence*. But we imagine this

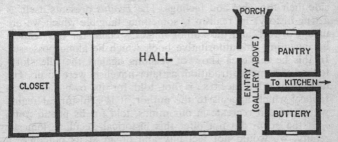

Floor plan of a fourteenth-century English house.

because we get the impression from the poem. He addresses us, the audience, directly—"Now herkeneth with a good intencioun" (I.52), or "if it hap in any wise / That here be any lover in this place" (II.29–30). Or he addresses the individual—"thou, reeder" (V.270). And he addresses us using standard devices of medieval rhetoric—for example, *occupatio*, the device of summarizing material under the guise of omitting it (as in III.491–504), or *apostrophe*, the device of using direct address to comment on the story (as in III.1317–18). These devices—there are dozens of others—were the artistic tools of a medieval poet, and like all tools they could be used skillfully or awkwardly. (When Chaucer made fun of them in *The Canterbury Tales*, for example in the Nun's Priest's Tale, he was, as so often, making fun of something he respected, or of its abuse.) In the *Troilus* he uses these devices with consummate skill and tact, and he added them to the work: there is much less of this rhetorical display in Boccaccio. The result is that Chaucer appears before us as a *writer* studying his old book and composing his version, and as a *performer* addressing us directly. At the end he turns the tables on us. We are made to imagine him putting his book aside, putting his own version down and bidding it farewell in the conventional *envoy* of medieval poems, then addressing a moral to the "younge, freshe folkes" of his audience, dedicating the book to some friends, and retreating into prayer and meditation: he seems to pass through a momentary state of panic, in which he lashes about among various sentiments and attitudes, and then to disappear.

Until the end of the poem we and the narrator are caught up in the everyday life of these upper-class Trojans, live inside their thoughts and feelings. The *Troilus* presents itself as a true history: its realism is something tangible which we are meant to feel, and the author makes a claim for this realism by inventing an authoritative book which he alone possesses. In this he makes a show of reacting against the idle storytelling of romance tradition, as later novelists were to do. His tale, unlike Boccaccio's, is not told for its own sake as a fantasy which appeals to the author; it is a historical reality which we can recreate in our minds, told for its poetic truth.

If the poem did not offer this historical, secular, domestic reality, we would not feel pity and dread at its outcome; it would only teach us that "all's for the best in the end." A Christian tragedy may teach this lesson but it teaches it the hard way—it makes us experience the beauty of the world and the dignity of man before showing us that this beauty will slip through our fingers and this dignity fail us. It wouldn't do for a tragic poet to make worldly loves seem trivial and contemptible; he must make us see their luster before he can make us feel the tragic side of loss and bad fortune. Yet when we come to the end we cannot dismiss this experience of a vivid, though transitory, beauty and cannot renounce it except in an intellectual way. The final moral sounds easy only to those who have never tried to live by it. Renounce *all* worldly loves? even when you are young? We can accept the abstraction "all nis but a fair, this world," but it is hard to imagine Chaucer seriously telling young folks they should never go to fairs, never dance, never sing. Chaucer teaches, rather, a frame of mind with which we must approach worldly loves: we must live in the world for a time and respond to it as God's creation knowing all the while that we must each leave it when we die and that it must be destroyed at the end of time. We have no choice but to enjoy and suffer the world as best we can from the short view, knowing that from the long view we must despise it. Chaucer meant us to see the events of the *Troilus* from both the short view and the long. He adapted his source to accomplish this: he made Boccaccio's tale more emotional, more exciting, more complex, more often funny, more poignant, and in the end more philosophical and more religious. In doing all this he gave it tragic proportions.

The most noticeable change he made in the story itself, the one which cast a sea-change over the whole work, was that he recreated the three principal characters, giving each more grandeur and complexity.

Chaucer made Troilus more sympathetic, more princely. He is a romance hero; he stands for those values which the poem explores and in the end rejects. When we first see him we see a young man who has never been in love making fun of love and lovers. This does not mean he's a virgin or an adolescent, as some think; it only means that he doesn't know the experience he laughs at, that of falling in love. (In Boccaccio, Troilo knows and is disillusioned with that experience—its joys are nothing, he says, compared to its torments.) The result is that in Chaucer, when Cupid strikes Troilus down for his pride, Troilus takes the experience more seriously. He goes off by himself and suffers all the griefs of traditional love-melancholy—he sighs, weeps, keeps the lady's name secret, assumes she could love no such wretch as himself. Yet the experience ennobles him—he behaves so as to deserve her admiration. He sees love in a far more idealistic way than his Italian counterpart: in the *Filostrato* you can't escape the feeling that the hero chiefly wants sexual satisfaction—when jilted, Troilo must accept the fact that young women are fickle, want many lovers, are vain. In Chaucer, Troilus when jilted grapples philosophically with the meaning of life and concludes that we are prisoners of fate, that though he knows Criseyde is not as fine as he had thought he can never "unlove" her.

It is hard for modern readers to take Troilus seriously because the conventions of "languishing for love" do not seem manly. These conventions of love were more familiar in Chaucer's day, but they are not unknown in ours: the experience of feeling depression, a loss of self-esteem, alienation, weariness, and loneliness when one falls in love for the first time with someone who doesn't respond is not at all outside the experience of young men in modern times. You take it seriously if it happens to you or a close friend; in a stranger, or an older man, or (when one grows older) in the young, it may seem laughable. So it seems to Troilus—after he is dead. Yet we misread the poem if we see him as a laughable adolescent from the start: he is already a great warrior and a prince. As a military hero he is very *macho* indeed; and as a private person he holds to his knightly ideals—his love is a matter of life and death to him, and it remains in his mind an unalterable devotion until his dying day. It is therefore true that the most unbearable part of the poem is the series of scenes where Troilus waits for Criseyde to return, stands gazing at her empty palace, rationalizes her failure to come when expected, dreams that awful dream in which he sees her kissing a boar, curses his sister Cassandra for a sorceress when she tells the meaning of his dream, receives that cruel letter from Criseyde, at last sees his own brooch, which he had given her at their parting, on Diomede's cloak, and knows that she "nas no longer on to triste" (V.1666). But it is just here, at this most chilling moment in the poem, that he returns home to lament her faithlessness and says,

> . . . I see that cleen out of your minde
> Ye han me cast. And I ne can nor may,
> For all this world, within mine herte finde
> To unloven you a quarter of a day.

In cursed time I born was, wailaway!
That you, that doon me all this woe endure,
Yet love I best of any creature. (V.1695–1701)

Criseyde, the object of Troilus's devotion, is Chaucer's most original creative accomplishment: the first fully successful literary portrait of a woman since the ancient world. She was in Chaucer's time and remains to this day a controversial figure. She is something different to everyone. At the end of the poem she is, from Troilus's viewpoint, no longer to be trusted but still his only love; from Pandarus's viewpoint she is to be hated; from Diomede's viewpoint, so far as we can intuit if from the way it is briefly sketched, she is only another woman, a pretty and appealing one of whom he can make use if she will have him and can forget about if she will not. From the narrator's viewpoint she has done wrong and is sufficiently punished: he can, he says, excuse her out of pity (V.1099).

What Chaucer thought *our* view of Criseyde should be is impossible to say. He provides us every opportunity to see things her way, to understand why when sent among the Greeks she takes up with Diomede and does not return to Troy. Before her choice he stops the action and, in an amazing passage (V.799–840), describes the three principal figures as if we had never seen them before—Diomede as a nobleman, Criseyde as a lovely woman "tender herted, sliding of courage," Troilus as a warrior. The passage "distances" us, asks us to observe with care as if from an altered perspective. Chaucer lets us understand that she is alone and needs help (he says so in V.1023–29), that there is danger, her father's intract-ability, Diomede's reassurances and his "greet estate," the war, the imminent fall of Troy, the passage of time. He lets us see her constitutional timidity, shyness, caution. And he lets us see that she hates herself for acting as she does—for he gives her a soliloquy (V.1058–85) which was in Benoit de Sainte-Maure's version of the story but which Boccaccio left out of the *Filostrato*. In it she says that no good word will ever be spoken of her—"O, rolled shall I been on many a tongue"—and that women will hate her most. But, she says, she sees "there is no better way," that it is "too late . . . for me to rewe." And, reiterating her admiration for Troilus as the one who "best can ay his lady honour keepe," she bursts into tears. She would be sorry to see him in adversity and knows he is guiltless—"But all shall pass, and thus take I my leeve." That is the last time we see her. At this point we

remember that she has lied to Diomede, telling him she loved
her husband and no other (974–78). So at this point we may
well ask whether she had lied to Troilus too. But the answer
is less certain.

This question about Criseyde's "trouthe" which arises at
the end of the poem naturally demands that we look back and
reexamine the way she fell in love with Troilus in the first
place.

Those earlier scenes are the heart of the story. When
Pandarus reveals to her that the prince Troilus is in love with
her, she allows him to go on with his long, persuasive speech;
then she says to herself, "I shall feelen what he meeneth, ywis,"
and asks him what he advises. He advises that she return
Troilus's love and reminds her that she will not be young
forever:

> . . . ere that age thee devoure,
> Go love, for, old, there will no wight of thee. (II.395–96)

At this she weeps: he, her uncle, who should counsel her
against a love affair, is advising her to enter into one. Boccaccio
had her weep when Pandaro told her Troilo's name; Chaucer
has her weep when Pandarus reminds her she is growing older.
For evidently what Chaucer wanted to do was to make her
doubts and restraints more complicated and more understand-
able. In Boccaccio, she is interested in the affair but fearful
for her reputation. In Chaucer we sense her interest and we
see that she is flattered—she is aware of her beauty, she says
to herself, though she quickly adds she wouldn't want anyone
to know she thought this. But she is afraid of more than the
danger to her reputation: she fears all the griefs and complexi-
ties of a love affair, the dangers of gossip and jealous people,
the loss of freedom. In a long scene, almost entirely Chaucer's
invention—II.596–931, a scene which repays very careful
reading—we see inside her mind and follow her thoughts as
she vacillates for and against engaging herself in a love affair.
We never see her make up her mind. In indecision, she joins
her ladies in the garden and hears Antigone sing a song
about a maiden who no longer fears love now that she tastes
its joys. Criseyde asks if there is such bliss among lovers, and
Antigone answers forcefully that only lovers can tell of love's
joys as only saints can tell of heaven. Criseyde makes no
answer but goes off to bed. Falling asleep she hears a night-
ingale sing its song of love. Then she dreams of a white eagle

who painlessly takes her heart and leaves in its place his own. If ever we see her predisposition tipped in favor of love, it is here at the deepest level of her unconscious.[5]

Even at that, she never agrees to do more than be friendly to Troilus: "love of friendship" is what she consents to. In the *Filostrato* Criseida consents to meet Troilo alone in her palace at night and go to bed with him—it's as simple as that. But in the *Troilus* she is *tricked* into going to bed with him. Pandarus invites her to *his* house, conceals Troilus in a secret room, and persuades Criseyde not to go home during the terrible storm raging outside. Having got her in a private chamber, he enters the room through a secret passage, leaving Troilus at the door. Troilùs evidently hears their conversation, including Pandarus's outrageous lie that Troilus has fallen into despair because of a rumor that she loves one Horaste. Inside, on Pandarus's prompting, Troilus kneels. She speaks of his jealousy and, declaring herself innocent, weeps and covers her face with the sheet. Troilus thinks to himself, "O Pandarus . . . alas, thy wile / Serveth of nought." He sinks to his knees, murmurs that "of this game / When all is wist, then am I not to blame." And then he faints.

That Troilus faints beside his lady's bed is always reckoned a comic touch; I am prepared to argue that it is serious—that Chaucer invented the episode *to underscore Criseyde's innocence.* Critics overlook the fact that Chaucer provided a detailed *medical* description of Troilus's fainting; I am prepared to argue that he did this *to underscore Troilus's sense of guilt.* In the passage (III.1081–92) he lets us see not just inside Troilus's mind but inside his body. What we see is a reality hard to grasp, because it is described in the language of medieval science; to understand the passage one would need to understand the medical ideas behind it and to determine whether Chaucer understood those ideas clearly. Judging from some other instances of fainting and faintness in Chaucer's works (especially *The Book of the Duchess,* lines 488–99), what seems to happen is this: a powerful emotion occurs in Troilus's heart—for the heart was con-

[5] I have offered a detailed demonstration of these aspects of the scene in "Experience, Language, and Consciousness: *Troilus and Criseyde*, II, 596–931," *Medieval Literature and Folklore Studies: Essays in Honor of Francis Lee Utley*, ed. J. Mandel and B. Rosenberg (New Brunswick, N.J.: Rutgers Univ. Press, 1970), pp. 173–92.

sidered the seat of emotions—and causes it to "shut." This
seems to signify a "chill" in the heart: his heart, as we would
say, "goes cold." As a result the blood rushes from his head
to his heart to warm it. The loss of blood in the head causes
the "spirits" (which were thought to control bodily functions)
to be so oppressed or "astoned" that each "knits in its vigor"
("his vigour in-knette," III.1088–89). With his "spirits" thus
paralyzed, Troilus is unable to give physical expression to his
emotion: tears cannot fall from his eyes (1087), the *feeling*
of his emotions is "fled . . . out of towne" (1090–91), and
he loses consciousness. It is all very scientific, and the science
is put into the passage to make us feel that it is possible and
reasonable. In a moment we are allowed to indulge any im-
pulse to laugh—for Pandarus is up enlisting Criseyde's help,
throws Troilus on the bed, removes his clothes, and the two
administer what first aid they can by rubbing his pulse and
palms, wetting his temples, she reassuring him and kissing
him. When he revives she asks, "Is this a manne's game?" and
forgives all. Pandarus issues a few more instructions—his
parting shot is, "Don't faint now"—and retreats to the fire-
place. The lovers are left alone to exchange vows and rings,
spend the night in bliss, and lament the coming of the dawn
with traditional dawn-songs.

It all happens so fast that readers manage to gloss over the
fundamental question: *why does Troilus faint?* Chaucer indi-
cates the answer: a powerful emotion overtakes him when he
realizes that he is there because of a trick Pandarus has
perpetrated and he allowed, and which seems to have failed.
And what is that emotion? Chaucer calls it "sorrow" or "fear"
or "aught elles" (1090–91). We can see that he feels fear and
sorrow because Pandarus has tricked her and deceived her,
because he has not intervened, and because now she is hurt:
she thinks he doesn't trust her and she weeps. We can suppose
that he fears this is the end of the affair, is sorrowful because
she is the injured party. But there is, Chaucer says, "aught
elles"—and what can this "something else" be but guilt? In his
last words before he faints he declares that "when all is wist,
then am I not to blame" (1085). Perhaps he is right. Perhaps
it is Pandarus who has compromised the best ideals in order
to get inside her chamber. And now that the compromise has
failed, perhaps Troilus can truly say that he permitted the
compromise out of the purest motives. But there is one argu-
ment against this. He would probably never have got inside
her chamber without compromising his ideals. And once into

such a deception there is no way out. Revived and in bed with her, when she demands that he say what made him jealous of Horaste and show it was not done in malice to "fonde" her, we are told that he must obey his lady's command—"And for the lesse harm, he muste feigne" (III.1158). He goes on to follow Pandarus's example and tell her a lie. True, it is a white lie. True, we know that in all the restraints of a strict aristocratic society some small amount of deception is inevitable in playing love's game. But none of this was necessary in Boccaccio's version—his story was purely erotic, and his heroine didn't need to be tricked but only reassured. Chaucer's story deals with more profound and complicated feelings and takes place in a more complicated world, one in which ideals are so high that they are not practicable—they have to be compromised by day-to-day necessities. It is the way of the world.

Both Troilus and Criseyde must decide whether to make the same kind of compromise with necessities when Criseyde must leave the city, and they decide not to. For Troilus to do anything but submit and wait for her return means breaking the secrecy of the affair or treating her like a possession which can be bargained for. This honorable line of conduct is clear to him: when Pandarus advises the pragmatic way out, Troilus brushes his arguments to one side and states with assurance what he knows is right. Pandarus—shockingly—suggests first that he has had enough of Criseyde and should find someone else to take her place. Troilus replies in a long speech that he cannot betray one who trusts him (IV.435–518) and points to the falseness—one might say the bad rhetoric—of Pandarus's suggestion: Pandarus has remained true to *his* lady-love though she has never responded to his devotion, so he must not even believe what he says. Pandarus then suggests that they "elope"—that Troilus take Criseyde away with him; Troilus replies with five reasons why this is out of the question (IV.547–81). Even then, when at the last minute Troilus has a change of heart and urges that they flee, Criseyde appeals to the canons of honorable conduct—and there is no necessary reason to suppose she is only stalling:

. . . moral virtue grounded upon trouthe—
That was the cause I first had on you routhe. (IV.1672–73)

Her plan, to go and then return in ten days, answers the objections she sees in eloping (IV.1555–96), objections having to do with honor and good reputation—and not just hers but Troilus's, for he would have to betray Troy to go off with her.

When we ask who meant well, who was false, and who is to blame, the answer is that everyone meant well, at one time or another everyone was false, and everyone is to blame. Despite all the attention Chaucer gives to the characters of the principal figures, it is not wholly the case in this story that "character is destiny." Destiny itself hovers over the story. We can wish that Calkas would not ask his daughter in return for Antenor (who we know is to betray the city), that the Trojan Parliament were not so easily swayed by the "noise of people," that Troilus would stand up as Hector has and turn the tide of public opinion, that Criseyde would risk her life to return. But all this is like saying we wish Troy would not fall. We wish it, but it is not to be. In the end historical necessity sweeps aside all human wishes.

Pandarus alone understands this necessity. That is why, with all his plotting, fast talking, "busyness" and trickery, he brings the affair about. Without him, Troilus would never have done more than worship his lady from afar. Without him, Criseyde would never have agreed to more than "love of friendship," if that. In Pandarus we have an inventor and manipulator inside the poem comparable to the poet outside it. The plot he oversees is, to him, like a work of art. Chaucer has him think of it in the words which the rhetorician Geoffrey of Vinsauf had applied to writing a poem, comparing it with building a house (I.1065–69). When Pandarus gets things planned adequately, Chaucer keeps up the comparison —"This timber is all redy up to frame" (III.530). When Pandarus finally gets the lovers safely together, he retires to a corner of the room and composes himself "As for to look upon an old romaunce" (III.980). And, like the poet-narrator, Pandarus then sees his invention assume an inscrutable shape of its own over which he has no control; in the end Pandarus, like the poet-narrator, stands helpless before events.

Pandarus is no more to blame for the tragic turn of events than anyone else. True, he seems like a tempter who teases, tricks, and cajoles the lovers into pursuing the affair. But this is not just because he takes a vicarious interest and has a mesmerizing gift of gab (though he does), it is because he sees that *the lovers both want the thing they shy away from.* In Boccaccio, Pandaro was Criseida's cousin and Troilo's friend: he was their age, and his role was simply that of confidant and messenger and arranger. Chaucer makes him Criseyde's *uncle*, so that we take him to be older. He makes him more worldly-wise and learned. And he makes him a more significant figure in the political life of Troy—he is intimate with the leading figures of the city. We even learn that he could not see Troilus on the day of Criseyde's departure because he spent the whole day in counsel with the King (V.281–86).

Pandarus is a nobleman of the highest rank, a counselor to princes, a man of dignity, importance, judgment. He is a glib persuader of enormous verbal skill, quick in thought and wit. He is keenly perceptive of other people—seems to guess what they are thinking and to know what argument or phrase will touch their true motives. Sometimes he seems almost a magician who can have the weather work into his schemes. This knowing, sensitive side of Pandarus at times approaches cynicism: he understands that his niece is not immune to fleshly desires (I.977–84) and later understands that she will not return to Troy. His worldly wisdom is based not alone on good instincts or experience or intelligence, but on learning. He knows and mentions books and "auctors." His store of proverbs is unsurpassed, and proverbs didn't mean platitudes or old saws: the medievals were very respectful of proverbs. Pandarus's proverbs are often from books, as it would seem, and he often presents them alongside specific examples and bookish references in elaborate analogies (as in I.624–72): his mind has a facility for abstract thought.

There is a reason in Pandarus's private emotional life which explains why he puts so much emotion into promoting the love affair. He is himself unhappy in love. He has, we are told, been in love with a certain unnamed lady for a long time, without success. Troilus knows about it and so does Criseyde. Troilus says, "How the devil can you help me if you can't help yourself?"—and Pandarus heaps up illustrations to show that one can teach what one cannot do: a whetstone is not a carving instrument, he says, but it can make carving tools sharp. The nature of his ill success is a mystery—he chose the wrong kind of woman, or had bad luck, or wasn't that deeply interested, or didn't successfully appeal to her. We do not know. We do know that he has learned to live with his disappointment. He can make a joke of it. Only once—but at a crucial point—we see him collapse into a depression: at the beginning of Book II he suffers a "tene" in love and retires to his bed tossing and turning. When he wakes the next day his first thought is the errand he must do for Troilus—his "greet emprise"—and he runs off to Criseyde's palace. What is missing in his own life he promotes and can enjoy vicariously in the lives of his friend and his niece. When the lovers are in love he is genuinely happy for them—there is not a hint of jealousy on his part. His interest in their affair may have a neurotic edge, but perhaps not more so than Troilus's singlemindedness or Criseyde's habitual fear. Whether he identifies more with Troilus or with Criseyde remains an open question.

What Pandarus has, which they do not, is a philosophy. It is, I believe, what Chaucer imagined the philosophies of the ancient world to be. It is a hodgepodge of ancient ideas of the kind which survived into the Middle Ages, and Chaucer had a good insight when he constructed this imaginary "pagan" philosophy. It is the most interesting side of Pandarus. And as philosophies of life go, his is a good one.

Pandarus believes in the world, in creatures. He sees creatures arranged in a hierarchy: he refers disparagingly to "bestialitee" (I.735) and speaks of "so noble a creature / As is a man" (V.384–85). I find no place where he expresses a belief in a superior being or a divine wisdom (though his oath in II.1734 could be so interpreted), but he does believe in a cycle or rhythm that may be perceived in human events. It is not a process—it doesn't move in the direction of progress or decline. It is only change, overseen by the goddess Fortune. There is nothing but the present moment, always at Fortune's mercy. He believes that Fortune is common to every "wight" (creature) and causes everything to pass away. Because he believes this, he believes that some favorable circumstance ("goodly aventure") is bound to occur in every creature's life (I.841–54). But it is up to the individual to take advantage of that "aventure"; if we pass it up, we cannot say that Fortune has deceived us—it is the fault of our own "slouth and wrecchednesse" (II.281–94).

If you asked Pandarus, "Then how do you think people should behave?" he would tell you first to be pragmatic, to behave according to the needs of the moment. He believes we should take advantage of the opportunity for pleasure when it presents itself and not trust tomorrow. Chaucer seems to have him quote Horace's famous phrase "seize the day" (*carpe diem*) when he tells Criseyde that she has found "good aventure" and should "Cacch it anon, lest aventure slacke" (II.291). This is not wholly hedonistic, for he believes that those pleasures will only last a little while and that we should resign ourselves when they desert us. It is opportunistic, for it holds that happiness is in the cards for everyone at one time or another and that we should grasp it while we can. But finally it is pessimistic, for it holds that no one will be happy long. In good "aventure" or bad, however, Pandarus believes we should always make an effort, should "seeken boote": we should seize our opportunities and find remedies for our troubles. Pandarus is for getting things done. He is against daydreaming or intellectualizing or procrastinating: he tells Criseyde that "alle thing hath time," that if a house is on fire one shouldn't stop to ask how the candle fell in the straw (III.855–59). He is against wallowing in misery and depression: he tells Troilus that it is the delight of fools to beweep their woe and not to "seeken boote" (I.762–63). But he is also against getting lost in joy. To take too much pleasure in one's happiness creates the possibility of a great disappointment when we lose that happiness, as we surely will: he warns Troilus that "as greet a craft is keepe well as winne" (III.1634).

Pandarus believes in the maxim *nothing to excess*. His notion is very like the classical idea of the Golden Mean, and indeed he says,

> . . . bothe two been vices—
> Mistrusten all, or elles alle leve.
> But well I wot, the meen of it no vice is. (I.687–89)

This moderation is designed to keep us human, to keep us from descending into "bestialitee." It is therefore totally unjust to accuse him of being "Machiavellian," of being cynically manipulative. True, he tells lies to get Troilus into Criseyde's chamber, but he would say he does it for a good end. True, he changes his mind about Criseyde, but only after *she* has changed. He may believe that the end justifies the means, but he would add that the end must be a good one; that ends must be sought and means used with moderation; and that all ends and all means should be judged by standards of honor and "gentilesse." Thus before he proceeds to the grand finale of his planning, he reminds Troilus of the need for discretion and declares that he has proceeded this far in arranging the affair —something he says he will never do again—because he knows Troilus's intentions are honorable (III.238–343).

One can call his frame of mind humanism. Pandarus believes that man is the measure, that no action should violate human dignity. He seems to believe that excess (like Troilus's despair in Book I or Criseyde's undue fear) does violate human dignity, for he disapproves of Troilus's extreme dependency and hates Criseyde for her final actions. Like all humanists he believes, too, that part of man's dignity lies in language. He is very reverential to books, authors, proverbs, and the "olde wise." They are the perdurable monument of the human mind, the only light he knows to guide us in the darkness of human life. To Pandarus, knowledge is relative. Of divine revelation he knows nothing. He believes that we know things by their opposites—we cannot know black without white or worthiness without shame. Each, set beside the other, has more meaning because of the other. "Of two contraries is one lore" (I.637–45). Pandarus stands at all times for the spirit of ancient paganism in its worldly and humanistic aspects. If Troilus stands for romance fantasies and idealism, Pandarus stands for rational conduct and sensible realism.

Neither Criseyde nor Troilus wholly absorbs the philosophy Pandarus offers. Their temperaments forbid it. Each maintains a measure of independence from his persuasions. Each ignores one whole side of his philosophy. And the sides they ignore are different ones, are indeed "two contraries":

(1) Criseyde at the end of the story has absorbed Pandarus's pragmatism but ignored his humanism.

Chaucer made Criseyde—unlike her Italian counterpart—constitutionally timid. When we first see her in the temple, she is standing *by the door*—she is one of those people who never get all the way into a room, but keep a ready access. Later we are told she was "the feerfulleste wight / That mighte be" (II.450–51). Nevertheless, she has a mind of her own. "I am mine owne woman" (II.750) she reminds herself. And in the early part of the poem we watch her little world of thoughts as it wends slowly toward an inclination—watch something happen which we scarcely ever watch in real life, an idea taking root. Pandarus has argued to her that one must take steps to attain happiness when an opportunity presents itself. This notion, the essence of his philosophy in its pragmatic aspect, comes into her thoughts as a proverb: "He which that nothing undertaketh, / Nothing n'acheveth" (807–808). She seems also to have absorbed, or to share, Pandarus's notion about moderation: "In every thing, I wot, there lieth mesure" (715), she argues to herself, giving the classic example of a mean between drunkenness and total abstinence. Then follows Antigone's song of love, the short conversation, the dream of the white eagle. Pandarus's *carpe diem* has after all got through to her.

With Troilus, then, she compromises her fears for her wishes; with Diomede she compromises her wishes for her fears. We are to assume that among the Greeks, as the days passed, she stumbled in the same way toward a determination to stay there. But it is not the same kind of determination and not made in the same spirit. It does not sound at all like *carpe diem*: it is verbalized with regret, sorrow, guilt (V.1058-85). The last word she speaks to herself, "But all shall pass" (1085), may sound like Pandarus, but the emotion is somber, resigned—very different from the perplexed, intrigued expectancy of her earlier emotion toward Troilus. It is now Diomede, not Pandarus, who is urging her. And Diomede's view of life is pragmatic and opportunistic, like Pandarus's— but it is only a warrior's *carpe diem*, not part of a philosophy. We even hear him say to himself, "For he that nought n'assayeth, nought n'acheeveth" (V.784). It sounds like the proverb Criseyde had uttered to herself, but there is a difference: he uses the word "assayeth," she used "undertaketh." For what she heard from Pandarus was a belief in "undertaking," in deliberate, rational action. Diomede believes in "assaying," in trying—taking what he can get and not worrying about what he can't. "For to assay," he tells himself just before this, "it nought ne greeveth" (783)—it can't hurt to try. By showing him trying and not caring, Chaucer points up the difference between him and Troilus: we saw Troilus at first caring and not trying.

Criseyde acts upon this callous kind of pragmatism and forgets Pandarus's humanism—his regard for honor, for "meaning well." Think of what she does! She gives to Diomede the brooch Troilus gave her on parting ("And that was litel need," the narrator allows himself to exclaim). And she writes a letter so harsh, so utterly insensitive—and this is *after* the narrator has said he can forgive her for pity—that we cannot be other than appalled. In it she accuses Troilus of selfishness, claims there has been gossip that he is only stringing her along. Her assurances (she cannot doubt that he is honorable) ring hollow, including her vague promise to return—for she cannot say "what yeer or what day" this will be. She concludes the letter with the worst kiss-off in literary history: let's be friends anyway, and I'm sorry this letter isn't longer. Is it any wonder Chaucer ended up apologizing to the ladies in his audience for giving women a bad name? What we see in Criseyde just at the end is *dehumanization*— perhaps the beginning of a process. She casts aside those values of delicacy with respect to emotions and honor with respect to principles which she might have learned from her uncle. She begins to behave like Diomede. She descends into that "bestialitee" to which Pandarus stands opposed. This is revealed to Troilus in his dream: he sees a boar with great tusks sleeping in the sun, in its arms, "kissing ay his lady bright, Criseyde" (V.1241)—and wakes crying "I n'am but deed!"

(2) Troilus at the end of the story is the "contrary" of Criseyde. He has absorbed Pandarus's humanism but ignored his pragmatism.

Chaucer made Troilus—unlike his Italian counterpart—a traditional "courtly lover" who sighs and weeps when he has fallen in love. Hence he seems like warm wax in Pandarus's hands. But, more princely and thoughtful than his Italian counterpart, he does not take *all* of Pandarus's advice. He composes his own song, writes his own letter, patiently explains to Pandarus why he cannot run off with Criseyde. Human dignity looms up large in his mind and he sees parts of honor which Pandarus fails to see. His unwillingness to compromise his devotion to his lady, even when she is false, comes across as a part of his noble, heroic stature. But seen from another viewpoint, perhaps one closer to Pandarus's, this unwillingness to compromise could be called rigidity. From such a viewpoint the portrait of him could be considered a critique of idealism when it takes this unbending, excessive form. To Pandarus it is simply a fact of human existence that circumstances alter cases and that we need to be adaptable. To Troilus this is unthinkable. True, he did accept Pandarus's pragmatism when he permitted Pandarus to lie and then kept up the lie "for the lesse harm" (III.1156– 62). But he is not capable even of that much compromise when he must give Criseyde up. This may mean that he has "grown," that he is more true to himself. But his frame of mind, in his last days, is singleminded: he is possessed, is passion's slave. Unable to "unlove" or to forget, he wants revenge against Diomede and his own death in battle. It is very different from Pandarus's spirit of resignation to Fortune, of compromise and moderation. All Troilus can see is his sorrow's crown of sorrows, the loss of his true love. He is obsessed, haunted, bereft—blind to any other reality. Only in death does he see his own life with clear vision.

It is for this reason that Troilus's *eyes* figure so prominently in the last two books of the poem. His eyes, which first saw Criseyde in the temple, through which Love's arrow first penetrated his heart—his eyes which communed with hers, those "humble nettes" which "wroughte me swich woe" (III. 1354–55)—are now deprived of the sight of her. They become empty holes through which he can weep but cannot see. Lamenting against Fortune, when he has heard that Criseyde must leave the city, he even compares himself with blinded Oedipus. He cries that he will "end . . . as Edippe, in darknesse / My sorrowful life" (IV.300–01), and goes on:

O woefull eyen two, sin your disport
Was all to seen Criseyde's eyen brighte,
What shall ye doon but, for my discomfort,
Standen for nought, and weepen out your sighte . . . (309–12)

In these lines Chaucer seems to have suggested a medieval image which is mentioned in Dante, *Purgatorio* 23: 31–33. A man's two eyes are like zeroes ("nought"), the nose and eyebrows like an M between them, spelling *omo* (Latin *homo*, man). Written out in an emblem with the medieval "gothic" letter M embracing the two O's it makes a ghostly abstraction of a face with empty eyes:

Such an image haunts us throughout the remainder of the work. (It is possibly why Chaucer points up, in V.813, the detail—found in earlier treatments but not in Boccaccio—that Criseyde's brows are joined together.) We see Criseyde's eyes with purple rings of sorrow (IV.869), Pandarus's eyes streaming tears (IV.872–73); but it is Troilus's eyes which dominate the imagery of the last two books. His "eyen two," we are told, "for pietee of herte, / Out streemeden as swifte welles twaye" (IV.246–47). Pandarus remarks that "in thine

heed thine eyen seemen deede" (IV.1092).[6] As he gazes on
the empty palace, we are told that Troilus cast his eyes on
Pandarus with a changed face, "pitous to beholde." When he
stands upon the city wall with Pandarus awaiting her return,
he cries "I *see* her!" (V.1158) and Pandarus must sadly point
out to him "That *I* see yond nis but a fare-carte." But in his
dream he sees (1238) the boar holding Criseyde in his arms.
Awake, he saw falsely what he hoped; in the inner vision of
the dream-world he sees truly what he fears. In his letter to
Criseyde he says that what is defaced can be blamed on his
tears, "which that fro mine eyen raine, / That wolden speke,
if that they coud, and plaine" (1336–37)—that his tears or
his eyes would speak for him if they could; he goes on to write

> Mine eyen two, in vain with which I see,
> Of sorrowful teeres salt aren woxen welles. (1373–74)

The eyes blinded by tears, deep and hollow as wells, de-
prived of the sight of her and especially the sight of her eyes,
where "Paradise stood formed" (817)—the "subtle streams"
praised earlier (I.305, III.129)—this image of hollowness and
emptiness prepares us for the ending. At line 1540 we are
told of Troilus "And thus he drieth forth his aventure." It is
the same phrase used at the end of Book I. We are back
where we started. Fortune, we are told in the next stanza, is
about to bring Troy's downfall. It is now that Troilus must
see the truth. First he sees and reads her letter. We are re-
minded that "at the laste, / For anything, men shall the
soothe see" (1639–40). Then he sees on Diomede's captured
cote-armor, inside the collar, the brooch he gave Criseyde
when they parted, for her to remember him by. In his lament
which follows he says, "I *see* that cleen out of your minde /
Ye han me cast" (1695–96); speaking to Pandarus he says,
"Now maist thou *see* thyself . . . How trew is now thy neece"
(1711–12).

This is the last thing Troilus "sees" in this world. After that
we learn that he proposes to seek death in arms; then we hear
of his death and ascent to the eighth sphere. There,

---

[6] When Criseyde has left and Troilus gazes at her empty palace,
lamenting "O thou lantern of which queint is the light" (V.543),
we get again, as earlier in IV.313, the image of light quenched,
and the double entendre in *queint*, which couples the spiritual light
with a solid fleshly reality.

. . . he saw, with full avisement,
The erratic stars, herkening harmonye,
With sounes full of hevenish melodye.

And down from thennes fast he gan avise
This litel spot of erth, that with the sea
Embraced is, and fully gan despise
This wrecched world, and held all vanitee
To respect of the plain felicitee
That is in hevene above. And at the laste,
Ther he was slain his looking down he caste—

And in himself he lough right at the woe
Of hem that wepten for his deeth so faste;
And dampned all our work that followeth so
The blinde lust, the which that may not laste. (V.1811–24)

In that final vision he sees what can never be clearly seen in
this world—that from the long view our blind pleasures,
which cannot last, deserve to be laughed at. But only to the
dead is it given to see and to laugh in that way. For the living,
the last and best counsel of the poem is to cast up the heart's
visage to God (1838–39), to ask Him to defend us from
visible and invisible foes (1866–67); but to follow that counsel
means being blind, willingly blind, to the world. From the
long view that is probably right: we live in the world for a
little while and try as we may to make the best of it, in the
end it is, if seen clearly, all emptiness and foolishness. But the
short view remains to haunt us. Our little joys and our best
efforts at nobility are all we can ever look back on. And what
more can we say, looking back, than what Pandarus says,
that "Alle thing hath time"?

A General Note
on the Text

The overall textual policy for the Signet Classic Poetry series attempts to strike a balance between the convenience and dependability of total modernization, on the one hand, and the authenticity of an established text on the other. Starting with the Restoration and Augustan poets, these guidelines have been followed:

Modern American spelling is used, although punctuation may be adjusted by the editor of each volume when he finds it advisable. In any case, syllabic final "ed" is rendered with grave accent to distinguish it from the silent one, which is written out without apostrophe (e.g., "to gild refinèd gold," but "asked" rather than "ask'd"). Archaic words and forms are kept, naturally, whenever the meter or the sense may require it.

In the case of poets from earlier periods, the text is more clearly a matter of the individual editor's choice, and the type and degree of modernization has been left to his decision. But in any event, archaic typographical conventions ("i," "j," "u," "v," etc.) have all been normalized in the modern way.

A Note on This Edition

The spelling is normalized, and made as modern as Middle English pronunciation will allow. We have attempted to adopt uniform spellings for Middle English words rather than keep the helter-skelter variants of Middle English manuscripts. From such variants we have chosen that spelling most like standard modern spelling (e.g., *had* for "hadde," *find* for "fynde," *sorrow* for "sorowe" or "sorwe"). Where Middle English had alternate pronunciations in Chaucer's dialect, we have often selected the pronunciation whose spelling approximates modern spelling (e.g., *enough*, not "enow"); but we have tried to preserve dialect doublets where Chaucer uses them to advantage. We have introduced no spellings which are exclusively modern (thus *heer* rather than "hair," *greet* rather than "great," *throt* rather than "throat"); and have altered no spellings which could substantially affect pronunciation (thus *yive*, *yaf* rather than "give," "gave," *weder* rather than "weather" or "wether," and *suster* rather than "sister").

The final *-e* is retained only under these conditions: (1) when it is pronounced (see pp. xxxviiff); (2) when the more nearly modern spelling ends in *-e* (as in *mine* or *have*; or in *there*, spelled in the modern way except when it means "where"); (3) when it is needed as an inflexional sign (as in *youre*= "yours," or *twiste*= "twisted"); (4) when its omission might cause confusion with similar words or other pronunciations (thus *hevene*, because it looks more like modern "heaven," whereas *heven* suggests a verb form); and (5) when it helps suggest the length of the preceding vowel (e.g., *speke*, not "spek" lest it suggest the pronunciation "speck").

Since perfect consistency is not possible, there remain in this text enough spelling variants to introduce the student to the mysteries of Middle English orthography. For example, words like *ordre* are so spelled when they seem to elide with the following word. Many old spellings are kept to preserve a rhyme or prosodic effect. And of course variants like *I/ich*, *ere/or*, *either/other/outher*, *als/also*, or *were/weren* themselves reflect variants in the speech of Chaucer's day.

Our purpose was not to preserve the appearance of Middle English on the page, nor to enforce a needless consistency, but by eliminating as best we could any nonfunctional old spellings to make a Middle English text which the student or general reader can read with ease and pronounce with accuracy.

The Introduction was written by Donald R. Howard. The text and Textual Notes were prepared by James Dean. Each reviewed carefully the other's work, and the remaining features of the book were prepared in collaboration.

On Pronouncing Chaucer

Pronouncing Chaucer's English as he pronounced it preserves rhythm and rhymes and brings out the richness of sound which distinguishes his verse. Mispronounced with modern sounds, Chaucer's poetry loses much of its prosodical energy and variousness. Although we cannot know certainly what English sounded like in fourteenth-century London, we can make a reasonable reconstruction from such evidence as rhymes or puns, and from the overall history of English pronunciation. The spelling in the present text is normalized or standardized as an aid to reading and pronouncing. The following rules of thumb will help.

1. *Pronounce all consonants.* Spelling was not standardized in Chaucer's time but roughly phonetic: people wrote what they expected to hear. Thus *knight* was pronounced with a *k* at the beginning, and with *gh* pronounced like German *ch*. *Folk* had an *l* pronounced, and *write* a *w*. Note also that *ch* was always pronounced as in *church*; and *r* was trilled or flapped, as it is today in parts of Britain. In words of French origin, there are two exceptions: initial *h* (as in *honour*) was not pronounced, and *gn* (as in *sign*) was pronounced *n*.

2. *Pronounce final -e at the end of a line, and elsewhere as rhythm requires.* Chaucer probably did not pronounce final *-e* in everyday speech, but he used it for poetical purposes. At the end of a line it is always pronounced. It has the reduced sound "uh" (as we pronounce the *e* in "mechanic" or "waited"). There are other syllabic *e*'s, not final, which may be pronounced—e.g., despaired, shippes, Engelond.

As an aid to learning how syllabic *e*'s work in the scansion of Chaucer's verse, the *e*'s which should be pronounced (but are not pronounced in modern English) have been marked in the Proem to Book I in the following manner:

> But ye lovers that bathen in gladnesse,
> If any drop of pitee in you be,
> Remembereth you on passed hevinesse
> That ye han felt, and on the adversitee
> Of other folk, and thinketh how that ye
> Han felt, that Love durste you displeese,
> Or ye han won him with too greet an eese.

The careful reader can easily develop an "ear" for Chaucer's verse with this much assistance; more would be a crutch. Besides, such marking cannot be authoritative—there are too many variables. For one thing, scholars disagree about the scansion; there is even a small minority who claim the verse scans without any pronounced *e*'s, and among the vast majority who agree that some *e*'s must be pronounced no two would agree on every line. It is not always certain where Chaucer meant to *write* a final *-e* since scribes who copied the manuscripts often added them indiscriminately. And not all those he *did* write have to be pronounced. The opening line of *The Canterbury Tales* is a good example:

> Whan that April with his showres soote

The manuscripts favor the spelling "Aprille,"[1] and a possible pronunciation of the word put the accent on the second syllable. Hence the line may read *Whán thăt Ápríl wíth . . .* or *Whán thăt Áprillĕ wíth . . .* (It may even read *Whán thăt Áprĭllĕ wíth . . .* , for it is perfectly possible to have two short syllables in a metrical foot; here the *-e* would normally be dropped, but coming before the caesura it might have been pronounced in a very reduced way or as a plus-juncture.) For that matter we cannot be absolutely certain if Chaucer said *Whán thăt* or *Whăn thát*. There are other variables as well. Some words may be pronounced in more than one way even in a single dialect (as was possibly the case with April/Aprill*e*). Moreover, English has now, and likely had then, four degrees of stress, so that the "weak and strong" stresses of the verse support a more elaborate and variable stress according to the meaning of sentences and the emphasis a performer wants to give them. (Thus above there are maximum stresses on "April," "showres," and "soote.")[2] Such

---

[1] See Robert O. Evans, "Whan that Aprill(e)?," *Notes and Queries*, n.s. 4(1957), 234–37.
[2] See M. Halle and S.J. Keyser, "Chaucer and the Study of Prosody," *College English*, 28 (1966), 187–219.

interpretative emphasis sometimes affects a final *-e*; for example, one can say *Yĕ háddĕ névĕr thíng sŏ líef, quŏd shé* (*Troilus*, III.870) or *Yé hăd névĕr thíng* . . . The difference depends on whether you emphasize "ye" or "had," but if you emphasize "had" you need a weak syllable after it. Again, there is nothing to prohibit two weak syllables (*Yé hăddĕ névĕr* . . .).

3. *Chaucer has six diphthongs.* A diphthong is two vowel sounds pronounced together as a continuing glide (not two letters in the spelling of a sound)—e.g., the "i" in modern *prize* is a diphthong ("ah-ee"), but "ea" in *meat* is not. In Modern English only some diphthongs are spelled with two letters; in Middle English nearly all were:

Spelling	Middle English Example	Pronounced as in Modern English
ei, ey, ai, ay	vein, pain, may	"pie"; or better yet, a sound halfway between "pie" and "pay": the vowel of "pat" plus the vowel of "be"
au, aw	cause, draw	"how"
ew	few, lewed, shew, beautee	the vowel of "bet" plus the vowel of "full." The sound occurs mainly in these four words.
ew, u	new, trew, knew, cure	the vowel of "be" plus the vowel of "Luke." (Thus *cure* was pronounced as it is in Modern English.)
oi, oy	boy	"boy"
ou, ow	thought, know	the vowel of "ought" plus the vowel of "full"

(Note: the spelling "ou" or "ow" was not always a diphthong, but sometimes a vowel pronounced like Modern English *root*; thus Middle English *house* would be pronounced like "hoos.")

The ending -ion (-ioun) was always pronounced in two syllables.

4. *Pronounce vowels with their "continental" values*, as in German or French.

Vowels might be long or short. The distinction refers to the length of time they were held while pronounced, plus the quality of the sound (see chart below). Roughly, vowels were long in stressed syllables unless immediately followed by two or more consonants in the same word.[3] Vowels which were short in stressed syllables are still "short" in modern English for the most part, and one's instincts can be trusted fairly well in pronouncing them (e.g., *love, God, pity, biddeth, wicked, live*).

The spellings "e" and "o" each represent two vowel pronunciations, called "open" and "close" (referring to the relative position of the lips while articulating them). The following rules will decide which is which in most cases, though there are exceptions:

Rule of thumb for close and open e: go by the modern spelling. Words spelled with double e ("ee") in Modern English (or sometimes "ie" as in "thief") had close *e* in Middle English and were pronounced as in modern "bait"; other long *e*'s were open, and were pronounced as in modern "bed."

Rule of thumb for close and open o: go by the modern pronunciation. Words pronounced in Modern English like *hope, so*, etc. had open *o* in Middle English, and were pronounced as in modern "law"; other long *o*'s were close, and were pronounced as in modern "low."

The Middle English examples are from the Proem to Book I.

---

[3] Exceptions: all vowels before *ld* are long, as are *i* and *o* before *mb*, and *i* and *u* before *nd*.

LONG VOWELS

Sound	Middle English Example	Pronounced as in Modern English
ā	bathen	"father"
close ē	weepen	"bait"
open ē	eese	"bed"
ī	write	"beet"
close ō	sooth	"low"
open ō	hope	"law"
ū	double	"Luke"
[ü	aventure ;	pronounced as in French *tu*; used for this vowel in words of French origin.]

SHORT VOWELS

Sound	Middle English Example	Pronounced as in Modern English
ă	that, after	"part"
ĕ	{ hem { joy*e*	"bet" "even"
ĭ	his	"bit"
ŏ	torment, of	"bottle"[4]
ŭ	purpose	"full"

---

[4] As pronounced in England and New England, i.e., rounded toward the sound in "bought," not as in American "*bah*ttle."

Chronology

1343 (?)   Born in London, son of John and Agnes Chaucer; had at least one sister, Catherine. Father and grandfather, wine merchants, both held public office, as Chaucer himself was to do. Schooling possibly at St. Paul's Cathedral School, London. By the time he reached maturity he knew Latin, French, and Italian.

1357   Served as a page in the household of Lionel, Earl of Ulster (the King's son) and Elizabeth, Countess of Ulster; this would have been a phase of his education.

1359–60   In France with the English army, was taken prisoner near Reims and released on ransom, to which the King contributed. Returned to England in May, then back to France during peace negotiations, serving as courier.

1361–66   Whereabouts unknown. He may have been for a time with Lionel in Ireland. He may also have been a student at the Inns of Court, where he would have received training in law and finance appropriate to his subsequent career as a public servant.

?   Married Philippa Roet. They had a son Thomas, a younger son Lewis. There are records of an Elizabeth and an Agnes "Chaucy" in the circle of John of Gaunt, possibly daughters of the poet.

1366   In Spain, probably on diplomatic mission.

1367	In the service of King Edward III; enrolled among the Esquires of the Royal Household. Beginning about this time and for the remainder of his life, Chaucer was in contact with the important people of his age, among them the chief poets of his day.
1368	Abroad in the King's service.
1369	In France, in military service, probably with John of Gaunt on a campaign in Picardy. Throughout this period of his life Chaucer was under the protection of John of Gaunt. Gaunt's wife, the Duchess Blanche, died in this year; Chaucer's *Book of the Duchess* is an elegy to her.
1370	Abroad in the King's service. During these early years Chaucer wrote some of his shorter works, such as the *ABC* and lyrics based on French models ("The Complaint of Venus," "To Rosemounde," "Merciless Beautee," etc.). Probably translated part of the *Romaunt of the Rose*.
1372–73	In Italy, to negotiate with Genoa about the use of an English port for commerce; visited Florence; undoubtedly bought some Italian books, among them Dante's *Divine Comedy*. From this period can be dated the influence of Italian literature on Chaucer. *The House of Fame* begun about this time, unfinished; *Anelida*; two tales later to show up in *Canterbury Tales* likely begun now—the legend of St. Cecilia (Second Nun's Tale) and the "tragedies" of the Monk's Tale.
1374	Took up residence in London at Aldgate (May). Appointed Controller of Customs and Subsidy of wools, skins, and hides in Port of London (June). Enjoyed great financial prosperity.
1376	On mission of secret service to the King.

1377   In Flanders on secret mission for the King; in
            France, in connection with negotiations for
            peace. Coronation of Richard II (June 22).
            The new king confirmed Chaucer's office as
            Controller of Customs. In France, evidently to
            negotiate a marriage between King Richard
            and the daughter of the King of France.

1378   In Italy (Lombardy) to secure help in the war
            with France. Probably from this trip he became
            acquainted with the work of Petrarch and
            Boccaccio, including Boccaccio's *Il Filostrato*,
            chief source for the *Troilus*, and Petrarch's
            song *S'amor non è*, which he translated and
            included in the *Troilus* as "Troilus's Song" (I.
            400–20).

1380   Released by one Cecily Chaumpaigne from
            legal action *"de raptu meo"*; it is not known
            whether *raptu* here means "rape" or "abduc-
            tion" or "seizure," nor is it known what, if
            anything, Chaucer had to do with the case.

1380–86   *Parliament of Fowls* written; *Palamon* (the
            antecedent of the Knight's Tale); translation of
            Boethius. Was writing various poems and
            ballads and working on *Troilus and Criseyde*.

1382   Appointed Controller of the Petty Customs on
            wines and other merchandise.

1385   Received permission to have a deputy in the
            wool custom; appointed Justice of the Peace
            in Kent and took up at least partial residence
            there, probably at Greenwich.

1386–87   *Troilus and Criseyde* completed.
            Began *Legend of Good Women* possibly at re-
            quest of the new queen, continued working on
            it for some years in a desultory way before
            abandoning it.

1386–89   Ended service in the Customs and left the
            house in Aldgate; the reason is unknown (the

hostility of Gloucester has been suggested). Fell into debt.

1386   Appointed Knight of the Shire; sat in Parliament only the one year, was not reappointed. The office was evidently secured by the King's influence, but Gloucester and his adherents now began to gain control over the young King.

1387 (?)   Death of his wife.
In Calais on official mission, its purpose unknown. During this period he was working on the General Prologue and the earlier Canterbury Tales. The idea of writing "some comedye" is mentioned at the end of *Troilus and Criseyde.*

1389–91   Richard II came of age; appointed Chaucer Clerk of the King's Works, an important office. He was in charge of royal palaces, chapels, parks, etc. Resigned commission in 1391, his reason unknown. Had many workmen under him on various projects, handled large amounts of money. The government owed him a considerable sum when he turned in his accounts. In September 1390, was twice robbed and once assaulted by the same band of robbers, public funds being involved.

1391   Appointed Deputy Forester of the royal forest of North Petherton; his son Thomas was later appointed to the same post.

1391–92   *Treatise on the Astrolabe.*

1393–1400   Worked on *The Canterbury Tales* plus a few short poems, e.g., "Envoy to Scogan" (1393), "Envoy to Bukton" (ca. 1396), "Complaint to his Purse" (its envoy written in 1399, addressed to new King Henry IV). It is very difficult to determine the order in which *The Canterbury Tales* were written. Those written earlier were doubtless revised. Chaucer worked on a number of poems at once, leaving many unfinished.

1399   Coronation of Henry IV. Chaucer's annuities
        renewed, additional annuity of forty marks
        granted. Took long-term lease on house in
        garden of Westminster Abbey. Was engaged in
        "arduous and urgent matters" in the King's
        service.

1400   Died October 25; buried in that part of West-
        minster Abbey which was to be known as the
        "poets' corner," the first poet buried there.

Selected Bibliography

EDITIONS

Root, Robert Kilburn (ed.). *The Book of Troilus and Criseyde*. Princeton, N.J.: Princeton University Press, 1926.

Baugh, Albert C. (ed.). *Chaucer's Major Poetry*. New York: Appleton-Century-Crofts, 1963.

Donaldson, E. Talbot (ed.). *Chaucer's Poetry: An Anthology for the Modern Reader*. 2nd ed. New York: Ronald Press, 1975.

Robinson, F. N. (ed.). *The Works of Geoffrey Chaucer*. 2nd ed. Boston: Houghton Mifflin, 1957.

Skeat, W. W. (ed.). *The Complete Works of Geoffrey Chaucer*. 7 vols. Oxford: Clarendon Press, 1894–97.

LIFE

Chute, Marchette. *Geoffrey Chaucer of England*. 1946; rpt. New York: E. P. Dutton, 1958.

Crow, M. M., and C. C. Olson (eds.). *Chaucer Life-Records*. Oxford: Clarendon; Austin: University of Texas Press, 1966.

COLLECTIONS

Brewer, D. S. (ed.). *Chaucer and Chaucerians: Critical Studies in Middle English Literature*. University, Alabama: University of Alabama Press, 1966.

—————— (ed.). *Geoffrey Chaucer*. (Writers and Their Background.) 1974; rpt. Athens, Ohio: Ohio University Press, 1975.

Cawley, A. C. (ed.). *Chaucer's Mind and Art*. Edinburgh and London: Oliver & Boyd, 1969.

Economou, George D. (ed.). *Geoffrey Chaucer: A Collection of Original Articles*. (Contemporary Studies in Literature.) New York: McGraw-Hill, 1975.

Newstead, Helaine (ed.). *Chaucer and His Contemporaries: Essays on Medieval Literature and Thought.* Greenwich, Conn.: Fawcett Publications, 1968.

Rowland, Beryl (ed.). *Companion to Chaucer Studies.* Toronto-New York-London: Oxford University Press, 1968.

Schoeck, Richard, and Jerome Taylor (eds.). *Chaucer Criticism II: Troilus and Criseyde & the Minor Poems.* Notre Dame, Ind.: University of Notre Dame Press, 1961.

Wagenknecht, Edward (ed.). *Chaucer: Modern Essays in Criticism.* New York: Oxford University Press, 1959.

BIBLIOGRAPHY

Hammond, E. P. *Chaucer: A Bibliographical Manual.* New York: Macmillan, 1908.

Griffith, D. D. *Bibliography of Chaucer: 1908–1953.* Seattle: University of Washington Press, 1955.

Crawford, W. R. *Bibliography of Chaucer: 1954–63.* Seattle: University of Washington Press, 1967.

Baugh, Albert C. *Chaucer.* (Goldentree Bibliographies in Language and Literature.) New York: Appleton-Century-Crofts, 1968.

Chaucer Review: A Journal of Medieval Studies and Literary Criticism. University Park, Pa.: Pennsylvania State University, 1966—. [Has annual bibliography.]

CRITICISM

Barney, Stephen. "Troilus Bound." *Speculum,* 47 (1972), 445–58.

Bloomfield, Morton W. "Distance and Predestination in *Troilus and Criseyde.*" *PMLA,* 72 (1957), 14–26.

Coghill, Nevill. *The Poet Chaucer.* 2nd ed. London-New York-Toronto: Oxford University Press, 1967.

David, Alfred. "The Hero of the *Troilus.*" *Speculum,* 37 (1962), 566–81.

Donaldson, E. Talbot. *Speaking of Chaucer.* Athlone Press, England, 1970; rpt. New York: W. W. Norton, 1972.

Gordon, Ida L. *The Double Sorrow of Troilus: A Study of Ambiguities in Troilus and Criseyde.* Oxford: Clarendon Press, 1970.

Hatcher, Elizabeth R. "Chaucer and the Psychology of Fear: Troilus in Book V." *ELH,* 40 (1973), 307–24.

Howard, Donald R. "Courtly Love and the Lust of the Flesh:

Troilus and Criseyde." In *The Three Temptations: Medieval Man in Search of the World.* Princeton, N.J.: Princeton University Press, 1966. Pp. 77–160.

————. "Experience, Language, and Consciousness: *Troilus and Criseyde,* II, 596–931." In *Medieval Literature and Folklore Studies: Essays in Honor of Francis Lee Utley.* Jerome Mandel and Bruce A. Rosenberg (eds.). New Brunswick, N.J.: Rutgers University Press, 1970. Pp. 173–92.

————. "Literature and Sexuality: Book III of Chaucer's *Troilus.*" *Massachusetts Review,* 8 (1967), 442–56.

Jordan, Robert M. "The Narrator in Chaucer's *Troilus.*" *ELH,* 25 (1958), 237–57.

Kirby, Thomas A. *Chaucer's Troilus: A Study in Courtly Love.* University, La.: Louisiana State University, 1940.

Kittredge, George L. *Chaucer and His Poetry.* Cambridge, Mass.: Harvard University Press, 1915.

Lewis, C. S. *The Allegory of Love: A Study in Medieval Tradition.* London: Oxford University Press, 1936.

————. "What Chaucer Really Did to *Il Filostrato.*" *E & S,* 17 (1932), 56–75.

McCall, John P. "Five-Book Structure in Chaucer's *Troilus.*" *MLQ,* 23 (1962), 297–308.

————. "The Trojan Scene in Chaucer's *Troilus.*" *ELH,* 29 (1962), 263–75.

Meech, Sanford B. *Design in Chaucer's Troilus.* Syracuse, N.Y.: Syracuse University Press, 1959.

Muscatine, Charles. *Chaucer and the French Tradition: A Study in Style and Meaning.* Berkeley and Los Angeles: University of California Press, 1957.

Payne, Robert O. *The Key of Remembrance: A Study of Chaucer's Poetics.* New Haven: Yale University Press, 1963.

Robertson, D. W., Jr. "Chaucerian Tragedy." *ELH,* 19 (1952), 1–37.

Sams, H. W. "The Dual Time-Scheme in Chaucer's *Troilus.*" *MLN,* 56 (1941), 94–100.

Steadman, John M. *Disembodied Laughter: Chaucer's Troilus and the Apotheosis Tradition.* Berkeley: University of California Press, 1972.

Tatlock, J. S. P. "The Epilog of Chaucer's *Troilus.*" *MP,* 18 (1921), 625–59.

Utley, Francis L. "Scene-Division in Chaucer's *Troilus and Criseyde.*" In *Studies in Medieval Literature in Honor of*

Professor Albert Croll Baugh. Philadelphia, Pa.: University
of Pennsylvania Press, 1961. Pp. 109–38.

LANGUAGE AND REFERENCE

Baugh, Albert C. *A History of the English Language.* 2nd ed.
New York: Appleton-Century-Crofts, 1957.

Kökeritz, Helge. *A Guide to Chaucer's Pronunciation.* 1954;
rpt. New York: Holt, Rinehart & Winston, 1961.

Middle English Dictionary. H. Kurath and S. Kuhn (eds.).
Ann Arbor Mich.: University of Michigan Press, 1956—
(in progress).

Mossé, Fernand. *A Handbook of Middle English.* James A.
Walker (trans.). Baltimore, Md.: The Johns Hopkins University Press, 1952.

Pyles, Thomas. *The Origins and Development of the English
Language.* New York: Harcourt, Brace & World, 1964.

Tatlock, J. S. P., and A. G. Kennedy. *Concordance to the
Complete Works of Geoffrey Chaucer.* Washington, D.C.:
Carnegie Institution, 1927.

COLLECTIONS OF PHOTOGRAPHS

Halliday, Frank Ernest. *Chaucer and His World.* London:
Thames & Hudson, 1968.

Hussey, Maurice. *Chaucer's World: A Pictorial Companion.*
Cambridge, Eng.: Cambridge University Press, 1967.

Loomis, Roger Sherman. *A Mirror of Chaucer's World.*
Princeton, N.J.: Princeton University Press, 1965.

BACKGROUND

Bowden, Muriel. *A Reader's Guide to Geoffrey Chaucer.*
1964; rpt. New York: Noonday Press, 1966.

Brewer, D. S. *Chaucer in His Time.* London: Thomas Nelson,
1963.

Coulton, G. G. *Chaucer and His England.* 1908; rpt. New
York: Russell & Russell, 1957.

Curry, Walter Clyde. *Chaucer and the Medieval Sciences.*
2nd ed. New York: Barnes & Noble, 1960.

Hussey, Maurice, A. C. Spearing, and James Winny. *An Introduction to Chaucer.* Cambridge, Eng.: Cambridge University Press, 1965.

McKisack, May. *The Fourteenth Century, 1307–1399*. Oxford: Oxford University Press, 1959.

Rickert, Edith (comp.). *Chaucer's World*. C. C. Olson and M. M. Crow (eds.). New York: Columbia University Press, 1948.

Robertson, D. W., Jr. *Chaucer's London*. New York: Wiley, 1968.

Smyser, H. M. "The Domestic Background of *Troilus and Criseyde*." *Speculum*, 31 (1956), 297–315.

Scene Outline of Chaucer's *Troilus*

The following scenario divides the five books of the poem into their component scenes and offers a synopsis of the action, with line numbers. Three asterisks have been placed in the text of the poem where one scene ends and a new one begins. The outline is meant to be used as a guide or roadmap in helping the reader through the complicated action of the poem.

BOOK I

Proem: 1–56   Addressed to Tisiphone, one of the Furies, in the form of a bidding-prayer to lovers. The Proem tells us the form of the work and its theme, and forewarns us of its outcome.

57–133   Calkas, the soothsayer, knowing that Troy will fall, deserts to the Greeks (57–91). His daughter Criseyde, left behind by her father, seeks the protection of Hector.

134–546   April. Troilus sees Criseyde in the temple of Palladion and as he mocks lovers is struck by the God of Love (134–322). In his palace he thinks of her and sings of Love, complaining of his plight.

547–1092   Pandarus persuades Troilus to reveal what lady he loves, has him repent to the God of Love, and promises help. At the end we see Pandarus conceiving a plan, and Troilus ennobled by Love.

BOOK II

BOOK III

BOOK IV

29–343   Calkas arranges to have Criseyde exchanged for Antenor, and Troilus complains against Fortune, collapsing into despair.

344–658   Pandarus and Troilus discuss what is to be done; Pandarus suggests a new love affair (393–427), but Troilus rejects the idea out of hand. Pandarus then suggests they elope, but Troilus explains why he cannot in honor do anything to stop her departure or abduct her.

659–945   At her palace Criseyde is visited by some women and hides her dread at leaving Troy (659–735). Alone, she meditates sorrowfully on this turn of events (736–805); Pandarus tells her of Troilus's distress and urges her to give encouragement.

946–1127   Troilus in a temple meditates upon predestination (946–1082, a passage drawn from Boethius). Pandarus reassures him, and sends him to her.

1128–1701   Troilus visits Criseyde. Criseyde faints and Troilus, thinking she is dead, is about to kill himself but she revives and restrains him (1149–1246). They speak of the exchange. Troilus at the last moment suggests they elope, but she presents idealistic arguments against eloping and promises to deceive her father and return to Troy in ten days. Troilus leaves in the morning with foreboding.

BOOK V

1–14   The narrator darkly mentions the Fates. Three years have passed since Troilus first saw Criseyde in the temple.

15–196   Troilus consigns Criseyde to the Greeks and Diomede; Diomede immediately offers Criseyde his friendship and protection.

197–686   Troilus alone in woe; he has bad dreams (197–273). Pandarus tries to cheer him up at Sarpedon's villa, but they leave after only a week (274–518). Troilus miserably awaits her return, remembering the past.

687–1099   Criseyde among the Greeks expresses her determination to return, but two months are to pass (687–770). On the tenth day after leaving Troy, Criseyde entertains Diomede, who speaks of love (771–1015). Criseyde decides to remain with the Greeks and to accept Diomede as her lover.

1100–1666   On the tenth day after parting, Troilus and Pandarus wait for Criseyde's return. Pandarus sees, and Troilus slowly realizes, that she will not return. He dreams of a boar embracing Criseyde and writes her a letter (1233–1421); her reply, only described, is brief and vague. Cassandra interprets the dream of the boar correctly, but Troilus rejects the interpretation (1440–1533). Troilus writes her often; she sends a tasteless reply, quoted in full, which Troilus regards as "strange" (1583–1645). Hope lost, Troilus finds on the captured coat of Diomede his own brooch that he had given her, and knows she is no longer to be trusted.

1667–1743   Troilus complains of his ill fortune, the worse because he still loves her. Pandarus can only say that he hates Criseyde and is sorry.

1744–1869   The narrator, with an apology for giving women a bad name (1765–85), bids farewell to his book (1786–1799), briefly recounts Troilus's death in battle and his ascent to the eighth sphere (1744–1827), draws a moral about the transience of earthly joys and the inadequacy of paganism (1828–55), dedicates his poem to Gower and Strode, asks the protection of the Trinity and prays that we be worthy of Christ's mercy.

TROILUS AND CRISEYDE

Book One

PROEM

The double sorrow° of Troilus to tellen
That was the king Priamus' son of Troye,°
In loving how° his aventures fellen°
Fro woe to wele, and after out of joye,°
My purpose is, ere that I parte fro ye.°   5
Thesiphone,° thou help me for t'endite°
These woeful vers that weepen° as I write.

To thee clepe° I, thou goddess of torment,
Thou cruel fury, sorrowing ever in paine:
Help me that am the sorrowful instrument   10
That helpeth lovers, as I can, to plaine.°

1 double sorrow the narrator suggests the theme and structure of the *Troilus* with this opening phrase. Troilus will pass from the woe of love to happiness, then back to woe as he loses both his lady and his life. The narrative begins in the high style with a reverse construction whose subject and verb occur in line 5: "My purpose is . . . to tell the double sorrow of Troilus" **2 That . . . Troye** who was the son of King Priam of Troy **3 In . . . how** how in loving **3 fellen** went **4 Fro . . . joye** i.e., in a circular manner. Chaucer here and in the Proem to Book IV places his romance in the tradition of medieval tragedy based upon the turning of Fortune's wheel. Though Fortune can bring prosperity (*wele*), she inevitably causes suffering and death. In The Monk's Prologue to *The Canterbury Tales*, Chaucer defines tragedy as "a certain storye . . . Of him that stood in greet prosperitee,/ And is y-fallen out of high degree/ Into misery, and endeth wrecchedly" **5 ere . . . ye** Chaucer imagines himself reading before an audience **6 Thesiphone** Tisiphone, one of the three classical Furies. The Furies avenged crimes and were associated with grief and pain. While Chaucer invokes pagan gods in his proems, he will close his work with a hymn to the Trinity and the Virgin Mary **6 t'endite** to compose **7 vers . . . weepen** verses which weep. The ending *-en* is plural **8 clepe** call, call upon **11 That . . . plaine** (instrument)

For well sit it, the soothe for to sayne,°
A woeful wight to han a dreery fere
And to a sorrowful tale a sorry cheere.°

For I, that God of Love's servants serve,°   15
Ne dare to Love, for mine unlikelinesse,
Prayen for speed, al sholde I therefore sterve°—
So far am I from his help in darknesse.
But natheless, if this° *may doon*° *gladnesse*
To any lover, and his cause availe,   20
Have he my thank,° *and mine be this travaille.*°

But ye lovers that bathen in gladnesse,
If any drop of pitee in you be,
Remembereth you on passed hevinesse°
That ye han felt, and on the adversitee   25
Of other folk, and thinketh how that ye
Han felt, that Love durste° *you displeese,*
Or° *ye han won him with too greet an eese.*

And prayeth° *for hem that been in the cas*
Of Troilus, as ye may after heere,°   30
That Love hem bring in hevene to solas.°
And eek for me prayeth to God so deere
That I have might to shew in some mannere

that, so far as I am able, helps lovers to complain   **12 well ...
sayne** it is entirely appropriate, to tell the truth   **13–14 A ...
cheere** for an unhappy person to have a mournful companion
(Tisiphone), and for a sorrowful tale to have a dreary face
15 that ... serve who serve the servants of the God of Love.
Chaucer's calling himself a servant of lovers perhaps alludes to
the Pope's epithet as "servant of the servants of God." Troilus and
Criseyde will make a religion of love; and Chaucer here suggests
his own role as a high priest in this worship   **16–17 Ne ... sterve**
dare not, because of my unworthiness, pray to Love for my own
success—even though I might therefore die   **19 this** i.e., the tale,
though it could refer back to *plaine* (line 11)   **19 doon** bring
21 Have ... thank may he have my blessing   **21 travaille** labor
24 Remembereth ... hevinesse recall past grief   **27 that ... durste**
when Love dared to   **28 Or** or else   **29–46 prayeth ... plesaunce**
the requests for prayers in these lines parallel ecclesiastical "bid-
ding prayers," in which the priest asks the congregation to pray for
various people. Chaucer carries on this function as the high priest of
Love   **30 after heere** hear after this   **31 solas** pleasure

Swich° pain and woe as Love's folk endure
In Troilus' unsely° aventure.   35

And biddeth eek for hem that been despaired
In love that never nill recovered be,°
And eek for hem that falsely been apaired°
Through wicked tongues, be it he or she.
Thus biddeth God, for his benignitee,   40
To grant hem soon out of this world to passe
That been despaired out of Love's grace.

And biddeth eek for hem that been at eese,°
That God hem grant ay good perseveraunce,°
And send hem might hir ladies so to pleese   45
That it to Love be worship and plesaunce.°
For so hope I my soule best avaunce°
To pray for hem that Love's servants be,
And write hir woe, and live in charitee,

And for to have of hem compassioun   50
As though I were hir owne brother deere.
Now herkeneth with a good intencioun:°
For now will I goon° straight to my mattere,
In which ye may the double sorrows heere
Of Troilus in loving of Criseyde,   55
And how that she forsook him ere she deide.°

It is well wist° how that the Greekes, stronge
In armes, with a thousand shippes wente
To Troyewardes,° and the citee longe
Assegeden, nigh ten yeer ere they stente,°   60

---

34 **Swich** such   35 **unsely** unhappy   36–37 **biddeth . . . be** pray
also for those who are despairing of love (and) who will never
recover. *Nill*= *ne will,* will not   38 **apaired** harmed. The danger of
gossip or slander in a love affair was a constant preoccupation
43 **at eese** in gladness—i.e., not despairing of love   44 **ay . . . per-
severaunce** always good continuance   45–46 **send . . . plesaunce**
send them the power to please their ladies in such a way that it is a
worship and delight to the God of Love   47 **avaunce** to profit
52 **herkeneth . . . intencioun** listen with a good will   53 **goon** go
(cf. *doon*= to do)   56 **deide** died   57 **wist** known   59 **To Troye-
wardes** to Troy   60 **Assegeden . . . stente** besieged nearly ten years

In diverse wise and in one intente
The ravishing to wreken of Heleine,
By Paris doon, they wroughten all hir paine.°

Now fell it so° that in the town there was
Dwelling a lord of greet auctoritee,   65
A greet divine that cleped was° Calkas,
That in science° so expert was that he
Knew well that Troye shold destroyed be,
By answer of his god that highte° thus:
Daun° Phebus or Apollo Delphicus.   70

So when this Calkas knew by calkulinge,°
And eek by answer of this Apollo,
That Greekes sholden swich a people bringe
Through which that Troye muste been fordo,°
He cast anon° out of the town to go.   75
For well wist he by sort° that Troye sholde
Destroyed been, yea, wolde whoso nolde.°

For which for to departen softely
Took purpose full this foreknowinge wise,°
And to the Greekes' host° full prively   80
He stal anon. And they in courteis wise
Him diden bothe worship and service,°
In trust that he hath konning hem to reede°
In every peril which that is to dreede.°

The noise up rose when it was first espied°   85
Through all the town and generally was spoken
That Calkas traitor fled was and allied

before they stopped   61–63 **In . . . paine** in different ways, but with
a single intention, they did all they could to avenge the abduction of
Helen by Paris   64 **fell . . . so** it so happened   66 **divine . . . was**
soothsayer who was named   67 **science** i.e., of soothsaying   69
highte was called   70 **Daun** lord   71 **calkulinge** forecasting; with
a pun on Calkas's name   74 **fordo** destroyed   75 **cast anon** de-
cided soon   76 **sort** divination   77 **wolde . . . nolde** whoever
should wish it or not; *nolde= ne wolde*, would not   78–79 **For . . .
wise** on this account this foreknowing wise man fully decided to
depart quietly   80 **host** army   81–82 **they . . . service** they in a
courteous fashion did him both honor and service   83 **In . . . reede**
trusting that he has the skill to advise them   84 **which . . . dreede**
which is to be feared   85 **espied** noticed

With hem of Greece, and casten to be wroken°
On him that falsely had his faith so broken,
And saiden he and all his kin at ones   90
Been worthy for to brennen, fell and bones.°

Now hadde Calkas left in this mischaunce,
Al unwist of this false and wicked deede,
His daughter, which that was in greet penaunce,°
For of her life she was full sore in dreede,   95
As she that niste what was best to reede;°
For both a widow was she and alone
Of any freend to whom she durst her mone.°

Criseyde was this lady° name al right—
As to my doom° in all Troye's citee   100
Nas none so fair; for, passing every wight,°
So angelic was her natif beautee°
That like a thing immortal seemed she,
As doth an hevenish parfit° creature
That down was sent in scorning of nature.°   105

This lady which that alday herde at eere°
Her fader's shame, his falseness and treesoun,
Well nigh out of her wit for sorrow and feere,
In widow's habit large of samite brown,°
On knees she fell beforn Hector adown,   110
With pitous voice and tenderly weepinge,
His mercy bade, herselven excusinge.°

Now was this Hector pitous of nature,
And saw that she was sorrowfully begon°

88 **casten . . . wroken** (the Trojans) determined to be avenged 90–
91 **all . . . bones** all his kin together were worthy to burn, skin and
bones 94 **penaunce** suffering 95–96 **For . . . reede** for she was
very afraid for her life, as she didn't know what was the best advice
to give herself. *Niste= ne wiste*, didn't know 97–98 **alone . . .
mone** without any friend to whom she dared complain about her
situation 99 **lady** lady's 100 **As . . . doom** in my opinion 101
passing . . . wight surpassing every creature 102 **natif beautee**
natural beauty 104 **parfit** perfect (cf. Fr. *parfait*) 105 **in . . .
nature** to scorn natural (worldly) things 106 **alday . . . eere**
everyday heard with her ears 109 **In . . . brown** in a flowing
widow's dress of brown samite silk 112 **herselven excusinge** pro-
claiming her innocence 114 **begon** situated

And that she was so fair a creature,   *115*
Of his goodness he gladded her° anon
And saide, "Let your fader's treeson goon
Forth with mischance,° and ye yourself in joye
Dwelleth with us, while you good list,° in Troye.

And all th'honour that men may doon you° have,   *120*
As ferforth as° your fader dwelled here,
Ye shull have, and your body shall men save°
As far as I may aught enquere or heere."°
And she him thanked with full humble cheere,°
And ofter wold, and° it had been his wille,   *125*
And took her leeve, and home,° and held her stille.

And in her house she abode with swich meinee
As till her honour neede was to holde.°
And while she was dwelling in that citee
Kept her estate,° and both of young and olde   *130*
Full well beloved; and well men of her tolde.°
But whether that she children had or noon,
I reed it not; therefore I let it goon.

*   *   *

The thinges fellen as they doon of werre°
Betwixen hem of Troy and Greekes ofte.   *135*
For some day boughten they of Troy it derre,
And eft the Greekes founden nothing softe
The folk of Troy.° And thus Fortune on lofte,
Now up, now down, gan hem to wheelen bothe
After her course ay while that they were wrothe.   *140*

116 **gladded her** made her glad   117–18 **goon . . . mischance** i.e.,
go to the devil   119 **while . . . list** as long as it pleases you   120
doon you cause you to   121 **As . . . as** as much as when   122
save protect, keep inviolate   123 **As . . . heere** i.e., to the extent
that I have anything to say about it   124 **cheere** face, manner
125 **And . . . and** and would have done so more often, if   126
home went home   127–28 **with . . . holde** with such a house-
hold company as she needed to retain for the sake of her honor.
The medieval nobles always retained and traveled with servants,
and Chaucer imagines that the Trojan nobility did the same
130 **Kept . . . estate** maintained her social position   131 **tolde**
spoke   134 **of werre** in war   136–38 **For . . . Troy** for on one
day the Trojans had a worse time of it (lit. "bought it dearer"),
and on another day the Greeks found the Trojans not at all soft

But how this town came to destruccion
Ne falleth not to purpose me to telle;°
For it were° here a long digression
Fro my matter, and you too long to dwelle.°
But the Trojan gestes° as they felle   145
In Homer or in Dares or in Dite,°
Whoso that can may reed hem as they write.

But though that Greekes hem of Troye shetten°
And hir citee beseeged all aboute,
Hir olde usage nolde they not letten   150
As for to honour hir goddes full devoute;°
But aldermost° in honour, out of doute,
They had a relic hight Palladion°
That was hir trust aboven everichoon.

And so befell when comen was the time   155
Of Aperil, when clothed is the meede°
With newe green, of lusty Ver° the prime,
And swoote smellen° flowers white and rede,
In sundry wises shewed, as I reede,
The folk of Troy hir observances olde,   160
Palladione's feste for to holde.

And to the temple in all hir beste wise
In general there wente many a wight
To herkenen of Palladion the service.
And namely,° so many a lusty knight,   165
So many a lady fresh and maiden bright,
Full well arrayed, both the most and leeste°—
Yea, bothe for the seeson and the feste.

---

142 **Ne . . . telle** does not suit my purpose to relate   143 **were** would be   144 **dwelle** delay   145 **gestes** stories   146 **Homer . . . Dite** Chaucer had no first-hand knowledge of any of these writers. Dares of Phrygia and Dictys of Crete were the supposed authors of eyewitness prose accounts of the Troy story, each sympathetic to a different side. Chaucer does not cite these historians as his sources, for he maintains later on that he is translating a writer named Lollius; he is assigning them for outside reading   148 **shetten** shut in   150–51 **Hir . . . devoute** they (the Trojans) wouldn't give up their ancient custom of devoutly honoring their gods   152 **aldermost** most of all   153 **hight Palladion** called the Palladium (a statue of Pallas Athena)   156 **meede** meadow   157 **Ver** Spring   158 **swoote smellen** smell sweet   165 **namely** especially   167 **Full . . . leeste** very well dressed, both the important and less important

Among these other folk was Criseyda,
In widow's habit black. But natheless,   *170*
Right as our firste letter is now an A,°
In beautee first so stood she makeless.°
Her goodly looking gladded all the press.
Nas never yet seen thing to been praised derre,°
Nor under cloude black so bright a sterre,°   *175*

As was Criseyde—as folk said everichoone°
That her behelden in her blacke weede.°
And yet she stood full low° and still, alone,
Behinden other folk, in litel brede°—
And nigh the door, ay under shame's dreede°—   *180*
Simple of attire and debonaire of cheere,°
With full assured looking and mannere.

This Troilus, as he was wont to guide°
His younge knightes, led hem up and down
In thilke° large temple on every side,   *185*
Beholding ay the ladies of the town,
Now here, now there, for no devocioun
Had he to none to reven him his reste,°
But gan to praise and lacken° whom him leste.

And in his walk full fast he gan to wayten°   *190*
If knight or squier of his compaignye
Gan for to sigh, or let his eyen baiten°
On any woman that he coud espye.
He wolde smile and holden it follye
And say him thus: "God wot° she sleepeth softe   *195*
For love of thee, when thou turnest° full ofte.

people   171 **A** possibly a compliment to Richard II's wife, Queen
Anne   172 **makeless** matchless   173–74 **Her . . . derre** her seemly
appearance gladdened the whole company. There was never yet seen
anything to be praised more highly   175 **sterre** star   176 **everi-
choone** every one   177 **weede** clothes   178 **low** humbly   179 **in
. . . brede** i.e., taking up little space   180 **under . . . dreede** in the
timidity of modesty   181 **debonaire . . . cheere** gracious of manner
(cf. Fr. *de bon aire*)   183 **wont . . . guide** accustomed to com-
mand   185 **thilke** that   187–88 **for . . . reste** for he had no com-
mitment to any of them to lose sleep over   189 **lacken** disparage
190 **wayten** observe   192 **eyen baiten** eyes feed   195 **wot** knows
196 **turnest** toss and turn (in bed)

"I have herde told, pardieux,° of your livinge,
Ye lovers, and your lewed observaunces!°—
And which a labour folk han in winninge
Of love, and in keeping which doutaunces!°   *200*
And when your prey is lost, woe and penaunces!
O verray fooles, nice° and blind be ye!
There nis not one can ware by other be!"°

And with that word he gan cast up the browe°
Ascaunces,° "Lo, is this not wisely spoken?"   *205*
At which the God of Love gan looken rowe
Right for despite, and shop for to been wroken.°
He kidde° anon his bowe nas not broken.
For suddenly he hit him at the fulle°—
And yet as proud a pecock can he pulle!°   *210*

O blinde world!° O blind intencioun!
How often falleth all the effect contraire
Of surquidry and foul presumpcioun!°
For caught is proud and caught is debonaire:
This Troilus is clomben° on the staire   *215*
And litel weeneth that he mot° descenden,
But alday faileth thing that fooles wenden.°

As proude Bayard° ginneth for to skippe
Out of the way, so pricketh him his corn,°

197 **pardieux** by God, certainly 198 **lewed observaunces** stupid
rites 199–200 **which . . . doutaunces** what pains people take to get
love and what anxieties they have to keep it 202 **nice** silly 203
There . . . be there is not one who can take warning from another
204 **gan . . . browe** raised his eyebrows 205 **Ascaunces** as if to say
206–7 **gan . . . wroken** glowered contemptuously, and planned to
be revenged (*rowe*= lit. "roughly") 208 **kidde** showed 209 **at the
fulle** i.e., squarely 210 **yet . . . pulle** even now he can pluck as
proud a peacock (as Troilus) 211 **O . . . world!** Chaucer launches
into a rhetorical style called *exclamatio*, as he addresses an "apos-
trophe" to the reader or listener, in which he comments on the story.
Cf. the Pardoner's apostrophe on gluttony in Chaucer's *Canterbury
Tales:* "O womb, O belly, O stinking cod!" 212–13 **How . . . pre-
sumpcioun!** how often does pride and wretched presumption bring
about the contrary (of what we hope or expect) 215 **is clomben**
has climbed 216 **litel . . . mot** little thinks that he must 217 **al-
day . . . wenden** "what fools believe constantly fails" (a proverb)
218 **Bayard** a characteristic name for a bay horse in medieval
literature (cf. "Dobbin," "Old Paint") 219 **so . . . corn** i.e., as he

Till he a lash have of the longe whippe;   220
Then thinketh he, "Though I prance all beforn
First in the trays, full fat and newe shorn,°
Yet am I but an horse, and horses' lawe
I mot endure and with my feres drawe."°

So ferde it by° this fierce and proude knight.   225
Though he a worthy kinge's sone were,
And wende nothing hadde had swich might
Agains his will that shold his herte steere,°
Yet with a look his herte wex a-feere,
That he that now was most in pride above   230
Wex suddenly most subjet unto Love.

Forthy ensample taketh of° this man,
Ye wise, proud, and worthy folkes alle,
To scornen Love, which that so soone can
The freedom of your hertes to him thralle.   235
For ever it was and ever it shall befalle
That Love is he that alle thing may binde;
For may no man fordo the Law of Kinde.°

That this be sooth hath preved and doth yet.°
For this trow° I ye knowen all or some: 240
Men reeden° not that folk han greeter wit
Than they that han be most with Love y-nome,°

feels his oats   221–22 **all . . . shorn** before everyone, first in the
horses' team, well fattened and newly clipped   224 **with . . . drawe**
draw (the wagon)` with my companions. Chaucer begins the
rhetorical exclamation in the high style but concludes with a rustic
comparison between Troilus and a hackney. Horses sometimes
symbolized animal lust   225 **So . . . by** so it went with   227–28
wende . . . steere believed nothing had such might as to steer his
heart against his will   232 **Forthy . . . of** therefore take a lesson
from   238 **fordo . . . Kinde** ignore the Law of Nature. Medieval
theologians distinguished natural law—what men know and respond
to innately—from the received or Mosaic Law (the "old" law).
Medieval historians identified three historical eras: *ante legem*,
before the Law, *sub lege*, under the Law, and *sub gratia*, under
Grace (the Christian era or "new" law). Troilus lived in the first
era, which was governed by natural law   239 **hath . . . yet** has
been and is still being proved   240 **trow** believe   241 **reeden**
think   242 **han . . . y-nome** have been most smitten with love;

And strengest° folk been therewith overcome,
The worthiest and greetest of degree.
This was and is, and yet men shall it see.   *245*

And trewelich it sit well° to be so.
For alderwisest° han therewith been pleesed,
And they that han been aldermost° in woe
With Love han been comforted most and eesed,
And oft it hath the cruel herte appesed,   *250*
And worthy folk made worthier of name,
And causeth most to dreeden vice and shame.

And sith it may not goodly been withstonde,°
And is a thing so vertuous in kinde,
Refuseth not to Love for to been bonde,°   *255*
Sin, as himselven list, he may you binde.
"The yerd is bet that bowen will and winde
Than that that brust."° And therefore I you reede
To followen him that so well can you leede.

But for to tellen forth in special   *260*
Of this kinge's son of which I tolde,
And leten other things collateral,°
Of him think I my tale forth to holde°
Both of his joy and of his cares colde;
And all his work as touching this mattere   *265*
For I it gan, I will therefore refere.°

Within the temple he went him forth playinge,
This Troilus, of every wight aboute—
On this lady and now on that lookinge,
Wherso° she were of town or of withoute.   *270*
And upon cas befell that through a route°

y-nome= taken, seized 243 **strengest** strongest 246 **trewelich . . .
well** truly it is appropriate 247 **alderwisest** the wisest of all
248 **aldermost** most of all 253 **sith . . . withstonde** since (Love)
may not be well withstood 255 **Refuseth . . . bonde** do not refuse
to be bound to Love 257–58 **The . . . brust** "the rod that will
bow and bend is better than one that breaks" (proverb) 262 **leten
. . . collateral** pass over other less pertinent things 263 **holde**
continue 265–66 **And . . . refere** and because I began it, I will
return (*refere*) to all his actions (*work*) concerning this matter
270 **Wherso** whether 271 **upon . . . route** by chance it occurred
that through a crowd

His eye perced, and so deep it wente
Till on Criseyde it smote, and there it stente.°

And suddenly he wex therewith astoned,°
And gan her bet behold in thrifty· wise.°　　　　275
"O mercy God!" thought he, "where hast thou woned°
That art so fair and goodly to devise?"°
Therewith his herte gan to spred° and rise,
And softe sighed lest men might him heere,
And caught again his firste playing cheere.　　　　280

She nas not with the leest of her stature,°
But all her limmes° so well answeringe
Weren to womanhood, that creature
Was never lesse mannish° in seeminge.
And eek the pure wise of her mevinge°　　　　285
Shewed well that men might in her guesse
Honour, estate, and womanly noblesse.°

To Troilus right wonder° well withalle
Gan for to like her moving° and her cheere,
Which somedeel deignous was,° for she let falle　　　　290
Her look a lite aside in swich mannere
Ascaunces,° "What, may I not standen here?"
And after that her looking gan she lighte,°
That never thought him° seen so good a sighte.

And of her look in him there gan to quicken°　　　　295
So greet desire and swich affeccioun
That in his herte bottom gan to sticken
Of her his fixe and deep impressioun,°
And though he erst had poured° up and down,

273 **stente** stopped　274 **astoned** amazed　275 **gan . . . wise** began
to look on her better in prudent fashion　276 **woned** dwelt　277
devise see　278 **spred** swell　281 **She . . . stature** she was not
among the shortest of women　282 **limmes** limbs　284 **mannish**
masculine　285 **wise . . . mevinge** way of moving　287 **noblesse**
nobility　288 **wonder** wonderfully　289 **moving** bearing　290 **some-
deel . . . was** was somewhat proud　292 **Ascaunces** as if to say
293 **lighte** brighten　294 **never . . . him** never did he think he had
295 **of . . . quicken** from her look there began in him to grow
297–98 **That . . . impressioun** that his fixed and deep impression of
her lodged in the bottom of his heart　299 **erst . . . poured** before
had gazed

He was tho glad his hornes in to shrinke;°　　　　　*300*
Unnethes wist he how to look or winke.°

Lo, he that leet himselven so konninge°
And scorned hem that Love's paines drien,°
Was full unware that Love had his dwellinge
Within the subtil streemes° of her eyen—　　　　*305*
That suddenly him thought he felte dien,
Right with her look, the spirit in his herte.°
Blessed be Love, that can thus folk converte!

She, this in black, liking to Troilus
Over all thing,° he stood for to beholde.　　　　*310*
Ne his desire, ne wherefore° he stood thus,
He neither cheere made,° ne worde tolde.
But from afar, his manner for to holde,
On other thing his look sometime he caste,
And eft° on her, while that the service laste.　　*315*

And after this, not fullich all awhaped,°
Out of the temple all eesilich° he wente,
Repenting him that he had ever y-japed
Of Love's folk,° lest fully the descente°
Of scorn fell on himself. But what he mente,°　*320*
Lest it were wist on any manner side,°
His woe he gan dissimulen° and hide.

300 **tho ... shrinke** glad then to pull in his horns (to stop swaggering) 301 **Unnethes ... winke** i.e., he scarcely knew whether to look or close his eyes 302 **leet ... konninge** considered himself to be so clever 303 **hem ... drien** those who suffer Love's pains 305 **streemes** beams 306–07 **suddenly ... herte** suddenly—straightway from her look—he thought he felt the spirit in his heart die. Chaucer alludes to a medieval medical theory. The "spirit in the heart" is one of the "vital spirits," which governs breath and pulse. Troilus felt his heart stop and his breath fail when his "vital spirit" was affected by the subtle beams of Criseyde's eyes—the "beams" which the eye was thought to send out with its look 309–10 **this ... thing** this woman in black, pleasing to Troilus more than anything else 311 **wherefore** why 312 **cheere made** i.e., revealed anything by his face 315 **eft** again 316 **not ... awhaped** not fully stupefied 317 **eesilich** easily, i.e., calmly 318–19 **y-japed ... folk** made fun of Love's servants 319 **descente** brunt 320 **mente** felt 321 **wist ... side** known by anyone 322 **dissimulen** disguise

When he was fro the temple thus departed,
He straight anon unto his palais turneth,
Right with her look through-shoten and through-darted.°   325
Al feigneth he in lust that he sojourneth,°
And all his cheer and speech also he bourneth,°
And ay of Love's servants every while,
Himself to wrye,° at hem he gan to smile,

And saide, "Lord, so ye live all in lest,°   330
Ye lovers, for the conningest° of you,
That serveth most ententiflich° and best,
Him tit as often harm thereof as prow.°
Your hire is quit again°—yea, God wot how!
Not well for well,° but scorn for good service.   335
In faith, your order is ruled in good wise!

"In non-certain° been all your observaunces,
But it a sely fewe pointes be,°
Ne nothing asketh° so greet attendaunces
As doth your law, and that know alle ye!   340
But that is not the worst, as mot I thee°—
But told I you the worste point, I leve,
Al said I sooth, ye wolden at me greeve.°

"But take this: that ye lovers oft eschewe,°
Or elles doon of good intencioun,   345
Full oft thy lady will it misconstrewe,
And deem it harm in her opinioun.
And yet if she for other enchesoun°

---

325 **Right . . . through-darted** with her look wholly shot through
and pierced (i.e., smitten)   326 **Al . . . sojourneth** although he pre-
tends that he travels in pleasure   327 **bourneth** polishes   329 **wrye**
conceal   330 **lest** pleasure   331 **conningest** most knowing   332 **en-
tentiflich** earnestly   333 **Him . . . prow** he as often derives harm
from it as profit. *Him tit=* "it betides him" or "happens to him"
334 **hire . . . again** wage is paid back   335 **well . . . well** good
deed for good deed   337 **non-certain** uncertainty   338 **But . . . be**
except for a few trivial things   339 **asketh** requires   341 **as . . .
thee** so may I prosper (a mild but common oath)   342–43 **But . . .
greeve** but if I told you the worst thing, I believe, although I told
the truth, you would be upset with me   344 **take . . . eschewe** con-
sider this: what you lovers often avoid   348 **enchesoun** reason

Be wroth, then shalt thou have a groyn anon.°
Lord, well is him that may of you been oon!"°   350

But for all this, when that he saw his time,
He held his peece. Noon other boot him gained,°
For Love began his fethers so to lime,°
That well unneth, until his folk, he feigned
That other bisy needes him destrained.°   355
For woe was him that what to doon he niste—
·But bade his folk to goon where that hem liste.°

And when that he in chamber was alone,
He down upon his bedde's feet° him sette,
And first he gan to sigh and eft to groone,°   360
And thought ay on her so, withouten lette,°
That as he sat and woke, his spirit mette°
That he her saw at temple, and all the wise
Right of her look, and gan it new avise.°

Thus gan he make a mirrour of his minde,   365
In which he saw all hoolly° her figure,
And that he well coud in his herte finde.°
It was to him a right good aventure
To love swich one, and if he did his cure°
To serven her, yet might he fall in grace,°   370
Or elles for one of her servants passe—

Imagininge that travaille nor grame
Ne mighte for so goodly one be lorn
As she, ne him for his desire no shame,

---

349 **have . . . anon** soon have a gripe   350 **well . . . oon** he is lucky
who is one of you! (a sarcasm)   352 **Noon . . . gained** he got no
other relief   353 **fethers . . . lime** to spread lime on his feathers.
Birds were sometimes caught by putting lime, a sticky material, on
tree branches   354–55 **That . . . destrained** so that he barely pre-
tended to his friends that other needs pressed him   357 **where . . .
liste** where they wanted. *Hem liste*= it pleased them   359 **bedde's
feet** foot of his bed   360 **eft . . . groone** then to groan   361 **lette**
stopping   362 **mette** dreamed   363–64 **wise . . . avise** exactly the
way she looked, and considered it anew   366 **hoolly** wholly   367
And . . . finde i.e., he had no difficulty in remembering *that*
369 **did . . . cure** did his best   370 **fall . . . grace** come into her
good graces   372–76 **travaille . . . beforn** a difficult passage:
"Neither work nor suffering might be lost for so goodly a woman
as she, nor that he should have shame on account of his desire,

Al were it wist, but in pris and up-born   375
Of alle lovers well more than beforn.°
Thus argumented he in his ginninge,°
Full unavised of his woe cominge.

Thus took he purpose Love's craft to suwe,°
And thought he wolde worken prively,°   380
First to hiden his desire in muwe
From every wight y-born, all outrely°—
But he might aught recovered be thereby°—
Remembering him that Love too wide y-blowe°
Yelt° bitter fruit, though sweete seed be sowe.   385

And overal° this yet muchel more he thoughte—
What for to speke and what to holden inne,
And what to arten° her to love he soughte,
And on a song anon-right° to beginne,
And gan loud on his sorrow for to winne.°   390
For with good hope he gan fully assente
Criseyde for to love, and nought repente.

And of his song not only the sentence°
(As writ mine auctor called Lollius)°

even if it were known, but that he should be prized and esteemed
by all lovers more than (lovers have been praised) before"
377 **argumented . . . ginninge** he debated with himself in the be-
ginning (of his love for Criseyde) 379 **suwe** follow 380 **prively**
secretly 381–82 **in . . . outrely** utterly in concealment from every
man alive. A *mew* was a cage for hawks or other birds during
moulting 383 **But . . . thereby** in case he might somehow benefit
from doing so 384 **y-blowe** broadcast 385 **Yelt** yields. *Yelt* is
a syncopated form (for *yeldeth*) 386 **overal** besides 388 **what
. . . arten** how to entice 389 **anon-right** at once 390 **gan . . .
winne** began to complain loudly of his sorrow. To compose a
"lover's complaint" to one's lady was a convention of "courtly"
love. Troilus's impulse to start work on a song is as automatic as
ours would be to get her phone number. Chaucer's short poems,
Merciless Beautee and *The Complaint of Venus,* are "lover's com-
plaints" 393 **sentence** meaning (the *sentence* is the inner meaning
as opposed to the style which embodies that meaning) 394 **As . . .
Lollius** as my author (i.e., my source), named Lollius, wrote. The
song of Troilus is actually a translation of Petrarch's sonnet
S'amor non è. On Lollius see Introduction, pp. xiii–xiv

But plainly, save our tongue's difference,°   395
I dare well sayn in all° that Troilus
Said in his song—lo, every word right thus
As I shall sayn. And whoso list it heere,°
Lo, next this verse he may it finden here:

Troilus's Song

If no love is,° O God, what feel I so?   400
And if love is, what thing and which is he?
If love be good, from whennes cometh my woe?
If it be wicke, a wonder thinketh me°
When every torment and adversitee
That cometh of him may to me savory thinke;°   405
For ay thirst I the more that ich° it drinke.

And if that at mine owne lust I brenne,°
From whennes cometh my wailing and my plaint?
If harm agree me, whereto plain I thenne?°
I noot ne why, unwery,° that I fainte.   410
O quicke deeth,° O sweete harm so quainte,°
How may of thee in me swich quantitee,
But if that I consente that it be?°

395 **save ... difference** except for the difference in our languages
396 **I ... all** I don't hesitate to speak of everything   398 **whoso
... heere** whoever wishes to hear it   400 **If ... is** if there is no
love   403 **If ... me** if it is wicked, I think it is a wonder   405
That ... thinke that comes from it may seem pleasant to me   406
ich I   407 **if ... brenne** if I burn from my own desire (but it also
means "at my own pleasure")   409 **If ... thenne?** if I like being
hurt, why then do I complain?   410 **I ... unwery** I don't know
why, not weary   411 **quicke deeth** living death. Troilus uses the
rhetorical device of oxymoron, a form of paradox in which two
seemingly contradictory terms characterize a single experience, to
explain his love. *Sweete harm* is also an oxymoron   411 **quainte**
strange (with a possible pun on *queint*= pudendum)   412–13 **How
... be?** how may there be such a quantity of you within me unless
I consent that it be so?

And if that I consent, I wrongfully
Complain, ywis. Thus possed° to and fro,　　　　　　415
All steereless° within a boot am I,
Amid the sea betwixen windes two
That in contrarye standen evermo.°
Alas, what is this wonder° maladye?
For heet of cold, for cold of heet I die.°　　　　　　420

And to the God of Love thus saide he
With pitous voice: "O Lord, now youres is
My spirit, which that oughte youres be.
You thank I, Lord, that han me brought to this.
But whether goddess or woman, ywis,　　　　　　425
She be, I noot, which that ye do me serve;
But as her man I will ay live and sterve.°

"Ye standen in her eyen mightily,°
As in a place unto your virtue digne.°
Wherefore, Lord, if my service or I　　　　　　430
May liken° you, so beeth to me benigne.
For mine estate royal I here resigne
Into her hand, and with full humble cheere
Become her man, as to my lady deere."°

In him ne deigned spare blood royal　　　　　　435
The fire of Love° (the wherefro God me blesse!),

---

415 possed knocked (related to Mod.E. *push*; *possen* was often used
to describe waves against a boat)　**416 steereless** rudderless　**418**
That . . . evermo that forever stand in contrariety, i.e., oppose one
another　**419 wonder** wondrous　**420 For . . . die** i.e., I am dying
through burning with cold and freezing with heat. Troilus complains
of the "lover's malady"—the paradoxical feelings of love by which
joy and grief, hope and fear, laughter and tears are all bound up
with one another. Such paradoxes were conventional in medieval
love lyrics and are from a modern perspective chiefly associated
with Petrarch, author of the poem which Chaucer here translates
427 sterve die　**428 Ye . . . mightily** you (Love) exist powerfully
in her eyes (a standard notion of "courtly" love)　**429 digne** worthy
431 liken please　**432–34 For . . . deere** The language in this pas-
sage is very formal and typical of a vow of fealty　**435–36 In . . .**
Love the fire of Love did not deign to spare the royal blood in him
(he had no royal prerogative as Priam's son)

Ne him forbare in no degree, for° all
His virtue° or his excellent prowesse,
But held him as his thrall, low in distresse,
And brende° him so sundry wise ay newe,   *440*
That sixty time a day he lost his hewe.°

So muche, day by day, his owne thought
For lust to her gan quicken° and increese,
That every other charge° he set at nought.
Forthy° full oft, his hote fire to ceese,°   *445*
To seen her goodly look he gan to presse.°
For thereby to been eesed well he wende,
And ay the neer° he was the more he brende.

For ay the neer the fire the hotter is—
This, trow I, knoweth all this compaignye.°   *450*
But were he far or neer, I dare say this:
By night or day, for wisdom or follye,
His herte (which that is his breeste's eye)
Was ay on her, that fairer was to seene
Than ever were Heleynè or Polixene.°   *455*

Eek of the day there passed not an houre
That to himself a thousand time he saide
"Good goodly,° to whom serve I and laboure
As I best can—now wolde° God, Criseyde,
Ye wolden on me rew ere that I deide.°   *460*

437 **for** despite   438 **virtue** strength, manhood. This word, usually
spelled *vertu* in the manuscripts, retains in Chaucer's English its
Latin and Old French sense of "that which is proper to a man"
(Lat. *vir*, man); hence it is often named as a quality of princes and
nobles   440 **brende** burned   441 **hewe** hue, color (the lover's pale-
ness was also traditional)   443 **For . . . quicken** about his desire
for her came alive   444 **charge** concern   445 **Forthy** therefore
445 **ceese** dampen   446 **presse** press for, strive   448 **neer** nearer
450 **compaignye** Chaucer imagines himself reading before a courtly
gathering, an audience which can perceive the analogy he makes
between fire and the passions of love   455 **Heleyne or Polixene**
Helen, cause of the Trojan War; Polixena, sister of Troilus and
loved by Achilles   458 **Good goodly** goodly one   459 **wolde** would
to   460 **rew . . . deide** take pity before I die

My deere herte, alas, mine hele and hewe°
And life is lost, but° ye will on me rewe."

All other dreedes weren from him fledde,
Both of the assege and his salvacioun;°
N'in him desire none other fownes° bredde   465
But arguments to this conclusioun:
That she of him wold han compassioun,
And he to been her man while he may dure—
Lo, here his life,° and from the deeth his cure.

The sharpe shoures fell°, of armes preve,   470
That Hector or his other bretheren diden,
Ne made him only therefore ones meve.°
And yet was he, wherso men went or riden,
Found one the best, and longest time abiden
Ther peril was,° and did eek swich travaille   475
In armes that to think it was marvaile.

But for noon hate he to the Greekes hadde,
Ne also for the rescous of the town,
Ne made him thus in armes for to madde,°
But only, lo, for this conclusioun: 480
To liken her the bet for° his renown.
Fro day to day in armes so he spedde°
That the Greekes, as the deeth, him dredde.°

461 hele . . . hewe health and complexion 462 but unless 464
salvacioun safety, but with a double meaning suggesting Christian
Salvation 465 fownes fawns or young animals. "Fawns" represent
the offspring of desire or "little desires" 469 her . . . life his life
was hers 470 sharpe . . . fell sharp, dreadful attacks. *Shoures*=
attacks, assaults; *armes*= deeds of arms which are put to the proof
(*preve*) in battle conditions 472 Ne . . . meve made him give way
not even once on their account. Troilus did as well in battle as
Hector and his other brothers 474–75 and . . . was and remained
for the longest time where there was danger 477–79 But . . .
madde Troilus did not rage(*madde*) thus in battle because of any
hate he had for the Greeks, nor for the town's rescue 481 liken
. . . for please her the better because of 482 spedde did well
483 as . . . dredde feared him like the plague

And fro this forth tho reft him Love his sleepe,°
And made his mete° his foe, and eek his sorrwe   *485*
Gan multiplye, that, whoso took keepe,°
It shewed in his hew both eve and morrwe.
Therefore a title he gan him for to borrwe°
Of other sickness, lest men of him wende
That the hote fire of love him brende,   *490*

And said he had a fever and ferde amiss.°
But how° it was certain can I not saye,
If that his lady understood not this,
Or feigned her she niste°—one of the twaye.
But well I reed that by no manner waye   *495*
Ne seemed it that she of him roughte,°
Or of his pain, or whatsoever he thoughte.

But thenne felt this Troilus swich woe
That he was well nigh wood°—for ay his dreede
Was this, that she some wight° had loved so   *500*
That never of him she wold han taken heede,
For which him thought he felt his herte bleede,
Ne of his woe ne durst he not beginne
To tellen her, for all this world to winne.

But when he had a space from his care,°   *505*
Thus to himself full oft he gan to plaine:
He said, "O fool, now art thou in the snare,
That whilom japedest at° love's paine.
Now art thou hent,° now gnaw thine owne chaine!
Thou were ay wont eech lover reprehende   *510*
Of thing fro which thou canst thee not defende.°

"What will now every lover sayn of thee
If this be wist, but ever in thine absence

484 **fro . . . sleepe** from this time forth Love deprived him of his
sleep 485 **mete** food; Troilus lost his appetite 486 **keepe** note
488 **a . . . borrwe** i.e., he said his love sickness was something else
491 **ferde amiss** fared poorly 492 **how** whether 494 **feigned . . .
niste** pretended she didn't know 496 **roughte** cared about 499
wood mad 500 **wight** man 505 **a . . . care** i.e., a moment free
from his business 508 **That . . . at** (you) who formerly made fun
of 509 **hent** captured 510–11 **wont . . . defende** accustomed to
rebuke each lover for the thing from which you can't defend yourself

Laughen in scorn and sayn, 'Lo, there goeth he
That is the man of so greet sapience,°   515
That held us lovers leest in reverence!
Now thanked be God he may goon in the daunce°
Of hem that Love list feebly for to avaunce.'°

"But O thou woeful Troilus, God wolde,
Sith thou must loven through thy destinee,   520
That thou beset were on swich one° that sholde
Know all thy woe, al lacked her° pitee.
But also cold in love towardes thee
Thy lady is° as frost in winter moone,
And thou fordone° as snow in fire is soone.   525

"God wold I were arrived in the port
Of deeth, to which my sorrow will me leede!
Ah, Lord, to me it were a greet comfort—
Then were I quit° of languishing in dreede.
For be mine hidde sorrow y-blowe on brede,°   530
I shall bejaped been° a thousand time
More than that fool of whose folly men rime.

"But now help God and thee, sweete, for whom
I plain, y-caught—yea, never wight so faste°—
O mercy, deere herte, and help me from   535
The deeth! For I, while that my life may laste,
More than myself will love you to my laste.
And with some freendly look gladdeth me, sweete,
Though never more thing ye me behete."°

These wordes and full many another too   540
He spake, and called ever in his complainte

515 **sapience** wisdom   517 **goon ... daunce** go in the dance. Chaucer often refers to love as a dance. Pandarus, for example, knew well "the olde dance" (III.695) of love, i.e., the intricacies of the game of love   518 **Of ... avaunce** of those whom it pleases Love to promote only halfheartedly   521 **beset ... one** were determined on such a woman   522 **al ... her** although she lacked   523–24 **But ... is** a reverse construction: But your lady is as cold towards you in love as (*also ... as*= as ... as)   525 **fordone** destroyed   529 **quit** rid   530 **For ... brede** for if my hidden sorrow is blown abroad (*on brede*= in breadth, or widely)   531 **bejaped been** be made the fool   533–34 **for ... faste** for whom I complain, caught —indeed, never a man (caught) so securely   539 **behete** promise

Her name, for to tellen her his woe,
Till nigh that he in salte teeres dreinte.°
All was for nought. She herde not his plainte.
And when that he bethought on° that follye,   545
A thousandfold his woe gan multiplye.

*   *   *

Bewailing in his chamber thus alone,
A freend of his that called was Pandare
Came ones in unware° and herde him groone,
And saw his freend in swich distress and care.   550
"Alas," quod he, "who causeth all this fare?°
O mercy, God, what unhap° may this meene?
Han now thus soone Greekes made you leene?°

"Or hast thou some remorse of conscience,
And art now falle in some devocioun,   555
And wailest for thy sin and thine offence,
And hast, forfered, caught attricioun?°
God save hem that beseeged han our town,
That so can lay our jolitee on presse°
And bring our lusty folk to holinesse!"   560

These wordes said he for the nones alle,
That with swich thing he might him angry maken,
And with anger doon his woe to falle,
As for the time,° and his corage awaken.
But well he wist, as far as tongues spaken,°   565
There nas a man of greeter hardinesse
Than he, ne more° desired worthinesse.

"What cas,"° quod Troilus, "and what aventure
Hath guided thee to seen me languishinge,
That am refus of° every creature?   570
But for the love of God, at my prayinge,

543 **dreinte** drowned   545 **bethought on** thought about   549 **unware**
unexpectedly   551 **fare** fuss   552 **unhap** misfortune   553 **Han . . .
leene?** have now the Greekes so quickly made you lean? Pandarus
wonders whether Troilus has lost his appetite out of cowardice
557 **forfered . . . attricioun** frightened, decided to be contrite
559 **That . . . presse** who can so put our joviality on the rack
564 **As . . . time** for the time being   565 **as far . . . spaken** i.e., as
everyone said   567 **ne more** nor a man who more   568 **cas** chance
570 **refus of** rejected by

Go hennes away, for certes my deyinge
Will thy diseese, and I mot needes deye.°
Therefore go way, there is no more to saye.

"But if thou wene I be thus sick for dreede,   575
It is not so. And therefore scorne not.
There is another thing I take of heede,°
Well more than aught the Greekes han yet wrought,°
Which cause is of my deeth for sorrow and thought.
But though that I now tell it thee ne leste,°   580
Be thou not wroth. I hide it for the beste."

This Pandar, that nigh malt° for woe and routhe,
Full ofte said, "Alas, what may this be?"
"Now freend," quod he, "if ever love or trouthe
Hath been, or is, betwixen thee and me,   585
Ne do thou never swich a crueltee
To hiden fro thy freend so greet a care.
Wost thou not well that it am I, Pandare?

"I will parten° with thee all thy paine,
If it be so I do thee no comfort,°   590
As it is freende's right, sooth for to sayne,
To entreparten woe as glad disport.°
I have and shall, for trew or false report,°
In wrong and right, y-loved thee all my live.
Hide not thy woe fro me, but tell it blive!"?   595

Then gan this sorrowful Troilus to sike,°
And said him° thus: "God leve it be my beste°
To tell it thee! For sith it may thee like,
Yet will I tell it, though mine herte brestè—
And well wot I thou maist do° me no reste.   600

573 **mot . . . deye** must needs die   577 **take . . . heede** am con-
cerned about   578 **aught . . . wrought** anything the Greeks have
yet done   580 **though . . . leste** though I don't wish to tell it to
you now   582 **nigh malt** nearly melted   589 **parten** share   590 **If
. . . comfort** even if it be the case (if it turns out) that I give you
no comfort   592 **To . . . disport** to share woe just as to share joy
and sport   593 **for . . . report** i.e., despite what people may say
595 **blive** immediately   596 **sike** sigh   597 **God . . . beste** God
grant it be the best thing for me   600 **do** give

But lest thou deem I truste not to thee,
Now herke, freend, for thus it stant° with me:

"Love—agains the which whoso defendeth
Himselven most, him alderleest availeth°—
With desespair so sorrowfully me offendeth°   605
That straight unto the deeth mine herte saileth.
Thereto desire so brenningly° me assaileth,
That to been slain it were a greeter joye
To me, than king of Greece been° and Troye.

"Sufficeth this, my fulle freend Pandare,   610
That I have said, for now wost thou my woe.
And for the love of God, my colde care
So hide it well; I told it never to mo.°
For harmes mighten followen mo than two
If it were wist. But be thou in gladnesse,   615
And let me sterve, unknowe,° of my distresse."

"How hast thou thus unkindely° and longe
Hid this fro me, thou fool?" quod Pandarus.
"Peraunter thou might after swich oon longe
That mine avis anon may helpen us."°   620
"This were a wonder thing," quod Troilus.
"Thou coudest never in love thyselven wisse;°
How devil° maist thou bringe *me* to blisse?"

"Yea, Troilus, now herke," quod Pandare,
"Though I be nice, it happeth often so   625
That one that excess doth full evil fare,°
By good counseil can keep his freend therefro.
I have myself eek seen a blind man go°

602 **stant** stands   603–4 **agains . . . availeth** against which whoever
guards himself most gains the least (*alderleest*= least of all; cf.
aldermost)   605 **me offendeth** attacks me   607 **brenningly** burn-
ingly   609 **than . . . been** than . . . to be   613 **mo** any other
616 **unknowe** unknown   617 **unkindely** unnaturally   619–20 **Per-
aunter . . . us** perhaps you might long for such a one that my
advice now can help us   622 **wisse** manage   623 **How devil** how
the devil   625–26 **Though . . . fare** though I am foolish, it often
happens that one whom excess (of passion) causes to fare badly
628 **go** walk

Ther-as he fell that coude looken wide.°
A fool may eek a wise man oft guide.   *630*

"A whetstone is no kerving° instrument,
But yet it maketh sharpe kerving tooles.
And ther thou wost that I have aught miswent,
Eschew thou that, for swich thing to thee scole is.°
Thus often wise men been ware° by fooles..   *635*
If thou do so, thy wit is well bewared.°
By his° contrary is every thing declared.°

"For how might ever sweetness han been knowe
To him that never tasted bitternesse?
Ne no man may been inly° glad, I trowe,   *640*
That never was in sorrow or some distresse.
Eek white by black, by shame eek worthinesse—
Eech, set by other, more for other seemeth,°
As men may see, and so the wise it deemeth.°

"Sith thus of two contraries is oo lore,°   *645*
I, that have in love so oft assayed
Grevances, oughte konne—and well the more—
Counseilen thee of that thou art amayed.°
Eek thee ne oughte not been evil apayed°
Though I desire with thee for to bere°   *650*
Thine hevy charge: it shall thee lesse dere.°

"I wot well that it fareth thus by me°
As to thy brother Paris, an herdesse,

---

629 **Ther-as . . . wide** i.e., where a sighted man ("he who could
look wide") fell   631 **kerving** carving   633–34 **And . . . is** and
where you know I have gone astray in any way, avoid that, for
such a thing is (like a) school to you   635 **been ware** are made
aware   636 **bewared** spent, expended (see OED *beware*, v²). Pan-
darus plays on words: *been ware/bewared*   637 **his** its   637 **de-
clared** clarified   640 **inly** inwardly   643 **Eech . . . seemeth** each
thing set by its contrary seems more distinct   644 **wise . . . deemeth**
the wise man judges it to be   645 **Sith . . . lore** since thus from
two contraries comes one lesson   646–48 **assayed . . . amayed** ex-
perienced setbacks, ought to know how to counsel you concerning
what you are dismayed about   649 **evil apayed** displeased   650
bere bear, shoulder   651 **thee . . . dere** trouble you the less   652 **it
. . . me** i.e., my situation is this   653–54 **an . . . Oënone** a shepher-
dess, who was called Oënone. She wrote a letter to Paris pleading

Which that y-cleped was Oënone,°
Wrote in a complaint of her hevinesse.   655
Ye saw the letter that she wrote, I guesse?"
"Nay, never yet, ywis," quod Troilus.
"Now," quod Pandare, "herkne—it was thus:

" 'Phebus that first fond° art of medicine,'
Quod she, 'and kouth in every wighte's care   660
Remedy and reed by herbes he knew fine,°
Yet to himself his conning was full bare;°
For Love had him so bounden in a snare,
All for the daughter of the king Amete,
That all his craft ne coud his sorrows bete.'°   665

"Right so fare I, unhappily for me—
I love one best, and that me smerteth sore.°
And yet peraunter can I reeden thee,
And not myself. Repreve° me no more.
I have no cause, I wot well, for to soore°   670
As doth an hawk that listeth for to playe,
But to thine help yet somewhat can I saye.

"And of oo thing right siker° maist thou be:
That certain, for to dien in the paine,°
That I shall nevermo discoveren° thee.   675
Ne, by my trouth,° I keepe not° restraine
Thee fro thy love, though that it were Heleyne,
That is thy brother° wife, if ich it wiste—
Be what she be, and love her as thee liste.

"Therefore as freend fullich in me assure.°   680
But tell me plat, what is th'enchesoun°
And final cause of woe that ye endure?

with him not to desert her for Helen of Troy   659 **fond** invented
660–61 **and . . . fine** and knew for every man's trouble a remedy
and aid by delicate herbes that he knew   662 **conning . . . bare**
knowledge was completely useless   665 **bete** remedy   667 **that . . .
sore** that hurts me deeply   669 **Repreve** reproach (cf. "reprove")
670 **soore** soar   673 **right siker** entirely sure   674 **for . . . paine**
though I die under torture   675 **discoveren** betray   676 **trouth**
pledge, honor (the word survives in the phrase of the marriage
ceremony, "I plight thee my troth")   676 **keepe not** don't mean to
678 **brother** brother's   680 **fullich . . . assure** have full confidence
in me   681 **plat . . . th'enchesoun** flatly, what is the reason

For douteth nothing, mine intencioun
Nis not to you of reprehencioun
To speke as now;° for no wight may bereeve°   685
A man to love till that him *list* to leeve.°

"And witeth well that bothe two been vices—
Mistrusten all, or elles alle leve.°
But well I wot, the meen of it° no vice is.
For to trusten some wight is a preve   690
Of trouth; and forthy wold I fain remeve
Thy wrong conceit, and do thee some wight triste,°
Thy woe to tell—and tell *me*, if thee liste.

"The wise saith, 'Woe him that is alone,
For and he fall, he hath noon help to rise.'   695
And sith thou hast a fellow, tell thy mone.°
For this nis not, certain, the nexte wise°
To winnen love—as teechen us the wise—
To wallow and weep as Niobe° the queene,
Whose teeres yet in marble been y-seene.   700

"Let be thy weeping and thy drerinesse,
And let us lissen° woe with other speeche.
So may thy woeful time seeme lesse.
Delite not in woe thy woe to seeche,°

684–85 **Nis . . . now** is not to reprehend you, to speak of the present
moment   685 **bereeve** prevent   686 **till . . . leeve** until it pleases
him to stop (i.e., until he chooses to stop loving)   688 **Mistrusten
. . . leve** to mistrust everyone or else to believe everyone   689 **meen
. . . it** middle way (between the two vices)   691–92 **fain . . . triste**
gladly remove your wrong opinion, and cause you to trust some
man   696 **mone** complaint (lit. "moan")   697 **nexte wise** nearest
(simplest) way. The rhyme *wise* ("way") in this line with *wise*
("wise people") in line 698 is an example of identical rhyme (*rime
riche*), in which a word appears to rhyme with itself but actually
rhymes with a word of a different part of speech or, as here, with
a word of different meaning. In medieval poetry this verbal wit
was thought to be elegant   699 **Niobe** she boasted about her chil-
dren and angered the goddess Artemis, who slew them all. Niobe
so sorrowed for her dead children that she turned into a marble
statue but continued to weep. She was an emblem of weeping: as
Hamlet says of his mother, "Like Niobe all tears"   702 **lissen**
alleviate   704 **Delite . . . seeche** don't take pleasure in seeking the

As doon these fooles that hir sorrows eche°   705
With sorrow, when they han misaventure,
And listen not to seech hem other cure.°

"Men sayn, 'To wrecch° is concolacioun
To have another fellow in his paine.'
That oughte well been our opinioun,   710
For bothe thou and I of love we plaine.
So full of sorrow am I, sooth for to sayne,
That certainly no more harde grace°
May sit on me—forwhy there is no space.

"If God will, thou art not aghast° of me   715
Lest I wold of thy lady thee beguile.°
Thou wost thyself whom that I love, pardee,
As I best can, gone sithen longe while.°
And sith thou wost I do it for no wile,
And sith I am he that thou trustest most,   720
Tell me somewhat—sin all my woe thou wost."

Yet Troilus for all this no word saide,
But long he lay as still as he deed were.°
And after this with sighing he abraide,°
And to Pandarus' voice he lent his eere,°   725
And up his eyen caste, that in feere
Was Pandarus lest that in frenesye°
He sholde fall, or elles soone die,

And cried, "*Awake!*" full wonderlich and sharpe.
"*What!* Slumberest thou as in a litargye?°   730
Or art thou like an asse to the harpe,
That heereth soun° when men the stringes plye,
But in his mind of that° no melodye

woe in your woe (Pandarus tries to dissuade him from self-pity)
705 **eche** increase   707 **And . . . cure** and don't wish to seek for
themselves other cure   708 **wrecch** a wretched man   713 **harde
grace** bad luck   715 **aghast** afraid   716 **of . . . beguile** i.e., dis-
suade you from loving her   718 **gone . . . while** i.e., for a long
time now   723 **as he . . . were** as if he were dead   724 **abraide**
started up   725 **eere** ear   727 **frenesye** frenzy   730 **litargye** lethargy
732 **soun** sound   733 **of that** of the sound

May sinken, him to gladden, for that he
So dull is of° his bestialitee?"   735

And with that, Pandar of his wordes stente.
And Troilus yet him nothing answerde—
Forwhy to tellen nas not his intente
To never no man for whom that he so ferde.°
For it is said, "Man maketh oft a yerde°   740
With which the maker is himself y-beeten
In sundry manner"—as these wise treeten:°

And namelich in his counseil tellinge
That toucheth love, that oughte been secree;°
For of himself° it will enough out springe,   745
But if that it the bet governed be.
Eek sometime it is a craft to seeme flee°
Fro thing which in effect men hunte faste.
All this gan Troilus in his herte caste.°

But natheless, when he had herde him crye   750
"Awake!" he gan to sighen wonder sore,
And saide, "Freend, though that I stille lie,
I am not deef.° Now peece, and cry no more;
For I have herde thy wordes and thy lore.
But suffer me my mischief° to bewaile,   755
For thy proverbes may me nought availe.

"Nor other cure canst thou° none for me.
Eek I nill not been° cured. I will deye.
What know I of the queene Niobe?
Let be thine old ensamples,° I thee praye."   760
"No," quod Pandarus, "therefore I saye,
Swich is delite of fooles, to beweepe
Hir woe, but seeken boote they ne keepe.°

735 of because of   739 for . . . ferde for whose sake he was acting
this way   740 yerde stick   742 as . . . treeten as these wise men
say   743–44 And . . . secree and particularly in telling one's secrets
which have to do with love, that should be secret   745 of himself
by itself   747 a . . . flee wise to seem to flee   749 caste turn over
753 deef deaf   755 suffer . . . mischief allow me my misfortune
757 canst thou do you know   758 I . . . been I don't want to be
760 ensamples exemplary stories   763 seeken . . . keepe but they
don't care to seek a remedy

"Now know I that reeson in thee faileth.
But tell me, if I wiste what she were,°   765
For whom that thee all this misaunter° aileth,
Durst thou° that I told in her eere
Thy woe, sith thou durst not thyself for feere,
And her besought on thee to han some routhe?"
"Why, nay," quod he, "by God and by my trouthe!"   770

"What, not as bisily,"° quod Pandarus,
"As though mine owne life lay on this neede?"
"No, certes, brother," quod this Troilus.
"And why?" "For that thou sholdest never speede."°
"Wost thou that well?"° "Yea, that is out of dreede,"   775
Quod Troilus, "for all that ever ye conne,°
She nill to none swich wrecch as I been wonne."°

Quod Pandarus, "Alas! what may this be,
That thou despaired art thus causeless?
What, liveth° not thy lady, *ben'dic'te?*°   780
How wost thou so that thou art graceless?°
Swich evil is not alway booteless.°
Why, put not impossible thus thy cure,°
Sin thing to come is oft in aventure.°

"I grante well that thou endurest woe   785
As sharp as doth he Ticius° in helle,
Whose stomach fowles tiren evermo,
That highten vultures, as bookes telle.
But I may not endure that thou dwelle°
In so unskilful° an opinioun,   790
That of thy woe is no curacioun.°

765 **what . . . were** who she is   766 **misaunter** unhappiness (*misaunter*= syncopated form of *misaventure*)   767 **Durst thou** would you dare   771 **What . . . bisily** what, not even if I acted as forcefully   774 **For . . . speede** because you would never succeed   775 **Wost . . . well?** i.e., do you know that for a fact?   776 **for . . . conne** despite whatever you can do   777 **She . . . wonne** she won't be won over to a wretch like me   780 **liveth** i.e., isn't she alive?   780 **ben'dic'te** a Latin interjection, *benedicite*, "bless me," pronounced *bendistay*, accent on first syllable   781 **graceless** unfavored   782 **booteless** without remedy   783 **put . . . cure** don't thus judge your cure impossible   784 **in aventure** uncertain   786 **he Ticius** that man Tityus   789 **may . . . dwelle** cannot stand that you remain   790 **unskilful** uninformed   791 **curacioun** cure

"But ones nilt thou°—for thy coward herte,
And for thine ire and foolish willfulnesse,
For wantrust°—tellen of thy sorrows smerte?°
Ne to thine owne help doon bisinesse°   795
As much as speke a reeson more or lesse,
But liest as he that lest of nothing recche?°
What woman coude loven swich a wrecche?

"What may she deemen other° of thy deeth,
If thou thus die and she noot° why it is,   800
But that for feer is yolden up thy breeth°
For Greekes han beseeged us, ywis?
Lord, which a thank° then shalt thou han of this!
Thus will she sayn, and all the town at ones,
'The wrecch is deed, the devil have his bones!'   805

"Thou maist alone here weep and cry and kneele—
But love a woman that she wot it not,
And she will quite it that° thou shalt not feele:
Unknowe, unkist, and lost, that is unsought!
What! many a man hath love full deer y-bought   810
Twenty winter that his lady wiste,°
That never yet his lady° mouth he kiste.

"What! shold he therefore fallen in despaire?
Or be recreant for his owne teene?°
Or sleen himself, al be his lady faire?   815
Nay, nay! but ever in oon° be fresh and greene
To serve and love his deere herte's queene,
And think it is a guerdon° her to serve
A thousandfold more than he can deserve!"

792 **nilt thou** won't you. The thought is completed in line 794:
"won't you . . . tell"   794 **wantrust** lack of trust   794 **smerte** pain-
ful   795 **doon bisinesse** do something constructive   797 **lest . . .
recche** who chooses to care for nothing   799 **What . . . other** what
else can she think   800 **noot** not know (*ne wot*)   801 **yolden . . .
breeth** your breath (or life) has been yielded up   803 **which . . .
thank** such thanks   808 **quite . . . that** requite it in such a way
810–11 **love . . . wiste** very dearly paid for a love that his lady
knew about twenty years. (Pandarus here puts forth an argument
for the idealistic notion that service to Love is its own reward)
812 **lady** lady's   814 **recreant . . . teene** cowardly for his own
distress   816 **ever in oon** always   818 **guerdon** reward

Of *that* word took heede Troilus;   820
And thought anon what folly he was inne,
And how that sooth him saide Pandarus—
That for to sleen himself might he not winne,°
But bothe doon unmanhood° and a sinne,
And of his deeth his lady nought to wite,   825
For of his woe, God wot, she knew full lite,

And with that thought he gan full sore sike,
And said, "Alas, what is me best to do?"
To whom Pandar answered, "If thee like,
The best is that thou tell me all thy woe.   830
And have my trouth, but thou it finde so
I be thy boot ere that it be full longe,
To pieces do me draw and sithen honge."°

"Yea, so thou saist," quod Troilus tho, "alas,
But God wot, it is not the rather so.°   835
Full hard were it to helpen in this cas,
For well find I that Fortune° is my foe.
Ne all the men that riden can or go
May of her cruel wheel the harm withstonde;
For as her list she playeth with free and bonde."°   840

Quod Pandarus, "Then blamest thou Fortune
For thou art wroth? Yea, now at erst° I see!
Wost thou not well that Fortune is commune
To every manner wight° in some degree?
And yet thou hast this comfort, lo, pardee: 845
That as her joyes moten overgone,°
So mot her sorrows passen everichoone.

"For if her wheel stint anything to turne
Then ceesed she Fortune anon to be.
Now sith her wheel by no way may sojourne,°   850

823 **winne** gain anything (or, win his lady)   824 **doon unmanhood**
do an unmanly thing   831–33 **but . . . honge** unless you find that
I am your cure before very long, have me drawn to pieces and then
hanged   835 **not . . . so** not so for that (because you *say* it)   837
Fortune Troilus views his love affair with Criseyde fatalistically
and pessimistically, thinking of Fortune's wheel (cf. note to I.4)
840 **free . . . bonde** free man and slave   842 **erst** last   843–44
commune . . . wight common to every kind of person   846 **moten
overgone** must pass away   850 **sojourne** stop

What wost thou if her mutabilitee
Right as thyselven list will doon by thee,°
Or that she be not far fro thine helpinge?
Peraunter thou hast cause for to singe.

"And therefore wost thou what I thee beseeche?   855
Let be thy woe and turning to the grounde,
For whoso list have heeling of his leeche,°
To him behooveth first unwry° his wounde.
To Cerberus in hell ay be I bounde°—
Were it for my suster all thy sorrwe,   860
By my will she shold all be thine tomorrwe.

"Look up, I say, and tell me what° she is
Anon, that I may goon about thy neede.°
Know ich her aught? For my love, tell me this!
Then wold I hopen rather° for to speede."   865
Tho gan the vein of Troilus to bleede,
For he was hit, and wex all red for shame.
"Aha!" quod Pandar, "here beginneth game."

And with that word he gan him for to shake,
And saide, "Theef! thou *shalt* her name telle!"   870
But tho gan sely° Troilus for to quake
As though men shold han led him into helle,
And said, "Alas, of all my woe the welle,°
Then is my sweete foe called . . . Criseyde"—
And well nigh with the word for feer he deide.   875

And when that Pandar herde her name nevene,°
Lord, he was glad, and saide, "Freend so deere,
Now fare aright, for Jove's name in hevene!
Love hath beset thee well! Be of good cheere.
For of good name and wisdom and mannere   880

851–52 **What . . . thee** how do you know if her fickleness won't
behave for you just as you yourself wish 857 **leeche** doctor 858
To . . . unwry it behooves him first to disclose 859 **To . . . bounde**
let me be bound in hell to Cerberus forever. Cerberus is the three-
headed mastiff that stands guard at the entrance to the classical
Hades 862 **what** who 863 **goon . . . neede** i.e., help you 865
rather sooner 871 **sely** poor 873 **welle** source 876 **nevene** named

She hath enough, and eek of gentilesse.°
If she be fair, thou wost thyself, I guesse.

"Ne I never saw a more bountevous
Of her estate, ne a gladder,° ne of speeche
A freendlier, ne a more gracious   885
For to do well, ne less had neede seeche°
What for to doon—and all this bet to eche°
In honour, too, as far as she may strecche.°
A kinge's herte seemeth by hers a wrecche.

"And forthy look of good comfort° thou be,   890
For certainly the firste point is this:
Of noble corage, and well ordainee,°
A man to have peece with himself, ywis.
So oughtest thou; for nought but good it is
To loven well and in a worthy place.   895
Thee oughte not to clepe it hap, but grace.°

"And also think and therewith gladde thee
That, sith thy lady virtuous is all,
So followeth it that there is some pitee
Amonges all these other° in general.   900
And forthy see that thou in special
Requere nought that is agains her name;°
For virtue streccheth not himself to shame.

"But well is me° that ever that I was born,
That thou beset art in so good a place!   905
For by my trouth, in love I durst have sworn°
Thee sholde never han tid° thus fair a grace.
And wost thou why? For thou were wont to chase

881 **gentilesse** nobility 883–84 **a . . . gladder** a more magnanimous
person in her social circumstances, nor a happier 886 **For . . .
seeche** nor, to do well, had less need to figure out 887 **bet . . .
eche** the better to increase 888 **strecche** reach 890 **comfort** cheer
892 **ordainee** under control 896 **clepe . . . grace** call it chance,
but good luck 900 **other** i.e., other virtues 902 **agains . . . name**
prejudicial to her reputation 904 **well . . . me** i.e., thank goodness
(cf. "woe is me") 906 **in . . . sworn** in respect to love I would
dare have sworn 907 **tid** happened 908–09 **wont . . . Love** ac-

At Love° in scorn, and for despite him calle
'Saint Idiot, lord of these fooles alle.'   910

"How often hast thou made thy nice japes,°
And said that Love's servants everichoone
Of nicetee been verray Godde's apes.°
And some wolde mucch hir mete° alone,
Lying abed, and make hem for° to groone.   915
And some, thou saidest, had a blaunche fevere°
And praydest God he sholde never cevere.°

"And some of hem took on hem for the cold°
More than enough, so saidest thou full ofte.
And some han feigned ofte time, and told   920
How that they waken when they sleepen softe.
And thus they wold han brought hemself alofte,°
And natheless were under° at the laste—
Thus saidest thou, and japedest full faste.

"Yet saidest thou that for the more part   925
These lovers wolden speke in general,°
And thoughten that it was a siker art
For failing for t'assayen overal.°
Now may I jape of thee, if that I shall.
But natheless, though that I sholde deye,   930
That thou art none of tho I durste saye.

"Now beet thy breest and say to God of Love,
'Thy grace, Lord, for now I me repente
If I misspake,° for now myself I love'—
Thus say with all thine herte in good intente."   935
Quod Troilus: "Ah, Lord, I me consente,

customed to harass Love   911 **nice japes** silly jokes   913 **Of . . .
apes** because of foolishness are true apes of God (i.e., natural born
fools)   914 **mucch . . . mete** munch their food   915 **make . . . for**
set out (or, perhaps, pretend)   916 **blaunche fevere** white fever, or
love sickness, which turns its victims pale and causes chills   917
cevere recover   918 **took . . . cold** made a fuss because of the fever
chills   922 **wold . . . alofte** wanted to make themselves succeed (by
faking traditional symptoms of love, so Troilus used to say)   923
were under i.e., failed   926 **in general** i.e., not of any particular
lady   927–28 **it . . . overal** a sure method not to fail was to try
everywhere   934 **misspake** spoke incorrectly

And pray to thee my japes thou foryive,°
And I shall nevermore while I live."

"Thou saist well," quod Pandarus, "and now I hope
That thou the Godde's wrath hast all appeesed.   *940*
And sithen thou hast wopen° many a drope,
And said swich thing wherewith thy God is pleesed,
Now wolde never God but thou were eesed!°
And think well she of whom rist° all thy woe
Hereafter may thy comfort be also.   *945*

"For thilke ground that ber'th the weedes wicke
Bereth eek these hoolsome herbes as full ofte.
Next the foule nettle, rough and thicke,
The rose waxeth swoot° and smooth and softe.
And next the valley is the hill alofte.   *950*
And next the darke night the glade morrwe.
And also joy is next the fin° of sorrwe.

"Now looke that attempre be thy bridel;°
And for the best ay suffer to the tide,°
Or elles all our labour is on idel.   *955*
He hasteth well that wisely can abide.
Be diligent and trew, and ay well hide.°
Be lusty, free.° Persevere in thy service.
And all is well if thou work in this wise.

"But he that parted is in every place°   *960*
Is nowhere hool, as writen clerkes° wise.
What wonder is though swich oon have no grace?
Eek wost thou how it fareth of some service:°
As° plant a tree or herb in sundry wise
And on the morrow pull it up as blive,°   *965*
No wonder is though it may never thrive.

937 **foryive** forgive 941 **wopen** wept 943 **wolde . . . eesed** i.e.,
let God grant nothing but your comfort 944 **of . . . rist** from
whom arises 949 **swoot** sweet 952 **next . . . fin** next to the end
953 **looke . . . bridel** see to it that your bridle is restrained 954
suffer . . . tide endure the circumstances 957 **hide** be discreet
958 **lusty, free** active, generous 960 **parted . . . place** i.e., spreads
himself thin 961 **clerkes** scholars 963 **of . . . service** with some
services (to a lady) 964 **As** as if to 965 **blive** fast

"And sith that God of Love hath thee bestowed
In place digne unto thy worthinesse,
Stand faste; for to good port hast thou rowed.
And of thyself, for any hevinesse,　　　　　　　　970
Hope alway well; for but if drerinesse
Or overhaste our bothe labour shende,°
I hope of this to maken a good ende.

"And wost thou why I am the less afered
Of this mattere with my neece treete?°　　　　975
For this have I herde said of wise lered,°
'Was never man or woman yet begete°
That was unapt to sufferen love's heete—
Celestial, or elles love of kinde.'°
Forthy some grace I hope in her to finde.　　　980

"And for to speke of her in special,
Her beautee to bethinken° and her youthe,
It sit her not to been celestial
As yet—though that her liste both, and couthe.°
But trewely it sat her well right nowthe°　　　985
A worthy knight to loven and cherice.°
And but she do, I hold it for a vice.

"Wherefore I am and will been ay redy
To paine me° to do you this service;
For bothe you to pleese thus hope I　　　　　990
Hereafterward; for ye ben bothe wise,
And can it counseil° keep in swich a wise
That no man shall the wiser of it be.
And so we may been gladded alle three.

971–72 but . . . shende unless laziness or too much haste ruin the
work of us both　975 with . . . treete to broach with my niece
976 of . . . lered by learned wise men　977 begete begotten　979
Celestial . . . kinde i.e., heavenly or earthly love; *love of kinde*=
natural love, love between the sexes　982 bethinken consider
983–84 It . . . couthe it doesn't suit her to be celestial (i.e., spiritual
in her love) at her age—even if she wanted both (kinds of love)
and was capable of this. (Tatlock translated "though she would
and could." Pandarus's wry remark, though its grammar is difficult,
clearly suggests that Criseyde is not beyond carnal desires)　985 it
. . . nowthe it would suit her well at the moment　986 cherice
cherish　989 paine me take pains　992 counseil secret

"And, by my trouth, I have right now of thee 995
A good conceit in my wit,° as I guesse—
And what it is I will now that thou see:
I think (sith that Love of his goodnesse
Hath thee converted out of wickednesse)
That thou shalt been the beste post,° I leve, 1000
Of all his law, and most his foes to greeve.°

"Ensample why:° see now these wise clerkes
That erren aldermost° again a lawe,
And been converted from hir wicked werkes
Through grace of God that list hem to Him drawe, 1005
Then are these folk° that han most God in awe,
And strengest faithed° been, I understande,
And can an errour alderbest withstande."

When Troilus had herde Pandar assented
To been his help in loving of Criseyde, 1010
Wex of his woe, as who saith, untormented.°
But hotter wex his love, and thus he saide,
With sober cheer, although his herte playde,°
"Now blissful Venus, help, ere that I sterve!
Of thee, Pandar, I mowe some thank deserve.° 1015

"But, deere freend, how shall my woe be lesse
Till this be done? And good,° eek tell me this—
How wilt thou sayn of me and my distresse,
Lest she be wroth—this dreed I most, ywis—
Or nill not heer or trowen how it is? 1020
All this dreed I, and eek for the mannere
Of thee, her em,° she nill no swich thing heere."

995–96 of . . . wit for you a good idea in my mind 1000 post
support 1001 most . . . greeve most likely to give his foes grief
1002 Ensample why for example 1003 erren aldermost transgress
most of all 1006 these folk i.e., the converts 1007 strengest
faithed strongest in faith. Pandarus, who has a seemingly inexhaust-
ible store of folk wisdom, here voices the traditional notion that
religious converts—or converts to Love—are the most forceful
spokesmen for their new faith 1011 Wex . . . untormented he
grew, as one might say, less tormented by his woe 1013 playde
danced, raced 1015 Of . . . deserve may I deserve some thanks
from you, Pandar (i.e., in return for an equal favor) 1017 good
good friend 1020 Or . . . is or will not hear or believe how things
stand 1021–22 eek . . . em i.e., also, considering the fact that you

Quod Pandarus: "Thou hast a full greet care
Lest that the cherl° may fall out of the moone!
Why, lord, I hate of thee thy nice fare.° 1025
Why! entremete of that thou hast to doone.°
For Godde's love, I bidde thee a boone:°
So let me alone, and it shall be thy beste."
"Why, freend," quod he, "now do right as thee leste.

"But herke, Pandar, oo word; for I nolde 1030
That thou in me wendest so greet follye
That to my lady I desiren sholde
That toucheth harm or any villainye.°
For dreedeless, me were levere die
Than she of me aught elles understoode 1035
But that that mighte sounen° into goode."

Tho lough this Pandar, and anon answerde,
"And I thy borwe?° Fie, no wight doth but so.
I roughte not° though that she stood and herde
How that thou saist. But farewell. I will go. 1040
Adieu. Be glad. God speed us bothe two!
Yif° me this labour and this bisinesse,
And of my speed be thine all that sweetnesse."°

Tho Troilus gan down on knees to falle
And Pandar in his armes hente faste° 1045
And saide, "Now, fie on the Greekes alle!
Yet, Pandar, God shall help us at the laste.
And dreedeless, if that my life may laste,
And God toforn,° lo, some of hem shall smerte!—
And yet m'athinketh that this avaunt me sterte.° 1050

are her uncle   1024 **cherl** the man in the moon. Pandarus cleverly
belittles Troilus's concerns and puts him on the defensive   1025 **of
. . . fare** in you your idiotic behavior   1026 **entremete . . . doone**
i.e., meddle in things which concern you   1027 **I . . . boone** I ask
you a favor   1033 **That . . . villainye** something that involves
harm or anything ill-bred   1036 **sounen** turn   1038 **And . . .
borwe?** and am I your guarantee? A *borwe* in Middle English was
a pledge or security   1039 **I . . . not** I don't care   1042 **Yif** give
1043 **And . . . sweetnesse** and let all the sweetness of my success
be yours   1045 **hente faste** grabbed firmly   1049 **God toforn** be-
fore God   1050 **And . . . sterte** and yet I repent that this boast
escaped me

"Now, Pandare, I can no more saye
But thou wise, thou wost, thou maist, thou art all.
My life, my deeth hool° in thine hand I laye.
Help now!" Quod he, "Yis, by my trouth I shall."
"God yeeld° thee, freend, and this in special,"   1055
Quod Troilus, "that thou me recommande°
To her that to the deeth me may commande."

This Pandarus, tho desirous to serve
His fulle freend, then said in this mannere:
"Farewell, and think I will thy thank deserve—   1060
Have here my trouth—and that thou shalt well heere,"°
And went his way thinking on this mattere,
And how he best might her beseech of grace,
And find a time thereto, and a place.

For every wight that hath an house to founde°   1065
Ne runneth not the work for to beginne
With rakel° hand, but he will bide a stounde,°
And send his herte's line out fro withinne,°
Alderfirst his purpose for to winne.°
All this Pandar in his herte thoughte,   1070
And cast his work full wisly ere he wroughte.°

But Troilus lay tho no longer down,
But up anon upon his steede bay,°
And in the feeld he played the leoun.
Woe was that Greek that with him met a-day!°   1075
And in the town his manner tho forth ay°
So goodly was, and gat° him so in grace,
That eech him loved that looked on his face.

1053 **hool** wholly 1055 **yeeld** reward 1056 **recommande** commend
1061 **and . . . heere** and (think) that you will hear good news
1065 **founde** build 1067 **rakel** a rash 1067 **bide . . . stounde**
wait awhile 1068 **send . . . withinne** i.e., the builder first con-
ceives the plan in his mind (*herte*) and then carries it out. (Chaucer
took this passage from the opening lines of Geoffrey of Vinsauf's
Poetria Nova, which describes the writing of a poem) 1069 **Alder-
first . . . winne** first of all to attain his purpose 1071 **And . . .
wroughte** and laid his groundwork very carefully before he acted
1073 **steede bay** bay steed (horse) 1075 **a-day** that day 1076 **tho
. . . ay** always from that time forth 1077 **gat** got

For he became the freendlieste wight,°
The gentilest, and eek the moste free,   *1080*
The thriftiest, and oon° the beste knight
That in his time was or mighte be.
Deed were his japes and his crueltee,
His highe port,° and his manner estraunge°—
And eech of tho° gan for a virtue chaunge.   *1085*

Now let us stint of Troilus a stounde,°
That fareth like a man that hurt is sore,
And is somedeel of aching of his wounde
Y-lissed well, but heeled no deel more,°
And as an eesy pacient the lore   *1090*
Abit of him that goeth about° his cure—
And thus he drieth forth his aventure.°

1079 **freendlieste wight** Troilus experiences the ennobling power of
love. According to love conventions, the lover becomes brave,
virtuous, and generous through the force of his passion and an
all-consuming desire to serve and please his lady. This "service"
to the lady also represents the lover's humbling and repentance in
the court of Love, to whose devotion he has become a recent
convert (cf. I.1002–08)   1081 **thriftiest . . . oon** worthiest, and one
of   1084 **highe port** haughty bearing   1084 **estraunge** aloof   1085
tho i.e., those vices   1086 **stounde** while   1089 **Y-lissed . . . more**
well relieved, but no closer to being healed   1090–91 **eesy . . .
about** a patient at ease awaits the wisdom of the one who is
working for   1092 **drieth . . . aventure** continues to endure his
fortune

Book Two

PROEM

Out of these blacke wawes° for to saile—
O wind, O wind, the weder ginneth cleere—°
For in this sea the bòot hath swich travaille
Of my conning that unneth I it steere.°
This sea clepe° I the ţempestous mattere   5
Of desespair that Troilus was inne:
But now of hope the kalendes° beginne.

O lady mine, that called art Cleo,°
Thou be my speed fro this forth,° and my muse,
To rime well this book till I have do.°   10
Me needeth here noon other art to use.
Forwhy to every lover I me excuse
That of no sentiment° I this endite,
But out of Latin° in my tongue it write.

Wherefore I nill have neither thank ne blame   15
Of all this work, but pray you meekely,
Disblameth° me if any word be lame,
For as mine auctor saide so say I.
Eek though I speke of love unfeelingly,
No wonder is, for it no thing of new is:°   20
A blind man cannot judgen well in hewis.°

1 **wawes** waves 2 **ginneth cleere** begins to clear 3–4 **boot . . . steere** boat of my ability (*conning*) has such difficulty that I can scarcely steer it 5 **clepe** call 7 **kalendes** first days 8 **Cleo** Clio, muse of history 9 **speed . . . forth** help from this time forth 10 **do** finished 13 **sentiment** personal experience 14 **out . . . Latin** Chaucer continues to maintain the fiction that he is merely a translator of "his author," Lollius (see I.394) 17 **Disblameth** excuse 20 **it . . . is** it is nothing new 21 **in hewis** with respect to

43

Ye know eek that in form of speech is chaunge°
Within a thousand yeer, and wordes tho
That hadden pris now wonder nice° and straunge
Us thinketh hem, and yet they spake hem so,   25
And sped as well in love as men now do.
Eek for to winnen love in sundry ages,
In sundry landes sundry been usages.°

And forthy if it hap in any wise
That here be any lover in this place,°   30
That herkeneth as the story will devise
How Troilus came to his lady grace,
And thinketh, "So nold I not love purchase,"°
Or wondreth on his speech or his doinge,
I noot, but it is me no wonderinge.   35

For every wight which that to Rome went
Halt not oo path or alway oo mannere;°
Eek in some land were all the game shent°
If that they ferde° in love as men doon here,
As thus—in open doing, or in cheere,   40
In visiting, in form, or said hir sawes.°
Forthy men sayn, "Eech contree hath his lawes."

Eek scarcely been there in this place three
That have in love said like and done in all,
For to thy purpose this may liken thee,   45
And thee right nought:° yet all is said, or shall.
Eek some men grave in tree,° some in stone wall,

colors (proverb) 22 in . . . chaunge there is change in the form
of speech 23–24 tho . . . nice that then had substance now won-
derfully foolish 28 In . . . usages in different lands there are
different customs 30 this place Chaucer here directs his poem to
an audience. Cf. I.5 33 So . . . purchase I wouldn't win love in
such a fashion 36–37 every . . . mannere every man who goes to
Rome does not adhere to one route or one mode of travel. Went=
wendeth; halt= holdeth 38 were . . . shent the game (of love)
would be ruined 39 ferde fared, i.e., behaved 40–41 As . . .
sawes for example—in open actions, in appearance, in visiting, in
polite behavior, or in expressing themselves 45–46 to . . . nought
for your purpose one thing may please you, and not you at all.
(Chaucer seems to be pointing at various members of his audience)
47 grave . . . tree carve in wood

As it betit.° But sin I have begunne,
Mine auctor shall I followen if I conne.

In May, that moder° is of monthes glade,   50
That freshe flowers blew and white and rede
Been quick° again, that winter deede made,
And full of baum is fleeting every meede°—
When Phebus doth his brighte beemes sprede
Right in the white Bull,° it so betidde°   55
As I shall sing, on Maye's day the thridde,

That Pandarus, for all his wise speeche,
Felt eek his part of Love's shottes keene,°
That coud he never so well° of loving preeche,
It made his hew a-day full ofte greene.   60
So shope it that him fell that day a teene
In love,° for which in woe to bed he wente,
And made, ere it was day, full many a wente.°

The swallow Proigne° with a sorrowful lay,°
When morrowen came, gan make her waymentinge   65
Why she forshapen was;° and ever lay
Pandar abed, half in a slumberinge,
Till she so nigh him made her chatteringe,
How Tereüs gan forth her suster take,
That with the noise of her he gan awake,   70

48 **betit** happens 50 **moder** mother 52 **quick** alive 53 **full . . . meede** every meadow is awash with balm (*fleeting*= "floating"). In Chaucer's day balm was much prized for its fragrance and restorative properties 55 **Right . . . Bull** in the midpoint of the sun's passage through the astrological sign Taurus, the Bull 55 **betidde** happened. This is the main verb of the stanza completing the suspended thought "In May . . ." 58 **part . . . keene** share of Love's sharp darts 59 **coud . . . well** however well he could 61–62 **So . . . love** it so happened that there came to him that day a pang in love 63 **wente** tossing and turning 64 **swallow Proigne** Procne helped her sister, Philomela, revenge her rape by Tereus and was subsequently turned into a swallow; Philomela was turned into a nightingale, the bird who traditionally sang of love 64 **lay** song 65–66 **gan . . . was** made her sorrowing for why she was metamorphosed (into a swallow). The myth explains the bird's song, which was thought to be plaintive

And gan to call, and dress him° up to rise,
Remembering him° his errand was to doone°
From Troilus, and eek his greet emprise;°
And cast, and knew in good plight was the moone
To doon viage;° and took his way full soone   75
Unto his neece's palais there beside.°
Now Janus,° god of entree, thou him guide!

When he was come unto his neece's place,
"Where is my lady?" to her folk quod he.
And they him told, and he forth in gan passe,   80
And found two other ladies set° and she
Within a paved parlour; and they three
Herden a maiden reden hem° "The Geste
Of the Siege of Thebes"° while hem leste.

Quod Pandarus: "Madame, God you see,°   85
With all your book and all the compaignye."
"Ey! Uncle mine! Welcome, ywis," quod she,
And up she rose and by the hand in hie°
She took him fast, and saide, "This night thrie—
To goode mot it turn—of you I mette."°   90
And with that word she down on bench him sette.

"Yea, neece, ye shall faren well the bet,°
If God will, all this yeer," quod Pandarus.
"But I am sorry that I have you let
To herken of° your book ye praisen thus.   95

71 **call . . . him** call (his servants), and prepare   72 **Remembering him** remembering (the verb is often used in this reflexive way, like Fr. *se souvenir*)   72 **to doone** to be done   73 **emprise** enterprise   74–75 **cast . . . viage** consulted his horoscope, and knew that the moon was in a good position (for him) to make a journey   76 **there beside** nearby   77 **Janus** the two-faced god of doors and openings (*of entree*), who looks both forward and backward. The action of Pandarus's "greet emprise" begins exactly at this point   81 **set** sitting   83 **Herden . . . hem** were listening to a maiden (who) read to them   83–84 **Geste . . . Thebes** They hear the story (*geste*) of a doomed city—as we are hearing a story of doomed Troy. We learn in V.936 that Thebes existed but a generation ago; yet in II.107 Pandarus remarks that it has been written about: it is already history   85 **God . . . see** may God look after you   88 **hie** haste   89–90 **thrie . . . mette** three times—may it turn out well—I dreamed of you   92 **well . . . bet** even better   94–95 **you . . . of** kept you from listening to

For Godde's love, what saith it? Tell it us.
Is it of love? O, some good ye me lere!"°
"Uncle," quod she, "your maistress° is not here."

With that they gonnen laugh, and tho she saide,
"This romance is of Thebes that we reede,   *100*
And we han herde how that King Laius deide
Through Edipus his son, and all that deede.
And here we stinten at these letters rede,°
How the bishop, as the book can telle,
Amphiorax,° fell through the ground to helle."   *105*

Quod Pandarus: "All this know I myselve,
And all the assege of Thebes and the care,
For hereof been there maked bookes twelve.°
But let be this, and tell me how ye fare.
Do way your barbe,° and shew your face bare!   *110*
Do way your book! Rise up, and let us daunce.
And let us doon to May some observaunce."°

"I? God forbede," quod she. "Be ye mad?
Is that a widow's life, so God you save?
By God, ye maken me right sore adrad°—   *115*
Ye been so wild, it seemeth as ye rave.

97 some . . . lere teach me something good **98 maistress** Pandarus's girl friend **103 stinten . . . rede** paused at these red letters. Red capital letters, or rubrics, by convention designated a new section of the manuscript **105 Amphiorax** Like Criseyde's father, Amphiorax was a soothsayer. He predicted disasters resulting from the Theban war along with his own death. The *Roman de Thèbes*, a twelfth-century romance based on Statius's *Thebaid*, calls Amphiorax an *arcevesque*, archbishop, and John Lydgate in his translation of the *Roman*, the *Siege of Thebes* (1420–22), terms him a *bishop*. Chaucer was familiar with both the *Thebaid* (see V.1792) and the *Roman* **108 For . . . twelve** for of this (the *assege* and *care*) twelve books have been written. There are twelve books in the *Thebaid* of Statius **110 Do . . . barbe** do away with your barb. (The *barb* was a kind of veil extending from the chin midway to the waist, worn by upper-class widows and some nuns. A number of manuscripts read *wimpel* for *barbe*) **112 doon . . . observaunce** i.e., observe the rites of spring (rather than reading an old romance indoors). Medieval nobles commonly ventured into the countryside "on Maying" in early spring **115 adrad**

It satte me well bet° ay in a cave
To bid° and reed on holy saintes' lives.
Let maidens goon to daunce, and younge wives."

"As ever thrive I," quod this Pandarus,   *120*
"Yet coud I tell a thing to doon you playe . . ."
"Now uncle deere," quod she, "tell it us,
For Godde's love. Is then the assege awaye?°
I am of Greeks so fered that I deye!"
"Nay, nay," quod he, "as ever mot I thrive,   *125*
It is a thing well bet than swiche five."°

"Yea, holy God!" quod she, "what thing is that?
What, bet than swiche five? Ey! nay, ywis.
For all this world ne can I reeden° what
It sholde been—some jape I trow is this.   *130*
And but yourselven tell us what it is
My wit is for to areed it all too leene.°
As help me God, I noot not what ye meene."

"And I your borwe, ne never shall for me
This thing be told to you, as mot I thrive."   *135*
"And why so, uncle mine, why so?" quod she.
"By God," quod he, "that will I tell as blive:
For prouder woman is there none on live,°
And ye it wist,° in all the town of Troye.
I jape not, as ever have I joye."   *140*

Tho gan she wonderen more than beforn
A thousandfold, and down her eyen caste.
For never sith the time that she was born
To knowe thing desired she so faste.
And with a sigh she said him at the laste: *145*
"Now uncle mine, I nill you not displeese,
Nor asken more that may do you diseese."°

afraid 117 **It . . . bet** it would be far more suitable for me
118 **bid** pray 123 **awaye** lifted 126 **well . . . five** much better
than five such things 129 **reeden** guess 132 **My . . . leene** my
imagination is all too scant to interpret it 134 **And . . . borwe**
and I promise you (see I.1038) 138 **on live** alive 139 **And . . .
wist** if you knew it 147 **do . . . diseese** make you uncomfortable

So after this, with many wordes glade
And freendly tales and with merry cheere,
Of this and that they played and gonnen wade 150
In many an uncouth,° glad, and deep mattere,
As freendes doon when they been met yfere,
Till she gan asken him how Hector ferde,
That was the towne's wall and Greeke's yerde.°

"Full well, I thank it God," quod Pandarus, 155
"Save in his arm he hath a litel wounde.
And eek his freshe brother Troilus,
The wise, worthy Hector the secounde,
In whom that alle virtue list abounde—
As alle trouth and alle gentilesse, 160
Wisdom, honour, freedom, and worthinesse."

"In good faith, em,"° quod she, "that liketh me,
They faren well—God save hem bothe two;
For trewelich, I hold it greet deintee°
A kinge's son in armes well to do, 165
And been of good condicions° thereto:
For greet power and moral virtue here
Is selde y-seen in oo person yfere."°

"In good faith, that is sooth," quod Pandarus.
"But, by my trouth, the king hath sones twaye— 170
That is to meen, Hector and Troilus—
That certainly, though that I sholde deye,
They been as void of vices, dare I saye,
As any men that liven under the sunne:
Hir might is wide y-know, and what they conne.° 175

"Of Hector needeth it no more for to telle.
In all this world there nis a better knight
Than he, that is of worthinesse welle—
And he well more virtue hath than might.
This knoweth many a wise and worthy wight. 180

150–51 **gonnen . . . uncouth** delved into many a strange 154 **wall
. . . yerde** protection and scourge of the Greeks 162 **em** uncle
164 **I . . . deintee** I believe it is a noble thing 166 **condicions**
character 168 **selde . . . yfere** seldom seen together in one person.
(Criseyde's interest in power and in moral character are to be noted
here) 175 **Hir . . . conne** their strength, and what they can do, is
widely known

The same pris° of Troilus I saye.
God help me so—I know not swiche twaye!"

"By God," quod she, "of Hector that is sooth;
Of Troilus the same thing trow I.
For dreedeless, men tellen that he doth   *185*
In armes day by day so worthily—
And bereth him here at home so gently
To every wight—that alle pris hath he
Of hem that me were levest praised be."°

"Ye say right sooth, ywis," quod Pandarus;   *190*
"For yesterday, whoso had with him been,
He might han wondered upon Troilus.
For never yet so thick a swarm of been
Ne fleigh as Greekes fro him gonne fleen.°
And through the feeld,° in every wighte's eere,   *195*
There nas no cry but 'Troilus is there.'

"Now here, now there, he hunted hem so faste,
There nas but Greekes' blood and Troilus.
Now him he hurt, and him° all down he caste.
Ay where he went it was arrayed thus:°   *200*
He was hir deeth, and sheeld and life for us,
That as that° day there durste none withstande,
While that he held his bloody sword in hande.

"Thereto he is the freendlieste man
Of greet estate that ever I saw my live;°   *205*
And where him list best fellowshipe can
To swich as him thinketh able for to thrive."°
And with that word tho Pandarus as blive
He took his leeve, and said, "I will goon henne."°
"Nay! blame have I,° mine uncle," quod she thenne,   *210*

181 **pris** praise   189 **Of . . . be** of those I should most wish to be
praised by   193–94 **been . . . fleen** bees (never) flew as Greeks fled
from him   195 **feeld** field (of battle)   199 **him . . . him** this one
. . . another   200 **Ay . . . thus** wherever he went, the situation was
this   202 **That . . . that** so that on that   205 **my live** in my life
206–7 **And . . . thrive** and where it pleases him he can bestow the
best friendship on such a man as he thinks is able to benefit from it
209 **henne** away   210 **blame . . . I** I am to blame

What aileth you to be thus wery soone—
And namelich of women? Will ye so?°
Nay, sitteth down. By God, I have to doone°
With you to speke of wisdom° ere ye go."
And every wight that was about hem tho   215
That herde that gan far away to stande,
While they two had all that hem list in hande.°

When that her tale all brought was to an ende
Of her estate and of her governaunce,°
Quod Pandarus, "Now is time I wende.   220
But yet say I, ariseth, let us daunce,
And cast your widow's habit to mischaunce!°—
What list you thus yourself to disfigure,°
Sith you is tid thus fair an aventure?"

"Ah! well bethought, for love of God," quod she.   225
"Shall I not witen what ye meen of this?"
"No, this thing asketh leiser,"° tho quod he,
"And eek me wolde muche greeve, ywis,
If I it told and ye it took amiss.
Yet were it bet my tongue for to stille,°   230
Than say a sooth that were agains your wille.

"For, neece, by the goddess Minerve,
And Jupiter, that maketh the thunder ringe,
And by the blissful Venus that I serve,
Ye been the woman in this world livinge—   235
Withouten paramour°—to my witinge°
That I best love and loothest° am to greeve.
And that ye witen well yourself, I leve."

---

212 **so** do so (go away)   213 **to doone** i.e., business   214 **wisdom**
i.e., to get your advice   217 **had . . . hande** dealt with everything
they wished   218–19 **When . . . governaunce** Her social position
and her behavior—presumably as a widow and abandoned daughter
—constitute the *wisdom* (line 214) about which Criseyde consulted
Pandarus   222 **to mischaunce** to the devil   223 **disfigure** obscure
your beauty   224 **Sith . . . aventure** since such an attractive fortune
has befallen you   227 **asketh leiser** requires time   230 **stille** hold
236 **Withouten paramour** except (my) lady love. Skeat suggests,
"excepting sweethearts [reading *paramours* for *paramour*]; or, ex-
cepting by way of passionate love. The latter is the usual sense in
Chaucer"   236 **witinge** knowledge   237 **loothest** most loath (un-
willing)

"Ywis, my uncle," quod she, "graunt mercy.°
Your freendship have I founden ever yet.°   240
I am to no man holden,° trewely,
So much as you—and have so litel quit.°
And with the grace of God, emforth° my wit,
As in my guilt,° I shall you never offende:
And if I have ere this, I will amende.   245

"But for the love of God, I you beseeche,
As ye been he that I love most and triste,
Let be to me your fremde° manner speeche,
And say to me, your neece, what you liste."
And with that word her uncle anon her kiste   250
And saide, "Gladly, leve neece deere.
Take it for good, that I shall say you here."

With that she gan her eyen down to caste.
And Pandarus to coughe gan a lite,
And saide, "Neece, alway, lo, to the laste,   255
How so it be that some men hem delite
With subtil art hir tales for to endite,°
Yet for all that, in hir intencioun,
Hir tale is all for some conclusioun.°

"And sith the end is every tale's strengthe—   260
And this matter is so behoovely°—
What shold I point or drawen it on lengthe°
To you, that been my freend so faithfully?"
And with that word he gan right inwardly°
Beholden her, and looken on her face,   265
And said, "On swich a mirrour goode grace!"°

239 **graunt mercy** many thanks (= Shakespeare's "gramercy") 240
founden . . . yet always found true   241 **holden** beholden   242
quit paid back ("requited")   243 **emforth** to the limit of   244 **As
. . . guilt** through my fault   248 **fremde** strange   256–57 **How . . .
endite** howsoever it is that some men amuse themselves in writing
their tales with a subtle art   259 **for . . . conclusioun** with some
purpose or end in sight   261 **behoovely** valuable   262 **What . . .
lengthe** why should I embellish it or drag it out   264 **inwardly**
intimately   266 **grace** favor. By calling her a *mirrour* Pandarus
suggests that Criseyde is a model of womanhood; or he may suggest
that by looking at her face "inwardly," i.e., into her eyes, he sees
his own soul, a medieval notion

Then thought he thus: "If I my tale endite
Aught hard, or make a process° any while,
She shall no savour han therein but lite,
And trow I wold her in my will beguile;°   270
For tender wittes weenen all be wile,°
Ther-as they cannot plainly understande.
Forthy her wit to serven will I fonde"°—

And looked on her in a bisy wise.°
And she was ware that he beheld her so,   275
And saide, "Lord, so fast ye me avise!°
Saw ye me never ere now? What, say ye no?"
"Yis, yis!" quod he, "and bet will ere I go.
But by my trouth, I thoughte° now if ye
Be fortunate, for now men shall it see.   280

"For to every wight some goodly aventure°
Some time is shape,° if he it can receiven.°
But if that he will take of it no cure°
When that it com'th, but wilfully it waiven,°
Lo, neither cas ne Fortune him deceiven,   285
But right his verray slouth° and wrecchednesse—
And swich a wight is for to blame, I guesse.

"Good aventure, O belle° neece, have ye
Full lightly founden, and ye conne it take;
And for the love of God, and eek of me,   290
Cacch° it anon, lest aventure slacke.
What shold I longer process of it make?
Yif me your hand, for in this world is noon,
If that you list, a wight so well begon.°

267–68 **endite . . . process** i.e., tell it in a way that is at all difficult,
or make a long story   269–70 **no . . . beguile** take but small
pleasure in it, and think I mean to willfully deceive her   271 **tender
. . . wile** sensitive minds believe that everything is guile   273 **serven
. . . fonde** I will try to accommodate myself to   274 **in . . . wise**
intently   276 **fast . . . avise** closely you scrutinize me   279 **thoughte**
wondered   281 **aventure** fortune   282 **shape** destined   282 **receiven**
take advantage of   283 **take . . . cure** pay no attention to it   284
waiven ignore   286 **right . . . slouth** just his very laziness   288
belle fair   291 **Cacch** seize. The phrase may echo Horace's *carpe
diem*, "seize the day" (see II.396)   293–94 **noon . . . begon** no
. . . creature so fortunate

"And sith I speke of° good intencioun,   295
As I to you have told well herebeforn—
And love as well your honour and renown
As creature in all this world y-born—
By all tho oothes that I have you sworn,
And ye be wroth therefore, or ween° I lie, 300
Ne shall I never seen you eft with eye.

"Beeth not aghast, ne quaketh not. Whereto?
Ne changeth not for feere so your hewe;
For hardily,° the worst of this is do.
And though my tale as now° be to you newe, 305
Yet trust alway ye shall me finde trewe.
And were it thing that me thought unsittinge,°
To you wold I no swiche tales bringe."

"Now, my good em, for Godde's love, I praye,"
Quod she, "come off,° and tell me what it is. 310
For both I am aghast what ye will saye,
And eek me longeth it to wite,° ywis!
For whether it be well or be amiss,
Say on! Let me not in this feere dwelle."
"So will I doon. Now herkeneth. I shall telle. 315

"Now, neece mine, the kinge's deere sone,
The goode, wise, worthy, fresh and free°—
Which alway for to doon well is his wone°—
The noble Troilus so loveth thee
That, but ye help, it will his bane° be. 320
Lo, here is all. What shold I more saye?
Do what you list to make him live or deye.

"But if ye let him die, *I* will sterve.
Have here my trouthe, neece, I nill not lien—
Al° shold I with this knife my throote kerve."° 325
With that the teeres brust out of his eyen,
And said, "If that ye doon us bothe dien

<hr>

295 **of** with 300 **ween** believe 304 **hardily** assuredly 305 **as now**
for the moment 307 **thing . . . unsittinge** something that seemed
to me unsuitable 310 **come off** come on 312 **me . . . wite** I long
to know it 317 **free** generous 318 **wone** wont, habit 320 **bane**
ruin 325 **Al** even if 325 **kerve** cut

Thus guilteless, then have ye fished faire.°
What mende ye though that we both apaire?°

"Alas, he which that is my lord so deere,   *330*
That trewe man, that noble, gentil knight,
That nought desireth but your freendly cheere—
I see him dien ther he goeth upright,°
And hasteth him with all his fulle might
For to been slain, if his fortune assente.   *335*
Alas, that God you swich a beautee sente!

"If it be so that ye so cruel be
That of his deeth you listeth nought to recche,
That° is so trew and worthy, as ye see,
No more than of a japer or a wrecche—   *340*
If ye be swich your beautee may not strecche°
To make amendes of so cruel a deede:
Avisement is good before the neede.°

"Woe worth° the faire gemme virtueless!°
Woe worth that herb also that doth no boote!°   *345*
Woe worth that beautee that is routheless!°
Woe worth that wight that tret eech° under foote!
And ye that been of beautee crop and roote,°
If therewithal in you there be no routhe,
Then is it harm ye liven, by my trouthe.   *350*

"And also, think well that this is no gaude,°
For me were lever thou and I and he
Were hanged, than I sholde been his bawde,°
As high as men might on us all y-see.
I am thine em. The shame were to me,   *355*
As well as thee, if that I shold assente,
Through mine abet, that he thine honour shente.°

328 fished faire i.e., made a fine catch   **329 What . . . apaire?** how are you improved if we both are harmed?   **333 dien . . . upright** i.e., dying on his feet   **339 That** who (i.e., Troilus)   **341 strecche** suffice   **343 Avisement . . . neede** i.e., "forewarned is forearmed" (proverb)   **344 Woe worth** woe come to   **344 gemme virtueless** gem without power. Medieval scientists believed that precious stones contained magical medicinal and astrological powers ("virtues")   **345 doth . . . boote** brings about no cure   **346 routheless** pitiless   **347 that . . . eech** who treads each man   **348 crop . . . roote** plant and root   **351 gaude** trick   **353 bawde** pimp, go-between   **357 Through . . . shente** through my assistance, that he destroyed your

"Now understand: for I you not requere°
To binde you to him through no beheste,°
But only that ye make him better cheere   360
Than ye han done ere this, and more feste,°
So that his life be saved at the leeste.
This all and some,° and plainly our intente—
God help me so, I never other mente.

"Lo, this request is nought but skile,° ywis,   365
Ne dout of reeson, pardee, is there noon.
I set the worste°—that ye dreeden this:
Men wolde wonderen seen° him come or goon.
Ther-agains° answer I thus anon:
That every wight—but he be fool of kinde°—   370
Will deem° it love of freendship in his minde.

"What! Who will deemen, though he see a man
To temple go, that he the images eeteth?°
Think eek how well and wisly that he can
Govern himself, that he nothing forgeteth;   375
That, where he com'th, he pris and thank him getteth;°
And eek thereto he shall come here so selde.°
What force were it,° though all the town behelde?

"Swich love of freendes regneth° all this town,
And wry you in that mantel° evermo.   380
And God so wis be my salvacioun,
As I have said, your best is to do so.
But alway, goode neece, to stint his woe,
So let your daunger sucred been a lite,°
That of his deeth ye be not for to wite."°   385

reputation   358 I . . . requere I don't ask you   359 beheste pro-
mise   361 feste welcome   363 This . . . some this is all there is to
it   365 skile reasonable and right   367 set . . . worste suggest the
worst that can happen   368 seen to see   369 Ther-agains in re-
sponse to that   370 but . . . kinde unless he is a natural born fool
371 deem judge. ("Love of friendship" signified a "platonic" rela-
tionship which would be above reproach)   373 he . . . eeteth that
he eats the idols   376 That . . . getteth that wherever he goes he
receives praise and thanks   377 selde seldom   378 What . . . it
what would it matter   379 regneth prevails in   380 wry . . . mantel
wrap yourself in that cloak (i.e., the pretext of friendship)   384 So
. . . lite let your aloofness be a little sweetened (sucred= sugared)
385 wite blame

Criseyde, which that herde him in this wise,
Thought, "I shall feelen° what he meeneth, ywis."
"Now em," quod she, "what wolde ye devise?°
What is your reed I sholde doon of this?"
"That is well said," quod he. "Certain, best is   *390*
That ye him love again° for his lovinge
As love for love is skilful guerdoninge.°

"Think eek how elde wasteth° every houre
In eech of you a partie° of beautee;
And therefore, ere that age thee devoure,   *395*
Go love,° for, old, there will no wight of thee.°
Let this proverb a lore° unto you be:
'Too late y-ware,° quod Beautee, when it paste.'°
And elde daunteth daunger° at the laste.

"The kinge's fool is wont to cryen loude   *400*
When that him thinketh a woman ber'th her hye:°
'So longe mot ye live, and alle proude,
Till crowes' feet be grown under your eye!
And send you then a mirrour in to prye,°
In which that ye may see your face amorrwe.'°   *405*
Neece, I bidde wish you no more sorrwe."°

With this he stint and cast adown the heed.°
And she began to brust aweep anon,°
And said, "Alas for woe! Why nere I deed?°
For of this world the faith is all agon.   *410*
Alas! what sholden strange° to me doon,

---

387 feelen find out   **388 devise** suggest   **391 again** in return   **392 skilful guerdoninge** a reasonable reward   **393 elde wasteth** age erodes   **394 partie** part   **396 Go love** Pandarus here expresses the conventional literary sentiment of *carpe diem,* "seize the day," in which a lyric poet urges a maiden to yield to her lover before the advent of old age and death. Cf. Herrick's "Gather ye rosebuds while ye may"   **396 for . . . thee** for nobody will want you when you are old   **397 lore** lesson   **398 y-ware** aware   **398 paste** passed   **399 elde . . . daunger** old age conquers haughtiness   **401 ber'th . . . hye** carries herself (acts) proudly   **404 in . . . prye** to gaze into   **405 amorrwe** in the morning (when the crow's feet would be most noticeable)   **406 I . . . sorrwe** I don't mean to wish you any more sorrow   **407 the heed** his head   **408 brust . . . anon** burst into tears at once   **409 nere . . . deed** weren't I dead   **411 strange** strangers

When he that for my beste freend I wende°
Ret° me to love, and shold it me defende?°

"Alas, I wold han trusted, douteless,
That if that I through my disaventure   415
Had loved outher° him° or Achilles,
Hector, or any manne's creature,°
Ye nold han had no mercy ne mesure°
On me, but alway had me in repreve.
This false world, alas, who may it leve?°   420

"What! Is this all the joy and all the feste?°
Is this your reed? Is this my blissful cas?
Is this the verray meed of your beheste?°
Is all this painted process° said, alas,
Right for this fin?° O lady mine, Pallas,°   425
Thou in this dreedful cas for me purveye,°
For so astoned° am I that I deye."

With that she gan full sorrowfully to sike.
"Ah, may it be no bet?" quod Pandarus,
"By God, I shall no more come here this wike°—   430
And God aforn—that am mistrusted thus.
I see full well that ye set lite° of us,
Or of our deeth. Alas, I, woeful wrecche!
Might *he* yet live—of *me* is not to recche . . .

"O cruel God, O despitouse Marte!°   435
O furies° three of hell—on you I crye!
So let me never out of this house departe,
If that I mente harm or villainye.°

412 wende took (i.e., believed)   **413 Ret** advises (= *reedeth*)   413
defende forbid   **416 outher** either   **416 him** i.e., Troilus   417
manne's creature i.e., any man alive   **418 mesure** moderation   420
it leve believe in it   **421 feste** rejoicing   **423 meed . . . beheste**
fulfillment of your promise (*meed*= reward)   **424 painted process**
elaborate argument. By saying "painted," Criseyde may refer to the
rhetorical nature of Pandarus's previous speech, with its rhetorical
devices, or "*colours*" of rethorik"   **425 fin** end   **425 Pallas** Pallas
Athena, patron goddess of the Palladium (I.153), was a virgin   426
for . . . purveye provide for me   **427 astoned** stunned   **430 wike**
week   **432 set lite** think little   **435 despitouse Marte** pitiless Mars
436 furies the furies revenged crimes against natural law (cf. I.6)
438 villainye impropriety

But sith I see my lord mot needes die,
And I with him, here I me shrive° and saye   *440*
That wickedly ye doon us bothe deye.

"But sith it liketh you that I be deed,
By Neptunus, that god is of the sea:
Fro this forth shall I never eeten breed,
Till I mine owne herte blood may see;   *445*
For certain I will die as soon as he."
And up he sterte, and on his way he raughte,°
Till she again him by the lappe° caughte.

Criseyde, which that well nigh starf° for feere—
So as she was the feerfulleste wight   *450*
That mighte be—and herde eek with her eere,
And saw the sorrowful ernest of the knight,
And in his prayer eek saw noon unright,°
And for the harm that might eek fallen more,
She gan to rew and dredde her° wonder sore,   *455*

And thoughte thus: "Unhappes fallen thicke
Alday° for love, and in swich manner cas
As men been cruel in hemself and wicke;°
And if this man slee here himself, alas,
In my presence, it will be no solas.°   *460*
What men wold of it deem I cannot saye.
It needeth me full slyly for to playe."

And with a sorrowful sigh she saide thrie,
"Ah, lord! What me is tid a sorry chaunce!°
For mine estate lieth now in jupartye,°   *465*
And eek mine eme's life is in balaunce.
But natheless, with Godde's governaunce,
I shall so doon mine honour shall I keepe,
And eek his life"—and stinte for to weepe.

440 **me shrive** confess myself 447 **raughte** went 448 **lappe** fold
of a garment (cf. "lapel") 449 **starf** died 453 **noon unright** no
wrong 455 **dredde her** was frightened 456–57 **Unhappes . . . Al-
day** misfortunes occur in droves all the time 458 **wicke** evil 460
solas comfort (or, as Baugh suggests, "no laughing matter") 464
What . . . chaunce! what bad luck has befallen me! 465 **jupartye**
jeopardy

"Of harmes two the less is for to chese:°   *470*
Yet have I lever maken him good cheere°
In honour than mine eme's life to lese.°
Ye sayn ye nothing elles me requere?"°
"No, wis," quod he, "mine owne neece deere."
"Now, well," quod she, "and I will doon my paine: *475*
I shall mine herte agains my lust° constraine.

"But that I nill not holden him in honde,°
Ne love a man ne can I not, ne may,
Agains my will. But elles will I fonde,°
Mine honour sauf,° pleesen him fro day to day.   *480*
Thereto nold I not ones han said nay,
But that I dredde, as in my fantasye.°
But ceese cause, ay ceeseth maladye.°

"But here I make a protestacioun:°
That, in this process, if ye deeper go,   *485*
That certainly, for no salvacioun
Of you,° though that ye sterven bothe two—
Though all the world on oo day be my foe—
Ne shall I never of him han other routhe."°
"I grante well," quod Pandar, "by my trouthe."   *490*

"But may I truste well thereto," quod he,
"That of this thing that ye han hight° me here
Ye will it holden trewely unto me?"
"Yea, douteless," quod she, "mine uncle deere."
"Ne that I shall han cause in this mattere,"   *495*
Quod he, "to plain, or after you to preeche?"°
"Why no, pardee." What needeth more speeche?

470 **Of . . . chese** i.e., one must choose the lesser of two evils.
Criseyde's remark suggests a pessimistic and skeptical view of life
471 **have . . . cheere** would I rather be good to him (Troilus) 472
lese lose   473 **nothing . . . requere** require nothing else of me.
Criseyde now speaks aloud to Pandarus 476 **lust** desire, wishes
477 **But . . . honde** except I won't lead him on 479 **fonde** try
480 **Mine . . . sauf** saving my honor 482 **fantasye** imagination
483 **But . . . maladye** but when the cause ceases then the disease
always ceases (a proverb) 484 **protestacioun** exception 486–87
for . . . you not (even) to save you 489 **routhe** pity (i.e., other
than what she agreed to in lines 479–80) 492 **hight** promised
496 **plain . . . preeche** complain, or to preach to you

Tho fellen they in other tales glade,°
Till at the last—"O good em," quod she tho,
"For his love which that us bothe made 500
Tell me how first ye wisten of his woe?
Wot none of it but ye?" He saide, "No."
"Can he well speke of love?" quod she. "I praye,
Tell me, for I the bet me shall purveye."°

Tho Pandarus a litel gan to smile, 505
And saide, "By my trouth, I shall you telle.
This other day, not gone longe while,
Inwith° the palais garden, by a welle,
Gan he and I well half a day to dwelle,
Right for to speken of an ordinaunce,° 510
How we the Greekes mighten disavaunce.°

"Soon after that begunne we to leepe
And casten with our dartes° to and fro,
Till at the last he said he wolde sleepe,
And on the grass adown he laid·him tho. 515
And I afar gan romen to and fro,
Till that I herde, as that I welk° alone,
How he began full woefully to groone.

"Tho gan I stalk him softely behinde,
And sikerly, the soothe for to sayne, 520
As I can clepe° again now to my minde,
Right thus to Love he gan him for to plaine.
He saide, 'Lord, have ruth upon my paine.
Al have I been rebel in mine intente,°
Now *mea culpa*,° Lord! I me repente. 525

" 'O God, that at thy disposicioun°
Leedest the fin° by juste purveyaunce°

498 **Tho . . . glade** then they fell (to talking) of other happy matters
504 **for . . . purveye** so that I shall better prepare myself. (One
must note here Criseyde's interest in "speaking of love"—and Pan-
darus's reaction in the next line) 508 **Inwith** within 510 **ordin-
aunce** plan 511 **disavaunce** set back 513 **casten . . . dartes** throw
our javelins 517 **welk** walked 521 **clepe** recall 524 **intente** in-
tentions. Troilus uses Christian theological language and makes a
Christian-like confession to the pagan God of Love 525 **mea culpa**
the blame is mine 526 **disposicioun** i.e., disposing 527 **Leedest
. . . fin** direct the end 527 **purveyaunce** foresight, providence

Of every wight—my low° confessioun
Accept in gree,° and send me swich penaunce
As liketh thee; but from disesperaunce,   *530*
That may my ghost depart away fro thee,
Thou be my sheeld,° for thy benignitee.

" 'For certes, Lord, so sore hath she me wounded,
That stood in black with looking of her eyen,°
That to mine herte's bottom it is y-sounded,°   *535*
Through which I wot that I mot needes deyen.
This is the worst, I dare me not bewrayen;°
And well the hotter been the gledes° rede
That men hem wryen° with ashen pale and deede.'

"With that he smote his heed adown° anon,   *540*
And gan to mutter I noot what, trewely.
And I with that gan still° away to goon
And let thereof as nothing wist had I°—
And came again anon, and stood him by,
And said, 'Awake! ye sleepen all too longe.   *545*
It seemeth not that love doth you longe,°

" 'That sleepen so that no man may you wake.
Who saw ever ere this so dull a man?'
'Yea, freend,' quod he, 'do ye your heedes ache°
For love—and let me liven as I can.'   *550*

---

528 **low** humble   529 **in gree** graciously (cf. "agreeable")   530–32 **from . . . sheeld** be thou my shield from despair which may separate my spirit from you. Of Christian despair Chaucer's Parson on the Canterbury pilgrimage remarks: "This horrible sin is so perilous that he that is despaired, there nis no felony ne no sin that he douteth [fears] for to do." In Troilus's religion of Love despair would be to give up hope not of God's grace but of the lady's "grace"   543 **looking . . . eyen** a look from her eyes. Eye-contact was traditionally the beginning of love   535 **is y-sounded** has plunged   537 **me . . . bewrayen** reveal myself (my love)   538 **gledes** coals   539 **wryen** cover   540 **smote . . . adown** cast his head down. Although Chaucer elsewhere uses the word *smiten* in its usual sense of "to strike," it appears that in this context the word *smote* partakes of its earliest signification of "throwing" (see OED, s.v. *smite*)   542 **still** quietly   543 **And . . . I** and acted as though I had known nothing about it   546 **It . . . longe** it doesn't seem that love concerns you (*longe*= to belong to, or befit)   549 **do . . . ache** make your heads ache (*your heedes*= the heads of your lovers)

But though that he for woe was pale and wan,
Yet made he tho as fresh a countenaunce
As though he shold have led the newe daunce.°

"This passed forth till now, this other day,
It fell that I came roming all alone   555
Into his chambre, and found how that he lay
Upon his bed. But man so sore groone
Ne herde I never! And what that was his mone
Ne wist I not,° for as I was cominge
All suddenly he left his complaininge.   560

"Of which I took somewhat suspicioun.
And neer° I came, and found he wepte sore;
And God so wis be my salvacioun
As never of thing had I no ruthe more.
For neither with engyne, ne with no lore,   565
Unnethes might I fro the deeth him keepe,°
That yet feel I mine herte for him weepe.

"And, God wot, never sith that I was born
Was I so bisy no man for to preeche,
Ne never was to wight so deep y-sworn   570
Ere he me told who mighte been his leeche.°
But now to you rehersen all his speeche,
Or all his woeful wordes for to soune,°
Ne bid me not, but ye will see me swoune.°

"But for to save his life—and elles nought—   575
And to noon harm of you thus am I driven;
And for the love of God that us hath wrought,°
Swich cheer him doth° that he and I may liven.
Now have I plat° to you mine herte shriven,°

552–53 **made . . . daunce** cf. "to put a bright face on things." Root
cites Gower's "the newefot" (a kind of dance) in his note to "the
newe daunce." Chaucer on several occasions refers to the courtship
ritual as a dance or "the old dance" (cf. I.517)   558–59 **what . . .
not** what his complaint was I didn't know   562 **neer** nearer   565–
66 **For . . . keepe** for neither with stratagems nor with learning
scarcely could I keep him from death   571 **leeche** doctor (i.e., cure)
573 **for . . . soune** to utter   574 **but . . . swoune** unless you wish
to see me swoon   577 **wrought** created   578 **Swich . . . doth** show
him such favor   579 **plat** plainly   579 **shriven** confessed

And sith ye wot that mine intent is cleene,°   580
Take heed thereof, for I noon evil meene.

"And right good thrift° I pray to God have ye,
That han swich oon y-caught withouten net.
And be ye wise as ye be fair to see,
Well in the ring then is the ruby set.   585
There were nevere two so well y-met,
When ye been his all hool as he is youre . . .°
Ther mighty God yet grant us see that houre!"

"Nay, thereof spake I not—ha, ha," quod she,
"As help me God, ye shenden every deel!"°   590
"O, mercy, deere neece," anon quod he,
"What so I spake, I mente nought but well.
By Mars, the god that helmed° is of steel,
Now beeth not wroth, my blood, my neece deere."
"Now well," quod she, "foryiven be it here."   595

* * *

With this he took his leeve, and home he wente.
And Lord, so he was glad and well begon.°
Criseyde arose—no longer she ne stente°—
But straight into her closet° went anon,
And set her down as still as any ston,   600
And every word gan up and down to winde°
That he had said, as it came her to minde,

And was somedeel astoned° in her thought
Right for the newe cas. But when that she
Was full avised,° tho found she right nought   605
Or peril why she ought afeered be.
For man may love, of possibilitee,
A woman so his herte may to-breste,°
And she not love again,° but if her leste.

But as she sat alone and thoughte thus,   610
Ascry arose at scarmuch all withoute,°

580 **cleene** pure   582 **thrift** luck   587 **hool . . . youre** wholly as
he is yours   590 **shenden . . . deel** spoil every bit   593 **helmed**
helmeted   597 **well begon** well pleased (cf. "woe begone")   598
stente stayed   599 **closet** bedroom   601 **winde** turn over   603 **as-
toned** astonished   605 **Was . . . avised** had fully considered   608
to-breste burst   609 **love again** i.e., return his love   611 **Ascry**

And men cried in the street—"See, Troilus
Hath right now put to flight the Greekes' route!"°
With that gan all her meinee° for to shoute:
"Ah, go we see! Cast up the lattice° wide,   615
For through this street he mot to palais ride,

"For other way is fro the gate noon
Of Dardanus. There open is the chaine."
With that came he and all his folk° anon
An eesy pace, riding in routes twaine,°   620
Right as his happy day was, sooth to sayne,
For which° men sayn: 'May nought disturbed be
That shall betiden of necessitee.'

This Troilus sat on his baye steede
All armed, save his heed, full richely;   625
And wounded was his horse, and gan to bleede,
On which he rode a pace full softely.°
But swich a knightly sighte, trewely,
As was on him was not, withouten faile,
To look on Mars,° that god is of bataille.   630

So like a man of armes and a knight
He was to seen, fulfilled of high prowesse,
For both he had a body and a might
To doon that thing, as well as hardinesse;
And eek to seen him in his geer him dresse—   635
So fresh, so young, so weeldy° seemed he
It was an hevene upon him for to see.°

. . . **withoute** an uproar arose at a skirmish outside   613 **route**
horde   614 **meinee** household (cf. Fr. *ménage*)   615 **lattice** a win-
dow screened by crossed or barred strips of wood or iron   619 **folk**
troops   620 **routes twaine** two companies   622 **For which** i.e., for
such lucky days   627 **a . . . softely** a gait very slowly   628–30
But . . . Mars truly to look upon Mars was not so knightly a sight,
without doubt, as to look upon Troilus   636 **weeldy** vigorous,
agile. The OED, which cites this passage from the *Troilus* as the
earliest occurrence of this word, glosses as follows: "Capable of
easily 'wielding' one's body or limbs, or a weapon, etc." (s.v. *wieldy*)
631–37 **So . . . see** The main clause of this suspended—and non-
parallel—sentence occurs in the stanza's final line. In a rough
paraphrase: "He was, to look upon, so like a man of arms . . . ;
and also, to see him carry himself in his armor, so vigorous, so
young, so active he seemed, (that) it was heaven to see him"

His helm to-hewen° was in twenty places
That by a tissue heng his back behinde.°
His sheeld to-dashed° was with swords and maces,°   640
In which men mighte many an arrow finde,
That thirled hadde horn and nerf and rinde;°
And ay the people cried, "Here cometh our joye,
And next his brother,° holder up of Troye!"

For which he wex a litel red for shame,   645
When he the people upon him herde cryen,
That to behold it was a noble game
How soberlich he caste down his eyen.
Criseyde gan all his cheer espien,
And let it so soft in her herte sinke   650
That to herself she said, "Who yaf me drinke?"°

For of her owne thought she wex all red,
Remembering her° right thus: "Lo, this is he
Which that mine uncle swereth he mot be deed,
But I on him have mercy and pitee."   655
And with that thought, for pure ashamed, she
Gan in her heed to pull, and that as faste,
While he and all the people foreby paste,

And gan to cast° and rollen up and down
Within her thought his excellent prowesse,   660
And his estate,° and also his renown—
His wit, his shape, and eek his gentilesse.
But most her favour was for° his distresse
Was all for her, and thought it was a routhe
To sleen swich oon, if that he mente trouthe.°   665

Now mighte some envious° jangle thus:
"This was a sudden love. How might it be

638 **to-hewen** cut to pieces   639 **by . . . behinde** hung down behind his back by a band   640 **to-dashed** battered   640 **maces** heavy clubs equipped with metal heads for smashing armor and often furnished with spikes   642 **That . . . rinde** that had pierced its bone and sinew and hide. The shield was made of a tough animal skin. A *nerf* was a ligament or *corde* which governs the movement of limbs   644 **next . . . brother** second (only to) Hector, his brother   651 **drinke** something intoxicating, a love potion or strong wine   653 **Remembering her** See II.72n   659 **cast** reflect   661 **estate** social position (son of Priam)   663 **for** because   665 **mente trouthe** meant (to be) sincere   666 **envious** envious person

That she so lightly° loved Troilus
Right for the firste sighte. Yea, pardee!"
Now who saith so mot he never y-thee,°   670
For every thing a ginning hath it neede
Ere all be wrought,° withouten any dreede.

For I say not that she so suddenly
Yaf him her love, but that she gan encline
To like him first, and I have told you why.   675
And after that, his manhood and his pine°
Made love within her herte for to mine,°
For which by process and by good service
He got her love, and in no sudden wise.

And also blissful Venus, well arrayed,   680
Sat in her seventh house of hevene tho,
Disposed well and with aspectes payed,°
To helpe sely Troilus of his woe.
And, sooth to sayn, she nas not all° a foe
To Troilus in his nativitee.   685
God wot that well the sooner spedde he.

Now let us stint of Troilus a throwe,°
That rideth forth,° and let us turne faste
Unto Criseyde, that heng her heed full lowe
Ther-as she sat alone, and gan to caste   690
Whereon she wold appoint her at the laste,°

668 **lightly** easily (with a pun on *light*= "wanton"?)   670 **mot . . . y-thee** may he never prosper   671–72 **a . . . wrought** must have a beginning before the whole is done   676 **pine** pain   677 **mine** bore, penetrate (cf. "undermine")   680–82 **And . . . payed** The references here are astrological: Venus, the planet as well as the goddess of love, is in the seventh "house" or division of the celestial sphere, a most propitious location (*well arrayed*), particularly for lovers. Hence Venus is called *blissful*, or beneficent. Venus also resides in a favorable zodiacal sign (*well disposed*), and the other planets are situated fortunately with respect to Venus (*with aspectes payed*). The heavens seem to conspire to create favorable conditions for the development of love. But it is of course the nature of heavenly bodies to alter their positions   684 **all** entirely   687 **a throwe** (for) a time   688 **That . . . forth** As Troilus rides off, Criseyde has been considering his virtues since she saw him riding beneath her window and said, "Who yaf me drinke?" (II.651)   691 **Whereon . . . laste** what she should do finally .

If it so were her em ne wolde ceese
For Troilus upon her for to presse.

And Lord, so she gan in her thought argue
In this matter of which I have you tolde,   695
And what to doon best were, and what eschewe,
That plited° she full oft in many folde.
Now was her herte warm, now was it colde;
And what she thoughte somewhat shall I write,
As to mine auctor listeth for to endite.°   700

She thoughte well that Troilus' persone
She knew by sight, and eek his gentilesse.
And thus she said: "Al were it not to doone°
To grant him love yet, for his worthinesse,
It were honour° with play and with gladnesse   705
In honestee° with swich a lord to deele,
For mine estate, and also for his hele.°

"Eek well wot I my kinge's son is he;
And sith he hath to see me swich delit,
If I wold outrelich° his sigh' flee,   710
Peraunter he might have me in despit,°
Through which I mighte stand in worse plit.°
Now were I wise me hate to purchase°
Withouten need, ther I may stand in grace?

"In every thing, I wot, there lieth mesure:°   715
For though a man forbede drunkenesse,

697 **plited** bent, folded. In arguing with herself she goes back and
forth, as we see in her meditation which follows   700 **As . . .
endite** as (much as) it pleases my author (the fictional Lollius) to
set it forth   703 **Al . . . doone** although it wouldn't be proper
705 **honour** an honorable thing   706 **In honestee** respectably (with
a pun on *honest*= chaste?)   707 **hele** welfare (lit. "health")   710
outrelich utterly   711 **have . . . despit** despise me   712 **plit** plight
713 **were . . . purchase** would I be wise to incur hatred for myself
715 **mesure** proportion. Criseyde refers to one of the fundamental
medieval assumptions concerning the nature of the cosmos: that
there is harmony in everything. Theologians based their thinking
on Boethius's *Consolation of Philosophy* and on Wisd. 11:20: "thou
hast ordered all things in measure and number and weight." At the
same time Criseyde here exposes her own philosophy concerning
excess and restraint. Among medieval nobles, "mesure" was the
virtue of acting with moderation and avoiding excess

He not forbet° that every creature
Be drinkeless for alway, as I guesse.
Eek, sith I wot for me is his distresse,
I ne oughte not for that thing him despise,   720
Sith it is so he meeneth in good wise.°

"And eek I know of longe time agon
His thewes° good, and that he is not nice,
N'avauntour, saith men, certain is he noon.°
Too wise is he to doon so greet a vice.   725
Ne als I nill him never so cherice°
That he may make avaunt by juste cause.°
He shall me never bind in swich a clause.°

"Now set a case:° the hardest° is, ywis,
Men mighten deemen that he loveth me.   730
What dishonour were it unto me, this?
May ich him let of that?° Why nay, pardee.
I know also, and alday heer and see,
Men loven women, al beside hir leeve;°
And when hem list no more—let hem leeve.   735

"I think eek how he able° is for to have,
Of all this noble town, the thriftieste°
To been his love, so she her honour save.
For out and out° he is the worthieste,
Save only Hector, which that is the beste.   740
And yet his life all lieth now in my cure.°
But swich is love, and eek mine aventure.

"Ne me to love° a wonder is it not.
For well I wot myself, so God me speede—

---

717 **not forbet** doesn't forbid   721 **he . . . wise** he means well
723 **thewes** qualities of character   724 **N'avauntour . . . noon** and,
men say, he is certainly no braggart   726 **Ne . . . cherice** also I
will never so cherish him   727 **make . . . cause** boast with cause
(i.e., of a sexual conquest)   728 **clause** agreement (as in a legal
contract)   729 **set . . . case** i.e., consider this. Criseyde in this pas-
sage sounds like a lawyer weighing the various arguments of a
situation   729 **hardest** worst   732 **May . . . that?** may I stop him
from that (loving me)?   734 **al . . . leeve** although without their
permission   736 **able** worthy   737 **thriftieste** most estimable woman
739 **out . . . out** far and away   741 **cure** care   743 **Ne . . . love**
that he loves me

Al wolde I that none wist° of this thought—   745
I am one the fairest,° out of dreede,
And goodlieste, who that taketh heede,
And so men sayn, in all the town of Troye.
What wonder is though he of me have joye?

"I am mine owne woman, well at eese,   750
I thank it God, as after mine estat,°
Right young, and stand untied in lusty leese,°
Withouten jalousy or swich debat.
Shall noon husbande sayn to me, 'Checkmat!'
For either they been full of jalousye,   755
Or maisterful, or loven novelrye.°

"What shall I doon? To what fin live I thus?
Shall I not love, in case if that me leste?
What, *pardieux,* I am not religious.°
And though that I mine herte set at reste   760
Upon this knight, that is the worthieste,
And keep alway mine honour and my name,
By alle right it may do me no shame."

But right as when the sunne shineth brighte
In March, that changeth ofte time his face,   765
And that° a cloud is put with wind to flighte,
Which oversprad° the sun as for a space,
A cloudy thought gan through her soule passe,
That oversprad her brighte thoughtes alle,
So that for feer almost she gan to falle.   770

That thought was this: "Alas, sin I am free,
Shold I now love and put in jupartye

---

745 **Al . . . wist** although I'd wish that no one knew. Criseyde's
appraisal of herself in these lines seems to confirm Pandarus's ob-
servation about her that "prouder woman is there none on live"
(II.138), though he may only mean that she has the dignity and
manner appropriate to her social position   746 **one . . . fairest** one
of the most beautiful   750–51 **well . . . estat** fully assured—I thank
God for it—with respect to my social position   752 **stand . . . leese**
remain free in a delightful pasture (with a play on *lust*= desire)
756 **Or . . . novelrye** or are overbearing, or want novelty   759 **re-
ligious** a nun   766 **that** i.e., when   767 **oversprad** overspreads

My sikerness,° and thrallen libertee?
Alas, how durst I thinken that follye?
May I not well in other folk espye 775
Hir dreedful joy, hir constraint, and hir paine?
There loveth none that she ne hath way to plaine.°

"For love is yet the moste stormy lif,
Right of himself,° that ever was begunne.
For ever some mistrust or nice strif 780
There is in love: some cloud is over that sunne.
Thereto we wrecched women nothing conne,°
When us is woe,° but weep and sit and thinke.
Our wrecch° is this: our owne woe to drinke.

"Also these wicked tongues been so preste 785
To speke us harm°—eek men been so untrewe—
That right anon as ceesed is hir leste
So ceeseth love—and forth to love a newe.°
But harm y-done is done, whoso it rewe;
For though these men for love hem first to-rende,° 790
Full sharp beginning breketh oft at ende.°

"How ofte time hath it y-knowen be,°
The treeson that to women hath been do.
To what fin is swich love I cannot see,
Or where becometh it when it is ago.° 795
There is no wight that wot, I trowe so,
Where it becometh. Lo, no wight on it spurneth:°
That erst was no thing into nought it turneth.

773 **sikerness** security   777 **There . . . plaine** no one loves who
does not have cause to complain   779 **Right . . . himself** just in
itself   782 **conne** can do   783 **us . . . woe** unhappiness is upon us
784 **wrecch** wretchedness   785–86 **preste . . . harm** eager to speak
harm of **us**. Jealous gossip which harms one's reputation was a
traditional danger of love affairs   787–88 **That . . . newe** that just
as soon as their desire has ceased, their love ceases as well—and
(they are) off to love another   790 **hem . . . to-rende** at first tear
themselves apart   791 **Full . . . ende** a very sharp beginning often
breaks at the end. The idea, which seems proverbial, is that the love
affair which begins most ardently is liable to be broken off at the
last   792 **y-knowen be** been known   795 **where . . . ago** what be-
comes of it when it is gone   797 **spurneth** stumbles (i.e., it is no-
where)

"How bisy, if I love, eek must I be
To pleesen hem that jangle of love and dreemen,   *800*
And coy hem,° that they say noon harm of me.
For though there be no cause, yet hem seemen
All be for harm that folk hir freendes quemen;°
And who may stoppen every wicked tongue,
Or soun of belles,° while that they been runge?"   *805*

And after that her thought gan for to cleere,°
And said, "He which that nothing undertaketh
Nothing n'acheveth, be him looth or deere."°
And with another thought her herte quaketh.
Then sleepeth hope, and after dreed awaketh—   *810*
Now hot, now cold. But thus betwixen twaye,°
She rist her up, and went her° for to playe.

Adown the stair anonright tho she wente
Into the garden with her neeces three,
And up and down they made many a wente°—   *815*
Flexippe, she, Tarbe, and Antigone—
To playen that it joye was to see.
And other of her women,° a greet route,
Her followed in the garden all aboute.

This yard was large, and railed all the alleys,°   *820*
And shadowed well with blossomy boughes greene,
And benched new,° and sanded all the wayes,°
In which she walketh arm in arm betweene;

800–01 **To . . . hem** to please those who gossip about love, and
daydream about it, and to quiet them (*coy*= L. *quietus,* "to set at
rest") 802–3 **yet . . . quemen** yet to them (those who gossip about
love) all things seem to be harmful that people (do) to please their
friends (i.e., gossipers are overly suspicious about love affairs and
skeptical when a woman tries to please a man) 805 **soun . . . belles**
the sound of bells. (Wagging tongues were often compared to the
clapper of a bell) 806 **cleere** brighten. Cf. the "cloudy thought"
of II.768 807–8 **He . . . deere** he who undertakes nothing will
achieve nothing, whether (the undertaking) be unpleasant or delight-
ful. Cf. Pandarus's previous advice to her in II.281–91 811 **twaye**
two (states of mind) 812 **rist . . . her** gets up and goes 815 **wente**
turn 818 **women** attendants 820 **railed . . . alleys** all the paths
were enclosed (or, perhaps, hedged) 822 **benched new** newly fur-
nished with grassy benches 822 **wayes** pathways

Till at the last, Antigone the sheene,°
Gan on a Trojan song to singen cleere,   825
That it an hevene was her voice to heere.

Antigone's Song

She said, "O Love, to whom I have and shall
Been humble subjet, trew in mine intente
As I best can—to you, Lord, yive ich all
For evermo mine herte's lust to rente.°   830
For never yet thy grace no wight sente
So blissful cause as me,° my life to leede
In alle joy and suretee, out of dreede.

"Ye, blissful God, han me so well beset°
In love, ywis, that all that bereth lif   ·   835
Imaginen ne coud how to be bet.
For, Lord, withouten jelousy or strif,
I love one which that most is ententif°
To serven well, unwery or unfeigned,°
That ever was, and leest with harm distained,   840

"As he that is the well of worthinesse,
Of trouthe ground, mirrour of goodliheed,
Of wit Apollo, stone of sikernesse,
Of virtue root, of lust finder and heed,°
Through which is alle sorrow fro me deed.   845
Ywis, I love him best, so doth he me:
Now good thrift° have he, whereso that he be.

"Whom shold I thanken but you, God of Love,
Of all this bliss, in which to bathe I ginne?
And thanked be ye, Lord, for that I love.   850
This is the righte life that I am inne,

824 **sheene** fair (cf. Ger. *schön*) 830 **to rente** as tribute 831–32
For . . . me for never yet has your grace sent to any creature such
cause for bliss as to me 834 **beset** established 838 **ententif** atten-
tive 839 **unwery . . . unfeigned** (most) tireless and without pre-
tense 844 **of . . . heed** of pleasure (or desire) the discoverer and
origin 847 **thrift** success

To flemen° alle manner vice and sinne.
This doth me so to virtue for to intende,°
That day by day I in my will amende.°

"And whoso saith that for to love is vice,   855
Or thralldom, though he feel in it distresse,
He outher is envious, or right nice,°
Or is unmighty, for his shrewednesse,°
To loven. For swich manner folk, I guesse,
Defamen Love as nothing of him knowe:°   860
They speken, but they benten never his bowe.°

"What is the sunne worse, of kinde right,°
Though that a man, for feebless of his eyen,
May not endure on it to see for bright?°
Or love the worse, though wrecches on it cryen?°   865
No wele is worth that may no sorrow drien.°
And forthy who that hath an heed of verre
Fro cast of stones ware him in the werre.°

"But I, with all mine herte and all my might,
As I have said, will love unto my laste   870
My deere herte and all mine owne knight,
In which mine herte growen is so faste—
And his in me—that it shall ever laste.
Al dredde I first to love him to beginne,
Now wot I well there is no peril inne."°   875

And of her song right with that word she stente,
And therewithal, "Now neece," quod Criseyde,

852 **flemen** drive out   853 **doth . . . intende** causes me so to strive for virtue   854 **amende** improve. It was one of the cardinal tenets of "courtly" love that the lover should acquire virtues he has never known through the strength of his (or her) loving. Troilus has already experienced the ennobling power of love (I.1072–85)   857 **right** nice just plain foolish   858 **unmighty . . . shrewednesse** unable, because of his wickedness   859–60 **swich . . . knowe** such folk defame Love as know nothing about him   861 **bowe** i.e., Cupid's bow   862 **of . . . right** in its own nature   864 **for bright** because of (its) brightness   865 **on . . . cryen** denounce it   866 **No . . . drien** he is worthy of no happiness who can endure no sorrow   867–68 **who . . . werre** "let whoever has a glass head beware the casting of stones in war" (proverb)   875 **inne** in (loving him)

"Who made this song now with so good intente?"
Antigone answered anon and saide,
"Madame, ywis, the goodlieste maide   880
Of greet estate in all the town of Troye,
And let° her life in most honour and joye."

"Forsoothe, so it seemeth by her song,"
Quod tho Criseyde, and gan therewith to sighe,
And saide, "Lord, is there swich bliss among   885
These lovers, as they conne fair endite?"°
"Yea, wis," quod fresh Antigone the white,
"For all the folk that han or been on live
Ne conne well the bliss of love descrive.

"But weene ye° that every wrecche wot   890
The parfit bliss of love? Why, nay, ywis!
They weenen *all* be love if *one* be hot—
Do way, do way, they wot nothing of this.
Men musten ask at saintes if it is
Aught fair° in hevene. Why? For *they* can telle.   895
And asken feendes° is it foul in helle."

Criseyde unto that purpose° nought answerde,
But said, "Ywis, it will be night as faste . . ."
But every word which that she of her herde,
She gan to printen° in her herte faste,   900
And ay gan love less her for to aghaste°
Than it did erst, and sinken in her herte,
That she wex somewhat able to converte.°

The daye's honour and the hevene's eye,
The nighte's foe—all these clepe I the sunne°—   905

---

882 **let** leads 886 **as . . . endite** that they can express it so beauti-
fully 890 **weene ye** do you suppose 895 **Aught fair** at all lovely
896 **asken feendes** ask fiends. Just as one must ask saints about
heaven and fiends about hell, one must ask a true lover—not one
who believes "all be love if one be hot"—about the nature of love
897 **purpose** subject 900 **printen** impress 901 **ay . . . aghaste**
ever did love frighten her the less 903 **That . . . converte** so that
she became somewhat (more) able to be converted 904–05 **The
. . . sunne** The narrator here waxes rhetorical in the high style:
three conceited metaphors (*traductiones*) follow one another in
rapid succession in parallel formation (*frequentatio*); but the grand
effect is deflated by his quotidian explanation, "all this I call the
sun"

Gan westren° fast and downward for to wrye,°
As he that had his daye's course y-runne,
And white thinges wexen dim and dunne°
For lack of light, and starres for to appere,
That she and all her folk in went yfere.   *910*

So when it liked her to go to reste,
And voided° weren they that voiden oughte,
She saide that to sleepen well her leste.
Her women soone till her bed her broughte.
When all was hust,° then lay she still and thoughte   *915*
Of all this thing. The manner and the wise
Reherse it needeth not,° for ye been wise.

A nightingale, upon a cedir greene,
Under the chamber wall ther-as she lay,
Full loude sang again the moone sheene,°   *920*
Peraunter, in his bridde's wise, a lay°
Of love that made her herte fresh and gay.
That herkened she so long in good intente,
Till at the last the deede sleep her hente.°

And as she slep, anonright tho her mette°   *925*
How that an eegle, fethered white as bon,°
Under her brest his longe clawes sette,
And out her herte he rent,° and that anon,
And did his herte into her brest to goon—
Of which she nought agroos, ne nothing smerte,°   *930*
And forth he fleigh,° with herte left for herte.

                              *   *   *

Now let her sleep, and we our tales holde°
Of Troilus, that is to palais riden
Fro the scarmuch° (of the which I tolde),

906 **Gan westren** moved in the west   906 **wrye** turn   908 **dunne**
dun, dark and gray   912 **voided** departed   915 **hust** hushed   917
Reherse . . . not there is no need to rehearse. (Note that the
narrator again addresses the audience or reader.) On the nightingale
in the following stanza see II.64n   920 **again . . . sheene** in the
moonlight   921 **bridde's . . . lay** bird's fashion, a song   923 **That
. . . hente** she listened to that song a long while attentively, until
at last dead sleep took hold of her   925 **her mette** she dreamed
926 **fethered . . . bon** with feathers white as bone   928 **rent** tore
930 **nought . . . smerte** was not at all frightened, and felt no pain
931 **fleigh** flew   932 **holde** continue   934 **scarmuch** skirmish (line
611)

And in his chamber sit and hath abiden,°   935
Till two or three of his messages yeden°
For Pandarus, and soughten him full faste,
Till they him found, and brought him at the laste.

This Pandarus came leeping in at ones
And saide thus, "Who hath been well y-beete°   940
Today with swordes and with slinge-stones
But Troilus, that hath caught him an heete?"°
—And gan to jape, and said, "Lord, so ye swete!°
But rise, and let us sup and go to reste."
And he answered him, "Do we as thee leste."   945

With all the haste goodly that they mighte°
They sped hem fro the supper unto bedde;
And every wight out at the door him dighte°
And, where him list, upon his way he spedde.
But Troilus, that thought his herte bledde   950
For woe, till that he herde some tidinge,°
He saide, "Freend, shall I now weep or singe?"

Quod Pandarus: "Lie still and let me sleepe,
And don thine hood.° Thy needes spedde be,°
And chese° if thou wilt sing or dance or leepe.   955
At shorte wordes thou shalt trowen me.
Sire, my neece will do well by thee,
And love thee best, by God and by my trouthe,
But lack of pursuit make it in thy slouthe.°

"For thus ferforth° I have thy work begunne   960
Fro day to day, till this day by the morrwe°
Her love, of freendship, have I to thee wonne;°

---

935 **sit . . . abiden** sits and has waited   936 **messages yeden** messengers went   940 **y-beete** beaten   942 **heete** fever   943 **so . . . swete** how you sweat   946 **With . . . mighte** with as much seemly haste as they could manage   948 **him dighte** left (lit. "betook himself")   951 **tidinge** news   954 **don . . . hood** put on your hat (and leave)   954 **spedde be** are taken care of   955 **chese** choose   959 **But . . . slouthe** unless there's a lack of pursuit through your negligence   960 **thus ferforth** as far as this   961 **this . . . morrwe** this morning   962 **of . . . wonne** have I won for you her "love of friendship" (cf. II.371)

And also hath she laid her faith to borwe°—
Algate a foot is hameled of thy sorrwe."°
What shold I longer sermon of it holde?°   965
As ye han herde before, all he him tolde.

But right as flowers, through the cold of night
Y-closed, stoupen° on hir stalkes lowe,
Redressen hem again the sunne bright°
And spreden on hir kinde course by rowe°—   970
Right so gan tho his eyen up to throwe
This Troilus, and said, "O Venus deere:
Thy might, thy grace, y-heried° be it here."

And to Pandar he held up both his hondes,
And saide, "Lord, all thine be that I have,   975
For I am hool, and brusten been my bondes.
A thousand Troyes whoso that me yave,
Eech after other, God so wise me save,
Ne mighte me so gladden.° Lo, mine herte
It spredeth so for joy it will to-sterte.°   980

"But Lord, how shall I doon? How shall I liven?
When shall I next my deere herte see?
How shall this longe time away be driven,
Till that thou be again at her fro me?
Thou maist answer, 'Abide, abide'; but he   985
That hangeth by the necke, sooth to sayne,
In greet diseese° abideth for the paine."

"All eesily, now, for the love of Marte,"°
Quod Pandarus, "for everything hath time.°
So long abide till that the night departe;   990
For also siker as thou liest here by me,
And God to-forn, I will be there at prime,°

963 **laid . . . borwe** pledged her faith   964 **Algate . . . sorrwe** at
least a foot of your sorrow is cut off   965 **holde** make   968 **stoupen**
droop   969 **Redressen . . . bright** stand up once more against the
bright sun   970 **spreden . . . rowe** open up, in their natural course,
in rows   973 **y-heried** praised   977–79 **A . . . gladden** whoever
gave me a thousand Troys each one after the other, as God may
surely save me, might not make so glad   980 **to-sterte** burst apart
987 **diseese** discomfort   988 **Marte** Mars   989 **everything . . . time**
"everything has its time" (a favorite proverb of Pandarus's)   992
prime 9 a.m.

And forthy work somewhat as I shall saye—
Or on some other wight this charge° laye.

"For pardee, God wot I have ever yit   995
Been redy thee to serve, and to this night°
Have I not feigned° but, emforth my wit
Done all thy lust, and shall, with all my might.
Do now as I shall sayn and fare aright.
And if thou nilt, wite all thyself thy care°—   1000
On me is nought along thine evil fare.°

"I wot well that thou wiser art than I
A thousandfold; but if I were as thou—
God help me so—as I wold outrely°
Of mine owne hand write her right now   1005
A letter, in which I wold her tellen how
I ferde amiss, and her beseech of routhe.
Now help thyself, and leeve it not for slouthe.

"And I myself will therewith to her goon;
And when thou wost that I am with her there,   1010
Worth thou upon a courser° right anon—
Yea, hardily, right in thy beste geere—
And ride forth by the place, as nought it were,°
And thou shalt find us, if I may, sittinge
At some window into the street lookinge.   1015

"And if thee list, then may thou us salewe,°
And upon me make thou thy countenaunce.°
But, by thy life, be ware, and fast eschewe
To tarryen aught°—God sheeld us fro mischaunce.
Ride forth thy way, and hold thy governaunce,°   1020
And we shall speke of thee somewhat, I trowe,
When thou art gone, to doon thine eeres glowe.°

994 **charge** responsibility   996 **to . . . night** tonight   997 **feigned** failed (in my obligation)   1000 **wite . . . care** blame only yourself for your problem   1001 **On . . . fare** your misfortune is nothing of my doing   1004 **outrely** without fail   1011 **Worth . . . courser** mount a courser (a swift horse)   1013 **as . . . were** as if nothing were planned   1016 **us salewe** greet us   1017 **make . . . countenaunce** direct your look of recognition   1018–19 **be . . . aught** be wary, and for sure avoid lingering at all   1020 **hold . . . governaunce** maintain your composure   1022 **to . . . glowe** to make your ears glow red

"Touching thy letter: thou art wise enough.
I wot thou nilt it dignelich endite;°
Ne make it with these argumentes tough;°   *1025*
Ne scrivenish, or craftily° thou it write.
Be-blot it with thy teeres eek a lite.°
And if thou write a goodly word all softe,°
Though it be good, reherse° it not too ofte.

"For though the beste harper upon live   *1030*
Wold on the beste souned jolly harpe
That ever was, with all his fingers five
Touch ay oo string, or ay oo werbul harpe°—
Were his nailes pointed never so sharpe—
It sholde maken every wight to dulle   *1035*
To heer his glee, and of his strokes fulle.°

"Ne jumper° eek no discordant thing yfere
As thus: to usen termes of physik
In love's termes.° Hold of thy mattere
The form° alway, and do that it be lik.°   *1040*
For if a painter wolde paint a pik°
With asse's feet, and heed it as° an ape,
It 'cordeth not, so nere it but a jape."

This counseil liked well unto Troilus,
But as a dreedful lover he said this: *1045*
"Alas, my deere brother Pandarus!
I am ashamed for to write, ywis,
Lest of mine innocence° I said amiss,

1024 **it . . . endite** write it in an affected style   1025 **make . . . tough** make it bristle with academic-sounding arguments   1026 **scrivenish . . . craftily** in a stilted or a studied manner   1027 **Be-blot . . . lite** sprinkle it with your tears a little also   1028 **all softe** tenderly   1029 **reherse** repeat   1033 **ay . . . harpe** always a single string, or always play a single melody   1035–36 **to . . . fulle** bored to hear his music and fed up with his harp-strokes. Pandarus's advice to Troilus in the matter of letter writing makes playful use of the ancient proverb "to harp on a single string or theme." His lesson in prose composition focuses more on tone than on content —doubtless a wise emphasis when it comes to writing love letters 1037 **jumper** jumble   1038–39 **termes . . . termes** terminology of medicine together with love's terms   1040 **form** proper style   1040 **do . . . like** make sure it's suitable   1041 **pik** pike (fish)   1042 **heed . . . as** give it the head of   1048 **innocence** inexperience

Or that she nold it for despite receive—
Then were I deed: there might it nothing weive."°   *1050*

To that Pandar answered, "If thee lest,
Do that I say, and let me therewith goon.
For by that Lord that formed eest and west,
I hope of it to bring answer anon
Right of her hand.° And if that thou nilt noon—   *1055*
Let be! And sorry mot he been his live
Agains thy lust that helpeth thee to thrive."°

Quod Troilus: "*Depardieux*, ich assente.
Sith that thee list, I will arise and write.
And blissful God pray ich with good intente   *1060*
The viage° and the letter I shall endite,
So speed it. And thou, Minerva the white,
Yif thou me wit my letter to devise!"
—And set him down and wrote right in this wise:

First he gan her his righte lady calle,   *1065*
His herte's life, his lust, his sorrow's leeche,
His bliss—and eek these other termes alle
That in swich case these lovers alle seeche.
And in full humble wise as in his speeche°
He gan him recommaund unto her grace—   *1070*
To tell all how, it asketh muchel space.°

And after this full lowly he her prayde
To be not wroth, though he of his follye
So hardy was to her to write—and saide
That Love it made—or elles must he die;   *1075*
And pitously gan *mercy* for to crye.
And after that he said, and leigh full loude,°
Himself was litel worth, and less he koude.

1050 **weive** avert   1055 **of . . . hand** (written) in her hand   1056–
57 **sorry . . . thrive** may he be sorry all his life who helps you
succeed against your will (i.e., if you don't want an answer you
don't deserve any help)   1061 **viage** undertaking   1069 **as . . .
speeche** in his writing   1071 **it . . . space** it requires (too) much
time   1077 **leigh . . . loude** lied openly. Chaucer makes fun of the
conventional language of love. Chaucer's source, Boccaccio, quotes
Troilus's letter in its entirety whereas Chaucer condenses it in in-
direct discourse

And that he shold han his conning° excused,
That litel was, and eek he dredde her so;   1080
And his unworthiness ay he accused.
And after that then gan he tell his woe—
But that was endeless, withouten ho°—
And said he wold in trouth alway him holde
—And redde it over, and gan the letter folde.   1085

And with his salte teeres gan he bathe
The ruby in his signet,° and it sette
Upon the wax deliverlich and rathe.
Therewith a thousand times ere he lette°
He kiste tho the letter that he shette,   1090
And saide, "Letter, a blissful destinee
Thee shapen is: my lady shall thee see."

This Pandar took the letter, and that betime°
Amorrow, and to his neece's palais sterte—
And fast he swore that it was passed prime,°   1095
And gan to jape and said, "Ywis, mine herte,
So fresh it is, although it sore smerte,
I may not sleepe never a Maye's morrwe.
I have a jolly woe, a lusty sorrwe."

Criseyde, when that she her uncle herde,   1100
With dreedful herte and desirous to heere
The cause of his coming, thus answerde:
"Now by your fay,° mine uncle," quod she, "deere,
What manner windes guideth you now here?
Tell us your jolly woe and your penaunce.   1105
How ferforth be ye put° in Love's daunce?"

"By God," quod he, "I hop alway behinde."
And she to laugh it thought her herte brest.°
Quod Pandarus: "Look alway that ye finde
Game in mine hood,° but herkeneth if you lest.   1110
There is right now come into town a gest,°

1079 **conning** ability   1083 **ho** end   1087 **signet** seal (signet-ring)
1088 **deliverlich . . . rathe** deftly and at once   1089 **ere . . . lette**
before he gave it up   1093 **betime** early   1095 **passed prime** past
9 a.m.   1103 **fay** faith   1106 **How . . . put** how far have you
progressed   1108 **to . . . brest** thought her heart would burst from
laughing   1109–10 **Look . . . hood** make sure you always find
cause to make fun of me   1111 **gest** stranger

A Greek espy, and telleth newe thinges,
For which I come to tell you new tidinges.

"Into the garden go we, and ye shall heere
All prively of this a long sermoun."°   *1115*
With that they wenten arm in arm yfere
Into the garden from the chamber down.°
And when that he so far was that the soun
Of that he spake there no man heeren mighte,
He said her thus, and out the letter plighte:°   *1120*

"Lo, he that is all hoolly youres free,
Him recommaundeth lowly to your grace,
And sente° you this letter here by me.
Aviseth you on it when ye han space,
And of some goodly answer you purchase°—   *1125*
Or help me God, so plainly for to sayne,
He may not longe liven for his paine."

Full dreedfully tho gan she standen stille,
And took it not, but all her humble cheere
Gan for to change, and saide, "Scrit ne bille,°   *1130*
For love of God, that toucheth swich mattere,
Ne bring me none. And also, uncle deere,
To mine estate have more reward, I praye,
Than to his lust.° What shold I more saye?

"And looketh now if this be resonable,   *1135*
And letteth° not, for favour ne for slouthe,
To sayn a sooth. Now were it convenable°
To mine estate, by God and by your trouthe,
To taken it or to han of him routhe,
In harming of myself, or in repreve?   *1140*
Bere it again, for him that ye on leve."

This Pandarus gan on her for to stare,
And saide, "Now is *this* the greetest wonder

1115 **sermoun** tale 1117 **from . . . down** The living quarters of
medieval houses were almost always above the first floor (cf. II.813)
1120 **plighte** plucked 1123 **sente** sends 1125 **you purchase** provide
yourself 1130 **Scrit . . . bille** writing (script) nor letter (or petition)
1133–34 **To . . . lust** have more regard (reward) for my social posi-
tion, I pray, than for his desire 1136 **letteth** fail 1137 **were . . .**

That ever I saw. Let be this nice fare!°
To deethe mot I smitten be with thunder   *1145*
If, for the citee which that standeth yonder,
Wold I a letter unto you bring or take
To harm of you. What list you thus it make?°

"But thus ye faren well nigh all and some,
That he that most desireth you to serve,   *1150*
Of *him* ye recche leest wher he become,°
And whether that he live or elles sterve.
But for all that that ever I may deserve,
Refuse it not," quod he—and hent her faste,
And in her bosom the letter down he thraste,   *1155*

And saide her, "Now cast it away anon,
That folk may seen and gauren° on us twaye."
Quod she: "I can abide till they be gon"—
And gan to smile, and said him, "Em, I praye,
Swich answer as you list yourself purveye,   *1160*
For trewely I nill no letter write."
"No? Than will *I*," quod he "—so *ye* endite."

Therewith she lough, and saide, "Go we dine."°
And he gan at himself to jape faste,
And saide, "Neece, I have so greet a pine°   *1165*
For love that everich other day I faste"°—
And gan his beste japes forth to caste,
And made her so to laugh at his follye
That she for laughter wende for to die.

And when that she was comen into halle,°   *1170*
"Now em," quod she, "we will go dine anon."
And gan some of her women to her calle,
And straight into her chamber gan she goon.
But of her bisinesses this was oon:

---

convenable would it be fitting   1144 **Let . . . fare!** stop this foolish
behavior!   1148 **What . . . make?** why do you want to take it this
way (as an evil action on my part)?   1151 **wher . . . become** what
becomes of him   1157 **gauren** gawk   1163 **Go . . . dine** let's go
dine. Dinner in the Middle Ages was served about 10 a.m.   1165
pine pain   1166 **everich . . . faste** I can't eat—every other day
1170 **halle** the main hall of the house (where people dined)

Amonges other thinges, out of dreede,   *1175*
Full prively this letter for to reede;

Avised° word by word in every line,
And found no lack,° she thought he koude good;°
And up it put, and went her in to dine.
But Pandarus, that in a study stood,°   *1180*
Ere he was ware, she took him by the hood,°
And saide, "Ye were caught ere that ye wiste."
"I vouche sauf,"° quod he, "do what you liste."

Tho weshen° they and set hem down and ete,
And after anon full slyly Pandarus   *1185*
Gan draw him° to the window next° the streete,
And saide, "Neece, who hath arrayed° thus
The yonder house that stant aforyein us?"
"Which house?" quod she, and gan for to beholde,
And knew it well, and whose it was him tolde—   *1190*

And fellen forth in speech of thinges smalle,
And setten in the window bothe twaye.
When Pandarus saw time unto his tale,°
And saw well that her folk were all awaye,
"Now, neece mine, tell on," quod he, "I saye,   *1195*
How liketh you the letter that ye wot?
Kan he thereon?° For by my trouth, I noot."

Therewith all rosy-hewed tho wex she,
And gan to hum, and saide, "So I trowe . . ."
"Aquit° him well for Godde's love," quod he;   *1200*
"Myself to meedes° will the letter sowe."°
And held his handes up and sat on knowe.°

1177 **Avised** she considered 1178 **lack** fault 1178 **koude good**
knew what was fitting 1180 **in . . . stood** stood meditating 1181
Ere . . . him before he was aware of it, she grabbed him 1183
vouche sauf admit it 1184 **weshen** washed 1186 **Gan . . . him**
went over 1186 **next** next to, facing out upon 1187 **arrayed**
decorated 1188 **stant aforyein** stands opposite 1193 **his tale** his
own concern (i.e., Troilus) 1197 **Kan . . . thereon?** i.e., does he
know how to write well of love? 1200 **Aquit** repay 1201 **to
meedes** as a reward 1201 **sowe** seal, or sew together 1202 **sat
. . . knowe** knelt down. Holding the hands up was a gesture of
supplication; cf. II.974. Pandarus urges her to write a reply, then
begs permission to sew the leaves, fold it up, etc.

"Now good neece, be it never so lite,
Yif me the labour it to sow and plite."°

"Yea, for aught _I_ kan° so writen," quod she tho,   1205
"And eek I noot what I shold to him saye."
"Nay, neece," quod Pandare, "say not so.
Yet at the leeste thanketh him, I praye,
Of his good will, and doth him not to deye.
Now for the love of me, my neece deere,   1210
Refuseth not at this time my prayere."

"_Depardieux_," quod she, "God leve° all be well!
God help me so, this is the firste letter
That ever I wrote—yea, all, or any deel."°
And into a closet for to avise her better   1215
She went alone, and gan her herte unfetter°
Out of disdaine's prison but a lite;
And set her down and gan a letter write.

Of which to tell in short is mine intente
The effect,° as far as I can understonde: 1220
She thanked him of all that he well mente
Towardes her; but holden him in honde°
She nolde not, ne make herselven bonde
In love; but as his suster, him to pleese,
She wolde fain to doon his herte an eese.   1225

She shut it, and into Pandar gan goon
Ther-as he sat and looked into the streete,
And down she set her by him on a ston
Of jasper, upon a quishin gold y-bete,°
And said, "As wisly help me God the greete,   1230
I never did a thing with more paine
Than writen this, to which ye me constraine"—

And took it him. He thanked her and saide,
"God wot, of thing full often looth° begonne
Cometh ende good. And neece mine, Criseyde,   1235

1204 **plite** fold   1205 **for . . . writen** for all _I_ know about writing
that way. "Yea" refers to line 1203: it will be "lite" indeed! See
textual note, p. 306   1212 **leve** grant that   1214 **deel** part (of one)
1216 **gan . . . unfetter** unchained   1219–20 **Of . . . effect** my intent
is to tell briefly the purport of which (letter)   1222 **holden . . .
honde** deceive him, lead him on   1229 **quishin . . . y-bete** cushion
embroidered with gold   1234 **looth** reluctantly

That ye to him of hard° now been y-wonne
Ought he be glad, by God and yonder sonne.
Forwhy men saith: 'Impressiounes lighte
Full lightly been ay redy to the flighte.'°

"But ye han played the tyrant nigh too longe,   *1240*
And hard was it your herte for to grave.°
Now stint, that ye no longer on it honge,°
Al wolde ye the form of daunger save;°
But hasteth you to doon him joye have.
For, trusteth well, too long y-done hardnesse   *1245*
Causeth despite full often for distresse."°

And right as they declamed° this mattere,
Lo, Troilus, right at the streete's ende,
Came riding with his tenthe-some° yfere
All softly, and thiderward gan bende   *1250*
Ther-as they set,° as was his way to wende
To palais-ward; and Pandarus him espide,
And saide, "Neece, y-see who com'th here ride.°

"O flee not in—he seeth us, I suppose—
Lest he may thinken that ye him eschewe."°   *1255*
"Nay, nay," quod she, and wex as red as rose.
With that he gan her humbly to salewe
With dreedful cheer, and oft his hewes mewe,°
And up his look debonairly he caste,
And becked on° Pandar, and forth he paste.   *1260*

God wot if he sat on his horse aright,
Or goodly was beseen that ilke day.

1236 **of hard** with difficulty   1238–39 **Impressiounes . . . flighte**
"light (hasty) impressions are always very lightly (easily) ready to
take flight" (proverb)   1241 **your . . . grave** to engrave upon your
heart (i.e., to make an impression on you)   1242 **on . . . honge**
hang on it (i.e., leave the situation dangling, or "up in the air")
1243 **the . . . save** keep the appearance of aloofness   1245–46 **too
. . . distresse** hard-heartedness kept up for too long very often
causes spite (in the lover) because of his distress   1247 **declamed**
talked about   1249 **his tenthe-some** ten of his men (cf. "foursome")
1250–51 **thiderward . . . set** turned in the direction in which they
sat   1253 **ride** riding   1255 **eschewe** avoid   1258 **his . . . mewe**
his hues changed (i.e., he blushes in different shades of red)
1260 **becked on** nodded to

God wot whether he was like a manly knight.
What shold I drecch° or tell of his array?°
Criseyde, which that all these thinges say,°   *1265*
To tell in short, her liked all in fere°—
His person, his array, his look, his cheere,

His goodly manner, and his gentilesse—
So well that never sith that she was born
Ne hadde she swich ruth of his distresse.   *1270*
And how so she hath hard been herebeforn,
To God hope I she hath now caught a thorn,
She shall not pull it out this nexte wike°
—God sende mo swich thornes on to pike!°

Pandar, which that stood her faste by,   *1275*
Felt iren hot, and he began to smite,°
And saide, "Neece, I pray you hertely,
Tell me that I shall asken you a lite:
A woman that were of his deeth to wite,
Withouten his guilt, but for her lacked routhe,°   *1280*
Were it well done?" Quod she, "Nay, by my trouthe."

"God help me so," quod he, "ye say me sooth.
Ye feelen well yourself that I not lie.
Lo, yond he rit."° Quod she, "Yea, so he doth."
"Well," quod Pandar, "as I have told you thrie,   *1285*
Yet be your nice shame° and your follye,
And speke with him in eesing of his herte.
Let nicetee not do you bothe smerte."

But thereon was to heeven and to doone;°
Considered alle thing, it may not be.   *1290*
And why?—for shame; and it were eek too soone

1264 **drecch** delay 1264 **array** dress 1265 **say** saw 1266 **her . . . fere** it pleased her altogether 1273 **wike** week 1274 **mo . . . pike** to others such thorns to pluck out. Chaucer here, as elsewhere in the narrative, is a partisan for love affairs—a "servant of the servants of Love" 1276 **Felt . . . smite** Cf. the proverbial expression in Chaucer's Melibee from *The Canterbury Tales:* "While that iren is hot, men sholden smite" 1280 **Withouten . . . routhe** not through any fault of his, but because she lacked pity 1284 **rit** rides 1286 **nice shame** silly modesty 1289 **was . . . doone** there was (much yet) to move ("to heave") and to do

To granten him so greet a libertee.
For plainly her intent, as saide she,
Was for to love him unwist, if she mighte,
And guerdon° him with nothing but with sighte.   1295

But Pandarus thought: "It shall not be so,
If that I may. This nice opinioun
Shall not be holden fully yeeres two."
What shold I make of this a long sermoun?
He must assent on that conclusioun,   1300
As for the time. And when that it was eve,
And all was well, he rose and took his leeve.

And on his way full fast homeward he spedde;
And right for joy he felt his herte daunce.
And Troilus he found alone abedde,   1305
That lay as do these lovers in a traunce
Betwixen hope and dark desesperaunce.°
But Pandarus, right at his in-cominge,
He sang, as who saith "Somewhat I bringe"—

And saide, "Who is in his bed so soone   1310
Y-buried thus?" "It am I, freend," quod he.
"Who, Troilus? Nay, help me so the moone,"°
Quod Pandarus, "thou shalt arise and see
A charme that was sent right now to thee,
The which can heelen thee of thine accesse,°   1315
If thou do forthwith all thy bisinesse."

"Yea, through the might of God," quod Troilus.
And Pandarus gan him the letter take,
And saide, "Pardee, God hath holpen us!
Have here a light and look on all this blacke."°   1320
But ofte gan the herte glad and quake
Of Troilus, while that he gan it reede,
So as the wordes yaf him hope or dreede.

But finally he took all for the beste
That she him wrote, for somewhat he beheld   1325
On which him thought he might his herte reste,

1295 **guerdon** reward   1307 **desesperaunce** despair   1312 **help . . .
moone** so help me the moon (which was thought to be helpful in
love matches)   1315 **accesse** illness   1320 **this blacke** i.e., ink

Al covered she the wordes under sheeld.°
Thus to the more worthy part he held,
That what for hope and Pandarus' beheste
His greete woe foryede° he at the leeste.   1330

But as we may alday ourselven see,
Through more wood or cool the more fir,°
Right so increese of hope, of what it be,
Therewith full oft increeseth eek desir;
Or as an ook cometh of a litel spir,°   1335
So through this letter which that she him sente
Increesen gan desire, of which he brente.

Wherefore I say alway that, day and night,
This Troilus gan to desiren more
Than he did erst through hope, and did his might   1340
To pressen on as by Pandarus' lore,°
And writen to her of his sorrows sore
Fro day to day. He let it not refreyde,°
That, by Pandar, he wrote somewhat or saide;

And did also his other observaunces   1345
That til a lover longeth° in this cas.
And after that these dees turned on chaunces,°
So was he other glad or said "alas,"
And held after his gestes ay his pas.°
And after swich answeres as he hadde,   1350
So were his dayes sorry other gladde.

But to Pandar alway was his recours,
And pitously gan ay til him to plaine,
And him besought of reed and some succours;°
And Pandarus, that saw his woode paine,   1355
Wex well nigh deed for ruthe, sooth to sayne,
And bisily, with all his herte, caste
Some of his woe to sleen, and that as faste,

1327 **Al . . . sheeld** i.e., although she concealed her real meaning
1330 **foryede** let go of   1332 **fir** fire   1335 **spir** sprout   1341 **lore**
instruction   1343 **refreyde** grow cool   1346 **til . . . longeth** is ap-
propriate for a lover   1347 **after . . . chaunces** i.e., according to
the throws of the dice (Fortune's whims)   1349 **held . . . pas** main-
tained his pace always according to what happened (see textual
note. p. 306)   1354 **succours** help

And saide, "Lord and freend and brother deere—
God wot that thy diseese doth me woe,   *1360*
But wilt thou stinten all this woeful cheere
And, by my trouth, ere it be dayes two,
And God to-forn, yet shall I shape it so
That thou shalt come into a certain place
Ther-as thou maist thyself her pray of grace.   *1365*

"And certainly (I noot if thou it wost,
But tho that been expert in love it saye)
It is one of the thinges furthereth most°
A man to han a leiser° for to praye,
And siker place his woe for to bewraye;°   *1370*
For in good herte it mot some ruth impresse°
To heer and see the guiltless in distresse.

"Peraunter thinkest thou: Though it be so
That Kinde wolde doon her to beginne
To have a manner° ruth upon my woe,   *1375*
Saith Daunger,° 'Nay, thou shalt me never winne.'
So ruleth her her herte's ghost° withinne
That, though she bende, yet she stant on roote.°
What in effect is this unto my boote?

"Think here-agains:° When that the sturdy ook,   *1380*
On which men hacketh ofte for the nones,
Received hath the happy falling strok,°
The greete sweigh doth it come all at ones,°
As doon these rockes or these milnestones:°

1368 **thinges . '. . most** things which most helps   1369 **a leiser** opportunity   1370 **siker . . . bewraye** a safe (private) place to reveal his woe   1371 **impresse** inspire   1375 **a manner** some kind of   1376 **Daunger** the personification of maidenly modesty. In courtly literature, Daunger appears as a personification of the lady's aloofness or haughtiness. Pandarus describes Daunger as part of Criseyde's mental questionings, the other side being represented by *Kinde*, Criseyde's natural impulses   1377 **So . . . ghost** so does her heart's spirit rule her   1378 **stant . . . roote** stands firm (well-rooted). Pandarus continues the botanical conceit in the next stanza   1380 **here-agains** on the other hand   1382 **falling strok** blow that fells it   1383 **The . . . ones** i.e., the oak's great sway or weight causes it to fall at once, whereas a tree of lighter mass would topple more slowly. The point of the comparison is that Troilus, when he finally inspires Criseyde's affections, should win her love all at once   1384 **milnestones** millstones

For swifter course cometh thing that is of wighte,°   *1385*
When it descendeth, than doon thinges lighte.

"And reed that boweth down for every blast,
Full lightly, ceese wind, it will arise;
But so nill not an ook when it is cast.°
It needeth me not thee longe to forbise.°   *1390*
Men shall rejoicen of a greet emprise
Acheved well, and stant withouten doute,°
Al han men been the longer there-aboute.°

"But Troilus, yet tell me if thee lest
A thing now which that I shall asken thee: *1395*
Which is thy brother that thou lovest best,
As in thy verray herte's privetee?"
"Ywis, my brother Deiphebus," quod he.
"Now," quod Pandar, "ere houres twies twelve,
He shall thee eese, unwist of it himselve.   *1400*

"Now let m'alone, and worken as I may,"
Quod he. And to Deiphebus went he tho,
Which had his lord and greete freend been ay.
Save Troilus, no man he loved so.
To tell in short, withouten wordes mo,   *1405*
Quod Pandarus, "I pray you that ye be
Freend to a cause which that toucheth me."

"Yis, pardee," quod Deiphebus. "Well thou wost
In all that ever I may, and God to-fore,
Al nere it but for man° I love most,   *1410*
My brother Troilus. But say wherefore
It is; for sith that day that I was bore,°
I nas, ne nevermo to been I thinke,
Agains a thing that mighte thee forthinke."°

1385 **For ... wighte** for something of weight comes (in a) swifter
course   1389 **cast** thrown to the ground   1390 **forbise** give ex-
amples   1392 **stant ... doute** one which stands secure   1393 **Al**
... there-aboute although men have taken longer to bring it about.
The point of all Pandarus's elaborate comparisons is that in spite of
the heavy difficulties they may hope for success   1410 **Al ... man**
unless it were for the man. (He seems to mean that he would do as
much for Pandarus as for anyone except Troilus)   1412 **bore** born
1413–14 **I ... forthinke** I never was, nor ever more intend to be,
against a thing if it might displease you

Pandar gan him thank, and to him saide,   *1415*
"Lo, sire, I have a lady in this town
That is my neece and called is Criseyde,
Which° some men wolden doon oppressioun,
And wrongfully han her possessioun.°
Wherefore I of your lordship you beseeche   *1420*
To been our freend, withouten more speeche."

Deiphebus him answered, "O, is not this,
That thou spekest of to me thus straungely,°
Criseyde, my freend?" He saide, "Yis."
"Then needeth," quod Deiphebus, "hardily,   *1425*
No more to speke: for trusteth well that I
Will be her champion with spur and yerde;°
I roughte not though all her foes it herde.

"But tell me, thou that wost of this mattere,
How I might best availen?" "Now let see . . ."   *1430*
Quod Pandarus, "if ye, my lord so deere,
Wolden as now do this honour to me
To prayen her tomorrow, lo, that she
Come unto you, her plaintes to devise,°
Her adversaries wold of it agrise.°   *1435*

"And if I more durst praye you as now,
And chargen° you to han so greet travaile
To han some of your bretheren here with you,
That mighten to her cause bet availe,
Then wot I well she mighte never faile   *1440*
For to been holpen, what at your instaunce,°
What with her other freendes' governaunce."

Deiphebus, which that comen was of kinde°
To all honour and bountee to consente,

1418 **Which** to whom   1419 **her possessioun** possession of her (i.e., her property). The charge, which Pandarus trumps up, is not as implausible as it may seem, since Criseyde's father has deserted to the Greeks; also, Criseyde has had legal run-ins with Polyphete in the past   1423 **thus straungely** i.e., as if I didn't know her   1427 **spur . . . yerde** spur and whip (i.e., forcefully)   1434 **her . . . devise** to set forth her complaints   1435 **agrise** tremble   1437 **chargen** require   1441 **instaunce** urging   1443 **comen . . . kinde** was by nature

Answered, "It shall be done; and I can finde   *1445*
Yet greeter help to this in mine intente.
What wilt thou sayn if I for Heleyn sente
To speke of this? I trow it be the beste,
For she may leeden° Paris as her leste.

"Of Hector, which that is my lord, my brother,   *1450*
It needeth not to pray him freend to be;
For I have herde him oo time and eek other
Speke of Criseyde swich honour, that he
May sayn no bet, swich hap to him° hath she.
It needeth not his helpes for to crave: *1455*
He shall be swich right as we will him have.

"Speke thou thyself also to Troilus
On my behalf, and pray him with us dine."
"Sire, all this shall be done," quod Pandarus—
And took his leeve, and never gan to fine,°   *1460*
But to his neece's house as straight as line
He came, and found her fro the mete arise,°
And set him down, and speke right in this wise.

He said, "O verray God! So have I ronne!
Lo, neece mine, see ye not how I swete?   *1465*
I noot whether ye the more thank me conne.°
Be ye not ware how false Polyphete
Is now about eftsoones for to plete,°
And bring on you advocacies° newe?"
"I? no!"—quod she, and changed all her hewe.   *1470*

"What! Is he more aboute me to drecche°
And doon me wrong? What shall I doon, alas?
Yet of himself nothing ne wold I recche,
Nere it for Antenor and Eneas,°
That been his freendes in swich manner cas.   *1475*
But for the love of God, mine uncle deere,
No force of that: let him han all yfere.

1449 **leeden** guide (i.e., Paris will follow her lead in this matter)
1454 **hap . . . him** favor with him   1460 **fine** stop   1462 **fro . . .
arise** arising from dinner   1466 **conne** can   1468 **Is . . . plete** is
very soon going to bring suit   1469 **advocacies** lawsuits   1471
drecche harass   1474 **Eneas** Aeneas (who, along with Antenor,
proved to be a traitor; cf. IV.203–05)

Withouten that, I have enough for us."
"Nay," quod Pandar, "it shall nothing be so!
For I have been right now at° Deiphebus,   *1480*
At Hector, and mine other lordes mo,
And shortly maked eech of hem his° foe
That, by my thrift, he shall it° never winne,
For aught he can, when that so he beginne."

And as they casten what was best to doone,   *1485*
Deiphebus, of his owne curteisye,
Came her to pray in his proper persone,°
To hold° him on the morrow compaignye
At dinner, which she nolde not denye,
But goodly gan to his prayer obeye.   *1490*
He thanked her, and went upon his waye.

When this was done, this Pandar up° anon,
To tell in short, and forth gan for to wende
To Troilus, as still as any ston.
And all this thing he told him, word and ende,   *1495*
And how that he Deiphebus gan to blende,°
And said him, "Now is time, if that thou conne,
To bere thee well tomorrow, and all is wonne.

"Now speke, now pray, now pitously complaine.
Let nought° for nice shame, or dreed, or slouthe.   *1500*
Sometime a man mot tell his owne paine:
Beleeve it, and she shall han on thee routhe.
Thou shalt be saved by thy faith, in trouthe.
But well wot I thou art now in dreede—
And what it is I lay I can areede.°   *1505*

"Thou thinkest now: 'How shold I doon all this?
For, by my cheeres, mosten folk espye
That for her love is that I fare amiss.
Yet had I lever unwist for sorrow die.'°

1480 **at** to (cf. Fr. *chez*) 1482 **his** i.e., Polyphete's 1483 **it** i.e.,
the lawsuit 1487 **in . . . persone** i.e., in person (rather than by
envoy) 1488 **hold** keep 1492 **up** rose up 1496 **blende** deceive
1500 **Let nought** leave nothing undone 1505 **lay . . . areede** bet
I can guess 1509 **lever . . . die** rather die of sorrow undetected

Now think not so, for thou dost greet follye.   1510
For I right now have founden oo mannere°
Of sleighte, for to coveren all thy cheere.°

"Thou shalt goon overnight, and that bilive,
Unto Deiphebus' house, as thee to playe,
Thy malady away the bet to drive—   1515
Forwhy thou seemest sick, sooth for to saye.
Soon after that down in thy bed thee laye,
And say thou maist no longer up endure,
And lie right there, and bide thine aventure.°

"Say that thy fever is wont thee for to take   1520
The same time, and lasten till amorrwe;°
And let see now how well thou canst it make.°
For, pardee, sick is he that is in sorrwe.
Go now. Farewell. And Venus here to borwe,°
I hope, and thou this purpose holde ferme,   1525
Thy grace she shall fully there conferme."

Quod Troilus: "Ywis, thou needeless
Counseilest me that sicklich I me feigne:
For I am sick in ernest, douteless,
So that well nigh I sterve for the paine."   1530
Quod Pandarus: "Thou shalt the better plaine
And hast the lesse need to countrefete,
For him men deemen hot that men seen swete.°

"Lo, hold thee at thy tryste close,° and I
Shall well the deer unto thy bowe drive."   1535
Therewith he took his leeve all softely,
And Troilus to palais wente blive.
So glad ne was he never in all his live,

1511 **oo mannere** one way   1512 **sleighte . . . cheere** trickery, to
account for your behavior   1519 **bide . . . aventure** i.e., await what
happens   1520–21 **is . . . amorrwe** is used to come over you at the
same time (each day) and lasts till the next day. Pandarus asks
Troilus to feign a "quotidian fever"   1522 **how . . . make** i.e., how
well you can act   1524 **Venus . . . borwe** i.e., with Venus's aid
1533 **him . . . swete** men judge the man hot whom they see sweat
1534 **hold . . . close** keep yourself hidden at your station. In the
medieval hunt the *tryste* was the spot where the hunters awaited the
deer, which was driven toward them by the huntsmen and dogs

And to Pandarus' reed gan all assente,
And to Deiphebus' house at night he wente.   *1540*

What needeth you to tellen all the cheere
That Deiphebus unto his brother made?
Or his access,° or his sicklich mannere—
How men gan him with clothes for to lade°
When he was laid, and how men wold him glade?   *1545*
—But all for nought: he held forth ay the wise°
That ye han herde Pandar ere this devise.°

But certain is, ere Troilus him laide,
Deiphebus had him prayed overnight
To been a freend and helping to Criseyde.   *1550*
God wot that he it granted anonright
To been her fulle freend with all his might:
But swich a neede was to pray him thenne
As for to bid a wood man for to renne!

The morrowen came, and nighen gan the time   *1555*
Of meeltide, that° the faire queen Heleyne
Shop her° to been, an hour after the prime,°
With Deiphebus, to whom she nolde feigne.°
But as his suster,° homely,° sooth to sayne,
She came to dinner in her plain intente   *1560*
—But God and Pandar wist all what this mente.

Came eek Criseyde, all innocent of this,
Antigone, her suster Tarbe° also . . .
But flee we now prolixitee best is,°
For love of God, and let us faste go   *1565*
Right to the effect, withouten wordes mo,
Why all this folk assembled in this place,
And let us of hir saluinges passe.°

1543 **access** illness   1544 **gan . . . lade** covered him up with bed-
clothes   1546 **held . . . wise** i.e., kept up the pretense   1541–47
What . . . devise This stanza but particularly lines 1541–45 is an
occupatio, a rhetorical convention in which a writer summarizes
material by stating, sometimes at length, what he will not deal with
1556 **meeltide, that** mealtime, when   1557 **Shop her** arranged
1557 **hour . . . prime** ten a.m.   1558 **to . . . feigne** whom she
didn't wish to disappoint (by not keeping her appointment)   1559
suster i.e., sister-in-law   1559 **homely** familiarly   1563 **Antigone
. . . Tarbe** Criseyde's nieces   1564 **flee . . . is** it is best that we flee
prolixity   1568 **hir . . . passe** pass over their greetings

Greet honour did hem Deiphebus, certain,
And fed hem well with all that mighte like.   *1570*
But evermo "Alas!" was his refrain.
"My goode brother Troilus, the sicke,
Lieth yet"—and therewithal he gan to sighe.
And after that he pained him to glade
Hem as he might, and cheere good he made.   *1575*

Complained eek Heleyn of his sicknesse
So faithfully that pitee was to heere.
And every wight gan waxen for accesse
A leech anon,° and said, "In this mannere
Men curen folk . . ." "This charm I will you leere . . ."   *1580*
But there sat one—al list her not to teeche—
That thought, "Best coud *I* yet been his leeche."

After complaint, him gonnen they to praise,
As folk doon yet° when some wight hath begunne
To praise a man, and up with pris him raise   *1585*
A thousandfold yet higher than the sunne—
"He is, he can, that fewe lordes conne"—
And Pandarus, of that they wold afferme,
He not forgot hir praising to conferme.

Herde all this thing Criseyde well enough,   *1590*
And every word gan for to notifye,°
For which with sober cheer her herte lough.
For who is that ne wold her glorifye
To mowen° swich a knight doon live or die?
—But all pass I, lest ye too longe dwelle: *1595*
For, for oo fin° is all that ever I telle.

The time came fro dinner for to rise,
And as hem ought arisen everichoon,
And gonne a while of this and that devise.
But Pandarus brake° all this speech anon,   *1600*
And said to Deiphebus, "Will ye gon,
If it your wille be, as I you prayde,
To speke here of the needes of Criseyde?"

1578–79 **And . . . anon** and everyone suddenly became a physician
for the illness   1584 **yet** still   1591 **notifye** note   1594 **mowen** be
able   1596 **for . . . fin** for one purpose   1598 **as . . . everichoon**
everyone arose as he should (i.e., in order of rank)   1600 **brake**

Heleyne, which that by the hand her held,
Took first the tale° and saide, "Go we blive."   *1605*
And goodly on Criseyde she beheld,
And saide, "Joves let him never thrive
That doth you harm, and bring him soon of live;°
And yive me sorrow, but he shall it rewe,
If that I may, and alle folk be trewe."°   *1610*

"Tell thou thy neece's cas," quod Deiphebus
To Pandarus, "for thou canst best it telle."
"My lordes and my ladies, it stant thus—
What shold I longer," quod he, "do you dwelle?"°
He rung hem out a process° like a belle   *1615*
Upon her foe that highte Polyphete,
So heinous that men mighte on it spete.°

Answered of this eech worse of hem than other,°
And Polyphete they gonnen thus to warien:°
"An-hanged be swich one, were he my brother."°   *1620*
—"And so he *shall*, for it ne may not varyen."°
What shold I longer in this tale tarryen?
Plainlich, all at ones, they her highten°
To been her help in all that ever they mighten.

Spake then Heleyn and saide, "Pandarus,   *1625*
Wot aught my lord, my brother, this mattere—
I meene Hector? Or wot it Troilus?"
He saide, "Yea. But will ye now me heere?
Me thinketh this: sith that Troilus is here,
It were good, if that ye wold assente,   *1630*
She told herself him all this ere she wente.

"For he will have the more her grief at herte,
Because, lo, that she a lady is;
And, by your leeve, I will but in right sterte°

interrupted, broke off   1605 **Took . . . tale** i.e., was the first to
speak   1608 **of live** to destruction (*of*= from)   1610 **If . . . trewe**
if I have any say in the matter, and if all folk be trustworthy
1614 **do . . . dwelle** i.e., keep you waiting   1615 **process** story
1617 **spete** spit   1618 **Answered . . . other** each of them reacted
to this worse than the other   1619 **warien** curse   1620 **An-hanged
. . . brother** such a person should be hanged, even if he were my
brother   1621 **varyen** be otherwise   1623 **highten** promised   1634
but . . . sterte just pop in

And do you wite°—and that anon, ywis—   1635
If that he sleep, or will aught heer of this."
—And in he lept, and said him in his eere:
"God have thy soul, y-brought have I thy beere!"°

To smilen of this gan tho Troilus.
And Pandarus, withouten reckeninge,°   1640
Out went anon to Heleyn and Deiphebus,
And said hem, "So there be no tarryinge,
Ne more press,° he will well that ye bringe
Criseyde, my lady, that is here,
And as° he may enduren, he will heere.   1645

"But well ye wot the chamber is but lite,
And fewe folk may lightly make it warm.°
Now looketh ye°—for I will have no wite
To bring in press that mighte doon him harm,
Or him diseesen, for my better arm—   1650
Whe'r it be bet she bide till eftsoonis.°
Now looketh ye that knowen what to doon is.

"I say, for me, best is, as I can knowe,
That no wight in ne wente but ye twaye—
But it were I—for I can in a throwe°   1655
Reherse her case unlike that° she can saye.
And after this she may him ones praye
To been good lord, in short, and take her leeve;
This may not muchel of his eese him reve.°

"And eek, for she is strange,° he will forbere°   1660
His eese, which that him thar not for you.°

1635 do . . . wite let you know   1638 beere bier (a joke about
Troilus's "fever")   1640 withouten reckeninge without explanation
(to Troilus, who doesn't know what Pandarus is up to)   1643 Ne
. . . press and no longer crowd (just Criseyde and Deiphebus)
1645 as as long as   1647 may . . . warm i.e., can easily fill it up
1648 looketh ye consider. (The thought is completed in line 1651:
"looketh ye . . . Whe'r")   1651 Whe'r . . . eftsoonis whether it
would be better for her to wait until later   1655 throwe moment
1656 unlike that i.e., better than what   1659 reve deprive   1660
strange a stranger   1660 forbere forgo   1661 which . . . you
which would not be necessary for you (his family). Troilus, despite
his illness, will make a special effort for Criseyde. Pandarus says

Eek other thing that toucheth not to here°
He will you tell—I wot it well right now—
That secret is, and for the towne's prow."°
And they that nothing knew of this intente,   *1665*
Withouten more, to Troilus in they wente.

Heleyn, in all her goodly softe wise,
Gan him salue,° and womanly to playe,
And said, "Ywis, ye must always arise.°
Now, faire brother, be all hool, I praye"   *1670*
—And gan her arm right over his shulder laye,
And him with all her wit to reconforte.°
As she best coud, she gan him to disporte.

So after this, quod she, "We you biseeke,
My deere brother Deiphebus and I,   *1675*
For love of God—and so doth Pandar eeke—
To been good lord and freend right hertely
Unto Criseyde, which that certainly
Receiveth wrong, as wot well here Pandare,
That can her cas well bet than I declare."   *1680*

This Pandarus gan new his tongue affile,°
And all her cas reherse, and that anon.
When it was said, soon after, in a while,
Quod Troilus: "As soon as I may goon,°
I will right fain with all my might been oon—   *1685*
Have God my trouth—her cause to sustene."°
"Good thrift have ye!" quod Heleyne the queene.

Quod Pandarus: "And it your wille be
That she may take her leeve ere that she go . . ."
"Or elles God forbede it tho," quod he,   *1690*
"If that she vouche sauf for to do so."
And with that word, quod Troilus, "Ye two,
Deiphebus and my suster lief and deere,
To you have I to speke of oo mattere,

all this, of course, with an exquisite sense of irony **1662 toucheth
. . . here** doesn't concern her **1664 prow** advantage. Deiphebus
and the others assume that Pandarus is speaking of the war **1668
salue** greet **1669 ye . . . arise** you must by all means get well
1672 reconforte comfort **1681 affile** sharpen **1684 goon** walk
1686 sustene champion

"To been avised by your reed the better"   *1695*
—And found, as hap was, at his bedde's heed,
The copy of a tretise° and a letter
That Hector had him sent to asken reed
If swich a man was worthy to been deed°
(Wot I not who); but in a grisly° wise   *1700*
He prayed hem anon on it avise.

Deiphebus gan this letter for to unfolde
In ernest greet; so did Heleyn the queene,
And roming outward fast it gan beholde,°
Downward a stair, into an herber° greene.   *1705*
This ilke thing they redden hem betweene,
And largely, the mountance° of an houre,
They gan on it to reden and to poure.

Now let hem rede, and turne we anon
To Pandarus, that gan full faste prye°   *1710*
That all was well; and out he gan to goon
Into the greete chamber, and that in hie,
And saide, "God save all this compaignye.
Come, neece mine, my lady queen Heleyn
Abideth you and eek my lordes twaine.   *1715*

"Rise, take with you your neece, Antigone,
Or whom you list. Or no force, hardily,
The lesse press the bet. Come forth with me,
And looke that ye thanken humblely
Hem alle three. And when ye may goodly   *1720*
Your time see, taketh of hem your leeve,
Lest we too long his restes him bereeve."°

All innocent of Pandarus' intente
Quod tho Criseyde, "Go we, uncle deere."
And arm in arm inward with him she wente,   *1725*
Avising well her wordes and her cheere.
And Pandarus, in ernestful mannere,
Said, "Alle folk, for Godde's love, I praye,
Stinteth right here, and softely you playe.

1697 **tretise** document   1699 **deed** put to death   1700 **grisly** serious
1704 **roming . . . beholde** roaming outside (she) beheld it closely
1705 **herber** garden   1707 **largely . . . mountance** entirely, the
extent   1710 **faste prye** quickly inspect (i.e., make sure)   1722 **his**
. . . bereeve deprive him of his rest

"Aviseth you what folk been here withinne,   1730
And in what plight one is, God him amende."
And inward thus: "Full softely beginne.
Neece, I conjure and highly you defende,°
On his half which that soul us alle sende,°
And in the virtue of corounes twaine,°   1735
Slee not this man that hath for you this paine.

"Fie on the devil! Think which one he is,
And in what plight he lieth. Come off anon!
Think all swich tarried tide but lost it nis!°
—That will ye bothe sayn when ye been oon.   1740
Secoundely, there yet divineth noon
Upon you two.° Come off now, if ye conne.
While folk is blent,° lo, all the time is wonne!

"In tittering and pursuit and delayes
The folk divine at wagging of a stree.°   1745
And though ye wold han after merry dayes,
Then dare ye not—and why? For she and she°
Spake swich a word; thus looked he and he.
Less time y-lost! I dare not with you deele.°
Come off, therefore, and bringeth him to hele."   1750

But now to you, ye lovers° that been here:
Was Troilus not in a cankedort,°

1733 **defende** forbid 1734 **On . . . sende** on behalf of Him who
has sent souls to all of us 1735 **in . . . twaine** by the power of
two crowns. The two crowns have not been successfully explained;
they may be nuptial crowns or symbols of martyrdom and chastity
1739 **Think . . . nis!** think how all such delayed time is simply lost!
1741–42 **there . . . two** there is none who yet guesses about you two
1743 **blent** blinded (i.e., while the wool is over their eyes) 1744–
45 **In . . . stree** in hesitating and entreating and delaying people
suspect the waving of a straw (i.e., anything at all). His point is that
procrastination looks more suspicious than decisive action 1747
she . . . she such and such a woman 1749 **deele** haggle 1751 **you
. . . lovers** Chaucer once again steps out of the narrative to address
his hearers directly. He imagines his audience to be lovers and
those interested in questions of love. Chaucer's question here re-
sembles a lover's "demand" (*demande d'amour*)—a question or
point thrown open to the judgment of a courtly group—such as
occurs at the close of Part I of The Knight's Tale: "You lovers
ax I now this question:/ Who hath the worse, Arcite or Palamoun?"
1752 **cankedort** quandary (?)

That lay and mighte whispering of hem heere,
And thought "O lord, right now runneth my sort°
Fully to die, or han anon comfort . . ."   1755
And was the firste time he shold her praye
Of love? O mighty God—what shall he saye?

1754 **runneth . . . sort** runs my fortune

Book Three

PROEM

O blissful light,° of which the beemes cleere°
Adorneth all the thridde hevene° faire,
O sunne's lief, O Jove's daughter deere,
Pleasaunce of love, O goodly debonaire,
In gentil hertes ay redy to repaire,°   5
O verray cause of hele and of gladnesse,
Y-heried° be thy might and thy goodnesse.

In hevene and hell, in erth and salte sea
Is felt thy might, if that I well discerne.
As man, brid, beest, fish, herb, and greene tree   10
Thee feel in times with vapour eterne.°
God loveth, and to love will nought werne;°
And in this world no lives creature
Withouten love is worth, or may endure.

Ye Joves first to thilk effectes glade,   15
Through which that thinges liven all and be,

1 0 . . . light The invocation of this central Book is to Venus, both in her aspect as the planet—the light in the "third heaven" (line 2) —and as the goddess of love. In Book I, Chaucer invoked Tisiphone, one of the furies; in Book II, he petitioned Clio, the muse of history. Now his appeal becomes at once personal and reverential as he asks for help in describing the love consummation of Troilus and Criseyde. The Proem is a hymn of praise to Love's power and influence 1 cleere bright 2 thridde hevene Venus was the third concentric "sphere" outward from the earth in the medieval geocentric cosmos, above the spheres of the Moon and Mercury but below those of the Sun, Mars, Jupiter, and Saturn. Cf. also 2 Cor. 12:2 5 repaire lodge 7 Y-heried praised 11 Thee . . . eterne feel you in seasons by your eternal exhalation 12 to . . . werne (He) will deny nothing to love 15–17 Ye . . .

Commeveden;° and amorous him made
On mortal thing; and as you list ay ye
Yive him in love eese or adversitee;
And in a thousand formes° down him sente 20
For love in erth, and whom you list he hente.°

Ye fierce Mars appaisen° of his ire,
And as you list ye maken hertes digne:
Algates hem that ye will set afire,
They dreeden shame, and vices they resigne. 25
Ye do hem courteis be, fresh and benigne;
And high or low, after a wight intendeth,°
The joyes that he hath, your might him sendeth.

Ye holden reign and house in unitee;°
Ye soothfast cause of freendship been also; 30
Ye know all thilke covered° qualitee
Of thinges, which that folk on wonderen so
When they cannot construe how it may jo°
She loveth him, or why he loveth here°—
As why this fish, and not that, cometh to were.° 35

Ye folk a law han set in universe,
And this know I by hem that lovers be:
That whoso striveth with you hath the werse.
Now, lady bright, for thy benignitee,
At reverence of hem that serven thee, 40
Whose clerk° I am, so teecheth me devise
Some joy of that is felt° in thy service.

Commeveden you first to those same joyous impulses . . . incited
Jove. Chaucer continues to address Venus 20 **thousand formes**
Jove appeared to mortal women in a number of avatars in order
to make love to them 21 **hente** possessed 22 **Ye . . . appaisen**
you appease fierce Mars. Venus was Mars's lover, and their union
in medieval and Renaissance iconography represents the harmony
of opposites, or the marriage of love with wrath and hate 27 **And
. . . intendeth** and (as) high or low as a person aims 29 **Ye . . .
unitee** i.e., you hold in unity the political and domestic spheres
31 **covered** secret 33 **construe . . . jo** explain how it may occur
(that) 34 **here** her 35 **to were** in the wier (fish trap) 41 **clerk**
In Book I, Chaucer characterized himself as "servant of the ser-
vants of Love" (line 15), as if he were a priest ("clerk") of Love's
religion 42 **Some . . . felt** some of that joy which is felt

Ye in my naked herte sentiment
Inhield, and do me shew of thy° sweetnesse.
Calliope,° thy voice be now present,   45
For now is need: seest thou not my distresse,
How I mot tell anonright the gladnesse
Of Troilus to Venus' heryinge?°—
To which gladnesse, who need hath, God him bringe!°

Lay all this meenewhile Troilus,   50
Recording° his lesson in this mannere:
"*Ma fay*,"° thought he, "thus will I say and thus.
Thus will I plain unto my lady deere.
That word is good, and this shall be my cheere.
This nill I not forgotten in no wise."   55
God leeve him worken as he can devise!

And, Lord, so that his herte gan to quappe,°
Heering her come, and shorte for to sike.°
And Pandarus, that led her by the lappe,°
Came neer, and gan in at the curtain pike,°   60
And saide, "God do boot on alle sicke!°
See who is here you comen to visite!
Lo, here is she that is your deeth to wite."

Therewith it seemed as he wept almost.
"Aaah . . . ," quod Troilus so rewfully,   65
"Whe'r me be woe, O mighty God, thou wost!
Who is all there? I see nought, trewely."
"Sir," quod Criseyde, "it is Pandar and I."
"Ye, sweete herte? Alas, I may not rise
To kneel and do you honour in some wise"—   70

And dressed° him upward. And she right tho
Gan both her handes soft upon him laye.
"O, for the love of God, do ye not so
To me," quod she—"Ey, what is *this* to saye?°

43–44 **sentiment . . . thy** pour in feeling, and make me show your
45 **Calliope** Muse of epic poetry 48 **heryinge** praise 49 **who . . .
bringe** let/God bring him who has need 51 **Recording** rehearsing
52 **Ma fay** my faith 57 **quappe** beat 59 **lappe** a flap of her gar-
ment 60 **pike** peek 61 **God . . . sicke!** may God heal all sick
people! 71 **dressed** raised 74 **Ey . . . saye?** oh, what does *this*
mean? Criseyde feels that Troilus is too forward with her and takes
too much for granted. She quickly gets to the point of her visit as

Sir, comen am I to you for causes twaye: 75
First, you to thank, and of your lordship° eeke
Continuance I wolde you beseeke."   .

This Troilus, that herde his lady praye
Of lordship him, wex neither quick ne deed,°
Ne might oo word for shame to it saye,°   80
Although men sholde smiten off his heed.
But Lord, so he wex suddenliche red,
And sire, his lesson, that he wende conne
To prayen her, is through his wit y-runne.°

Criseyde all this espied well enough,   85
For she was wise and loved him never the lasse,
Al nere he malapert, or made it tough,°
Or was too bold to sing a fool a masse.°
But when his shame gan somewhat to passe,
His reesons,° as I may my rimes holde,   90
I you will tell as teechen bookes olde.

In changed voice, right for his verray dreede—
Which voice eek quoke, and thereto his mannere
Goodly abaist°—and now his hewes rede,
Now pale, unto Criseyde his lady deere,   95
With look downcast and humble y-yolden cheere,°
Lo, the alderfirste word that him asterte°
Was twies, "Mercy, mercy, sweete herte"—

And stint a while, and when he might out bringe,
The nexte word was, "God wot, for I have,   100
As faithfully as I have had conninge,°
Been youres all, God so my soule save,

she understands it and asks Troilus's help in her supposed legal
difficulties 76 **lordship** protection 79 **wex . . . deed** i.e., hovered
between life and death 80 **Ne . . . saye** nor might he say one word
to it because of shame. Troilus is embarrassed because his initial
familiar outburst to Criseyde—"Ye, sweete herte?"—has met with
a formal response 83–84 **And . . . y-runne** and, ladies and gentle-
men, his speech that he thought he knew to ask of her has passed
out of his mind 87 **Al . . . tough** because he wasn't impertinent
and didn't swagger 88 **too . . . masse** i.e., (didn't) spin her a pretty
story 90 **reesons** speeches 94 **Goodly abaist** graciously abashed
96 **y-yolden cheere** submissive look 97 **him asterte** started from
him 101 **conninge** ability

And shall, till that I, woeful wight, be grave.°
And though I dare, ne can, unto you plaine,
Ywis, I suffer not the lesse paine.   *105*

"Thus much as now, O womanliche wif,°
I may out bring. And if this you displeese,
That shall I wreke° upon my owne lif,
Right soon, I trow, and do your herte an eese,
If with my deeth your herte may appese.   *110*
But sin that ye han herde me somewhat saye,
Now recch I never how soone that I deye."

Therewith his manly sorrow to beholde
It might han made an herte of stone to rewe.
And Pandar weep as he to water wolde,°   *115*
And poked ever his neece new and newe,
And saide, "Woe-begone been hertes trewe!
For love of God, make of this thing an ende,
Or slee us both at ones ere ye wende."

"Ey, what!" quod she, "by God and by my trouthe,   *120*
I noot not what ye wilne° that I saye."
"Ey, what!"° quod he—"that ye han on him routhe,
For Godde's love, and doth him not to deye."
"Now thenne thus," quod she, "I wold him praye
To telle me the fin of his intente—   *125*
Yet wist I never well what that he mente."

"What that I meen! O sweete herte deere,"
Quod Troilus, "O goodly freshe free,
That with the streemes of your eyen cleere
Ye wolde sometime freendly on me see.   *130*
And then agreen that I may been he,
Withouten branch° of vice on any wise,
In trouth alway to doon you my service,

"As to my lady right and chief resort,°
With all my wit and all my diligence.   *135*
And I to han, right as you list, comfort°

103 **grave** buried 106 **wif** woman 108 **wreke** avenge 115 **wolde**
would turn 121 **wilne** want 122 **Ey, what!** Pandarus mimics her
132 **branch** subspecies (like the branch of a tree. Vices and virtues
were so represented in the Middle Ages) 134 **resort** refuge 136
comfort i.e., support

Under your yerd° egal to mine offence—
As deeth, if that I breke your defence.°
And that ye deigne me so much honoure
Me to commanden aught in any houre.   *140*

"And I to been youre°—verray, humble, trewe,
Secret, and in my paines pacient,
And evermo desiren freshly newe
To serve and been ay y-like diligent;
And with good herte all hoolly your talent°   *145*
Receiven well, how sore that me smerte—
Lo this meen I,° mine owne sweete herte."

Quod Pandarus: "Lo, here an hard requeste,
And reesonable a lady for to werne!°
Now neece mine, by natal Jove's feste,°   *150*
Were I a god, ye sholden sterve as yerne,°
That heeren well this man will nothing yerne°
But your honour, and seen him almost sterve,
And been so looth to sufferen him you serve."

With that she gan her eyen on him caste   *155*
Full eesily and full debonairly,
Avising her—and hied not too faste
With never a word, but said him softely,
"Mine honour sauf, I will well trewely,
And in swich form as he gan now devise,°   *160*
Receiven him fully to my service,

"Beseeching him, for Godde's love, that he
Wold in honour of trouth and gentilesse,
As I well meen, eek meenen well to me;

137 **yerd** rule 138 **defence** prohibition 141 **youre** yours 145 **talent**
desire 147 **this ... I** Troilus, after Criseyde said she didn't under-
stand his intentions (lines 124–26), has outlined a series of requests:
(1) regard me with friendly eyes; (2) let me serve you; (3) put me
under your governance; (4) ask me anything at any time. In return,
Troilus will agree to serve willingly and without complaint 149
werne deny 150 **by ... feste** "By the feast of Jupiter, who pre-
sides over nativities" (Skeat) 151 **as yerne** quickly 152 **yerne**
desire. The rhyme *yerne/ yerne* in lines 151–52 is a good example
of *rime riche* (see I.697n) 160 **he ... devise** he did now outline.
(Criseyde still speaks very formally through Pandarus in the third

And mine honour, with wit and bisinesse, 165
Ay keep. And if I may doon him gladnesse
From hennesforth, ywis, I nill not feigne.°
Now beeth all hool. No longer ye ne plaine.

"But natheless, this warn I you," quod she,
"A kinge's son although ye be, ywis, 170
Ye shall no more han sovereignetee°
Of me in love than right in that cas is.
N'I nill forbere, if that ye doon amiss,
To wrathe you; and while that ye me serve,
Cherissen you right after ye deserve. 175

"And shortly, deere herte and all my knight,
Beeth glad, and draweth you to lustinesse.°
And I shall trewely, with all my might,
Your bitter turnen all into sweetnesse.
If I be she that may you do gladnesse, 180
For every woe ye shall recover a blisse"—
And him in armes took, and gan him kisse.

Fell Pandarus on knees, and up his eyen
To hevene threw, and held his handes highe:
"Immortal God," quod he, "that maist not dien— 185
Cupid I meen—of this maist glorifye!°
And Venus, thou maist maken melodye!
Withouten hand, me seemeth that in the towne,
For this merveile, ich heer eech belle soune.°

"But ho! no more as now of this mattere, 190
Forwhy this folk will comen up anon
That han the letter red. Lo, I hem heere.
But I conjure thee, Criseyde, and oon,
And two, thou Troilus,° when thou maist goon,°

person. She addresses Troilus "ye" only in line 169) 167 **feigne**
hold back 171 **sovereignetee** mastery, governance 177 **draweth
. . . lustinesse** prepare yourself for activity (rather than idle sick-
ness) 186 **of . . . glorifye** in this you may triumph 188–89
Withouten . . . soune it seems that I hear in the town each bell
ring, without being pulled, for this miracle (a common detail in
saints' legends) 193–94 **conjure . . . Troilus** call upon you,
Criseyde and—one, two—you, Troilus (Pandarus perhaps makes a
gesture of counting them) 194 **maist goon** can walk

That at mine house ye been at my warninge,°   *195*
For I full well shall shape your cominge,

"And eeseth there your hertes right enough,
And let see which of you shall bere the belle°
To speke of love aright"—therewith he lough—
"For there have ye a leiser for to telle."   *200*
Quod Troilus: "How longe shall I dwelle
Ere this be done?" Quod he: "When thou maist rise,
This thing shall be right as I you devise."

With that Heleyn and also Deiphebus
Tho comen upward right at the staire's ende—   *205*
And lord! so then gan gronen Troilus,
His brother and his suster for to blende.°
Quod Pandarus: "It time is that we wende.
Take, neece mine, your leeve at alle three,
And let hem speke and cometh forth with me."   *210*

She took her leeve at hem full thriftily,
As she well coud, and they her reverence
Unto the fulle diden hardily,
And wonder well speken in her absence
Of her, in praising of her excellence—   *215*
Her governance, her wit, and her mannere
Commended, that it joye was to heere.

Now let her wend unto her owne place,
And turne we to Troilus again,
That gan full lightly of the letter passe,°   *220*
That Deiphebus had in the garden seen.
And of Heleyn and him he wolde fain
Delivered been,° and saide that him leste
To sleep, and after tales° have reste.

Heleyn him kissed and took her leeve blive,   *225*
Deiphebus eek, and home went every wight.
And Pandarus, as fast as he may drive,
To Troilus tho came as line right,
And on a paillet° all that glade night

195 **warninge** call   198 **bere . . . belle** win the prize   207 **blende**
deceive   220 **That . . . passe** who passed over the letter very
quickly   222–23 **he . . . been** he would gladly be rid of   224 **tales**
talks   229 **paillet** cot

By Troilus he lay with merry cheere 230
To tale°—and well was hem they were yfere.

* * *

When every wight was voided° but they two,
And all the doores weren fast y-shette,
To tell in short withouten wordes mo,
This Pandarus withouten any lette 235
Uprose, and on his bedde's side him sette,
And gan to speken in a sober wise
To Troilus, as I shall you devise:

"Mine alderlevest lord and brother deere,
God wot, and thou, that it sat me so sore 240
When I thee saw so languishing to-yere°
For love, of which thy woe wex alway more,
That I, with all my might and all my lore,
Have ever sithen done my bisinesse
To bringe thee to joy out of distresse; 245

"And have it brought to swich plight as thou wost,
So that, through me, thou standest now in waye°
To faren well. I say it for no boost°—
And wost thou why? For shame it is to saye,
For thee have I begun a gamen playe 250
Which that I never do shall eft for other,
Although he were a thousandfold my brother.

"That is to say, for thee am I becomen—
Betwixen game and ernest—swich a meene°
As maken women unto men to comen. 255
Al say I not°—thou wost well what I meene.
For thee have I my neece, of vices cleene,
So fully made thy gentilesse triste,
That all shall been right as thyselven liste.

"But God, that all wot, take I to witnesse, 260
That never I this for coveitise° wroughte,
But only for t'abregge° that distresse
For which well nigh thou deidest, as me thoughte.

231 **tale** talk   232 **was voided** had left   241 **to-yere** this year   247
through . . . waye because of my efforts (or, perhaps, with myself
as an intermediary) you are now ready   248 **boost** boast   254
meene intermediary   256 **Al . . . not** although I don't say it   261
coveitise gain   262 **t'abregge** to abridge, relieve

But, goode brother, do now as thee oughte,
For Godde's love, and keep her out of blame,   265
Sin thou art wise, and save alway her name.°

"For well thou wost, the name as yet of here
Among the people, as who saith, hallowed is;
For that man is unbore, I dare well swere,
That ever wiste that she did amiss.   270
But woe is me that I, that cause all this,
May thinken that she is my neece deere,
And I her em and traitor eek yfere!

"And were it wist that I, through mine engyn,°
Had in my neece y-put this fantasye°   275
To doon thy lust and hoolly to been thyn,
Why, all the world upon it wolde crye,°
And sayn that I the worste trecherye
Did in this cas that ever was begunne,
And she forlost—and thou right nought y-wonne!°   280

"Wherefore, ere I will ferther goon a pas,
Yet eft I thee beseech and fully saye
That privitee go with us in this cas—
That is to sayn, that thou us never wraye;°
And be not wroth, though I thee ofte praye   285
To holden secree swich an high mattere—
For skilful° is, thou wost well, my prayere.

"And think what woe there hath betid ere this
For making of avauntes,° as men rede,°
And what mischance in this world yet there is,   290
Fro day to day, right for that wicked deede;°
For which these wise clerkes that been deede°
Han ever thus proverbed to us younge,
That 'Firste virtue is to keepe tongue.'

---

266 **name** reputation   274 **engyn** contriving   275 **fantasye** notion
277 **upon . . . crye** would denounce it   280 **she . . . y-wonne** she
wholly lost—and you not at all ahead   284 **us . . . wraye** never
give us away   287 **skilful** reasonable   289 **avauntes** boasts   289
rede read of   291 **deede** i.e., boasting. To boast of any sexual
conquest—to "kiss and tell"—was an egregious social blunder and
an enormous breach of faith in medieval times   292 **clerkes . . .
deede** scholars who are dead (and therefore of great authority)

"And nere it that I wilne as now t'abregge   *295*
Diffusion of speech, I coud almost
A thousand olde stories thee allegge°
Of women lost through false and fooles' boost.
Proverbes kanst thyself° enough and wost
Agains that vice for to been a labbe,°   *300*
Al said men sooth as often as they gabbe.°

"O tongue,° alas! So often herebeforn
Hast thou made many a lady bright of hewe
Said° 'Wailaway, the day that I was born!'
And many a maide's sorrow for to newe;°   *305*
And for the more part all is untrewe
That men of yelp,° and it were brought to preve.
Of kinde noon avauntour is to leve.°

"Avauntour and a liar—all is oon.
As thus: I pose° a woman grante me   *310*
Her love, and saith that other will she noon;°
And I am sworn to holden it secree;
And after I go tell it two or three,
Ywis, I am avauntour, at the leeste,
And a liar, for I breke my beheste.   *315*

"Now looke then if they be not to blame,
Swich manner folk—what shall I clepe hem? what?—
That hem avaunt of women, and by name,
That yet behight hem never this ne that,
Ne knew hem more than mine olde hat.   *320*
No wonder is, so God me sende hele,
Though women dreeden with us men to deele.

"I say not this for no mistrust of you,
Ne for no wise men, but for fooles nice,
And for the harm that in the world is now,   *325*

----

297 **allegge** cite   299 **kanst thyself** you know yourself   300 **labbe**
blabbermouth   301 **gabbe** lie   302 **O tongue** Pandarus, conceding
that boasters aren't all liars, launches into an apostrophe (see
I.211n)   304 **Said** i.e., to have said   305 **newe** be renewed   307 **of
yelp** brag of   308 **Of . . . leve** by nature no braggart is to be
believed   310 **I pose** I put the case. Pandarus changes rhetorical
style from the preacher to the lawyer   311 **other . . . noon** she
wants no other (lover)

As well for folly oft as for malice.
For well wot I in wise folk that vice
No woman drat,° if she be well avised:
For wise been by fooles' harm chastised.°

"But now to purpose, leve brother deere.   *330*
Have all this thing that I have said in minde,
And keep thy close,° and be now of good cheere:
For at thy day° thou shalt me trewe finde.
I shall thy process set in swich a kinde°—
And God to-forn—that it shall thee suffise,   *335*
For it shall been right as thou wilt devise.

"For well I wot thou meenest well, pardee;
Therefore I dare this fully undertake.
Thou wost eek what thy lady granted thee,
And day is set, the charters up to make.°   *340*
Have now good night, I may no longer wake;
And bid° for me, sin thou art now in blisse,
That God me sende deeth or soone lisse."°

Who mighte tellen half the joy or feste°
Which that the soul of Troilus tho felte,   *345*
Heering the effect° of Pandarus' beheste?
His olde woe, that made his herte swelte,°
Gan tho for joye wasten and to-melte,°
And all the richess° of his sighes sore
At ones fled—he felt of hem no more.   *350*

But right so as these holtes and these hayes,°
That han in winter deede been and dreye,°
Revesten hem° in green when that May is,
When every lusty liketh best to playe—
Right in that selve° wise, sooth for to saye,   *355*

328 **drat** dreads   329 **wise . . . chastised** "wise men learn their les-
sons from fools' wrongdoing" (proverb)   332 **close** close-mouthed
(cf. "keep one's own counsel")   333 **at . . . day** i.e., at the proper
time   334 **thy . . . kinde** arrange your affair in such a way   340
the . . . make to draw up the legal papers (i.e., to get under way)
342 **bid** pray   343 **soone lisse** quick comfort   344 **feste** merriment
346 **effect** substance   347 **swelte** swoon   348 **wasten . . . to-melte**
dissolve and melt away   349 **richess** profusion   351 **holtes . . .
hayes** woods . . . hedges   532 **dreye** dry   353 **Revesten hem** dress
themselves again   355 **selve** same

Wax suddenlich his herte full of joye,
That gladder was there never man in Troye;

And gan his look on Pandarus up caste
Full soberly and freendly for to see,
And saide, "Freend, in Aperil the laste—   360
As well thou wost, if it remember thee—
How nigh the deeth for woe thou founde me,
And how thou didest all thy bisinesse
To know of me the cause of my distresse;

"Thou wost how long ich it forbare to saye°   365
To thee, that art the man that I best triste;
And peril noon was it to thee bewraye,°
That wist I well. But tell me, if thee liste,
Sith I so looth was that thyself it wiste,
How durst I mo tellen of this mattere,   370
That quake now, and no wight may us heere?

"But natheless, by that God I thee swere,
That as him list may all this world governe—
And if I lie, Achilles with his spere
Mine herte cleve,° al were my life eterne   375
As I am mortal, if I late or yerne°
Wold it bewray, or durst, or sholde conne,°
For all the good° that God made under sunne—

"That° rather die I wold, and determine,°
As thinketh me, now stocked° in prisoun,   380
In wrecchedness, in filth, and in vermine,
Caitiff to° cruel king Agamenoun;°
And this in all the temples of this town
Upon the goddes all, I will thee swere
Tomorrow day, if that it like thee heere.   385

365 **ich . . . saye** I restrained myself from telling it (the "cause,"
line 364)   367 **And . . . bewraye** and there was no danger in re-
vealing the cause to you   375 **cleve** cleave, split   376 **late . . . yerne**
cf. "sooner or later"   377 **sholde conne** could   378 **good** goods
(i.e., wealth)   379 **That** This line picks up the thought suspended at
line 372: "by that God I thee swere . . . That . . ."   379 **determine**
come to an end (cf. "terminate")   380 **stocked** put in stocks
382 **Caitiff to** captive of   382 **Agamenoun** Agamemnon, leader of
the Greeks

"And that thou hast so much y-done for me—
That I ne may it nevermore deserve—
This know I well, al might I now for thee
A thousand times on a morrow sterve.
I can no more, but that I will thee serve   ·390
Right as thy sclave,° whider so thou wende,
For evermore unto my live's ende.

"But here with all mine herte, I thee beseeche
That never in me thou deeme swich follye
As I shall sayn: me thoughte by thy speeche   395
That this, which thou me dost for compaignye,°
I sholde ween it were a bawderye.°
I am not wood, al if I lewed be!°
It is not so—that wot I well, pardee.

"But he that goeth, for gold or for richesse,   400
On swich message,° call him what thee list;
And this that thou dost, call it gentilesse,
Compassion, and fellowship, and trist.
Depart it so, for widewhere is wist
How that there is diversitee requered°   405
Betwixen thinges like, as I have lered.

"And that thou know I thinke not, ne weene,
That this service a shame be or jape,
I have my faire suster, Polixene,
Cassandre, Heleyn, or any of the frape,°   410
Be she never so fair or well y-shape:
Telle which thou wilt of everichone
To han for thine, and let me then alone.°

"But sith thou hast y-done me this servise
My life to save, and for noon hope of meede,°   415

391 sclave slave   396 compaignye comradeship   397 bawderye
pimp's arrangement   398 I . . . be! I'm not mad, even if I'm stupid!
401 message errand   404-5 Depart . . . requered distinguish it in
this way (from bawdry), for it is known far and wide that distinc-
tions must be made   410 frape bunch   413 let . . . alone i.e.,
leave the rest to me. Troilus's argument is weak: if Pandarus
would "have for his own" any of Troilus's sisters—or Helen, his
brother's wife!—Troilus will arrange it to prove that Pandarus's
service was not shameful and that he would equally trust Pan-
darus's honor   415 meede reward

So for the love of God, this greet emprise
Perform it out,° for now is moste neede.
For high and low, withouten any dreede,
I will alway thine hestes° alle keepe.
Have now good night, and let us bothe sleepe."   *420*

Thus held him eech of other well apayed,°
That all the world ne might it bet amende;°
And on the morrow, when they were arrayed,
Eech to his owne needes gan intende.
But Troilus, though as the fire he brende   *425*
For sharp desire of hope and of plesaunce,
He not forgot his goode governaunce.

But in himself with manhood gan restraine
Eech rakel° deed and eech unbridled cheere,
That alle tho that liven, sooth to sayne,   *430*
Ne shold han wist, by word or by mannere,
What that he ment as touching this mattere.
From every wight as far as is the cloude
He was, so well dissimulen° he coude.

And all the while which that I you devise   *435*
This was his life: with all his fulle might
By day he was in Marte's high service—
This is to sayn, in armes as a knight;
And for the more part, the longe night
He lay and thought how that he mighte serve   *440*
His lady best, her thank for to deserve.

Nill I not swere, although he laye softe,
That in his thought he nas somewhat diseesed,°
Ne that he turned on his pillows ofte,
And wold of that he missed han been seesed.°   *445*
But in swich cas men is not alway pleesed,
For aught I wot, no more than was he.
That can I deem of possibilitee.°

416–17 **this . . . out** carry out (to its end) this great enterprise. (The
tone of gentle urgency here does not wholly accord with Troilus's
protestations of honor)   419 **hestes** commands   421 **apayed** pleased
422 **bet amende** improve   429 **rakel** rash   434 **dissimulen** dissemble
443 **diseesed** troubled   445 **seesed** possessed (Chaucer won't swear
that Troilus didn't toss and turn thinking of Criseyde)   448 **That**

But certain is, to purpose for to go,
That in this while, as written is in geste,°   **450**
He saw his lady sometime, and also
She with him spake, when that she durst or leste;
And by hir both avis, as was the beste,
Appointeden full warly in this neede,°
So as they durste, how they wold proceede.   **455**

But it was spoken in so short a wise,
In swich await° alway, and in swich feere,
Lest any wight divinen or devise
Wold of hem two, or to it lay an eere,
That all this world so lief to hem ne were   **460**
As that Cupide wold hem grace sende
To maken of hir speech aright an ende.°

But thilke litel that they spake or wroughte,
His wise ghost° took ay of all swich heede
It seemed her he wiste what she thoughte   **465**
Withouten word, so that it was no neede
To bid him aught to doon, or aught forbede;
For which she thought that love, al come it late,
Of alle joy had opened her the gate.

And shortly of this process for to passe,   **470**
So well his work and wordes he besette,
That he so full stood in his lady grace,
That twenty thousand times, ere she lette,°
She thanked God that ever she with him mette.
So coud he him govern in swich service,   **475**
That all the world ne might it bet avise.°

Forwhy she found him so discreet in all,
So secret, and of swich obeisaunce,
That well she felt he was to her a wall
Of steel, and sheeld from every displesaunce;   **480**
That to been in his goode governaunce,°

... possibilitee i.e., I can see that is a possibility   **450 geste** story
454 Appointeden . . . neede arranged very warily in this affair
457 await watchfulness   **462 aright . . . ende** quickly an end (i.e.,
to the talking, and let them progress to actions)   **464 ghost** spirit,
power of perception   **473 lette** left off   **476 avise** devise   **481 been
... governaunce** While Criseyde has previously made Troilus agree

So wise he was, she was no more afeered—
I meen, as far as oughte been requered.

And Pandarus, to quick alway the fir,°
Was ever y-like prest° and diligent: 485
To eese his freend was set all his desir.
He shof° ay on, he to and fro was sent,
He letters bare when Troilus was absent,
That never man as in his freende's neede
Ne bare him bet than he, withouten dreede.   490

But now, peraunter, some man waiten° wolde
That every word, or soond,° or look, or cheere
Of Troilus that I rehersen sholde,
In all this while unto his lady deere;
I trow it were a long thing for to heere,   495
Or of what wight that stant in swich disjointe
His wordes all, or every look to pointe.°

Forsooth, I have not herde it done ere this
In story noon, ne no man here,° I weene.
And though I wold, I coude not, ywis;   500
For there was some epistle° hem betweene,
That wold, as saith mine auctor, well contene°
Nigh half this book, of which him list not write.°
How shold I then a line of it endite?

                        * * *

But to the greet effect.° Then say I thus: 505
That standing in concord and in quiete
These ilke two, Criseyde and Troilus,
As I have told, and in this time sweete—

that he will not have control (III.169–72), as he has offered to
serve her, Chaucer seems to concede that in such matters the man
does get the upper hand nonetheless **484 to . . . fir** to keep the
fire alive **485 prest** prompt **487 shof** pushed **491 waiten** expect
492 soond message **496–97 Or . . . pointe** to list (*pointe*) either
all the words, or every look, of a man who stands in such a
situation. This stanza is an elegant *occupatio* (cf. II.1541–47
and n) **499 ne . . . here** Chaucer again envisions an audience
501 some epistle correspondence (i.e., some letters) **502 well con-
tene** easily contain **503 of . . . write** of which (letters) he ("my
author," i.e., "Lollius") didn't wish to write **505 effect** point,
climax

Save only often mighte they not meete,
Ne leiser have hir speeches to fulfille—   510
That it befell right as I shall you telle,

That Pandarus—that ever did his might
Right for the fin that I shall speke of here
(As for to bringen to his house some night
His faire neece and Troilus yfere,   515
Wher-as at leiser all this high mattere,
Touching hir love, were at the full upbounde)°—
Had out of doute a time to° it founde.

For he with greet deliberacioun
Had everything that hereto might availe   520
Forncast,° and put in execucioun,
And neither left° for cost ne for travaille.
Come if hem list, hem sholde nothing faile;°
And for to been in aught espied there—
That, wist he well, an impossible were.   525

Dreedeless, it cleer was in the wind
From every pie and every lette-game.°
Now all is well, for all the world is blind
In this mattere, bothe fremd° and tame.
This timber is all redy up to frame:°   530
Us lacketh nought, but that we witen wolde
A certain hour in which she comen sholde.

And Troilus, that all this purveyaunce°
Knew at the full and waited on it ay,
Had hereupon eek made greet ordinaunce,°   535
And found his cause and thereto his array,°

517 were . . . upbounde should be fully concluded   518 to for. The
"it" refers to the meeting mentioned at lines 514–15   521 Forncast
prearranged   522 neither left spared nothing either   523 Come . . .
faile if they wished to come, nothing should be lacking   527 pie
. . . lette-game magpie (a gossipy bird) . . . spoilsport. There would
be nobody at Pandarus's house to gossip about Troilus and Criseyde,
so the wind would be still and free (cleer) of chatter   529 fremd
wild (fremd and tame= everyone)   530 This . . . frame i.e., the
house is ready to be built   533 purveyaunce planning   535 ordi-
naunce arrangements   536 And . . . array and made up his excuse
and moreover his pretext. This thought is completed in line 539:

If that he were missed night or day
Ther while he was aboute this service—
That he was gone to doon his sacrifise,

And must at swich a temple alone wake,°   540
Answered of Apollo for to be,
And first to seen the holy laurer quake,
Ere that Apollo spake out of the tree
To tell him next when Greekes sholden flee.°
And forthy let° him no man, God forbede,   545
But pray Apollo helpen in this neede.

Now is there litel more for to doone,
But Pandar up, and (shortly for to sayne)
Right soon upon the changing of the moone,
When lightless is the world oo night or twaine,   550
And that the welken shop him° for to raine,
He straight amorrow unto his neece wente—
Ye han well herde the fin of his intente.

When he was come, he gan anon to playe
As he was wont, and of himself to jape;   555
And finally he swore and gan her saye,
By this and that, she shold him not escape,
Ne longer doon him after her to gape°—
But certainly she muste, by her leeve,
Come suppen in his house with him at eve.   560

At which she lough, and gan her fast excuse,
And said, "It raineth! Lo, how shold I goon?"
"Let be," quod he, "ne stand not thus to muse.
This mot be done. Ye shall be there anon."
So at the last hereof they fell at oon,°   565

"... pretext that he should go to sacrifice" **540 wake** stay awake.
Troilus's elaborate—almost desperate—machinations for escaping
from his servants and friends underscore, as H.M. Smyser observes,
the lack of privacy in the Middle Ages (see *Speculum*, 31:311 ff.)
542-44 And ... flee Troilus says he is to watch for the sign from
Apollo's sacred tree, the laurel, which will first shake and then
deliver up the god's prediction of the Greek retreat. This elaborate
fiction is Troilus's *cause* (line 536) **545 let** hinder **551 that ...
him** when the sky prepared (itself) **558 doon ... gape** cause him
to chase after her **565 fell ... oon** agreed

Or elles (soft he swore her in her eere)
He nolde never comen ther she were.

Soon after this she gan to him to rowne,°
And asked him if Troilus were there.
He swore her nay, for he was out of towne,   570
And saide, "Neece, I pose that he were:
You thurste never han the more feere.°
For rather than men might him there espye,
Me were lever a thousandfold to die."

Not list mine auctor fully to declare   575
What that she thoughte when he saide so,
That Troilus was out of town y-fare—
As, if he saide thereof sooth or no;
But that, without await,° with him to go
She granted him, sith he her that besoughte,   580
And as his neece obeyed as her oughte.

But natheless yet gan she him beseeche,
Although with him to goon it was no feere,
For to be ware of goosish° peoples' speeche,   585
That dreemen° thinges which as never were,
And well avise him whom he broughte there;
And said him, "Em, sin I most on you triste,
Look all be well, and do now as you liste."

He swore her yis, by stockes and by stones,°
And by the goddes that in hevene dwelle,   590
Or elles were him lever, soul and bones,
With Pluto king as deepe been in Helle
As Tantalus.° What shold I more telle?
When all was well he rose and took his leeve,
And she to supper came when it was eve,   595

With a certain° of her owne men,
And with her faire neece, Antigone,
And other of her women nine or ten.

568 **rowne** whisper   572 **You . . . feere** you would never need to
be fearful on that account. *You thurste*= "it would be needful to
you" (from *thurfen*)   579 **await** delay   585 **goosish** people who
honk stupidly like geese   586 **dreemen** dream up   589 **by . . .
stones** i.e., by wooden or stone images (sacred idols)   593 **Tantalus**
who was "tantalized" in Hades for his wrongdoing by food and
drink just out of reach   596 **a certain** a certain number, a few

But who was glad now? Who, as trowe ye,
But Troilus, that stood and might it see 600
Throughout a litel window in a stewe,°
Ther he beshet sin midnight was in mewe,°

Unwist of every wight but of Pandare?
But to the point: now when that she was come,
With alle joy and alle freendes' fare,° 605
Her em anon in armes hath her nome,°
And after to the supper all and some,
When time was, full softe they hem sette.
God wot, there was no deintee for to fette.°

And after supper gonnen they to rise, 610
At eese well, with hertes fresh and glade;
And well was him that coude best devise°
To liken her,° or that her laughen made.
He sang; she° played; he tolde tale of Wade.°
But at the last, as everything hath ende, 615
She took her leeve, and needes wolde wende.

But O Fortune, executrice of wierdes!°
O influences of these hevenes highe!
Sooth is, that under God ye been our hierdes,°
Though to us beestes been the causes wrye. 620
This meen I now, for she gan homeward hie,
But execut was all, beside her leeve,
At the goddes' will, for which she muste bleve.°

The bente moone with her hornes pale,
Saturn, and Jove in Cancro joined were,° 625

601 **stewe** small room, or closet 602 **Ther . . . mewe** where he
was shut up since midnight in hiding 605 **fare** to-do (they greet
her warmly) 606 **nome** taken 609 **no . . . fette** no delicacy to be
fetched (i.e., nothing was lacking) 612 **devise** contrive 613 **liken
her** please her (a gentlewoman) 614 **He . . . she** one . . . another
614 **Wade** Germanic romance hero of the Middle Ages, very much
an anachronism here unless it refers generally to tales of knight-
hood 617 **executrice . . . wierdes** empress of men's fates (weirds)
619 **hierdes** herdsmen. Chaucer makes the point that men are sub-
ject to Fortune and the influence of the stars and planets 622–23
But . . . bleve but all was executed, irrespective of her desires, at
the gods' will, on account of which she must remain 625 **in . . .
were** the crescent (*bente*) moon, Saturn, and Jupiter were in con-

That swich a rain from hevene gan avale°
That every manner woman that was there
Had of that smoky rain a verray feere.
At which Pandar tho lough, and saide thenne:
"Now were it time a lady to goon henne!   *630*

"But, goode neece, if I might ever pleese
You anything, then pray ich you," quod he,
"To doon mine herte as now so greet an eese
As for to dwell here all this night with me—
Forwhy this is your owne house, pardee.°   *635*
For by my trouth, I say it not a-game,°
To wend as now it were to me a shame."

Criseyde, which that coud as muche good
As half a world,° took heed of his prayere;
And sin it ron,° and all was on a flood,   *640*
She thought, "As good chepe° may I dwellen here,
And grant it gladly with a freende's cheere,
And have a thank, as grucch° and then abide.°
For home to goon it may not well betide."

"I will," quod she, "mine uncle lief and deere.   *645*
Sin that you list, it skill° is to be so.
I am right glad with you to dwellen here.
I saide but a-game I wolde go."
"Ywis, graunt mercy,° neece," quod he tho,
"Were it a-game or no, sooth for to telle,   *650*
Now am I glad, sin that you list to dwelle."

Thus all is well. But tho began aright
The newe joy and all the feste again.
But Pandarus, if goodly had he might,°
He wold han hied her to bedde fain—   *655*
And saide, "Lord, this is an huge rain!
This were a weder° for to sleepen inne!—
And that I reed us soone to beginne.

junction in the zodiacal sign of Cancer (the Crab). This conjunction
causes the rain   626 **avale** descend   636 **a-game** in jest   638–39
which . . . world who knew (best) the good half of the world
640 **ron** rained   641 **good chepe** easily   643 **grucch** grumble   643
abide stay   646 **skill** reasonable   649 **graunt mercy** much thanks
654 **if . . . might** if it had been in his power   657 **a weder** weather

"And neece, wot ye where I will you laye°——
For that we shall not lien far asunder,°   *660*
And for ye neither shullen, dare I saye,
Heeren noise of raine nor of thunder?
By God, right in my litel closet° yonder.
And I will in that outer house alone
Be warden° of your women everichone.   *665*

"And in this middle chamber° that ye see
Shall your women sleepen well and softe;
And ther I saide shall yourselven be.
And if ye lien well tonight, come ofte,
And careth not what weder is alofte.   *670*
The wine° anon, and when so that you leste,
So go we sleep—I trow it be the beste."

There nis no more, but hereafter soone—
The voidee drunk, and travers° drawe anon—
Gan every wight that hadde nought to doone   *675*
More in the place out of the chamber gon.
And evermo so sternelich it ron,°
And blew therewith so wonderliche loude,
That well nigh no man heeren other coude.

Tho Pandarus, her em, right as him oughte,   *680*
With women swich as were her most aboute,°
Full glad unto her bedde's side her broughte,
And took his leeve, and gan full lowe loute,°
And said, "Here at this closet door withoute,

659 **you laye** put you   660 **asunder** apart   663 **closet** small room
665 **warden** guardian   666 **middle chamber** The company ate supper
in the great hall. Criseyde is to sleep in a small room (*closet*) which
connects with the great hall. The hall itself is to be partitioned by
a heavy curtain (*travers*, line 674). Criseyde's women attendants
will occupy the portion of the hall nearest Criseyde's room (*middle
chamber*), while Pandarus will sleep on the far side of the curtain
(*that outer house*)   671 **The wine** (bring) the wine. It was cus-
tomary for medieval people to drink wine—the *voidee* (line 674),
or "nightcap"—before retiring   674 **travers** curtain drawn to act
as a room divider (see note to line 666)   677 **so . . . ron** it rained
so fiercely   681 **her . . . aboute** usually with her   683 **loute** low

Right overthwart,° your women lien alle,   685
That, whom you list, of hem ye may her calle."

So when that she was in the closet laid,
And all her women forth by ordinaunce°
Abedde weren, ther-as I have said,
There was no more to skippen nor to traunce,   690
But boden go to bedde with mischaunce°
If any wight was stirring anywhere,
And let hem sleepen that abedde were.

But Pandarus, that well coud each a deel
The olde dance, and every point thereinne,   695
When that he saw that alle thing was well,
He thought he wold upon his work beginne,
And gan the stewe-door all soft unpinne.
And still as stone, withouten longer lette,
By Troilus adownright he him sette.   700

And shortly to the point right for to goon:
Of all this work he told him word and ende,
And saide, "Make thee redy right anon,
For thou shalt into hevene blisse wende."
"Now blissful Venus, thou me grace sende,"   705
Quod Troilus, "for never yet no neede
Had ich ere now, ne halvendeel° the dreede."

Quod Pandarus: "Ne dreed thee neveradeel,
For it shall be right as thou wilt desire.
So thrive I, this night shall I make it well,   710
Or casten all the gruel in the fire."°
"Yet, blissful Venus, this night thou me inspire,"
Quod Troilus, "as wis as I thee serve,
And ever bet, and bet shall, till I sterve.

"And if ich had, O Venus full of mirthe,   715
Aspectes bad of Mars or of Saturne,°

685 **Right overthwart** just opposite 688 **by ordinaunce** in due
order 690–91 **There . . . mischaunce** there was no more skipping
and prancing about, but any person was ordered (*boden*) to go to
bed, for shame, if . . . 707 **halvendeel** half 711 **casten . . . fire**
i.e., "throw in the towel" (apparently a proverb). *Gruel*= porridge
716 **Aspectes . . . Saturne** malevolent influences from Mars or

Or thou combust or let were° in my birthe,
Thy fader pray all thilke harm disturne
Of grace, and that I glad again may turne,°
For love of him thou lovedest in the shawe°— 720
I meen Adon, that with the boor was slawe.°

"O Jove eek, for the love of fair Europe,°
The which in form of bull away thou fette,°
Now help! O Mars, thou with thy bloody cope,°
For love of Cypress,° thou me nought ne lette. 725
O Phebus,° think when Dane herselven shette
Under the bark, and laurer wex for dreede;
Yet for her love, O help now at this neede!

"Mercurye,° for the love of Hierse eeke,
For which Pallas was with Aglauros wroth, 730
Now help! And eek Diane, I thee beseeke,
That this viage be not to thee looth.°
O fatal sustren which, ere any cloth
Me shapen was, my destinee me spunne,°
So helpeth to this work that is begunne." 735

Saturn (the most malignant planets). When Troilus says "if ich
had," he means at his nativity, for the position of the stars at birth
determines one's inclinations through life   717 **combust . . . were**
were burnt up or hindered (i.e., if your influence was in some way
neutralized by other baleful influences)   718–19 **Thy . . . turne**
beg your father (Jove, a benign planet) graciously to turn aside
all that evil influence, and that I may become glad (or fortunate)
again   720 **shawe** wood   721 **Adon . . . slawe** Adonis, who was
slain by the boar   722 **Europe** Jove appeared to Europa in the
form of a bull and carried her off (the "rape of Europa")
723 **fette** fetched   724 **cope** cloak   725 **Cypress** Venus, whom
Mars loved   726 **Phebus** Phoebus Apollo (the sun god), burning
with love, chased the nymph Daphne, but she was turned into a
laurel tree (*wex laurer*) before the god could catch her   729 **Mer-
curye** Mercury loved Herse, whose sister, Aglauros, was made
envious by Pallas (Minerva). When Aglauros tried to bar Mer-
cury's way into Herse's chamber, the god turned Aglauros into
stone. Chaucer read the stories of Venus and Adonis, Apollo and
Daphne, and Mercury and Herse in Ovid's *Metamorphoses*   732
looth Troilus hopes that the chaste moon goddess, Diana, will find
nothing profane in his "voyage" (*viage*) to Criseyde's bedchamber.
He has prayed to all of the planetary gods except Saturn, who
would be out of place in this company since his influences are
almost exclusively malignant   733–34 **O . . . spunne** O you sister

Quod Pandarus: "Thou wrecched mouse's herte—
Art thou aghast so that she will thee bite?
Why! don this furred cloke upon thy sherte,
And follow me, for I will han the wite.°
But bide, and let me goon beforn a lite." 740
And with that word he gan undoon a trappe,°
And Troilus he brought in by the lappe.°

The sterne° wind so loude gan to route°
That no wight other noise mighte heere;
And they that layen at the door withoute° 745
Full sikerly they slepten all yfere.
And Pandarus, with a full sober cheere,
Goeth to the door anon withouten lette
Ther-as they lay, and softely it shette.

And as he came againward° privily, 750
His neece awoke, and asked, "Who goeth there?"
"My deere neece," quod he, "it am I.
Ne wondereth not, ne have of it no feere."
And neer° he came, and said her in her eere: 755
"No word, for love of God, I you beseeche.
Let no wight rise and heeren of our speeche."

Fates who, before any cloth was fashioned for me (as clothing),
spun my destiny for me. Troilus concludes his prayer by enlisting
the help of those who have already determined his destiny 739
han . . . wite take the blame. Note the contrast between Troilus's
formal, reverent prayer to Venus and the planetary gods and
Pandarus's colloquial rebuke 741 **gan . . . trappe** unfastened a
trapdoor. It is not entirely clear how Pandarus and Troilus reach
Criseyde's "closet." Pandarus apparently goes from his room in
the "outer house" beyond the "travers" to Troilus's little room or
"stewe," somehow bypassing Criseyde's attendants in the "middle
chamber." From Troilus's "stewe" Pandarus and Troilus proceed
directly to Criseyde's bedroom. H.M. Smyser suggests that Troilus's
"stewe" is directly below Criseyde's "litel closet" and connects
with it by the trapdoor, passing through a secret passage or
possibly the privy (see lines 750, 787). See diagram on p. xv
742 **lappe** fold in his garment 743 **sterne** raging 743 **route** howl
745 **they . . . withoute** Criseyde's women, who are sleeping just
beyond Criseyde's door in the "middle chamber" 750 **againward**
back again 754 **neer** nearer

"What! Which way be ye comen, *ben'dic'te*?"
Quod she, "and how thus unwist of hem alle?"
"Here at this secree trappe door," quod he.
Quod tho Criseyde: "Let me some wight calle." 760
"Ey! God forbede that it sholde falle,"
Quod Pandarus, "that ye swich folly wroughte:
They mighte deemen thing they never ere thoughte.°

"It is not good a sleeping hound to wake,
Ne yive a wight a cause to divine.° 765
Your women sleepen all, I undertake,
So that, for hem, the house men mighte mine,
And sleepen willen° till the sunne shine.
And when my tale brought is to an ende,
Unwist° right as I came so will I wende. 770

"Now, neece mine, ye shall well understonde,"
Quod he, "so as ye women deemen alle,
That for to hold in love a man in honde,°
And him her lief and deere herte calle,
And maken him an houve above a calle°— 775
I meen, as love another in this meene while—
She doth herself a shame and him a guile.°

"Now whereby that I telle you all this:
Ye wot yourself, as well as any wight,
How that your love all fully granted is 780
To Troilus, the worthieste knight
One of this world, and thereto trouth y-plight,°
That, but it were on him along,° ye nolde
Him never falsen° while ye liven sholde.

"Now stant it thus: that sith I fro you wente, 785
This Troilus, right platly for to sayn,

---

763 **They . . . thoughte** they might suspect something they never thought of before   765 **Ne . . . divine** nor give a person cause to guess   767–68 **for . . . willen** for anything they could do, men might undermine the house, and (yet) they will sleep on   770 **Unwist** unobserved   773 **to . . . honde** to lead a man on in love   775 **maken . . . calle** i.e., fool him (lit. "make a hood above his cap")   777 **guile** trick   781–82 **the . . . y-plight** the single worthiest knight of this world, and also (you) pledged your faith   783 **but . . . along** unless it were his fault   784 **falsen** play false

Is through a gutter by a privee wente°
Into my chamber come in all this rain,
Unwist of every manner wight, certain,
Save of myself, as wisly have I joye,   790
And by the faith I shall° Priam of Troye.

"And he is come in swich pain and distresse
That, but he be all fully wood by this,
He suddenly mot fall into woodnesse,
But if God help—and cause why this is?   795
He saith him told is of a freend of his
How that ye shold loven one that hatte Horaste,°
For sorrow of which this night shall been his laste."

Criseyde, which that all this wonder herde,
Gan suddenly about her herte colde,°   800
And with a sigh she sorrowfully answerde:
"Alas, I wende, whoso tales tolde,
My deere herte wolde me not holde
So lightly false. Alas, conceites° wronge—
What harm they doon! For now live I too longe.   805

"Horaste, alas! And falsen Troilus!
I know him not, God help me so," quod she.
"Alas, what wicked spirit told him thus?
Now certes, em, tomorrow, and I him see,
I shall thereof as full excusen me   810
As ever dide woman, if him like."
And with that word she gan full sore sike.

"O God," quod she, "so worldly selinesse,°
Which clerkes callen false felicitee,
Y-meddled° is with many a bitternesse.   815
Full anguishous° then is, God wot," quod she,

---

787 through ... wente through a gutter by a secret passage (presumably part of the drainage system of the house, and perhaps the privy) **791 shall** owe **797 that ... Horaste** who is called Orestes **800 colde** grow cold **804 conceites** imaginings **813 so ... selinesse** how worldly happiness. Criseyde's philosophical observations about happiness, which may seem pessimistic and rather pagan, are adapted from a favorite book of medieval Christians, Boethius's *Consolation of Philosophy*, II, pr. 4 **815 Y-meddled** mingled **816 Full anguishous** most anguishing

"Condicioun of vain° prosperitee;
For either joyes comen not yfere,
Or elles no wight hath hem alway here.°

"O brotel wele° of manne's joy unstable,   820
With what wight so thou be or how thou playe,
Either he wot that thou, joy, art muable,°
Or wot it not: it mot been one of twaye.
Now if he wot it not, how may he saye
That he hath verray joy and selinesse,   825
That is of ignorance ay in darknesse?

"Now if he wot that joy is transitorye,
As every joy of worldly thing mot flee,
Then every time he *that* hath in memorye,
The dreed of lesing° maketh him that he   830
May in no parfit selinesse be.
And if to lese his joy he set a mite,°
Then seemeth it that joy is worth but lite.

"Wherefore I will define° in this mattere
That trewely, for aught I can espye,   835
There is no verray wele in this world here.
But O, thou wicked serpent, jelousye,
Thou misbeleved° and envious follye—
Why hast thou Troilus made to me untriste,°
That never yet aguilt° him, that I wiste?"   840

Quod Pandarus: "Thus fallen is this cas—"
"Why, uncle mine," quod she, "who told him this?
Why doth my deere herte thus, alas?"
"Ye wot, ye neece mine," quod he, "what is.
I hope all shall be well that is amiss,   845
For ye may quench° all this if that you leste.
And doth right so,° for I hold it the beste."

817 **vain** empty. Criseyde argues that happiness in the world is
transient and illusory because joy is always mixed up with or
followed by sorrow 818–19 **joyes . . . here** joys don't come to-
gether, or else no creature has them continuously in this world
820 **brotel wele** brittle prosperity (weal) 822 **muable** changeable,
mutable 830 **lesing** losing (joy) 832 **set . . . mite** cares at all
834 **define** conclude 838 **misbeleved** misbelieving 839 **to . . .
untriste** mistrust me 840 **aguilt** wronged 846 **quench** stop 847
doth . . . so do exactly that

"So shall I do tomorrow, ywis," quod she,
"And God to-forn, so that it shall suffise."
"Tomorrow? Alas, *that* were a fair,"° quod he.   850
"Nay, nay, it may not standen in this wise;
For, neece mine, thus writen clerkes wise,
That 'Peril is with drecching in y-drawe'°—
Nay, swich abodes been not worth an hawe.°

"Neece, alle thing hath time, I dare avowe;   855
For when a chamber afire is, or an halle,
Well more need is it suddenly rescowe°
Than to dispute and ask amonges alle
How the candel in the straw is falle.
Ah, *ben'dic'te*! for all among that fare°   860
The harm is done, and farewell feeldefare.°

"And, neece mine, ne take it not agrief,°
If that ye suffer him° all night in this woe,
God help me so, ye had him never lief°—
That dare I sayn. Now is there but we two . . .   865
But well I wot that ye will not do so.
Ye been too wise to doon so greet follye
To put his life all night in jupartye."

"Had I him never lief? By God, I wene
Ye hadde never thing so lief," quod she.   870
"Now by my thrift," quod he, "*that* shall be seene,
For sin ye make this ensample of me,
If ich all night wold him in sorrow see
For all the tresour in the town of Troye,
I bidde° God I never mot have joye.   875

"Now looke then, if ye that been his love
Shall put his life all night in jupartye
For thing of nought,° now by that God above,

850 **a fair** a fine thing (sarcasm)   853 **Peril . . . y-drawe** "danger
is drawn nearer by delay" (Skeat)   854 **swich . . . hawe** such delays
just aren't worth a bean (*hawe=* hawthorn fruit, useless as food for
humans)   857 **Well . . . rescowe** there is far more need to save it
right away   860 **all . . . fare** all during that action (the disputing)
861 **farewell feeldefare** "bye bye birdie" (apparently a proverb).
The fieldfare is a thrush   862 **agrief** amiss   863 **suffer him** let him
stay   864 **had . . . lief** never held him dear   875 **bidde** pray   878
For . . . nought i.e., for nothing at all, for no reason

Not only this delay cometh of follye
But of malice, if that I shall not lie.   *880*
What! platly, and ye suffer him in distresse,
Ye neither bountee doon ne gentilesse."

Quod tho Criseyde: "Will ye doon oo thing,
And ye therewith shall stint all his diseese?
Have here and bereth him° this blewe ring,   *885*
For there is nothing might him better pleese—
Save I myself—ne more his herte appeese;
And say my deere herte that his sorrwe
Is causeless—that shall be seen tomorrwe."

"A ring!" quod he, "ye hazelwoodes shaken!°   *890*
Yea, neece mine, that ring must han a ston
That mighte dede° men alive maken,
And swich a ring, trow I, that ye have noon.
Discrecion out of your heed is gon—
That feel I now," quod he, "and that is routhe.   *895*
O time y-lost, well maist thou cursen slouthe!

"Wot ye not well that noble and high corage
Ne sorroweth not, ne stinteth eek, for lite?°
But if a fool were in a jelous rage,
I nolde setten at his sorrow a mite,°   *900*
But feffe him with a fewe wordes white°
Another day, when that I might him finde.
But *this* thing stant all in another kinde.

"This° is so gentil and so tender of herte
That with his deeth he will his sorrows wreke;°   *905*
For trusteth well, how sore that him smerte,
He will to you no jelous wordes speke.
And forthy, neece, ere that his herte breke,
So speke yourself to him of this mattere;
For with oo word ye may his herte steere.   *910*

885 **Have . . . him** take and bear to him. The color blue symbolized constancy   890 **ye . . . shaken** a deprecatory idiom like mod. "big deal," "small potatoes," "peanuts." The idea probably was: shake hazelwood trees and what do you get? Hazelnuts   892 **dede** dead   897–98 **high . . . lite** (a) high spirit doesn't sorrow, or quit, for little things   900 **setten . . . mite** rate his sorrow at a mite   901 **feffe . . . white** bestow on him a few choice words   904 **This** this man   905 **wreke** vanquish

"Now have I told what peril he is inne,
And his ·coming unwist is to every wight—
Ne, pardee, harm may there be none, ne sinne:
I will myself be with you all this night.
Ye know eek how it is your owne knight,   915
And that by right ye most upon him triste,
And I all prest° to fecch him when you liste."

This accident° so pitous was to heere—
And eek so like a sooth at *prime face*,°
And Troilus her knight to her so deere,   920
His privee coming and the siker place°—
That, though that she did him as then a grace,
Considered alle thinges as they stoode,
No wonder is,° sin she did all for goode.

Criseyde answered, "As wisly God at reste   925
My soule bring, as me is for him woe!°
And em, ywis, fain wold I doon the beste,
If that I hadde grace for to do so.
But whether that ye dwell° or for him go,
I am—till God me better minde sende—   930
At dulcarnon,° right at my wittes' ende."

Quod Pandarus: "Yea, neece, will ye heere?
Dulcarnon called is 'fleming of wrecches.'°
It seemeth hard, for wrecches will not leere
For verray slouth or other willful tecches°—   935
This said by hem that been not worth two fecches.°
But *ye* been wise, and that we han on honde
Nis neither hard ne skilful° to withstonde."

"Then em," quod she, "doth hereof as you list;
But ere he come I will first up arise,   940

917 **prest** ready   918 **accident** turn of events   919 **sooth . . . face**
the truth on its face   921 **His . . . place** his secret coming (to
her bedchamber) and the safe place   922–24 **though . . . is** the
fact that she took pity on him . . . is no wonder   926 **for . . . woe**
woeful for him   929 **dwell** stay here   931 **At dulcarnon** in a
quandary   933 **fleming . . . wrecches** "flight of wretches"—the
name of a difficult proposition in Euclidean geometry (L. *fuga
miserorum*), the downfall of less gifted students (*wrecches*)
935 **tecches** shortcomings   936 **fecches** beans   938 **skilful** reason-

And for the love of God, sin all my trist
Is on you two, and ye been bothe wise,
So worketh now in so discreet a wise,
That I honour may have, and he plesaunce,
For I am here all in your governaunce."   945

"That is well said," quod he, "my neece deere!
Ther good thrift° on that wise gentil herte!
But lieth still and taketh° him right here:
It needeth not no ferther for him sterte.°
And eech of you eese other's sorrows smerte,   950
For love of God; and Venus, I thee herye,°
For soon hope I we shall been alle merrye!"

This Troilus full soon on knees him sette
Full soberly, right by her bedde's heed;
And in his beste wise his lady grette.°   955
But, Lord, so she wex suddenliche red!
Ne though men sholde smiten off her heed,
She coude not a word aright out bringe
So suddenly, for his sudden cominge.

But Pandarus, that so well coude feele°   960
In everything, to play anon began,
And saide, "Neece, see how this lord can kneele!
Now for your trouthe, see this gentil man."
And with that word he for a quishen° ran,
And saide, "Kneeleth now while that you leste,   965
Ther God your hertes bringe soon at reste."

Can I not sayn (for she bade him not rise)
If sorrow it put out of her remembraunce,
Or elles that she took it in the wise
Of duetee, as for his observaunce.°   970
But well find I she did him this plesaunce:
That she him kissed, although she sighed sore,
And bade him sit adown withouten more.

able 947 **Ther . . . thrift** may there be prosperity 948 **taketh**
receive 949 **sterte** move (because Troilus is already there, as we
see in line 953. We may infer that he has heard Pandarus's lie and
her reaction) 951 **herye** praise 955 **grette** greeted 960 **feele** un-
derstand 964 **quishen** cushion 969–70 **she . . . observaunce** she
understood it (his kneeling) as a duty, as his gesture of courtesy

Quod Pandarus: "Now will ye well beginne.
Now doth him sitte, goode neece deere,   975
Upon your bedde's side all there withinne,°
That eech of you the bet may other heere."
And with that word he drew him to the fere,°
And took a light, and foond his countenaunce
As for to° look upon an old romaunce.   980

Criseyde, that was Troilus' lady right,
And cleer stood on a ground of sikernesse,°
Al thoughte she her servant and her knight
Ne shold, of right, noon untrouth in her guesse,
Yet natheless, considered° his distresse,   985
And that love is in cause of swich follye,
Thus to him spake she of his jelousye:

"Lo, herte mine, as wold the excellence
Of love, agains the which that° no man may—
Ne ought eek—goodly make resistence;   990
And eek because I felte well and say°
Your greete trouth and service every day,
And that your herte all mine was, sooth to sayne,
This drove me for to rew upon your paine.

"And your goodness have I found alway yet,°   995
Of which my deere herte and all my knight
I thank it you, as far as I have wit—
Al can I not as much as it were right;
And I, emforth my konning and my might,°
Have and ay shall, how sore that me smerte,   1000
Been to you trew and hool with all mine herte.

"And dreedeless, that shall be found at preve.
But, herte mine, what all this is to sayne°

976 **withinne** i.e., within the bed curtains. In the interests of pri-
vacy, medieval beds were furnished with curtains all around   978
fere fireplace   979–80 **took . . . to** brought a candle, and assumed
an attitude as if he would   982 **And . . . sikernesse** who clearly
stood on secure ground (i.e., she knew she was faithful to Troilus)
985 **considered** considering   988–89 **as . . . that** as the excellence
of love requires, against which   991 **felte . . . say** sensed well
enough and saw   995 **found . . . yet** always experienced   999 **em-
forth . . . might** to the limit of my understanding and ability
1003 **to sayne** means

Shall well be told, so that ye nought you greve,
Though I to you right on yourself complaine. 1005
For therewith meen I finally the paine
That halt° your herte and mine in hevinesse
Fully to sleen, and every wrong redresse.

"My goode mine, noot I forwhy, ne how,
That jelousy, alas! that wicked wivere,° 1010
Thus causeless is croppen° into you,
The harm of which I wolde fain delivere.°
Alas, that he all hool, or of him slivere,°
Shold han his refut° in so digne a place,
Ther Jove him soon out of your herte arace!° 1015

"But O, thou Jove, O auctor of nature,
Is this an honour to thy deitee,
That folk unguiltif° sufferen hir injure,
And who that guiltif is, all quit goeth he?°
O, were it leful° for to plain on thee, 1020
That undeserved sufferest jelousye,°
Of *that* I wold upon thee plain and crye.

"Eek all my woe is this—that folk now usen°
To sayn right thus: 'Yea, jelousy is love,'
And wold a bushel venim all excusen, 1025
For that oo grain of love is on it shove.°
But that wot highe God that sit above,
If it be liker° love or hate or grame°—
And after that it oughte bere his° name.

"But certain is, some manner jelousye 1030
Is excusable more than some, ywis—

1007 **halt** holds   1010 **wivere** viper   1011 **is croppen** has crept
1012 **The . . . delivere** from the danger of which I would gladly
deliver you   1013 **he . . . slivere** it (the viper jealousy), wholly or
a piece of it   1014 **refut** refuge   1015 **arace** pluck   1018 **unguiltif**
guiltless   1019 **all . . . he** he goes scot-free   1020 **leful** lawful
1021 **That . . . jelousye** who permit undeserved jealousy   1023 **usen**
are accustomed   1025–26 **And . . . shove** and (folk) would entirely
overlook a bushel of venom because a single grain of love were
thrown upon it   1028 **If . . . liker** if it (jealousy) be more like
1028 **grame** wrath   1029 **his** its

As when cause is, and some swich fantasye
With pietee so well repressed is
That it unnethe doth or saith amiss,
But goodly drinketh up all his distresse;°   *1035*
And that excuse I for the gentilesse.

"And some° so full of fury is and despit
That it surmounteth his repressioun.°
But, herte mine, ye be not in that plit—
That thank I God; for which your passioun,°   *1040*
I will nought call it but illusioun
Of habundance of love and bisy cure,°
That doth your herte this diseese endure—

"Of which I am right sorry but nought wroth.
But for my devoir° and your herte's reste,   *1045*
Whereso you list, by ordeel or by ooth,
By sort,° or in what wise so you leste,
For love of God, let preve it° for the beste;
And if that I be guiltif, do me deye.
Alas, what might I more doon or saye?"   *1050*

With that a fewe brighte teeres newe
Out of her eyen fell, and thus she saide:
"Now God, thou wost, in thought ne deed, untrewe
To Troilus was never yet Criseyde."
With that her heed down in the bed she laide,   *1055*
And with the sheet it wreigh,° and sighed sore,
And held her peece—not oo word spake she more.

But now help God to quenchen all this sorrwe!
So hope I that he shall, for he best may.
For I have seen of a full misty morrwe   *1060*
Followen full oft a merry summer's day;

1032–35 As . . . distresse as when there is cause, and (when) some
fantastic idea of this kind is with pity so well restrained that it
hardly does or says anything amiss, but patiently drinks up its
distress (i.e., suffers without complaint)   1037 some i.e., some kind
of jealousy   1038 surmounteth . . . repressioun surpasses restraint
1040 passioun suffering (because of jealousy)   1042 bisy cure anx-
ious concern   1045 devoir duty   1047 sort divination   1048 let . . .
it put (my fidelity) to the test   1056 wreigh covered

And after winter followeth greene May.
Men seen alday, and reeden eek in stories,
That after sharpe shoures° been victories.

This Troilus, when he her wordes herde,   *1065*
Have ye no care, him liste not to sleepe!
For it thought him no strokes of a yerde°
To heer or seen Criseyde, his lady, weepe:
But well he felt about his herte creepe,
For every teer which that Criseyde asterte,°   *1070*
The cramp of deeth, to strain° him by the herte.

And in his mind he gan the time accurse
That he came there, and that that° he was born.
For now is wicke turned into° worse,
And all that labour he hath done beforn,   *1075*
He wend it lost. He thought he nas but lorn.°
"O Pandarus," thought he, "alas, thy wile°
Serveth of nought,° so wailaway the while!"

And therewithal he heng° adown the heed,
And fell on knees, and sorrowfully he sighte.   *1080*
What might he sayn? He felt he nas but deed,
For wroth was she that shold his sorrows lighte.
But natheless, when that he speken mighte,
Then said he thus: "God wot that of this game,
When all is wist, then am I not to blame."°   *1085*

Therewith the sorrow so his herte shette°
That from his eyen fell there not a teere,
And every spirit his vigour in-knette,°

1064 **shoures** battles   1067 **no . . . yerde** no (mere) strokes of a rod (i.e., it was much more painful)   1070 **asterte** started from   1071 **strain** grab   1073 **that that** the fact that   1074 **wicke . . . into** a wrong thing made   1076 **lorn** utterly lost (cf. "lovelorn," "forlorn," etc.)   1077 **wile** trick   1078 **Serveth . . . nought** accomplishes nothing   1079 **heng** hung   1085 **am . . . blame** The implication is that Pandarus is to blame (for the lie about Horaste). The reader must decide for himself whether Troilus shares the blame by allowing it   1086 **shette** closed up   1088 **every . . . in-knette** each of the three bodily spirits contracted or held in (*in-knette*) its power (*vigour*), with the result that he faints (line 1092). Earlier (I.306–07), Troilus felt faint because of failure of the "vital spirit" or "spirit of the heart," which controls pulse and breath. Now the "natural

So they astoned° or oppressed° were.
The feeling of his sorrow, or of his feere,   *1090*
Or of aught elles, fled were out of towne°—
And down he fell all suddenly a-swoune.

This was no litel sorrow for to see.
But all was hust,° and Pandar up as faste:
"O neece, peece, or we be lost!" quod he.   *1095*
"Beeth not aghast." But certain, at the laste,
For this or that he into bed him caste,
And said, "O theef, is this a manne's herte?"
And off he rent all to his bare sherte,°

And saide, "Neece, but ye help us now,   *1100*
Alas, your owne Troilus is lorn!"
"Ywis, so wold I, and I wiste how,
Full fain," quod she—"alas, that I was born."
"Yea, neece, will ye pullen out the thorn°
That sticketh in his herte?" quod Pandare.   *1105*
"Say 'All foryive,'° and stinte all this fare."

"Yea, that to me," quod she, "full lever were
Than all the good the sun aboute goeth"°—
And therewithal she swore him in his eere,
"Ywis, my deere herte, I am not wroth: *1110*
Have here my trouth and many another ooth.
Now speke to me, for it am I, Criseyde!"
But all for nought; yet might he not abraide.°

Therewith his pous and paumes° of his hondes
They gan to frote,° and wet his temples twaine;   *1115*
And to deliveren him fro bitter bondes

---

spirit" (liver) and "animal spirit" (brain) also contract. The passage reflects medieval medical theories. Evidently what happens inside Troilus is that a powerful emotion in his heart blocks the flow of the spirits from the liver to the brain. Hence his tears cannot flow (1087), he cannot feel emotion (1090–91), and ultimately cannot sustain consciousness 1089 **astoned** stunned 1089 **oppressed** assaulted 1091 **out . . . towne** away 1094 **hust** hushed 1099 **sherte** shirt (worn next to the skin) 1104 **thorn** cf. II.1272 1106 **All foryive** all is forgiven 1108 **good . . . goeth** property which the sun encircles (i.e., the whole world) 1113 **abraide** revive 1114 **pous . . . paumes** pulse and palms 1115 **frote** rub

She oft him kissed. And, shortly for to sayne,
Him to revoken° she did all her paine.
And at the last he gan his breeth to drawe,
And of his swough° soon after that adawe,°   *1120*

And gan bet mind and reeson to him take.°
But wonder sore he was abaist,° ywis,
And with a sigh, when he gan bet awake,
He said, "O mercy God, what thing is this?"
"Why do ye with yourselven thus amiss?"   *1125*
Quod tho Criseyde. "Is this a manne's game?°
What—Troilus, will ye do thus, for shame?"

And therewithal her arm over him she laide,
And all foryaf, and ofte time him keste.
He thanked her, and to her spake, and saide   *1130*
As fell to purpose for° his herte's reste;
And she to that answered him as her leste,
And with her goodly wordes him disporte
She gan, and oft his sorrows to comforte.

Quod Pandarus: "For aught I can espyen,°   *1135*
This light nor I ne serven here of nought:
Light is not good for sicke folkes' eyen.
But for the love of God, sin ye been brought
In this good plight, let now noon hevy° thought
Been hanging in the hertes of you twaye"—   *1140*
And bare the candle to the chimeneye.°

Soon after this, though it no neede were,
When she swich oothes as her list devise
Had of him take, her thoughte tho no feere,
Ne cause eek none, to bid him thennes rise.°   *1145*
Yet lesse thing than oothes may suffise

1118 revoken revive **1120 of . . . swough** out of his swoon **1120
adawe** awake **1121 to . . . take** get ahold of his **1122 abaist**
abashed **1126 manne's game** i.e., way of carrying on appropriate
for adults **1131 As . . . for** what best suited **1135 espyen** see
1139 hevy sad **1141 chimeneye** chimney-side **1143-45 When . . .
rise** when she had extracted from him such oaths as it pleased her
to think of, then she thought there was nothing to fear, nor reason
to ask him to get up

In many a cas, for every wight (I guesse)
That loveth well meeneth but gentilesse.°

But in effect she wolde wite° anon
Of what man, and eek where, and also why   *1150*
He jelous was, sin there was cause noon;
And eek the signe that he took it by,
She bade him that to tell her bisily,°
Or elles, certain, she bare him on honde
That this was done of malice, her to fonde.°   *1155*

Withouten more, shortly for to sayne,
He must obey unto his lady heste.°
And for the lesse harm, he muste feigne:°
He said her when she was at swich a feste,
She might on him han looked at the leeste—   *1160*
Noot I not what, al deer enough a rishe°—
As he that needes must a cause fishe.°

And she answered, "Sweet, al were it so,
What harm was that, sin I noon evil° meene?
For by that God that wrought us bothe two,   *1165*
In alle thing is mine intente cleene.
Swich arguments ne been not worth a beene.
Will ye the childish jelous counterfete?
Now were it worthy that ye were y-bete."°

Tho Troilus gan sorrowfully to sighe.   *1170*
Lest she be wroth, him thought his herte deide,
And said, "Alas, upon my sorrows sicke
Have mercy, sweete herte mine, Criseyde.
And if that in tho wordes that I saide

1148 **meeneth . . . gentilesse** intends only honorable conduct   1149
wite to know   1152–53 **signe . . . bisily** she asked him to tell her
promptly the evidence he understood to confirm it (her infidelity)
1154–55 **she . . . fonde** she would make the accusation against him
that this was done out of malice, to test her   1157 **lady heste** lady's
behest   1158 **And . . . feigne** and as the lesser of two evils he must
keep up the pretense (i.e., he must continue the lie about Horaste)
1161 **deer . . . rishe** worth no more than a straw   1162 **a . . . fishe**
fish up a reason. Troilus flounders around for a credible story
1164 **evil** harm   1169 **y-bete** beaten

Be any wrong, I will no more trespasse.   *1175*
Doth what you list, I am all in your grace."

And she answered, "Of guilt misericorde.°
That is to sayn, that I foryive all this,
And evermore on this night you recorde;°
And beeth well ware ye do no more amiss."   *1180*
"Nay, deere herte mine," quod he, "ywis."
"And now," quod she, "that I have done you smerte,
Foryive it me, mine owne sweete herte."

This Troilus, with bliss of that surprised,
Put all in Godde's hand, as he that mente   *1185*
Nothing but well. And suddenly avised,°
He her in armes faste to him hente.
And Pandarus, with a full good intente,
Laid him to sleep, and said, "If ye be wise,
Swouneth not now, lest more folk arise."   *1190*

What might or may the sely larke saye
When that the sparhawk hath it in his foot?
I can no more; but of these ilke twaye,
To whom this tale sucre be or soot,
Though that I tarry a yeer, sometime I mot   *1195*
After mine auctor tellen° hir gladnesse,
As well as I have told hir hevinesse.

Criseyde, which that felt her thus y-take,°
As writen clerkes in hir bookes olde,
Right as an aspe's leef° she gan to quake,   *1200*
When she him felt her in his armes folde.
But Troilus, all hool° of cares colde,
Gan thanken tho the blissful goddes sevene.°
Thus sundry paines bringen folk in hevene.

1177 **Of . . . misericorde** mercy for guilt. "For a crime, there is
mercy (to be had)" (Skeat) 1179 **recorde** remember 1186 **sud-
denly avised** quickly getting possession (of himself) 1193-96 **of
. . . tellen** of these two (lovers)—to whomsoever this tale be sweet
or bitter, though I waste a year, I must take some time to tell
(them), according to my author 1198 **y-take** seized 1200 **aspe's
leef** aspen leaf 1202 **hool** cured 1203 **goddes sevene** planetary
gods. Troilus had prayed to the gods before entering Criseyde's
bedchamber (III.712–35); now he thanks them for his present
success

This Troilus in armes gan her straine,°   1205
And said, "O sweet, as ever mot I goon,
Now be ye caught, now is there but we twaine.
Now yeeldeth you, for other boot° is noon."
To that Criseyde answered thus anon:
"N' had I ere now, my sweete herte deere,   1210
Been yold, ywis, I were now not here."°

O, sooth is said that heeled for to be°
As of a fever or other greet sicknesse,
Men muste drink, as men may ofte see,
Full bitter drink; and for to han gladnesse   1215
Men drinken ofte pain and greet distresse.
I meen it here as for this aventure
That through a pain hath founden all his cure.

And now sweetnesse seemeth more sweete
That bitternesse was assayed° beforn;   1220
For out of woe in blisse now they flete.°
Noon swich they felten sin they were born!
Now is this bet than bothe two be lorn!
For love of God, take every woman heede
To worken° thus, if it cometh to the neede!   1225

Criseyde, all quit° from every dreed and teene,°
As she that juste cause had him to triste,
Made him swich feste it joye was to seene,
When she his trouth and cleen intente wiste.
And as about a tree, with many a twiste,   1230
Betrent and writhe° the sweete woodebinde,
Gan eech of hem in armes other winde.°

1205 **straine** hold 1208 **boot** remedy 1210–11 **N'had . . . here** if
I hadn't before now . . . yielded myself, certainly, I would not be
here now 1212 **O . . . be** O, truth is spoken that in order to be
healed . . . Chaucer here interrupts with a few philosophical ob-
servations 1218 **hath . . . cure** has found its entire cure 1220
assayed experienced 1221 **flete** float. At the beginning of Book II,
Chaucer compared Troilus's love-torn situation to a tempestuous
"sea" (II.5). On the way to Criseyde's bedchamber, Troilus called
his movement a "voyage" (III.732). The sea of love, usually tempest-
tossed, has now become serenè as the lovers "float" on its waves
1225 **worken** act 1226 **quit** freed 1226 **teene** grief 1231 **Betrent**
. . . writhe winds round and folds 1232 **other winde** twine around
the other

And as the newe abaised° nightingale,
That stinteth first when she beginneth to singe,
When that she heereth any herde tale,°   *1235*
Or in the hedges any wight stirringe,
And after siker° doth her voice out-ringe—
Right so Criseyde, when her dreede stente,
Opened her herte and told him her intente.

And right as he that seeth his deeth y-shapen,   *1240*
And dien mot in aught that he may guesse,°
And suddenly rescous doth him° escapen,
And from his deeth is brought in sikernesse—
For all this world, in swich present gladnesse
Was Troilus, and hath his lady sweete.   *1245*
With worse hap° God let us never meete!

Her armes small, her straighte back and softe,
Her sides longe, fleshly, smooth, and white,
He gan to stroke, and good thrift bade full ofte
Her snowish throat,° her breestes round and lite.   *1250*
Thus in this hevene he gan him to delite,
And therewithal a thousand times her kiste,
That what to doon for joy unneth he wiste.

Then said he thus: "O Love, O Charitee,
Thy moder eek, Cytherea° the sweete,   *1255*
After thyself next heried° be she—
Venus meen I, the well-willy° planete.
And next that, Hymeneus,° I thee greete.
For never man was to you goddes holde°
As I, which ye han brought fro cares colde.   *1260*

"Benigne Love, thou holy bond of thinges,
Whoso will grace and list thee not honouren,
Lo, his desire will flee° withouten winges.

1233 **newe abaised** recently startled   1235 **herde tale** herdsman
speak   1237 **siker** safely   1241 **dien . . . guesse** must die for aught
that he can tell   1242 **rescous . . . him** rescue enables him to   1246
hap luck   1249–50 **good . . . throot** doing it right recommended
(bade) very often (that he stroke) her snowy throat   1255 **Cytherea**
Venus   1256 **heried** praised   1257 **well-willy** beneficent   1258 **next
. . . Hymeneus** next in order, Hymen (god of marriages, who would
naturally follow the gods of love)   1259 **holde** beholden   1263 **flee**

For noldest thou of bountee hem succouren
That serven best and most alway labouren,   1265
Yet were all lost, that dare I well sayn, certes,
But if thy grace passed our desertes.°

"And for thou me—that leest coude deserve
Of hem that numbered been unto thy grace—
Hast holpen, ther I likely was to sterve,°   1270
And me bestowed in so high a place
That thilke boundes may no blisse passe,°
I can no more: but laud° and reverence
Be to thy bountee and thine excellence."

And therewithal Criseyde anon he kiste,   1275
Of which, certain, she felte no disease.
And thus said he: "Now wolde God I wiste,
Mine herte sweet, how I you mighte pleese.
What man," quod he, "was ever thus at eese
As I, on which the fairest and the beste   1280
That ever I saw deigneth her herte reste?°

"Here may men seen that mercy passeth right:°
Th'experience of that is felt in me,
That am unworthy to so sweet a wight.
But, herte mine, of your benignitee,   1285
So thinketh, though that I unworthy be,
Yet mot I need amenden° in some wise
Right through the virtue of your high service.

"And for the love of God, my lady deere,
Sin God hath wrought me for I shall you serve,   1290

fly 1264–67 For . . . desertes for if you didn't wish, out of
magnanimity (*bountee*), to aid those who serve you best and who
most labor (for you), all would be lost, I dare say, for certain,
unless your grace surpassed our merit. (Troilus's argument here
parallels the Christian doctrine of grace: man by himself cannot
hope to achieve true love or lasting happiness without divine inter-
vention. Chaucer imitates this passage from Dante's address to the
Virgin Mary in *Paradiso*) 1268–70 And . . . sterve and because
you . . . have helped me, when I was likely to die 1272 That
. . . passe whose boundaries no bliss may surpass 1273 laud
praise 1281 deigneth . . . reste condescends to place her heart
1282 mercy . . . right mercy transcends justice 1287 mot . . .
amenden I must needs improve

As thus I meen, he will ye be my steere,°
To do me live—if that you list—or sterve,
So teecheth me how that I may deserve
Your thank, so that I through mine ignoraunce
Ne do nothing that you be displesaunce.   *1295*

"For certes, freshe womanliche wif,°
This dare I say: that trouth and diligence,
That shall ye finden in me all my lif.
N'I will not, certain, breeken your defence.°
And if I do, present or in absence,   *1300*
For love of God, let slee me with the deede,°
If that it like unto your womanheede."

"Ywis," quod she, "mine owne herte's lust,°
My ground of eese, and all mine herte deere,
Gramercy, for on that is all my trust.   *1305*
But let us fall away fro this mattere,
For it sufficeth this that said is here.
And at oo word, withouten repentaunce,
Welcome my knight, my peece, my suffisaunce!"

Of hir delit or joyes oon the leeste°   *1310*
Were impossible to my wit to saye,
But judgeth, ye that han been at the feste
Of swich gladness, if that hem liste playe.
I can no more but thus: these ilke twaye
That night, betwixen dreed and sikernesse,   *1315*
Felten in love the greete worthinesse.

O blissful night, of hem so long y-sought,
How blithe unto hem bothe two thou were!
Why n'ad *I* swich one° with *my* soul y-bought—
Yea, or the leeste joye that was there?   *1320*
Away, thou foule Daunger and thou Feere,
And let hem in this hevene blisse dwelle,
That is so high that all ne can I telle.

But sooth is, though I cannot tellen all,
As can mine auctor of his excellence,   *1325*

1291 **steere** rudder (guide)   1296 **wif** woman   1299 **defence** prohibition (i.e., whatever you forbid)   1301 **let . . . deede** have me slain right then   1303 **lust** desire   1310 **joyes . . . leeste** the least one of their joys   1319 **swich one** i.e., such a night

Yet have I said, and God to-forn, and shall
In everything all hoolly his sentence;°
And if that I, at Love's reverence,°
Have any word in eched for the beste,°
Doth therewithal right as yourselven leste.   *1330*

For mine wordes, here and every part,
I speke hem all under correccioun
Of you, that feeling han in Love's art,
And put it all in your discrecioun
To increese or maken diminucioun   *1335*
Of my langage, and that I you beseeche.
But now to purpose of my rather speeche.°

These ilke two, that been in armes laft,°
So looth to hem asunder goon it were°
That eech from other wende been beraft,°   *1340*
Or elles, lo, this was hir moste° feere:
That all this thing but nice dreemes were.°
For which full oft eech of hem said, "O sweete,
Clip ich you thus, or elles I it mete?"°

And Lord, so he gan goodly on her see,   *1345*
That never his look ne blente° from her face,
And said, "O deere herte, may it be
That it be sooth that ye been in this place?"
"Yea, herte mine, God thank I of his grace,"
Quod tho Criseyde, and therewithal him kiste,   *1350*
That where his spirit was, for joy he niste.

This Troilus full oft her eyen two
Gan for to kiss, and said, "O eyen cleere,
It weren ye that wroughte me swich woe,
Ye humble nettes° of my lady deere.   *1355*

1327 **all . . . sentence** wholly what he meant 1328 **at . . . reverence**
out of reverence for Love 1329 **in . . . beste** added in betterment
of the work 1337 **But . . . speeche** but now to the purpose of my
earlier subject 1338 **laft** left 1339 **So . . . were** they were so
loath to part 1340 **eech . . . beraft** each one away from the other
thought himself bereft 1341 **moste** greatest 1342 **but . . . were**
were only foolish dreams 1344 **Clip . . . mete?** do I embrace you
thus, or do I dream it? 1346 **ne blente** turned away 1355 **humble
nettes** modest nets (with which he is caught)

Though there be mercy written in your cheere,
God wot the text° full hard is, sooth, to finde.
How coude ye withouten bond me binde?"

Therewith he gan her fast in armes take,
And well an hundred times gan he sike— *1360*
Not swiche sorrowful sighes as men make
For woe₂ or elles when that folk been sicke,
But eesy sighes swich as been to like,°
That shewed his affeccioun withinne—
Of swiche sighes coude he not blinne.° *1365*

Soon after this they spake of sundry thinges
As fell to purpose° of this aventure,
And playing interchangeden hir ringes,
Of which I cannot tellen no scripture.°
But well I wot a brooch, gold and azure, *1370*
In which a ruby set was like an herte,°
Criseyde him yaf, and stak it on his sherte.°

Lord, trowe ye a coveitous° or a wrecche,
That blameth love and halt of it despit,°
That of tho pens that he can mokre and crecche° *1375*
Was ever yet y-yiven° him swich delit
As is in love, in oo point in some plit?°
Nay, douteless, for also God me save,
So parfit joye may no niggard have.

They will sayn "Yis." But Lord, so that° they lie— *1380*
Tho bisy wrecches, full of woe and dreede.
They callen love a woodness or follye,
But it shall fall° hem as I shall you reede:
They shall forgoon the white and eek the rede,°

1357 **text** i.e., the meaning   1363 **to like** pleasing   1365 **blinne** cease   1367 **fell . . . purpose** were appropriate   1369 **scripture** inscriptions. Medieval rings were often inscribed with moral or amorous mottoes   1371 **like . . . herte** in the shape of a heart   1372 **stak . . . sherte** pinned it on his shirt   1373 **coveitous** covetous person; the small-mindedness of the miser is here compared with the magnanimity of the person in love   1374 **halt . . . despit** holds it in contempt   1375 **of . . . crecche** from those pennies which he can hoard up and grab   1376 **y-yiven** given   1377 **in . . . plit** to one instance in any situation   1380 **so that** how   1383 **fall** befall   1384 **the . . . rede** white and red wine

And live in woe, ther God yive hem mischaunce!   *1385*
And every lover in his trouth avaunce.°

As wolde God tho wrecches that despise
Service of Love had eeres also longe
As hadde Mida,° full of coveitise,
And thereto drunken had as hot and stronge   *1390*
As Crassus° did for his affectes wronge,
To teechen hem that they been in the vice,°
And lovers not, although they hold hem nice.°

These ilke two of whom that I you saye,
When that hir hertes well assured were,   *1395*
Tho gonne they to speken and to playe,
And eek rehersen how and when and where
They knew hem first, and every woe or feere
That passed was. But all swich hevinesse—
I thank it God—was turned to gladnesse.   *1400*

And evermo when that hem fell to speke
Of anything of swich a time agon,
With kissing all that tale sholde breke,°
And fallen in a newe joy anon,
And diden all hir might, sin they were oon,°   *1405*
For to recoveren bliss and been at eese,
And passed woe with joye counterpeise.°

Reeson will not° that I speke of sleep,
For it accordeth not to° my mattere;

1386 And . . . avaunce and further (by comparison) every love in
his fidelity   1389 Mida Midas, who had the golden touch but also
asses' ears   1391 Crassus When he was killed on the battlefield,
Crassus, a Roman general, had his mouth filled with molten gold
because of his surpassing greed (*affectes wronge*)   1392 they . . .
vice they (*wrecches*) are in the wrong   1393 they . . . nice they
(the wrecches) believe lovers to be foolish. Chaucer wishes those
who are greedy and despise love and its rites would receive instruc-
tive punishment, so that they might learn the errors of their ways
and that lovers might be vindicated. Chaucer takes this section
about misers and greed from Boccaccio, whose father was a money-
lender   1403 breke break off   1405 oon at one   1407 passed . . .
counterpeise counterbalance past woe with joy   1408 Reeson . . .
not reason doesn't wish (i.e., it would be out of place here)
1409 accordeth . . . to doesn't suit

God wot, they took of that full litel keep.　　　　*1410*
But lest this night that was to hem so deere
Ne shold in vain escape in no mannere,
It was beset in joy and bisinesse
Of all that souneth into° gentilesse.

But when the cock, commune astrologer,°　　　　*1415*
Gan on his breest to beet and after crowe;
And Lucifer, the daye's messager,
Gan for to rise and out her° beemes throwe;
And eestward rose, to him that coud it knowe,
Fortuna Major°—that anon Criseyde,　　　　*1420*
With herte sore to Troilus thus saide:

"Mine herte's life, my trust, all my plesaunce,
That I was born, alas! What me is woe,
That day of us mot make disseveraunce;°
For time it is to rise and hennes go,　　　　*1425*
Or elles I am lost for evermo.
O night, alas, why nilt thou over us hove°
As long as when Almena° lay by Jove?

"O blacke night, as folk in bookes reede—
That shapen art by God this world to hide　　　　*1430*
At certain times with thy darke weede,°
That under that men might in rest abide—
Well oughten beestes plain and folk thee chide,
That ther-as day with labour wold us breste,
That thou thus fleest and deignest us not reste.°　　　　*1435*

1414 **souneth into** tends to　1415 **commune astrologer** common astrologer (because he announces the dawn to everybody)　1418 **her** Lucifer ("light-bringer") is the morning star, the planet Venus (hence *her*)　1420 **Fortuna Major** the planet Jupiter. Venus, also a beneficent planet—especially to lovers—was known as *Fortuna Minor*　1423–24 **What . . . disseveraunce** how woeful am I that day must cause us to part. Criseyde's song (lines 1422–42) is an *aubade*, a conventional lyric form concerning lovers' parting at dawn. Criseyde emphasizes the joys of night while Troilus, in his answering song (lines 1450–70), focuses on the unwelcome day　1427 **over . . . hove** linger over us　1428 **Almena** To prolong the pleasure of his lovemaking with Alcmena, Jove lengthened the duration of that night　1431 **weede** cloak　1434–35 **That . . . reste** that whereas day seeks to break our backs with labor, you (night) flee and grant us no respite

"Thou dost, alas, too shortly thine office,°
Thou rakel night, ther God, Maker of Kinde,
Thee for thine haste and thine unkinde vice
So fast ay to our hemisphere binde
That nevermore under the ground thou winde:°   *1440*
For now, for thou so hiest° out of Troye,
Have I forgone thus hastily my joye."

This Troilus—that with tho wordes felte,
As thought him tho, for pietous° distresse,
The bloody teeres from his herte melte,   *1445*
As he that never yet swich hevinesse
Assayed had out of so greet gladnesse°—
Gan therewithal Criseyde his lady deere
In armes strain, and said in this mannere:

"O cruel day, accusor° of the joye   *1450*
That night and love han stole and fast y-wryen,°
Accursed be thy coming into Troye,
For every bore° hath one of thy bright eyen.
Envious day, what list thee so to spyen?
What hast thou lost? Why seekest thou this place?   *1455*
Ther God thy light so quenche° for his grace!

"Alas, what have these lovers thee aguilt,°
Despitous° day? Thine be the pain of helle,
For many a lover hast thou slain, and wilt.
Thy pouring in will nowhere let hem dwelle.   *1460*
What proffrest thou thy light here for to selle?°
Go sell it hem that smalle seeles grave.°
We will thee nought. Us needeth no day have."

1436 **office** task   1437–40 **Thou . . . winde** you rash night, may
God, Creator of Nature, because of your haste and unnatural wrong-
doing, bind you so fast to our hemisphere that you shall nevermore
turn underground. (That is, may God forbid the night from leaving
ever again)   1441 **for . . . hiest** because you so speed   1444 **pietous**
piteous   1446–47 **swich . . . gladnesse** had experienced such sad-
ness (grow) out of such great happiness   1450 **accusor** betrayer
1451 **y-wryen** covered up   1453 **bore** chink   1456 **quench** extin-
guish   1457 **thee aguilt** wronged you   1458 **Despitous** spiteful
1461 **What . . . selle?** why do you offer your light for sale here?
1462 **hem . . . grave** to those who engrave small seals (and so have
need of strong light to see what they are doing)

And eek the sunne, Titan, gan he chide,
And said, "O fool, well may men thee despise, *1465*
That hast the Dawing° all night be thy side,
And sufferest her so soon up fro thee rise
For to diseese lovers in this wise.
What, hold° your bed there, thou, and eek thy Morrwe!
I bidde God, so yive you bothe sorrwe." *1470*

Therewith full sore he sighed, and thus he saide:
"My lady right, and of my wele or woe
The well and root, O goodly mine Criseyde,
And shall I rise, alas, and shall I go?
Now feel I that mine herte mot a-two,° *1475*
For how shold I my life an houre save,
Sin that with you is all the life ich have?

"What shall I doon? For certes, I noot how,
Ne when, alas, I shall the time see
That in this plight I may been eft with you. *1480*
And of my life, God wot, how that shall be,
Sin that desire right now so biteth me
That I am deed anon but I returne.
How shold I long, alas, fro you sojourne?

"But natheless, mine owne lady bright, *1485*
Yet were it so that I wist outrely
That I, your humble servant and your knight,
Were in your herte y-set so fermely
As ye in mine—the which thing, trewely,
Me lever were than these worldes twaine°— *1490*
Yet shold I bet enduren all my paine."

To that Criseyde answered right anon,
And with a sigh she said, "O herte deere,
The game, ywis, so ferforth now is gon°
That first shall Phebus° fallen fro his sphere, *1495*
And everich eegle been the dove's fere,°

1466 **the Dawing** Aurora. Chaucer confuses Titan with Tithonus, husband of the Dawn 1469 **hold** stay in (addressed to Titan) 1475 **mot a-two** must (break) in two 1490 **than . . . twaine** than two worlds like this 1494 **so . . . gon** has now gone so far 1495 **Phebus** the sun 1496 **fere** mate

And every rock out of his place sterte,°
Ere Troilus out of Criseyde's herte.

"Ye been so deep inwith mine herte grave°
That, though I wold it turn out of my thought—   1500
As wisly verray God me soule save—
To dien in the pain° I coude nought;
And for the love of God that us hath wrought,
Let in your brain noon other fantasye°
So creepe that it cause me to die.   1505

"And that ye me wold han as fast in minde
As I have you, that wold I you beseeche.
And if I wiste soothly that to finde,°
God mighte not a point° my joyes eche;°
But herte mine, withouten more speeche,   1510
Beeth to me trew, or elles were it routhe,
For I am thine, by God and by my trouthe.

"Beeth glad forthy, and live in sikernesse.°
Thus said I never ere this,° ne shall to mo.
And if to you it were a greet gladnesse   1515
To turn again° soon after that ye go,
As fain wold I° as ye it were so,
As wisly God mine herte bring to reste"—
And him in armes took and ofte keste.

Agains his will, sith it mot needes be,   1520
This Troilus up rose and fast him cledde,°
And in his armes took his lady free
An hundred time, and on his way him spedde.
And with swich wordes as his herte bledde
He said, "Farewell, my deere herte sweete,   1525
Ther God us grante sound and soon to meete."°

1497 out . . . sterte leap out of its place 1499 grave engraved
1502 To . . . pain even if I were to die in torture 1504 fantasye
Troilus first came to her, Criseyde thinks, because of his jealousy
of Horaste. Criseyde hopes this past evening will dispel any such
"fantasy" hereafter 1508 wiste . . . finde could truly count on
that 1509 point bit 1509 eche increase 1513 sikernesse confi-
dence 1514 ere this Criseyde suggests that love was not involved
in her marriage, not an unusual circumstance in medieval marriages,
which were socio-economic affairs 1516 turn again return 1517
As . . . I I would be as glad 1521 cleede clad 1526 sound

To which no word for sorrow she answerde,
So sore gan his parting her distraine.°
And Troilus unto his palais ferde,
As woebegone as he was, sooth to sayne: *1530*
So hard him wrung of sharp desire the paine,
For to been eft ther he was in plesaunce,
That it may never out of his remembraunce.

Returned to his royal palais soone,
He soft into his bed gan for to slinke   *1535*
To sleepe long, as he was wont to doone.
But all for nought—he may well lie and winke,°
But sleep ne may there in his herte sinke,
Thinking how she, for whom desire him brende,
A thousandfold was worth more than he wende.   *1540*

And in his thought gan up and down to winde
Her wordes all, and every countenaunce,
And fermely impressen in his minde
The leeste point that to him was plesaunce;
And verrailich, of thilke remembraunce,   *1545*
Desire all new him brend, and lust to breede
Gan more than erst°—and yet took he noon heede.

Criseyde also, right in the same wise
Of Troilus, gan in her herte shette
His worthiness, his lust, his deedes wise,   *1550*
His gentilesse, and how she with him mette,
Thanking Love he so well her besette,°
Desiring eft to han her herte deere
In swich a plight she durste make him cheere.°

* * *

Pandar, oo morrow which that comen was   *1555*
Unto his neece, and gan her faire greete,
Said, "All this night so rained it, alas,

. . . **meete** to meet soon and sound (in health; cf. "safe and sound") 1528 **distraine** pain 1537 **winke** close his eyes 1546–47 **Desire . . . erst** desire burned him anew, and craving (or, lust) grew more than before. Medieval moralists warned that fleshly desires could never be satisfied; gratification was temporary and fed desire anew. Troilus experiences this heaping of fuel upon the flames and takes no heed 1552 **besette** assigned her a place 1554

That all my dreed is that ye, neece sweete,
Han litel leiser had to sleep and mete.°
All night," quod he, "hath rain so do me wake,°   1560
That some of us, I trow, our heedes ache."

And neer he came and said, "How stant it now
This merry morrow, neece? How can° ye fare?"
Criseyde answered, "Never the bet for *you*,
Fox that ye been, God yive your herte care!   1565
God help me so, ye caused all this fare,
Trow I," quod she, "for all your wordes white.
O, whoso seeth you knoweth you full lite."

With that she gan her face for to wrye°
With the sheet, and wex for shame all red.   1570
And Pandarus gan under for to prye,°
And saide, "Neece, if that I shall be deed,
Have here a sword and smiteth off mine heed!"
With that his arm all suddenly he thriste°   1575
Under her neck, and at the last her kiste.

I pass all that which chargeth not to saye.°
What! God foryaf His deeth,° and she also
Foryaf, and with her uncle gan to playe,
For other cause was there none but so.
But of this thing right to the effect to go: 1580
When time was, home to her house she wente—
And Pandarus hath fully his intente.

Now turne we again to Troilus,
That resteless full long a-bedde lay,
And prively sent after Pandarus   1585
To him to come in all the haste he may.
He came anon, not ones said he nay,
And Troilus full soberly he grette,
And down upon his bedde's side him sette.

In . . . cheere in such a situation that she dared make him happy
1559 **mete** dream   1560 **do . . . wake** kept me awake   1563 **can**
do   1569 **wrye** cover   1571 **prye** peek   1574 **thriste** thrust   1576
chargeth . . . saye is insignificant to tell   1577 **His deeth** i.e., those
who killed Christ. (The narrator reminds us that he, like his audi-
ence, lives in Christian times)

This Troilus, with all the affeccioun 1590
Of freende's love that herte may devise,
To Pandarus on knees fell adown,
And ere that he wold of° the place arise,
He gan him thanken in his beste wise
An hundred sithe,° and gan the time blesse 1595
That he was born to bring him fro distresse.

He said, "O freend, of freends the alderbeste
That ever was, the soothe for to telle,
Thou hast in hevene y-brought my soul at reste
Fro Phlegeton, the fiery flood° of helle— 1600
That though I might a thousand times selle,
Upon a day, my life in thy service,
It mighte not a mote in that suffise.

"The sunne, which that all the world may see,
Saw never yet (my life that dare I laye)° 1605
So inly fair and goodly as is she,
Whose I am all, and shall, till that I deye.
And that I thus am heres,° dare I saye,
That thanked be the highe worthinesse
Of Love, and eek thy kinde bisinesse. 1610

"Thus hast thou me no litel thing y-yive,
For which to thee obliged be for ay
My life. And why? For through thine help I live,
Or elles deed had I been many a day."
And with that word down in his bed he lay, 1615
And Pandarus full soberly him herde,
Till all was said, and then he him answerde:

"My deere freend, if I have done for thee
In any cas, God wot, it is me lief,
And am as glad as man may of it be, 1620
God help me so. But take now not agrief
That I shall sayn: be ware of this mischief,
That ther-as thou now brought art in thy blisse,
That thou thyself ne cause it not to misse.°

1593 **of** from   1595 **sithe** times   1600 **flood** river   1605 **laye** wager
1608 **heres** hers   1624 **misse** to go amiss

"For of Fortune's sharp adversitee   1625
The worste kind of infortune° is this:
A man to han been in prosperitee,
And it rememberen when it passed is.
Th'art wise enough, forthy do not amiss;
Be not too rakel, though thou sitte warme,   1630
For if thou be, certain, it will thee harme.

"Thou art at eese, and hold thee well thereinne.
For also sure as red is every fir,
As greet a craft is keepe well as winne.°
Bridle° alway well thy speech and thy desir,   '1635
For worldly joy halt° not but by a wir.°
That preveth well—it brest alday° so ofte—
Forthy need is to worken with it softe."°

Quod Troilus: "I hope, and God to-forn,
My deere freend, that I shall so me bere°   1640
That in my guilt° there shall nothing be lorn,
N'I nill not rakel as for to greeven here.°
It needeth not this matter ofte stere,°
For wistest thou mine herte well, Pandare,
God wot, of this thou woldest litel care."°   1645

Tho gan he tell him of his glade night,
And whereof first his herte dredde, and how,
And saide, "Freend, as I am trewe knight—
And by that faith I shall° to God and you—
I had it never half so hot as now!   1650
And ay the more that desire me biteth,
To love her best the more it me deliteth!

"I noot myself not wisly what it is,
But now I feel a newe qualitee,
Yea, all another than I did ere this."   1655
Pandar answered and saide thus—that "He
That ones may in hevene's blisse be,

1626 **infortune** misfortune   1634 **As . . . winne** it is as great an
art to keep (what you have) as to get it   1635 **Bridle** curb   1636
halt holds, hangs on   1636 **wir** wire   1637 **That . . . alday** that
is easily proved—it (the wire) breaks every day   1638 **softe** gently
1640 **me bere** conduct myself   1641 **in . . . guilt** through my fault
1642 **rakel . . . here** act rashly to distress her   1643 **stere** urge, stir
up   1645 **care** worry   1649 **shall** owe

He feeleth otherwayes, dare I laye,
Than thilke time he first herde of it saye."

This is oo word for all: that Troilus   *1660*
Was never full° to speke of this mattere,
And for to praisen unto Pandarus
The bountee of his righte lady deere,
And Pandarus to thank and maken cheere.
This tale ay was span-newe to beginne,°   *1665*
Till that the night departed hem a-twinne.°

Soon after this, for that Fortune it wolde,
Y-comen was the blissful time sweete
That Troilus was warned that he sholde,
Ther he was erst, Criseyde his lady meete.   *1670*
For which he felt his herte in joye fleete,°
And faithfully gan all the goddes herie—
And let see now if that he can be merrye!

And holden° was the form and all the wise
Of her coming, and eek of his also,   *1675*
As it was erst, which needeth not devise.
But plainly to the effect right for to go,
In joy and suretee Pandarus hem two
A-bedde brought, when that hem bothe leste.
And thus they been in quiet and in reste.   *1680*

Not needeth it to you, sin they been met,
To ask at me if that they blithe were;
For if it erst was well, tho was it bet
A thousandfold—this needeth not inquere.
Ago was every sorrow and every feere,   *1685*
And both, ywis, they had—and so they wende—
As muche joy as herte may comprehende.°

This is no litel thing of for to saye;
This passeth every wit for to devise,
For eech of hem gan other's lust obeye.   *1690*
Felicitee, which that these clerkes wise

1661 **full** satisfied   1665 **span-newe . . . beginne** started brand new
over   1666 **departed . . . a-twinne** separated them   1671 **fleete**
float   1674 **holden** preserved   1687 **comprehende** contain

Commenden so, ne may not here suffice:
This joye may not written be with inke.
This passeth all that herte may bethinke.

But cruel day—so wailaway the stounde!°—   *1695*
Gan for t'approch, as they by signes knewe,
For which hem thoughte feelen deethe's wounde.
So woe was hem that changen gan hir hewe,
And day they gonnen to despise all newe,
Calling it traitor, envious, and worse,   *1700*
And bitterly the daye's light they curse.

Quod Troilus: "Alas, now am I war°
That Pyrous and tho swifte steedes three,
Which that drawen forth the sunne's char,°
Han gone some bypath in despite of me.°   *1705*
That maketh it so soone day to be,
And for the sun him hasteth thus to rise,
Ne shall I never doon him sacrifice."

But needes day depart hem° muste soone,
And when hir speeche done was and hir cheere,   *1710*
They twine° anon, as they were wont to doone,
And setten time of meeting eft yfere.
And many a night they wrought in this mannere.
And thus Fortune a time led in joye
Criseyde and eek this kinge's son of Troye.   *1715*

In suffisance,° in bliss, and in singinges,
This Troilus gan all his life to leede:
He spendeth, jousteth, maketh festeyinges,°
He yiveth freely oft, and changeth weede,°
And held about him alway—out of dreede—   *1720*
A world of folk, as came him well of kinde,°
The freshest and the best he coude finde;

1695 **so . . . stounde** alas the time   1702 **war** aware. This lament
is a small *aubade*. Cf. III.1423 ff.   1704 **char** car, chariot   1705
bypath . . . me short-cut to spite me   1709 **depart hem** separate
them   1711 **twine** embrace   1716 **suffisance** contentment   1718
jousteth . . . festeyinges jousts, makes feasts   1719 **changeth weede**
changes clothes   1721 **as . . . kinde** as became him well by nature
(because of his royal breeding)

That swich a voice was of him and a stevene°
Throughout the world, of honour and largesse,°
That it up rung unto the gates of hevene;   *1725*
And as in love he was in swich gladnesse
That in his herte he deemed, as I guesse,
That there nis lover in this world at eesè
So well as he; and thus gan Love him pleese.

The goodliheed or beautee which that Kinde   *1730*
In any other lady had y-set
Cannot the mountance of a knot unbinde
About his herte of all Criseyde's net.°
He was so narrow y-masked and y-knet°
That it undone on any manner side,   *1735*
That nill not been, for aught that may betide.°

And by the hand full oft he wolde take
This Pandarus, and into garden leede,
And swich a feste° and swich a process° make
Him of Criseyde and of her womanheede   *1740*
And of her beautee that, withouten dreede,
It was an hevene his wordes for to heere.
And then he wolde sing in this mannere:

Troilus's Song

"Love,° that of erth and sea hath governaunce;
Love, that his hestes° hath in hevene highe;   *1745*
Love, that with an hoolsome alliaunce

1723 **voice . . . stevene** report . . . reputation   1724 **largesse** gener-
osity (one of the important medieval courtly virtues)   1732–33
mountance . . . net extent of one knot in her knot of love. Troilus
has said that it was Criseyde's "nets," her eyes, which first caused
him to be bound "withouten bond" (III.1355–58). The metaphor is
conventional in love poetry   1734 **narrow . . . y-knet** closely en-
meshed and ensnared   1736 **betide** happen   1739 **swich . . . feste**
such rejoicing   1739 **process** story   1744–71 **Love . . .** Troilus's
hymn to love often receives special recognition in the manuscripts
as the *Canticus Troili*, the Song of Troilus. Boccaccio's Troilo also
has a song at this moment in the *Filostrato*, but Chaucer has used
that song already in his Proem to Book III (III.1–38); here, for
Troilus's song, he uses Boethius's *Consolation*, II, met. 8   1745
hestes behests

Halt peoples joined as him list hem gie;°
Love, that knitteth law of compaignye,°
And couples doth in virtue for to dwelle—
Bind this accord° that I have told and telle.   *1750*

"That that° the world, with faith which that is stable,
Diverseth so his stoundes concordinge;°
That elements that been so discordable°
Holden a bond perpetually duringe;°
That Phebus mot his rosy day forth bringe,   *1755*
And that the moon hath lordship over the nightes—
All this doth Love. Ay heried be his mightes!°

"That that the sea, that greedy is to flowen,°
Constraineth to a certain ende so
His floodes,° that so fiercely they ne growen   *1760*
To drenchen° erth and all for evermo.
And if that Love aught let his bridle go,
All that now loveth asunder sholde leepe,
And lost were all that Love halt now to-hepe.

"So wolde God, that auctor is of Kinde,   *1765*
That with his bond Love of his virtue liste
To circlen hertes all and faste binde,°
That from his bond no wight the way out wiste.
And hertes cold, hem wold I that he twiste°
To make hem love, and that him list ay rewe   *1770*
On hertes sore, and keep hem that been trewe."°

In alle needes for the towne's werre
He was, and ay the first in armes, dight;°

1747 **Halt . . . gie** holds people together as it pleases him to guide
them 1748 **compaignye** companionship (a form of love) 1750
accord union 1751 **That that** the fact that 1752 **Diverseth . . .
concordinge** varies so its harmonious seasons. Troilus praises Love's
ability to effect a reconciliation of opposites: the seasons are varied
and yet concordant 1753 **discordable** discordant, warring 1754
duringe lasting 1757 **mightes** powers 1758 **that . . . flowen** which
is eager to overflow (its bounds) 1760 **floodes** tides 1761 **drenchen**
drown 1766–67 **Love . . . binde** it pleased Love through his power
to encircle all hearts and bind them fast (together) 1769 **twiste**
bend 1770–71 **him . . . trewe** it may please him always to take
pity on grieving hearts, and protect those who are faithful 1772–
73 **In . . . dight** in all situations having to do with the town's war he

And certainly, but if that bookes erre,
Save Hector most y-dredde of any wight;   *1775*
And this increese of hardiness and might
Came him° of love,° his lady's thank to winne,
That altered his spirit so withinne.

In time of trewe° on-hawking wold he ride,
Or elles hunte boor, bere,° or lioun—   *1780*
The smalle beestes let he goon beside.
And when that he came riding into town,
Full oft his lady from her window down,
As fresh as faucon° comen out of muwe,°
Full redy was him goodly to saluwe.°   *1785*

And most of love and virtue was his speeche;
And in despite had alle wrecchednesse;
And douteless, no need was him beseeche
To honouren hem that hadden worthinesse,
And eesen hem that weren in distresse.   *1790*
And glad was he if any wight well ferde
That lover was,·when he it wist or herde.

For sooth to sayn, he lost held every wight
But if he were in Love's high servise—
I meene folk that ought it been, of right.°   *1795*
And overal this, so well coud he devise
Of sentiment, and in so uncouth wise
All his array, that every lover thoughte
That all was well, what so he said or wroughte.°

And though that he be come of blood royal,   *1800*
Him list of pride at no wight for to chase;°
Benigne he was to eech in general,
For which he got him thank in every place.
Thus wolde Love—y-heried be his grace—

was prepared—and he was always the first one in arms   1777 **him
to him**   1777 **of love** because of love   1779 **trewe** truce   1780
boor, bere boar, bear   1784 **faucon** falcon   1784 **muwe** cage
1785 **saluwe** greet   1795 **that . . . right** who should be (in) it, by
right   1796–99 **And . . . wroughte** And moreover so well could
he handle his own feeling, and in so marvelous a fashion all his
outward appearance, that every lover thought, whatever he said or
did, that all was well   1801 **for . . . chase** to trouble

That pride and ire, envy and avarice,   *1805*
He gan to flee, and everich other vice.

Thou lady bright, the daughter to Dione,°
Thy blind and winged son eek, Daun° Cupide,
Ye sustren nine° eek that by Helicone
In hill Parnaso listen for t'abide,°   *1810*
That ye thus far han deigned me to guide—
I can no more, but sin that ye will wende,
Ye heried been for ay withouten ende.

Through you have I said fully in my song
The effect and joy of Troilus' servise—   *1815*
Al be that there was some diseese among,°
As to mine auctor listeth to devise.°
My thridde book now end ich in this wise;
And Troilus in lust and in quiete
Is with Criseyde, his owne herte sweete.   *1820*

1807 daughter . . . Dione. Venus   1808 Daun lord   1809 Ye . . .
nine the nine Muses, who live on Mount Helicon. Chaucer mis-
takenly believes Helicon is a stream (he calls it "the clere welle" in
The House of Fame). He also errs in placing Helicon near Mount
Parnassus, though Parnassus was sacred to the Muses   1810 listen
. . . t'abide are pleased to dwell (in)   1816 diseese among distress
along with it   1817 to . . . devise it pleases my author to narrate

Book Four

PROEM

But all too litel, wailaway° the while,
Lasteth swich joy, y-thanked be Fortune,
That seemeth trewest when she will beguile,
And can to fooles so her song entune
That she hem hent and blent, traitor commune.°   5
And when a wight is from her wheel° y-throwe,
Then laugheth she, and maketh him the mowe.°

From Troilus she gan her brighte face
Away to writhe,° and took of him noon heede,
But cast him cleen out of his lady grace,   10
And on her wheel she set up Diomede.
For which mine herte right now ginneth bleede,
And now my pen, alas, with which I write,
Quaketh for dreed of that I must endite.

For how Criseyde Troilus forsook—   15
Or at the leest how that she was unkinde—
Mot hennesforth been matter of my book,
As writen folk through which it is in minde.°
Alas, that they shold ever cause finde

1 litel, wailaway short (a time), alas   5 she . . . commune she,
traitor to all, seizes and blinds them   6 wheel Fortune's wheel
constantly revolves, dispensing and withdrawing temporal goods.
Thus while a man for a time may experience prosperity and joy
(weal), he will inevitably come to know sorrow and misery (woe),
and vice-versa. Fortune, like Cupid, is a blind deity. She disregards
mankind's welfare, for she herself is an agent of God's Providence
7 maketh . . . mowe makes a face at him (mowe= Fr. moue,
"pouting grimace")   9 writhe turn   18 is . . . minde i.e., has been
preserved

To speke her harm! And if they on her lie,   20
Ywis, hemself shold han the villainye.°

O ye Erinyes,° Nighte's daughtren three,
That endless complainen ever in pine,°
Megera, Alete, and eek Thesiphone;
Thou cruel Mars eek, fader to Quirine,°   25
This ilke ferthe book me helpeth fine,
So that the loss of life and love yfere
Of Troilus be fully showed here.

Lying in host,° as I have said ere this,
The Greekes strong aboute Troye town,   30
Befell that when that Phebus shining is
Upon the breest of Hercules' lioun,°
That Hector, with full many a bold baroun,
Cast on a day with Greekes for to fighte,
As he was wont, to greve hem what° he mighte.   35

Noot I how long or short it was betweene
This purpose and that day they fighten mente.°
But on a day, well armed, bright and sheene,°
Hector and many a worthy wight out wente
With spere in hand and bigge bowes bente,   40
And in the berd, withouten longer lette,
Hir foemen in the feeld anon hem mette.°

The longe day with speres sharp y-grounde,
With arrows, dartes, swordes, maces felle,°
They fight and bringen horse and man to grounde,   45
And with hir axes out the braines quelle.°

21 hemself . . . villainye they themselves should have the reproach
22 Erinyes the furies: Megaera, Alecto, and Tisiphone. In this in-
vocation Chaucer recalls the opening lines of his poem, where he
turned to Tisiphone for aid in narrating the "double sorrow" of
Troilus 23 pine pain 25 Quirine Romulus 29 host a host (i.e.,
as an army) 31–32 Befell . . . lioun it happened that when Phoe-
bus the sun is shining in the midst of the sign of the Lion (i.e., in
late July and early August). Chaucer identifies the zodiacal sign of
Leo with the Nemean lion, one of Hercules's labors 35 greve . . .
what harass them however 37 fighten mente intended to fight 38
sheene shining 41–42 And . . . mette and face to face, without
longer delay, they met their foes straightway on the battlefield
44 felle cruel 46 quelle dash

But in the laste shour,° sooth for to telle,
The folk of Troy hemselven so misledden,°
That with the worse at night homeward they fledden.

At whiche day was taken Antenor,   50
Maugree° Polydamus or Monesteo,
Santippe, Sarpedon, Polynestor,
Polite, or eek the Trojan daun Rupheo,
And other lesse folk as Phebuseo,
So that, for harm,° that day the folk of Troye   55
Dredden to lese° a greet part of hir joye.

Of Priamus was yive at Greeks' requeste
A time of trewe,° and tho they gonnen treete,°
Hir prisoners to changen,° most and leste,
And for the surplus yiven summes° greete.   60
This thing anon was couth° in every streete,
Both in the assege,° in town, and everywhere,
And with the first it came to Calkas' eere.°

When Calkas knew this tretise sholde holde,°
In consistory° among the Greekes soone   65
He gan in thringe° forth with lordes olde
And set him ther-as he was wont to doone.
And with a changed face hem bade a boone,°
For love of God, to doon that reverence
To stinte noise and yive him audience.   70

Then said he thus: "Lo, lordes mine, ich was
Trojan, as it is knowen out of dreede;
And if that you remember, I am Calkas,
That alderfirst yaf comfort to your neede,
And tolde° well how that ye sholden speede.   75

47 **shour** assault   48 **hemselven . . . misledden** conducted them-
selves so poorly   51 **Maugree** despite the efforts of (to prevent the
capture of Antenor; on Antenor see II.1474n)   55 **for harm** be-
cause of their setbacks   56 **Dredden . . . lese** feared they might
lose   57–58 **Of . . . trewe** Priam extended, at request of the
Greeks, a time of truce   58 **treete** negotiate   59 **changen** exchange
60 **summes** sums of money (ransom)   61 **couth** known   62 **assege**
the siege camp (of the Greeks)   63 **Calkas' eere** the attention of
Calkas. Calkas is Criseyde's father   64 **tretis . . . holde** treaty
should go forward   65 **consistory** council   66 **in thringe** press in
68 **boone** favor   75 **tolde** foretold (see I.64–91)

For dreedeless through you shall, in a stounde,°
Been Troy y-brend and beeten down to grounde.

"And in what form or in what manner wise
This town to shend° and all your lust to acheve,
Ye han ere this well herde it me devise,
This knowe ye, my lordes, as I leve.   80
And for the Greekes weren me so leve,°
I came myself, in my proper persone,
To teech in this how you was best to doone,

"Having unto my tresoure ne my rente   85
Right no resport to respect of your eese.°
Thus all my good° I left and to you wente,
Weening in this you, lordes, for to pleese.
But all that loss ne doth me no diseese.
I vouchesauf, as wisly have I joye,   90
For you to lese° all that I have in Troye—

"Save of a daughter that I left, alas,
Sleeping at home when out of Troy I sterte.
O stern, O cruel fader that I was!
How might I have in that so hard an herte?   95
Alas, I n'ad y-brought her in her sherte!°—
For sorrow of which I will not live tomorrwe,
But if ye lordes rew upon my sorrwe.

"For by that cause I saw no time ere now
Her to deliver,° ich holden have my pees.   100
But now or never, if that it like you,
I may her have right soone, douteless.
O, help and grace amonges all this press!°
Rew on this olde caitiff° in distresse,
Sin I through you have all this hevinesse.   105

"Ye have now caught and fettered in prisoun
Trojans enough; and if your willes be,
My child with one may han redempcioun.°

76 **stounde** while   79 **shend** destroy   82 **leve** beloved   85–86 **Having
. . . eese** having for my wealth or my income no regard at all in
comparison with your comfort   87 **good** goods   91 **you . . . lese**
lose for your sake   96 **sherte** nightgown   100 **deliver** free   103
press group   104 **caitiff** wretch   108 **with . . . redempcioun** be ex-
changed with

Now for the love of God and of bountee,
One of so fele,° alas, so yive him me. *110*
What need were it this prayer for to werne,°
Sin ye shall both han folk and town as yerne?°

"On peril of my life, I shall not lie,
Apollo hath me told it faithfully;
I have eek found it by astronomye,° *115*
By sort,° and by augury° eek trewely—
And dare well say the time is faste by
That fire and flaumb° on all the town shall sprede,
And thus shall Troye turn to ashen deede.°

"For certain, Phebus and Neptunus bothe, *120*
That makeden the walles of the town,
Been with the folk of Troy alway so wrothe,
That they will bring it to confusioun,
Right in despite of° king Lameadoun.
Because he nolde payen hem hir hire, *125*
The town of Troye shall been set on fire."

Telling his tale alway, this olde graye,°
Humble in speech and in his looking eeke,
The salte teeres from his eyen twaye
Full faste runnen down by either cheeke. *130*
So long he gan of succour hem beseeke,
That for to heel him of his sorrows sore,
They yaf him Antenor withouten more.

But who was glad enough but Calkas tho?
And of this thing full soon his needes° laide *135*
On hem that sholden for the tretise go.
And hem for Antenor full ofte prayde

---

110 **fele** many 111 **werne** deny 112 **as yerne** very soon 115 **astronomye** astrology (he consulted the stars) 116 **sort** divination (by throwing lots) 116 **augury** prediction (by observing the flight and chirping of birds) 118 **flaumb** flame 119 **ashen deede** dead ashes 124 **in ... of** out of hatred for. Laomedon, father of Priam and founder of Troy, hired Apollo and Neptune to dedicate and build the walls of Troy but then refused to pay the gods for their work. The gods' wrath was one of the causes of Troy's fall 127 **graye** graybeard 135 **needes** requirements

To bringen home king Thoas and Criseyde.
And when Priam his save-garde° sente,
Th'ambassadours to Troye straight they wente.   *140*

The cause y-told of hir coming, the olde
Priam the king full soon in general
Let hereupon his parlement to holde,°
Of which the effect rehersen you I shall:
The ambassadours been answered for final,°   *145*
The eschange of prisoners and all this neede
Hem liketh well, and forth in they proceede.

This Troilus was present in the place
When asked was for Antenor Criseyde,
For which full soone changen gan his face,   *150*
As he that with tho wordes well nigh deide.
But natheless he no word to it saide,
Lest men shold his affeccion espye.°
With manne's herte he gan his sorrows drie,°

And full of anguish and of grisly dreede   *155*
Abode what lordes wold unto it saye.
And if they wolde grant—as God forbede!—
The eschange of her, then thought he thinges twaye.
First, how to save her honour. And, what waye
He mighte best the eschange of her withstonde.°   *160*
Full fast he cast how all this mighte stonde.

Love him made all prest to doon her bide,°
And rather dien than she sholde go.
But Reeson said him on that other side:
"Without assent of her ne do not so,   *165*
Lest for thy work she wolde be thy foe
And sayn that through thy meddling is y-blowe
Your bother love,° ther it was erst unknowe."

139 **save-garde** safe-conduct (to come into Troy) 143 **holde** assemble 145 **for final** as a final decision 153 **his . . . espye** notice his emotion 154 **drie** endure 160 **withstonde** oppose 162–68 **Love . . .** The conflict between Love and Reason was traditional 162 **prest . . . bide** anxious to make her remain 167–68 **is . . .**

For which he gan deliberen for the beste
That though the lordes wolde that she wente, 170
He wolde let hem grante what hem leste,
And tell his lady first what that they mente.°
And when that she had said him her intente,
Thereafter wold he worken also blive,
Though all the world again it wolde strive. 175

Hector, which that well the Greekes herde
For Antenor how they wold han Criseyde,
Gan it withstand,° and soberly answerde:
"Sires, she nis no prisoner," he saide.
"I noot on you who that this charge laide, 180
But, on my part, ye may eftsoon hem telle
We usen° here no women for to selle."

The noise of people up sterte then at ones,
As breme° as blaze of straw y-set on fire—
For infortune it wolde for the nones 185
They sholden her confusion desire.°
"Hector," quod they, "what ghost° may you inspire
This woman thus to sheeld, and doon us lese
Daun Antenor—a wrong way now ye chese°—

"That is so wise and eek so bold baroun? 190
And we han need of folk, as men may see.
He is eek one the greetest of this town.
O Hector, let tho fantasies be!
O King Priam," quod they, "thus seggen° we:
That all our voice is to forgoon° Criseyde." 195
And to deliveren Antenor they prayde.

O Juvenal,° lord! trew is thy sentence,
That litel witen folk what is to yerne,

bother love your mutual love is broadcast 172 mente intended
178 withstand oppose 182 usen are accustomed 184 breme fierce
185–86 For . . . desire for ill luck would have it on this occasion
that they should desire her ruin. (There is a divergence between
fortune and Criseyde's welfare, caused by the willful whims of "the
people"—i.e., by mob psychology) 187 ghost spirit. (They believe
Hector must be possessed to protect a mere woman when Antenor's
freedom is at stake) 189 chese choose 194 seggen say 195 voice
. . . forgoon decision is to give up 197 Juvenal Roman satirist,

That they ne find in hir desire offence,
For cloud of error let hem not discerne   *200*
What best is.° And lo, here ensample as yerne:°
This folk desiren now deliveraunce
Of Antenor, that brought hem to mischaunce!

For he was after traitor to the town
Of Troy. Alas, they quit him out too rathe!°   *205*
O nice world, lo, thy discrecioun:°
Criseyde, which that never did hem scathe,°
Shall now no longer in her blisse bathe;
But Antenor he shall come home to towne,
And she shall out—thus saide here and howne.°   *210*

For which delibered° was by parlement
For Antenor to yeelden out° Criseyde,
And it pronounced by the president,
Although that Hector "Nay" full ofte prayde.
And finally what wight that it withsaide,   *215*
It was for nought. It muste been and sholde,
For substance° of the parlement it wolde.

Departed out of parlement eech one.
This Troilus, withouten wordes mo,
Into his chamber sped him fast alone,   *220*
But if it were° a man of his or two,
The which he bade out faste for to go,
Because he wolde sleepen, as he saide—
And hastily upon his bed him laide.

And as in winter leeves been beraft,°   *225*
Eech after other, till the tree be bare,
So that there nis but bark and branch y-laft,

thought by medieval writers to be an authority on moral questions
(hence, "lord") 197–201 trew . . . is your saying is true that peo-
ple have little idea what is desirable, that they find no harm in their
will, for a cloud of error prevents them from discerning what is best
201 here . . . yerne he (is) an example at once   205 quit . . .
rathe freed him too quickly   206 discrecioun discernment   207
hem scathe harm to them   210 here . . . howne one and all (?)
211 delibered decided   212 yeelden out yield up   217 substance
majority   221 But . . . were except for   225 beraft stripped away

Lieth Troilus, beraft of eech welfare,
Y-bounden in the blacke bark of care,
Disposed wood out of his wit to braide,° 230
So sore him sat the changing of Criseyde.

He rist° him up and every door he shette
And window eek, and tho this sorrowful man
Upon his bedde's side adown him sette
Full like a deed image,° pale and wan. 235
And in his breest the heeped° woe began
Out brust, and he to worken in this wise
In his woodness, as I shall you devise.

Right as the wilde bull beginneth springe,
Now here, now there, y-darted° to the herte, 240
And of his deeth roreth in complaininge,
Right so gan he about the chamber sterte,
Smiting his breest ay with his fistes smerte,
His heed to the wall, his body to the grounde,
Full oft he swapt° himselven to confounde.° 245

His eyen two, for pietee of herte,
Out streemeden as swifte welles twaye.
The highe sobbes of his sorrows smerte
His speech him reft—unnethes might he saye
"O Deeth, alas, why nilt thou do° me deye? 250
Accursed be that day which that Nature
Shop° me to been a lives° creature!"

But after, when the fury and all the rage
Which that his herte twiste and faste threste,°
By length of time somewhat gan assuage, 255
Upon his bed he laid him down to reste.
But tho began his teeres more out breste,

230 **Disposed . . . braide** prepared suddenly to take leave of his
senses 232 **rist** rises (= *riseth*) 235 **deed image** lifeless statue
236 **heeped** stored up 240 **y-darted** pierced 245 **swapt** beat 245
confounde destroy 250 **do** let 252 **Shop** created 252 **lives** living
254 **twiste . . . threste** wrung and stabbed hard

That wonder is the body may suffise
To half this woe which that I you devise.

Then said he thus: "Fortune, alas the while!   260
What have I done? What have I thus aguilt?°
How mightest thou for ruthe me beguile?°
Is there no grace? And shall I thus be spilt?°
Shall thus Criseyde away, for that thou wilt?
Alas, how maist thou in thine herte finde   265
To been to me thus cruel and unkinde?

"Have I thee not honoured all my live—
As thou well wost—above the goddes alle?
Why wilt thou me fro joye thus deprive?
O Troilus, what may men now thee calle   270
But wrecch of wrecches, out of honour falle
Into misery, in which I will bewaile
Criseyde, alas, till that the breeth me faile?

"Alas, Fortune, if that my life in joye
Displeesed had unto thy foul envye,   275
Why n'haddest thou my fader, king of Troye,
Beraft the life, or doon my bretheren die,°
Or slain myself, that thus complain and crye?
I, cumber-world,° that may of nothing serve,
But ever die and never fully sterve.   280

"If that Criseyde alone were me laft,
Nought rought I whider thou woldest me steere.
And *her*, alas, then hast thou me beraft?
But evermore, lo, this is thy mannere:
To reve a wight that most is to him deere,   285
To preve in that thy gerful violence.°
Thus am I lost; there helpeth no defence.

261 **aguilt** done wrong   262 **for . . . beguile** i.e., have the heart to
deceive me   263 **spilt** ruined   276–77 **Why . . . die** why didn't you
take the life of my father, king of Troy, or cause my brothers to die
279 **cumber-world** an encumbrance to the world   285–86 **To . . .
violence** to take from a man what is most dear to him, to prove by
that your wanton violence

"O verray Lord of Love, O God, alas,
That knowest best mine herte and all my thought,
What shall my sorrowful life doon in this cas,   *290*
If I forgo that I so deer have bought?
Sin ye Criseyde and me han fully brought
Into your grace, and both our hertes seeled,
How may ye suffer, alas, it be repeeled?

"What shall I doon? I shall, while I may dure   *295*
On live in torment and in cruel paine,
This infortune or this disaventure,
Alone as I was born, ywis, complaine.
Ne never will I seen it shine or raine,
But end I will, as Edippe,° in darknesse   *300*
My sorrowful life, and dien in distresse.

"O wery ghost, that errest° to and fro,
Why nilt thou fleen out of the woefulleste
Body that ever might on grounde go?
O soule lurking in this woe unneste,°   *305*
Flee forth out of mine herte and let it breste,
And follow alway Criseyde, thy lady deere.
Thy righte place is now no longer here.

"O woeful eyen two, sin your disport
Was all to seen Criseyde's eyen brighte,   *310*
What shall ye doon but, for my discomfort,
Standen for nought,° and weepen out your sighte,
Sin she is queint° that wont was you to lighte?
In vain fro this forth have ich eyen twaye
Y-formed, sin your virtue° is awaye.   *315*

"O my Criseyde, O lady sovereigne
Of this woeful soule that thus cryeth,

300 **Edippe** Oedipus, who died in blindness, after blinding himself
302 **wery . . . errest** weary spirit, that wander   305 **unneste** ban-
ished from the nest (because deprived of Criseyde)   312 **Standen
. . . nought** be of no use. See Introduction, p. xxxi   313 **queint**
quenched, extinguished (with a possible pun)   315 **virtue** power

Who shall now yiven comfort to the paine?
Alas, no wight. But when mine herte dieth,
My spirit, which that so unto you hieth,   *320*
Receive in gree,° for that shall ay you serve.
Forthy no force is though the body sterve.

"O ye lovers, that high upon the wheel
Been set of Fortune in good aventure,
God leeve that ye find ay love of steel,   *325*
And longe mot your life in joy endure!
But when ye comen by my sepulture,
Remembereth that your fellow° resteth there—
For I loved eek, though ich unworthy were.

"O old, unhoolsome and mislived° man—   *330*
Calkas I meen—alas, what aileth thee
To been a Greek, sin thou art born Trojan?
O Calkas, which that wilt my bane be,
In cursed time was thou born for me!
As wolde blissful Jove, for his joye,   *335*
That I thee hadde where I wold in Troye."

A thousand sighes, hotter than the glede,°
Out of his breest eech after other wente,
Meddled° with plaintes new his woe to feede,
For which his woeful teeres never stente;   *340*
And shortly, so his plaintes him to-rente,°
And wex so maat,° that joye nor penaunce
He feeleth none, but lieth forth in a traunce.

*   *   *

Pandare, which that in the parlement
Had herde what every lord and burgeis° saide,   *345*
And how full granted was by one assent
For Antenor to yeelden so Criseyde,
Gan well nigh wood out of his wit to braide,°

321 **gree** favor   328 **fellow** fellow lover   330 **unhoolsome . . .
mislived** unsavory and ill-living   337 **glede** glowing coal   339
Meddled mingled   341 **to-rente** tore up   342 **wex . . . maat** (he)
grew so exhausted   345 **burgeis** townsman   348 **braide** go

So that for woe he niste what he mente;
But in a rees° to Troilus he wente.   *350*

A certain knight that for the time kepte
The chamber door undid it him anon.-
And Pandar, that full tenderliche wepte,
Into the darke chambre, as still as ston,
Toward the bed gan softely to goon,   *355*
So confus that he niste what to saye:
For verray woe his wit was nigh awaye.

And with his cheer and looking all to-torn°
For sorrow of this, and with his armes folden,
He stood this woeful Troilus beforn,   *360*
And on his pitous face he gan beholden.
But Lord! so ofte gan his herte colden,
Seeing his freend in woe, whose hevinesse
His herte slew, as thought him, for distresse.

This woeful wight, this Troilus, that felte   *365*
His freend Pandar y-comen him to see,
Gan as the snow again° the sunne melte,
For which this sorrowful Pandar, of pitee,
Gan for to weep as tenderlich as he.
And speechless thus been these ilke twaye,   *370*
That neither might oo word for sorrow saye.

But at the last this woeful Troilus,
Nigh deed for smert, gan brusten out to roore,
And with a sorrowful noise he saide thus
Among his sobbes and his sighes sore: *375*
"Lo, Pandar, I am deed withouten more.
Hast thou not herde at parlement," he saide,
"For Antenor how lost is my Criseyde?"

This Pandarus, full deed and pale of hewe,
Full pitously answered and saide, "Yis.   *380*
As wisly were it false° as it is trewe
That I have herde, and wot all how it is.
O mercy, God, who wold have trowed this?

350 **rees** rush   358 **to-torn** ravaged   367 **again** against (i.e., be-
neath)   381 **As . . . false** would it were surely as false

Who wold have wend that in so litel a throwe°
Fortune our joye wold han overthrowe?   385

"For in this world there is no creature,
As to my doom, that ever saw ruine
Stranger than this, through cas or aventure.
But who may all eschew or all divine?
Swich is this world. Forthy I thus define:°   390
Ne trust no wight to finden in Fortune
Ay propretee°—her giftes been commune.

"But tell me this: why thou art now so mad
To sorrowen thus? Why liest thou in this wise,
Sin thy desire all hoolly hast thou had,   395
So that by right it ought enough suffise?
But I, that never felt in my service
A freendly cheer or looking of an eye,
Let *me* thus weep and wailen till I die.

"And overal this, as thou well wost thyselve,   400
This town is full of ladies all aboùte;
And to my doom, fairer than swiche twelve
As ever *she* was, shall I find° in some route°—
Yea, one or two, withouten any doute.
Forthy be glad, mine owne deere brother: 405
If she be lost we shall recover another.

"What! God forbid alway that eech plesaunce
In oo thing were° and in none other wight.
If one can sing, another can well daunce;
If this be goodly, she is glad and light;   410
And this is fair, and that kan good aright.°
Eech for his virtue° holden is for deere,
Both heroner° and faucon for rivere.°

---

384 **throwe** space of time   390 **define** conclude   392 **propretee** satis-
faction of his own desires (from *propre*, what belongs to an indi-
vidual). Fortune cannot satisfy any one man since she dispenses her
favors to everyone: "her gifts are common to all"   402–03 **fairer
. . . find** I shall find (one who is) twelve times fairer than she ever
was   403 **route** crowd   407–08 **eech . . . were** every pleasure should
be in one woman   411 **kan . . . aright** knows how to conduct herself
412 **virtue** (own special) excellence   413 **heroner** falcon trained to
catch herons   413 **faucon . . . rivere** falcon beside the river, per-

"And eek, as writ Zanzis° that was full wis,
'The newe love out chaseth oft the olde.'   *415*
And upon newe cas lieth new avis.°
Think eek thy life to saven art thou holde.°
Swich fire, by process, shall of kinde colde,°
For sin it is but casuel plesaunce,°
Some cas shall put it out of remembraunce.   *420*

"For also sure as day cometh after night,
The newe love, labour, or other woe,
Or elles selde° seeing of a wight,
Doon old affeccions all over-go.°   *425*
And for thy part thou shalt have one of tho
To abridge with thy bitter paines smerte:
Absence of her shall drive her out of herte."

These wordes said he for the nones alle
To help his freend lest he for sorrow deide.
For douteless, to doon his woe to falle,°   *430*
He roughte not what unthrift° that he saide.
But Troilus, that nigh for sorrow deide,
Took litel heed of all that ever he mente.
One eer it herde, at other out it wente.

But at the last he answered and said, "Freend,   *435*
This leechecraft,° or heeled thus to be,
Were well sitting° if that I were a feend,
To traisen° her that true is unto me.
I pray God let this counseil never y-thee,°
But do me rather sterve anonright here   *440*
Ere I thus do as thou me woldest leere.

haps one trained to catch waterfowl. Pandarus compares the indi-
vidual virtues of women with the specializations of two kinds of
falcons 414 **writ Zanzis** writes Zanzis. The quotation in line 415
ultimately belongs to Ovid (via Boccaccio), but Pandarus, the
Trojan, can scarcely cite the Roman or Italian authors. Who
"Zanzis" was, if he was anybody, is not known 416 **upon . . .
avis** a new situation requires new consideration 417 **holde** bound
418 **by . . . colde** in due course, shall by nature grow cold 419
casuel plesaunce pleasure which comes about through chance
(*cas*) 423 **selde** seldom 424 **over-go** fade away 430 **falle** lessen
431 **roughte . . . unthrift** didn't care what unfortunate thing
436 **leechecraft** medical treatment 437 **well sitting** appropriate
438 **traisen** betray 439 **y-thee** succeed

"She that I serve, ywis, what so thou saye,
To whom mine herte enhabit is° by right,
Shall han me hoolly hers till that I deye.
For Pandarus, sin I have trouth her hight,　　　*445*
I will not been untrewe for no wight,
But as her man I will ay live and sterve,
And never other creature serve.

"And ther thou saist thou shalt as faire finde
As she—let be! Make no comparisoun　　　*450*
To creature y-formed here by kinde.
O leve Pandar, in conclusioun,
I will not be of thine opinioun
Touching all this. For which I thee beseeche,
So hold thy peece: thou sleest me with thy speeche.　　　*455*

"Thou biddest me I sholde love another
All freshly new, and let Criseyde go.
It lieth not in my power, leve brother.
And though I might, I wolde not do so.
But canst thou playen racket,° to and fro,　　　*460*
Nettle in, dock out°—now this, now that, Pandare?
Now foule fall her for thy woe that care!°

"Thou farest eek by me, thou Pandarus,
As he that, when a wight is woe-begon,
He cometh to him a pace° and saith right thus:　　　*465*
'Think not on smart° and thou shalt feele noon.'
Thou must me first transmewen in° a ston,
And reve me my passiones alle,
Ere thou so lightly do my woe to falle.

The deeth may well out of my breest departe°　　　*470*
The life, so longe may this sorrow mine;°

443 **enhabit is** is given　460 **racket** court tennis　461 **Nettle . . .
out** The opening words of a medieval folk charm: stinging nettle
goes in, dockweed takes it out. "Nettle in, dock out" was proverbial
for fickleness—first one thing and then another　462 **for . . . care**
who cares for your woe　463–65 **Thou . . . pace** you behave to me,
Pandarus, as one who, when a person is woe-begone, comes
shuffling up to him　466 **on smart** of pain　467 **transmewen in**
transform into　470 **departe** drive　471 **mine** undermine

But fro my soule shall Criseyde's darte°
Out° nevermo. But down with Proserpine,°
When I am deed, I will go wone in pine,°
And there I will eternally complaine   *475*
My woe, and how that twinned° be we twaine.

"Thou hast here made an argument for fin,°
How that it shold a lesse paine be
Criseyde to forgoon, for she was min,
And lived in eese and in felicitee.   *480*
Why gabbest° thou that saidest unto me
That 'Him is worse that is fro wele y-throwe
Than he had erst none of that wele y-knowe'?°

"But tell me, now, sin that thee thinketh so light°
To changen so in love ay to and fro,   *485*
Why hast thou not done bisily thy might
To changen her° that doth *thee* all *thy* wo?
Why nilt thou let *her* fro *thine* herte go?
Why nilt thou love another lady sweete,
That may thine herte setten in quiete?   *490*

"If thou hast had in love ay yet mischaunce,
And canst it not out of thine herte drive,
I, that lived in lust and in plesaunce
With her as much as creature on live,
How shold I that forget, and that so blive?   *495*
O, where hast thou been hid so long in mewe°
That canst so well and formally argue?

"Nay! God wot, nought worth is all thy reed.
For which, for what that ever may befalle,
Withouten wordes mo, I will be deed.   *500*

---

472 **darte** arrow (of her love) 473 **Out** go out. Troilus argues that
whereas his life may easily leave his body, the arrow of Criseyde's
love will remain in his breast forever 473 **Proserpine** queen of
Hades 474 **wone . . . pine** dwell in pain 476 **twinned** separated
477 **for fin** finally 481 **gabbest** talk nonsense 482–83 **Him . . .
y-knowe** it is worse for him who is cast out of happiness than (if)
he had known none of that happiness before (cf. Pandarus's utter-
ance in III.1625–28) 484 **thee . . . light** it seems to you so easy
487 **her** Pandarus's girl friend 496 **in mewe** cooped up

O Deeth, that ender art of sorrows alle,
Come now, sin I so oft after thee calle,
For sely is that deeth, sooth for to sayne,
That, oft y-cleped, com'th and endeth paine.

"Well wot I, while my life was in quiete— 505
Ere thou me slew—I wold have yiven hire;°
But now thy coming is to me so sweete
That in this world I nothing so desire.
O Deeth, sin with this sorrow I am afire,
Thou outher do me anon in teeres drenche, 510
Or with thy colde stroke mine heete quenche.°

"Sin that thou sleest so fele in sundry wise,
Agains hir will, unprayed,° day and night,
Do me, at my requeste, this service:
Deliver now the world—so dost thou right— 515
Of me, that am the woefulleste wight
That ever was; for time is that I sterve,
Sin in this world of right nought may I serve."

This Troilus in teeres gan distille,
As licour out of a lambik° full faste, 520
And Pandarus gan hold his tongue stille,
And to the ground his eyen down he caste.
But natheless thus thought he at the laste:
"What, pardee, rather than my fellow deye,
Yet shall I somewhat more unto him saye." 525

And saide: "Freend, sin thou hast swich distresse,
And sin thee list mine arguments to blame,
Why nilt thyselven helpen doon redresse
And with thy manhood letten all this grame?°
Go ravish° her! Ne canst thou not? For shame! 530
And outher let her out of towne fare,
Or hold° her still and leeve thy nice fare.

506 **yiven hire** given ransom (to ward off death)   511 **heete quenche**
(vital) heat extinguish   513 **unprayed** unasked   519–20 **in . . .
lambik** distilled into tears, as liquor out of an alembic (distilling
retort)   529 **letten . . . grame** stop all this sorrow   530 **ravish**
steal away   532 **hold** hold on to

"Art thou in Troy and hast noon hardiment
To take a woman which that loveth thee,
And wold herselven been of thine assent?°   *535*
Now is not this a nice vanitee?
Rise up anon, and let this weeping be,
And kith° thou art a man—for in this houre
I will been deed, or she shall bleven oure."°

To this answered him Troilus full softe,   *540*
And saide, "Pardee, leve brother deere,
All this have I myself yet thought full ofte,
And more thing than thou devisest here.
But why this thing is left° thou shalt well heere,
And when thou me hast yive an audience,°   *545*
Thereafter maist thou tell all thy sentence.°

"First, sin thou wost this town hath all this werre
For ravishing of women so by might,°
It sholde not be suffered *me* to erre,°
As it stant now, ne doon so greet unright.   *550*
I shold han also blame of every wight
My fadre's grant if that I so withstoode,°
Sin she is changed for the towne's goode.

"I have eek thought, so it were her assent,
To ask her at my fader, of his grace.   *555*
Then think I this were her accusement,°
Sin well I wot I may her not purchase:°
For sin my fader, in so high a place
As parlement, hath her eschange enseeled,°
He nill for me his letter be repeeled.°   *560*

535 of . . . assent in agreement with you   **538 kith** show   **539
bleven oure** remain ours   **544 left** left undone   **545 audience**
hearing (i.e., heard me out)   **546 sentence** opinion   **547–48 sin
. . . might** since you know this town has contracted this war be-
cause of the abduction of women thus by force. Telamon abducted
Priam's sister, Hesione, and in reprisal Paris, Priam's son, abducted
Helen, legal wife of the Greek king Menelaus. The Trojan war
followed as a result of these abductions   **549 be . . . erre** be
allowed for me to do wrong (in abducting her)   **522 My . . .
withstoode** if I so transgressed my father's command   **556 her
accusement** an accusation of her (because their love would be dis-
closed)   **557 purchase** obtain   **559 enseeled** guaranteed   **560 letter**

"Yet dreed I most her herte to perturbe
With violence, if I do swich a game.°
For if I wold it openly disturbe,°
It muste be disclaundre° to her name.
And me were lever deed than her defame—   565
As nolde God, but if I sholde have
Her honour lever than my life to save.

"Thus am I lost, for aught that I can see.
For certain is, sin that I am her knight,
I must her honour lever han than me   570
In every cas, as lover ought of right.°
Thus am I with Desire and Reeson twight:°
Desire for to disturben her me reedeth,
And Reeson nill not—so mine herte dreedeth."

Thus weeping that he coude never ceese,   575
He said, "Alas, how shall I, wrecche, fare?
For well feel I alway my love increese,
And hope is less and less alway, Pandare.
Increesen eek the causes of my care.
So wailaway, why nill mine herte breste?   580
For as in love there is but litel reste."

Pandar answered: "Freend, thou maist, for me,
Doon as thee list. But had ich it so hote,
And thine estate,° she sholde go with me,
Though all this town cried on this thing by note.°   585
I nolde set at all that noise a groote.°
For when men han well cried, then will they rowne;°
Eek wonder last but nine night° never in towne.

. . . repeeled decree be revoked 562 game trick 563 it . . .
disturbe openly disrupt (the exchange) 564 disclaundre slander
571 as . . . right as a lover should by rights. Troilus, having given
four reasons why he cannot steal off with her or intercede with his
father, shows that he has thought it over and that he has her
honor uppermost in his mind 572 twight pinched 584 estate
social station 585 by note in unison 586 groote groat (penny)
587 rowne whisper (i.e., quiet down) 588 wonder . . . night
astonishment never lasts but nine nights

"Divine° not in reeson ay so deepe,
Ne courteisly,° but help thyself anon.   590
Bet is that other than thyselven weepe—
And namely, sin ye two been all oon,
Rise up! For by mine heed she shall not goon.
And rather be in blame a lite y-founde
Than sterve here as a gnat withouten wounde.   595

"It is no shame unto you ne no vice
Her to withholden that ye love most.
Peraunter she might holden thee for nice
To let her go thus to the Greekes' host.
Think eek Fortune, as well thyselven wost,   600
Helpeth hardy man to his emprise°—
And waiveth wrecches° for hir cowardise.

"And though thy lady wold a lite her greve,
Thou shalt thyself thy peece hereafter make.
But as for me, certain I cannot leve   605
That she wold it as now for evil take.°
Why sholde then of-feered thine herte quake?
Think eek how Paris hath, that is thy brother,
A love—and why shalt thou not have another?

"And Troilus, oo thing I dare thee swere: 610
That if Criseyde, which that is thy lief,
Now loveth thee as well as thou dost here,°
God help me so, she nill not take agrief
Though thou do boot° anon in this mischief.
And if she wilneth° fro thee for to passe,   615
Then is she false—so love her well the lasse.

"Forthy take herte and think right as a knight:
Through love is broken alday every lawe.
Kith° now somewhat thy courage and thy might!
Have mercy on thyself, for any awe.°   620

589 **Divine** consider   590 **Ne courteisly** nor with regard to courtly
decorum. Pandarus advises Troilus to cast reason and caution to
the winds   601 **to . . . emprise** in his undertaking   602 **waiveth
wrecches** abandons wretched men   606 **for . . . take** take it ill
612 **here** her   614 **do boot** find a remedy   615 **wilneth** wishes   619
Kith show   620 **for . . . awe** despite any fear

Let not this wrecched woe thine herte gnawe,
But manly set the world on six and sevene°—
And if thou die a martyr, go to hevene.

"I will myself been with thee at this deede,
Though ich and all my kin, upon a stounde,°   625
Shall in a street as dogges lien deede,
Through-girt° with many a wide and bloody wounde.
In every cas I will a freend be founde.
And if thee list here sterven as a wrecche—
Adieu! The devil speede him that recche!"   630

This Troilus gan with tho wordes quicken,°
And saide, "Freend, graunt mercy, ich assente.
But certainly thou maist not so me pricken,°
Ne paine none ne may me so tormente,
That, for no cas, it is not mine intente,   635
At shorte wordes, though I dien sholde,
To ravish her, but if herself it wolde."

"Why, so meen I," quod Pandar, "all this day!
But tell me, then, hast thou her will assayed°
That sorrowest thus?" And he answered him, "Nay."   640
"Whereof art thou," quod Pandar, "then amayed°—
That noost not that she will been evil apayed—
To ravish her, sin thou hast not been there,
But if that Jove told it in thine ere?

"Forthy rise up, as nought ne were, anon,   645
And wash thy face, and to the king thou wende,
Or he may wonderen whider thou art gon.
Thou must with wisdom him and other blende
Or, upon cas, he may after thee sende
Ere thou be ware. And shortly, brother deere,   650
Be glad, and let me work in this mattere.

"For I shall shape it so that sikerly
Thou shalt this night sometime, in some mannere,
Come speken with thy lady privily,
And by her wordes eek as by her cheere   655

622 **set . . . sevene** i.e., hazard everything (as on a dice throw)
625 **upon . . . stounde** in short order   627 **Through-girt** pierced
through   631 **quicken** revive   633 **pricken** goad   639 **her . . .
assayed** consulted her wishes   641 **amayed** dismayed

Thou shalt full soon apperceive and well heere
All her intent, and in this cas the beste.°
And fare now well, for in this point I reste."

* * *

The swifte Fame,° which that false thinges
Egal° reporteth like the thinges trewe,   *660*
Was throughout Troy y-fled with preste° winges
Fro man to man and made this tale all newe—
How Calkas' daughter with her brighte hewe,
At parlement, withouten wordes more,
Y-granted was in change of Antenore.   *665*

The whiche tale anonright as Criseyde
Had herde, she which that of her fader roughte
As in this cas right nought, ne whe'r he deide,
Full bisily to Jupiter besoughte°
Yive hem mischance that this tretise broughte.   *670*
But shortly, lest these tales° soothe were,
She durst at no wight asken it for feere,

As she that had her herte and all her minde
On Troilus y-set so wonder faste
That all this world ne might her love unbinde,   *675*
Ne Troilus out of her herte caste:
She will been his while that her life may laste.
And thus she brenneth both in love and dreede,
So that she niste what was best to reede.

But as men seen in town and all aboute   *680*
That women usen freendes to visite,
So to Criseyde of women came a route,°
For pitous joy, and wenden her delite.°
And with hir tales—deer enough a mite°—
These women which that in the citee dwelle,   *685*
They set hem down and said as I shall telle.

Quod first that one: "I am glad, trewely,
Because of you that shall your fader see."

657 **the beste** the best thing to do   659 **Fame** rumor. In Chaucer's
House of Fame, this personified figure is hailed as "Goddess of
Renown or of Fame"   660 **Egal** equally   661 **preste** swift   669
besoughte prayed   671 **tales** rumors   682 **route** crowd   683 **wenden
. . . delite** thought to gladden her   684 **deer . . . mite** dear enough
at a mite. (The *mite* was a small Flemish coin made of copper)

Another said, "Ywis, so n'am not I,
For all too litel hath she with us be."   690
Quod tho the thrid: "I hope, ywis, that she
Shall bringen us the peece on every side,
That when she goeth almighty God her guide!"

Tho wordes and tho womanishe thinges,
She herde hem right as though she thennes were.°   695
For, God it wot, her herte on other thing is:
Although the body sat among hem there,
Her advertence° is alway elleswhere.
For Troilus full fast her soule soughte;
Withouten word on him alway she thoughte.   700

These women, that thus wenden her to pleese,
Aboute nought gan all hir tales spende.°
Swich vanitee ne can doon her noon eese,
As she that all this meenewhile brende
Of other passion than that they wende,   705
So that she felt almost her herte die
For woe and wery° of that compaignye.

For which no longer mighte she restraine
Her teeres, so they gonnen up to welle,
That yaven signes of the bitter paine   710
In which her spirit was and muste dwelle—
Remembering her fro hevene into which helle
She fallen was, sin she forgoth the sighte
Of Troilus. And sorrowfully she sighte.

And thilke fooles sitting her aboute   715
Wenden that she wept and sighed sore
Because that she shold out of that route
Depart, and never playe with hem more.
And they that had y-knowen her of yore
Saw her so weep, and thought it kindenesse,   720
And eech of hem wept eek for her distresse.

And bisily they gonnen her comforten
Of thing, God wot, on which she litel thoughte.

695 **right . . . were** just as if she were absent   698 **advertence**
attention   702 **Aboute . . . spende** squandered their chit-chat for
nothing   707 **wery** weariness

And with hir tales wenden her disporten,
And to be glad they often her besoughte.   *725*
But swich an eese therewith they her wroughte
Right as a man is eesed for to feele,
For ache of heed, to clawen him on his heele!

But after all this nice vanitee
They took hir leeve and home they wenten alle.   *730*
Criseyde, full of sorrowful pitee,
Into her chamber up went out of the halle,
And on her bed she gan for deed to falle,
In purpose never thennes for to rise.
And thus she wrought as I shall you devise: *735*

Her ounded heer that sunnish° was of hewe
She rent,° and eek her fingers long and smalle
She wrung full oft, and bade God on her rewe, .
And with the deeth to doon boot on her bale.°
Her hew, whilom bright that tho was pale,   *740*
Bare witness of her woe and her constrainte.°
And thus she spake, sobbing in her complainte:

"Alas," quod she, "out of this regioun
I, woeful wrecch and infortuned° wight,
And born in cursed constellacioun,°   *745*
Mot goon, and thus departen fro my knight.
Woe worth, alas, that ilke daye's light
On which I saw him first with eyen twaine,
That causeth me—and ich him—all this paine!"

Therewith the teeres from her eyen two   *750*
Down fell as shower in Aperil swithe;
Her white breest she beet, and for the woe
After the deeth she cried a thousand sithe,
Sin he that wont her woe was for to lithe,°
She mot forgoon;° for which disaventure   *755*
She held herself a forlost creature.

---

736 **ounded . . . sunnish** wavy hair that sunny   737 **rent** tore . 739
doon . . . bale remedy her trouble   741 **constrainte** distress   744
infortuned unfortunate   745 **in . . . constellacioun** in an accursed
configuration of planets   754 **lithe** ease   755 **mot forgoon** must
lose

She said, "How shall he doon—and ich also?
How shold I live if that I from him twinne?
O deere herte eek that I love so,
Who shall that sorrow sleen that ye been inne?   760
O Calkas, fader, thine be all this sinne!
O moder mine, that cleped were Argive,
Woe worth that day that thou me bere on live!

"To what fin shold I live and sorrowen thus?
How shold a fish withouten water dure?   765
What is Criseyde worth from Troilus?
How shold a plant or lives creature
Live without his kinde nouriture?°
For which full oft a byword° here I saye,
That 'Rooteless mot greene soone deye.'°   770

"I shall doon thus: sin neither sword ne darte
Dare I none handle for the crueltee,
That ilke day that I from you departe,
If sorrow of that nill not my bane be,
Then shall no mete° or drinke come in me   775
Till I my soul out of my breest unsheethe.°
And thus myselven will I doon to deethe.

"And, Troilus, my clothes everichoon
Shall blacke been in tokening, herte sweete,
That I am as out of this world agon,   780
That wont was you to setten in quiete.
And of mine order ay till deeth me meete,
The observance ever in your absence
Shall sorrow been, complaint, and abstinence.°

"Mine herte and eek the woeful ghost thereinne   785
Bequeeth I with your spirit to complaine
Eternally, for they shall never twinne;

768 **his . . . nouriture** its natural nourishment   769 **byword** proverb   770 **Rooteless . . . deye** "without roots green things must die"   775 **mete** food   776 **unsheethe** withdraw   782–84 **And . . . abstinence** Criseyde says she will devote herself to Troilus in his absence as a nun worships in her religion. She explains that the "observance" or mode of worship of her "order" will be—rather than the monastic vows of poverty, chastity, and obedience—sorrow, lamentation, and abstinence from "mete and drinke"

For though in erth y-twinned be we twaine,
Yet in the feeld of pitee, out of paine,
That hight Elysos,° shall we be yfere,   *790*
As Orpheus and Erudice his fere.°

"Thus, herte mine, for Antenor, alas.
I soone shall be changed, as I weene.
But how shall ye doon in this sorrowful cas—
How shall your tender herte this sustene?   *795*
But, herte mine, forget this sorrow and teene°
And me also. For soothly for to saye,
So° ye well fare, I recche nought to deye."

How might it ever y-red been or y-songe,°
The plainte that she made in her distresse?   *800*
I noot. But as for me, my litel tongue,
If I discriven wold her hevinesse,
It sholde make her sorrow seeme lesse
Than that it was, and childishly deface
Her high complaint. And therefore ich it passe.   *805*

Pandare, which that sent from Troilus
Was to Criseyde, as ye han herde devise,
That for the best it was accorded° thus—
And he full glad to doon him that service—
Unto Criseyde in a full secree° wise,   *810*
Ther-as she lay in torment and in rage,
Came her to tell all hoolly his message,

And found that she herselven gan to treete°
Full pitously, for with her salte teeres
Her breest, her face y-bathed was full wete.   *815*
The mighty tresses of her sunnish heeres°
Unbroiden° hangen all about her eeres,
Which yaf him verray signal of martyre
Of deeth,° which that her herte gan desire.

789–90 **feeld . . . Elysos** Elysian fields   791 **fere** mate. When Eury-
dice died, Orpheus followed her into Hades to try to win her back.
He failed, but was reunited with her in the Elysian fields, the after-
life of classical mythology   796 **teene** grief   798 **So** as long as
799 **y-red . . . y-songe** be read or sung   808 **accorded** agreed   810
secree secret   813 **gan . . . treete** behaved   816 **heeres** hair   817
Unbroiden unbraided   818–19 **Which . . . deeth** which gave him a

When she him saw, she gan for sorrow anon 820
Her teery face atwix her armes hide,
For which this Pandar is so woe-begon
That in the house he might unneth abide,
As he that pitee felt on every side:
For if Criseyde had erst complained sore, 825
Tho gan she plaine a thousand times more.

And in her aspre° plainte thus she saide:
"Pandare first of joyes mo than two
Was cause causing unto me, Criseyde,
That now transmuwed been in cruel woe.° 830
Whe'r shall I say to you 'Welcome' or no,
That alderfirst me brought into service
Of Love, alas, that endeth in swich wise?

"Endeth then love in woe? Yea, or men lieth,
And alle worldly bliss, as thinketh me. 835
The end of bliss ay sorrow it occupieth!°
And whoso troweth not that it so be,
Let him upon me, woeful wrecch, y-see,
That myself hate and ay my birth accorse,
Feeling alway fro wicke° I go to worse. 840

"Whoso me seeth, he seeth sorrow all atones:
Paine, torment, plainte, woe, distresse!
Out of my woeful body harm there noon is,°
As anguish, langour,° cruel bitternesse,
Annoy,° smart, dreed, fury, and eek sicknesse. 845
I trow, ywis, from hevene teeres raine
For pitee of mine aspre and cruel paine."

"And thou, my suster, full of discomfort,"
Quod Pandarus, "what thinkest thou to do?
Why n'hast thou to thyselven some resport?° 850
Why wilt thou thus thyself, alas, fordo?°

certain sign of martyrdom by death 827 **aspre** bitter 828–30
Pandare . . . woe Pandarus (was) first the cause of joys more than
two joys to me, Criseyde, which are now transformed into cruel woe
836 **The . . . occupieth!** sorrow always displaces the end of bliss!
840 **wicke** bad 843 **Out . . . is** there is no suffering outside my woe-
ful body (she contains all suffering within her) 844 **langour** sickness
845 **Annoy** vexation 850 **resport** regard 851 **fordo** destroy, do in

Leeve all this work° and take now heede to
That I shall sayn, and herken of good intente°
This that by me thy Troilus thee sente."

Turned her tho Criseyde, a woe makinge   855
So greet that it a deeth was for to see.
"Alas," quod she, "what wordes may ye bringe?
What will my deere herte sayn to me,
Which° that I dreede nevermo to see?
Will he han plaint or teeres ere I wende?   860
I have enough if he thereafter sende."°

She was right swich to seen in her visage
As is that wight that men on beere° binde:
Her face, like of Paradise the image,
Was all y-changed in another kinde.   865
The play, the laughter men was wont° to finde
In her, and eek her joyes everichoone
Been fled, and thus lieth now Criseyde alone.

About her eyen two a purpre° ring
Betrent, in soothfast tokening° of her paine,   870
That to behold it was a deedly thing—
For which Pandare mighte not restraine
The teeres from his eyen for to raine.
But natheless, as he best might, he saide
From Troilus these wordes to Criseyde: 875

"Lo, neece, I trowe ye han herde all how
The king with other lordes, for the beste,
Hath made eschange of Antenor and you,
That cause is of this sorrow and this unreste.
But how this cas doth Troilus moleste,°   880
That may noon erthly manne's tongue saye—
For verray woe his wit is all awaye.°

---

852 **work** behavior   853 **herken . . . intente** listen carefully   859
Which whom   861 **thereafter sende** sends for any   863 **beere** bier
866 **was wont** were accustomed   869 **purpre** purple   870 **Betrent
. . . tokening** encircles, in true betokening   880 **moleste** perturbs
882 **his . . . awaye** his mind is distracted

"For which we han so sorrowed, he and I,
That into litel both it had us slawe.°
But through my counseil this day finally   885
He somewhat is fro weeping now withdrawe,
And seemeth me that he desireth fawe°
With you to been all night, for to devise
Remedy in this, if there were any wise.

"This short and plain, th'effect of my message,   .   890
As ferforth as my wit can comprehende.
For ye, that been of torment in swich rage,
May to no long prologue as now intende;
And hereupon ye may answer him sende—
And for the love of God, my neece deere,   895
So leeve this woe ere Troilus be here."

"Greet is my woe," quod she, and sighed sore,
As she that feeleth deedly sharp distresse,
"But yet to me his sorrow is muchel more,
That love him bet than he himself, I guesse.   900
Alas, for me hath he swich hevinesse?
Can he for me so pitously complaine?
Ywis, this sorrow doubleth all my paine.

"Grevous to me, God wot, is for to twinne,"
Quod she, "but yet it harder is to me   905
To seen that sorrow which that he is inne,
For well wot I it will my bane be,
And die I will in certain," tho quod she.
"But bid him come ere deeth, that thus me threeteth,°
Drive out that ghost which in mine herte beeteth."   910

These wordes said, she on her armes two
Fell gruf,° and gan to weepen pitously.
Quod Pandarus: "Alas, why do ye so,
Sin well ye wot the time is faste by
That he shall come? Arise up hastily,   915
That he you not bewopen° thus ne finde—
But ye will have him wood out of his minde.

884 **into . . . slawe** it (sorrow) almost slew us both 887 **fawe**
gladly (*fawe*= dialectal variant of *fain*) 909 **threeteth** threatens
912 **gruf** prone 916 **bewopen** tear-stained

"For wist he that ye ferde in this mannere,
He wold himselven slee. And if I wende
To han this fare,° he sholde not come here   920
For all the good° that Priam may dispende.
For to what fin he wold anon pretende,°
That know I well. And forthy yet I saye,
So leeve this sorrow, or platly° he will deye.

"And shapeth you his sorrow for to abredge,°   925
And nought increese, leve neece sweete:
Beeth rather to him cause of flat than edge,°
And with some wisdom ye his sorrow bete.°
What helpeth it to weepen full a streete,°
Or though ye both in salte teeres dreinte?   930
Bet is a time of cure ay° than of plainte.

"I meene thus: when ich him hider bringe,
Sin ye been wise and both of one assent,°
So shapeth how disturbe your goinge,
Or come again soon after ye be went°—   935
Women been wise in short avisement°—
And let seen how your wit shall now availe,
And what that° I may help, it shall not faile."

"Go," quod Criseyde, "and uncle, trewely,
I shall doon all my might me to restraine   940
From weeping in his sight, and bisily
Him for to glad I shall doon all my paine,
And in mine herte seeken every veine;°
If to this sore there may be founden salve,
It shall not lacke, certain, on my halve."°   945

* * *

919–20 **I . . . fare** I believed I would meet with this behavior
921 **good** wealth   922 **pretende** pursue   924 **platly** flatly   925
shapeth . . . abredge plan to lessen his sorrow   927 **cause . . .
edge** cause of healing than of harm. Pandarus refers to the flat of a
sword which was thought to bestow a healing power as opposed to
its sharp edge   928 **bete** assuage   929 **full . . . streete** a street full
(of tears)   931 **Bet . . . ay** a time of recovery is always better
933 **assent** opinion   934–35 **So . . . wente** arrange a way to hinder
your leaving, or to return soon after you've gone   936 **in . . .
avisement** in quick decisions   938 **what that** however   943 **seeken
. . . veine** Criseyde alludes to the art of letting blood in medieval
leechcraft (here metaphorical for a psychological malady, hence
"in mine herte")   945 **halve** part

Goeth Pandarus, and Troilus he soughte
Till in a temple he found him all alone,
As he that of his life no longer roughte.
But to the pitous goddes everichoone
Full tenderly he prayed and made his mone,   *950*
To doon him soon out of this world to passe—
For well he thought there was noon other grace.

And shortly, all the soothe for to saye,
He was so fallen in despair that day
That outrely he shop him for to deye.   *955*
For right thus was his argument alway:
He said he nas but lorn,° so wailaway—
"For all° that cometh, cometh by necessitee:
Thus to be lorn, it is my destinee.

"For certainly this wot I well," he saide,   *960*
"That foresight of divine Purveyaunce°
Hath seen alway me to forgoon Criseyde,°
Sin God° seeth everything, out of doutaunce,
And hem disponeth, through his ordinaunce,
In hir merites° soothly for to be,   *965*
As they shall comen by predestinee.°

"But natheless, alas, whom shall I leve?
For there been greete clerkes, many oon,

---

957 **nas . . . lorn** was nothing but lost   958 **For all . . .** The
following passage (lines 958–1078), Troilus's meditation on man's
lack of free choice, is adapted from Boethius's *Consolation of Phi-
losophy*, V, pr. 2 and 3. Troilus here states the somewhat rambling
argument of the character Boethius in the *Consolation*: that be-
cause divine Providence (*Purveyaunce*) foresees everything, there-
fore everything is predetermined and man has no free choice. In
the *Consolation*, Lady Philosophy exposes the inaccuracy of this
viewpoint: that Providence foresees an event does not mean it
necessarily wills it, and hence man does have free choice. Lady
Philosophy's argument—the Christian perspective—does not occur
to Troilus in this passage   961 **Purveyaunce** Providence   962 **Hath
. . . Criseyde** always has seen that I should lose Criseyde   963
God Providence and God were often equated, but Providence,
strictly speaking, is an attribute of God. Providence is that divine
power which oversees the course of events in the world from the
beginning to the end of time. Providence also guarantees that God
will achieve his benign purposes in the world   964–65 **And . . .
merites** and disposes them, through his ordering law, according
to their merits   966 **predestinee** predestination

That destinee through argumentes preve;
And some men sayn that needely there is noon,° 970
But that free choice is yiven us everichoon.
O wailaway! So sly° arn clerkes olde
That I noot whose opinion I may holde.

"For some men sayn, 'If God seeth all beforn°—
Ne God may not deceived been, pardee— 975
Then mot it fallen, though men had it sworn,
That Purveyaunce hath seen before to be.'°
Wherefore I say that from eterne,° if he
Hath wist beforn our thought eek as our deede,°
We han no free choice as these clerkes reede. 980

"For other thought nor other deed also
Might never been, but swich as Purveyaunce—
Which may not been deceived nevermo—
Hath feeled beforn,° withouten ignoraunce.°
For if there mighte been a variaunce° 985
To writhen out fro Godde's purveyinge,°
There nere no prescience° of thing cominge.

"But it were rather an opinioun
Uncertain, and no stedfast° foreseeinge.
And certes that were an abusioun° 990
That God shold han no perfit cleer witinge°
More than we men, that han doutous weeninge.°
But swich an error upon God to guesse
Were false and foul and wicked cursednesse.

970 **needely . . . noon** of necessity there is none (no destiny) 972
sly clever 973 **beforn** beforehand 976–77 **Then . . . be** then it
must happen, though men had sworn the contrary, that Providence
has seen things before they occur 978 **eterne** eternity 979 **our
. . . deede** our thoughts as well as our deeds 984 **feeled beforn**
known beforehand 984 **withouten ignoraunce** i.e., without possi-
bility of ignorance. Troilus argues that if there is divine fore-
knowledge, then it must be absolute foreknowledge 985 **variaunce**
variance, alternative 986 **To . . . purveyinge** to twist out (of the
scope) of God's providence 987 **prescience** foreknowledge 989
stedfast certain 990 **abusioun** slander 991 **witinge** knowledge
992 **doutous weeninge** doubtful guessing (rather than certain knowl-
edge). Troilus first argues that either God has absolute foreknowl-
edge, or He does not. If He does, then man has no free choice
because what God has destined to occur will occur despite man's
will

"Eek this is an opinion of some   *995*
That han hir top full high and smooth y-shore.°
They sayn right thus: that thing is not to come
For that the prescience hath seen before
That it shall come; but (they sayn) that therefore
That it shall come, therefore the Purveyaunce   *1000*
Wot it beforn,° withouten ignoraunce.

"And in this manner this necessitee
Returneth in his part contrary again:°
For needfully behooveth it not to be
That thilke. thinges fallen in certain   *1005*
That been purveyed; but needly (as they sayn)
Behooveth it that thinges which that falle,
That they in certain been purveyed alle.°

"I meen as though I laboured me in this
To inqueren which thing cause of which thing be:°   *1010*
As whether that the prescience of God is
The certain cause of the necessitee
Of thinges that to comen been, pardee;
Or if necessitee of thing cominge
Be cause certain of the purveyinge.°   *1015*

"But now n'enforce I me not in showinge°
How the order of causes stant.° But well wot I·

996 **That . . . y-shore** who have the crowns of their heads very
high and smoothly shorn (the clerk's tonsure)   1001 **Wot . . . beforn**
knows it beforehand. The argument is that things do not come
about because they are foreknown, but are foreknown because they
will come about   1003 **Returneth . . . again** returns to the con-
trary argument   1004–08 **For . . . alle** for of necessity it need not
be that those things happen that are foreseen; but of necessity (as
they say) it is necessary that things which happen are all foreseen
certainly. (The argument here concerns foreknowledge: not every-
thing that God can foresee in His infinite mind must needs occur;
but,nothing can occur that God has not foreseen)   1009–10 **I . . .
be** I mean that I'm striving to do this, to inquire into which thing
causes which   1011–15 **As whether . . .** The argument here con-
cerns necessity: does it reside in God's foreknowledge, causing
events absolutely to occur? Or does it reside in the thing or event
itself, causing God's foreknowledge?   1016 **But . . . showinge** but
now I won't attempt (any longer) to show   1017 **stant** stands

That it behooveth that the befallinge
Of thinges wist beforen certainly
Be necessary, al seem it not thereby   *1020*
That prescience put falling necessaire
To thing to come, al fall it foul or faire.°

"For if there sit a man yond on a see,°
Then by necessitee behooveth it°
That, certes, thine opinion sooth be   *1025*
That weenest or conjectest° that he sit;
And furtherover now againward yit,°
Lo, right so is it of the part contrarye,°
As thus—now herken, for I will not tarrye—

"I say that if the opinion of thee   *1030*
Be sooth for that he sit, then say I this:
That he mot sitten by necessitee.
And thus necessitee in either is:
For in him need of sitting is, ywis,
And in thee need of sooth; and thus, forsoothe, *1035*
There mot necessitee been in you bothe.°

"But thou maist sayn the man sit not therefore
That thine opinion of his sitting sooth is,
But rather, for the man sit therebefore,
Therefore is thine opinion sooth, ywis.°   *1040*
And I say, though the cause of sooth of this
Cometh of his sitting, yet necessitee
Is entrechanged° both in him and thee.

"Thus in this same wise, out of doutaunce,
I may well maken, as it seemeth me,   *1045*

1018–22 **That it . . .** The argument is that things which are known
beforehand absolutely by Providencè must occur, although it seems
that foreknowledge—the fact that the events have been foreseen—
does not cause the events to occur   1023 **see** seat   1024 **by . . . it**
of necessity it follows   1026 **weenest . . . conjectest** supposes or
conjectures   1027 **And . . . yit** i.e., on the other hand   1028 **part
contrarye** contrary argument   1034–36 **For in . . .** There is an as-
pect of necessity both in the event (the sitting) and in the foreknowl-
edge of that event   1037–40 **But . . . ywis** but you may say that
the man doesn't sit because your opinion of his sitting is true, but
rather, because the man sits before being seen, then your opinion
is indeed true   1043 **entrechanged** intermingled

My reesoning of Godde's Purveyaunce°
And of the thinges that to comen be.
By whiche reeson men may well y-see
That thilke thinges that in erthe falle,°
That by necessitee they comen alle.   1050

"For although that for thing shall come, ywis,
Therefore is it purveyed certainly—
Not that it cometh for it purveyed is—
Yet natheless behooveth it needfully
That thing to come be purveyed, trewely,   1055
Or elles thinges that purveyed be,
That they betiden by necessitee.°

"And thus sufficeth right enough, certain,
For to destroy our free choice everydeel.
But now is this abusion to sayn   1060
That falling of the thinges temporel
Is cause of Godde's prescience eternel.°
Now trewely that is a false sentence,°
That thing to come shold cause his prescience.

"What might I ween, and I had swich a thought,   1065
But that God purveyeth thing that is to come
For that it is to come—and elles nought?°
So might I ween that thinges, all and some,
That whilom been befalle and overcome,
Been cause of thilke sovereign Purveyaunce   1070
That forewot all, withouten ignoraunce.

1046 **of . . . Purveyaunce** about God's Providence   1049 **falle** happen   1051–57 **For although . . .** I.e., although an event which shall certainly occur is foreseen (not that it occurs because it is foreseen), yet an event that is foreseen must occur from necessity. Troilus here restates the same argument in such a way as to give events that are foreseen the most deterministic and fatalistic appearance   1060–62 **But . . . eternel** but now it is a blasphemy to say that the occurrence of temporal things is the cause of God's eternal foreknowledge. (The argument is that if worldly events or things subject to time—temporal things—occur from a necessity of their own independent of God's foreknowledge, then they limit and prescribe that divine foreknowledge)   1063 **sentence** conclusion   1066–67 **God . . . nought** God foresees an event to come (simply) because it is to come—and otherwise not

"And overal this, yet say I more hereto:
That right as when I wot there is a thing,
Ywis, that thing mot needfully° be so;
Eek right so, when I wot a thing coming   *1075*
So mot it come. And thus the befalling
Of thinges that been wist before the tide,
They mow not been eschewed on no side."°

Then said he thus: "Almighty Jove in trone,°
That wost of all this thing the soothfastnesse,   *1080*
Rew on my sorrow or do me dien soone,
Or bring Criseyde and me fro this distresse!"
And while he was in all this hevinesse,
Disputing with himself in this mattere,
Came Pandar in, and said as ye may heere: *1085*

"O mighty God," quod Pandarus, "in trone,
Ey, who saw ever a wise man faren so?
Why, Troilus, what thinkest thou to doone?
Hast thou swich lust to been thine owne foe?
What, pardee, yet is not Criseyde ago!   *1090*
Why list thee so thyself fordoon for dreede,
That in thine heed thine eyen seemen deede?

"Hast thou not lived many a yeer beforn
Withouten her, and ferde full well at eese?
Art thou for her and for noon other born?   *1095*
Hath Kind thee wrought all only her to pleese?
Let be, and think right thus in thy diseese:
That in the dees right as there fallen chaunces,°
Right so in love there come and goon plesaunces.

"And yet this is a wonder most of alle,   *1100*
Why thou thus sorrowest, sin thou noost not yit,
Touching her going, how that it shall falle,°
Ne yif she can herself disturben° it;
Thou hast not yet assayed all her wit.°

1074 **mot needfully** must of necessity   1076–78 **the . . . side** the occurrence of things that are known before the time (of happening) may not be averted in any way   1079 **trone** throne   1098 **in . . . chaunces** as chance occurs in the throw of dice   1102 **falle** turn out   1103 **disturben** hinder   1104 **assayed . . . wit** determined her mind

A man may all betime his necke bede　　　　　　*1105*
When it shall off—and sorrowen at the neede.°

"Forthy take heed of that I shall thee saye:
I have with her y-spoke and long y-be°—
So as accorded° was betwix us twaye—
And evermore me thinketh thus, that she　　　　*1110*
Hath somewhat in her herte's privitee°
Wherewith she can, if I shall right areede,
Disturb° all this of which thou art in dreede.

"For which my counseil is, when it is night
Thou to her go and make of this an ende.　　　　*1115*
And blissful Juno through her greete might
Shall, as I hope, her grace unto us sende.
Mine herte saith, 'Certain, she shall not wende.'
And forthy put thine herte a while in reste,
And hold thy purpose, for it is the beste."　　　　*1120*

This Troilus answered and sighed sore:
"Thou saist right well, and I will doon right so."
And what him list he said unto it more.
And when that it was time for to go,
Full privily himself, withouten mo,°　　　　　*1125*
Unto her came as he was wont to doone.
And how they wrought I shall you tellen soone.

* * *

Sooth is that when they gonnen first to meete,
So gan the pain hir hertes for to twiste
That neither of hem other mighte greete,　　　　*1130*
But hem in armes took, and after kiste.
The lesse woeful of hem bothe niste
Where that he was, ne might oo word out bringe,
As I said erst, for woe and for sobbinge.

Tho woeful teeres that they leten falle　　　　*1135*
As bitter weren, out of teeres' kinde,°

1105–06 **all . . . neede** in good time offer his neck when it shall be
cut off—and grieve at the necessity　1108 **long y-be** been for a
long time　1109 **accorded** agreed　1111 **privitee** recess　1113 **Dis-
turb** prevent　1125 **mo** others (i.e., without his servants)　1136
out . . . kinde exceeding the nature of tears

For pain as is ligne-aloes or galle.°
So bitter teeres weep° not, as I finde,
The woeful Myrrha° through the bark and rinde—
That in this world there nis so hard an herte   *1140*
That nold han rewed on hir paines smerte.

But when hir woeful wery ghostes twaine
Returned been ther-as hem ought to dwelle,
And that somewhat to waiken° gan the paine
By length of plaint, and ebben gan the welle   *1145*
Of hir teeres, and the herte unswelle,°
With broken voice, all hoorse for-shright,° Criseyde
To Troilus these ilke wordes saide:

"O Jove, I die, and mercy I beseeche!
Help Troilus!" And therewithal her face   *1150*
Upon his breest she laid and loste speeche—
Her woeful spirit from his° proper place,
Right with the word, alway on point to passe.°
And thus she lieth with hewes pale and greene,
That whilom fresh and fairest was to seene.   *1155*

This Troilus, that on her gan beholde,
Cleping her name—and she lay as for deede,
Without answer, and felt her limmes° colde,
Her eyen throwen° upward to her heede—
This sorrowful man kan now noon other reede,   *1160*
But ofte time her colde mouth he kiste.
Whe'r him was woe, God and himself it wiste.

He rist him up, and long straight he her laide.°
For sign of life, for aught he kan or may,
Can he none find, in nothing, on Criseyde,   *1165*

1137 **ligne-aloes . . . galle** wood aloes (a bitter drug) or bile   1138
weep wept   1139 **Myrrha** Myrrha wept tears of myrrh—a bitter
gum—when, after tricking her father into an incestuous relation-
ship, she was turned into a myrrh tree   1144 **waiken** diminish
1146 **unswelle** emotion was thought to make the heart swell   1147
hoorse for-shright hoarse from shrieking   1152 **his** its   1153 **on
. . . passe** on the point of passing away   1158 **limmes** limbs   1159
throwen rolled   1163 **He . . . laide** he rose, and laid her stretched
out

For which his song full oft is, "Wailaway."
But when he saw that speecheless she lay,
With sorrowful voice and herte of bliss all bare,
He said how she was fro this world y-fare.

So after that he long had her complained,°   *1170*
His handes wrung, and said that was to saye,
And with his teeres salt her breest berained,°
He gan tho teeres wipen off full dreye,
And pitously gan for the soule praye,
And said, "O Lord, that set art in thy trone,   *1175*
Rew eek on me, for I shall follow her soone!"

She cold was and withouten sentiment,°
For aught he wot, for breeth ne felt he noon.
And this was him a pregnant° argument
That she was forth out of this world agon.   *1180*
And when he saw there was noon other woon,°
He gan her limmes dress° in swich mannere
As men doon hem that shall been laid on beere.°

And after this, with stern and cruel herte,
His sword anon out of his sheeth he twighte,°   *1185*
Himself to sleen, how sore that him smerte,
So that his soul her soule followen mighte,
Ther-as the doom of Minos wold it dighte,°
Sin Love and cruel Fortune it ne wolde
That in this world he longer liven sholde.   *1190*

Then said he thus, fulfilled of° high disdain:
"O cruel Jove, and thou, Fortune adverse,
This all and some—that falsely have ye slain
Criseyde; and sin ye may do me no worse,
Fie on your might and workes so diverse!   *1195*
Thus cowardly ye shall me never winne:
There shall no deeth me fro my lady twinne.

1170 **her complained** lamented for her   1172 **berained** rained down
upon   1177 **sentiment** feeling   1179 **pregnant** forceful   1181 **woon**
course   1182 **her . . . dress** to arrange her limbs   1183 **beere** bier
1185 **twighte** pulled   1188 **Ther-as . . . dighte** where the judgment
of Minos would decree. Minos was judge of the dead in Hades
1191 **fulfilled of** filled with

"For I this world, sin ye have slain her thus,
Will lete,° and follow her spirit low or hie.
Shall never lover sayn that Troilus   *1200*
Dare not for fere with his lady die;
For certain I will beer her compaignye.
But sin ye will not suffer us liven here,
Yet suffereth that our soules been yfere.

"And thou, citee, which that I leeve in woe;   *1205*
And thou, Priam, and bretheren all yfere;
And thou, my moder, farewell, for I go.
And Atropos,° make redy thou my beere;
And thou, Criseyde, O sweete herte deere,
Receive now my spirit," wold he saye,   *1210*
With sword at herte, all redy for to deye.

But as God wold, of swough therewith she abraide,°
And gan to sigh, and "Troilus!" she cride.
And he answered, "Lady mine, Criseyde,
Live ye yet?"—and let his sword down glide.   *1215*
"Yea, herte mine, that thanked be Cypride!"°
Quod she, and therewithal she sore sighte,
And he began to glad her as he mighte—

Took her in armes two and kissed her ofte,
And her to glad he did all his intente;   *1220*
For which her ghost that flickered ay on lofte,
Into her woeful herte again it wente.
But at the last, as that her eye glente°
Aside, anon she gan his sword espye
As it lay bare, and gan for fere crye,   *1225*

And asked him why he it had out drawe.
And Troilus anon the cause her tolde,
And how himself therewith he wold han slawe;°
For which Criseyde upon him gan beholde,
And gan him in her armes faste folde,   *1230*

1199 **lete** leave   1208 **Atropos** third of the Fates, who cuts the
thread of life (see V.1–4n)   1212 **of . . . abraide** with that she
awoke from her swoon   1216 **that . . . Cypride** may Venus be
thanked for it   1223 **glente** glanced   1228 **slawe** slain

And said, "O mercy, God, lo, which° a deede!
Alas, how nigh we weren bothe deede!

"Then if I ne hadde spoken, as grace was,°
Ye wold han slain yourself anon?" quod she.
"Yea, douteless." And she answered, "Alas,   1235
For by that ilke Lord that made me,
I nold a furlong way on live have be°
After your deeth, to han been° crowned queene
Of all that land the sun on shineth sheene, .

"But with this selve° sword which that here is,   1240
Myselve I wold han slain," quod she tho—
"But ho! for we han right enough of this,
And let us rise and straight to bedde go,
And there let us speken of our woe,
For by the morter° which that I see brenne   1245
Know I full well that day is not far henne."

When they were in her bed in armes folde,
Nought was it like tho nightes here-beforn;
For pitously eech other gan beholde
As they that hadden all hir bliss y-lorn,   1250
Bewailing ay the day that they were born;
Till at the last this sorrowful wight, Criseyde,
To Troilus these ilke wordes saide:

"Lo, herte mine, well wot ye this," quod she,
"That if a wight alway his woe complaine,   1255
And seeketh nought how holpen for to be,
It nis but folly and increese of paine;
And sin that here assembled be we twaine
To finde boot of woe that we been inne,
It were all time soone to beginne.   1260

"I am a woman, as full well ye wot,
And as I am avised suddenly,
So will I telle you, while it is hot,

1231 **which** what   1233 **as . . . was** i.e., as by grace I did   1237
I . . . be I wouldn't have been alive longer than the time it takes to
go a furlong   1238 **to . . . been** i.e., even if I were   1240 **selve**
self-same   1245 **morter** candle left burning all night

Me thinketh thus: that nouther ye nor I
Ought half this woe to maken, skilfully,° 1265
For there is art° enough for to redresse
That yet is miss,° and sleen this hevinesse.

"Sooth is, the woe the which that we been inne,
For aught I wot, for nothing elles is
But for the cause that we sholden twinne: 1270
Considered all, there nis no more amiss!
But what is then a remedy unto this,
But that we shape us soone for to meete?
This all and some, my deere herte sweete.

"Now that I shall well bringen it aboute 1275
To come again soon after that I go,
Thereof am I no manner thing° in doute;
For dreedeless within a week or two
I shall been here—and that it may be so,
By alle right, and in a wordes fewe 1280
I shall you well an heep of wayes shewe.

"For which I will not make long sermoun—
For time y-lost may not recovered be—
But I will goon to my conclusioun,
And to the best, in aught that I can see. 1285
And, for the love of God, foryive it me
If I speke aught agains your herte's reste,
For, trewely, I speke it for the beste,

"Making alway a protestacioun
That now these wordes, which that I shall saye, 1290
Nis but to shewen you my mocioun°
To find unto our help the beste waye;
And taketh it noon otherwise, I praye,
For in effect what so ye me commaunde,
That will I doon, for that is no demaunde.° 1295

"Now herkeneth this: ye han well understonde
My going granted is by parlement

1264–65 **nouther . . . skilfully** neither you nor I should reasonably
make half this woe   1266 **is art** are ways   1277 **miss** amiss   1277
no . . . thing not at all   1291 **Nis . . . mocioun** (words) are only
to show you my thinking   1295 **that . . . demaunde** there is no
question about that

So ferforth that it may not be withstonde
For all this world, as by my judgement.
And sin there helpeth noon avisement   *1300*
To letten° it, let it pass out of minde,
And let us shape a better way to finde.

"The sooth is this: that twinning of us twaine
Will us diseese and cruelich annoye.
But him behooveth some time han a paine   *1305*
That serveth Love, if that he will have joye.
And sin I shall no ferther out of Troye
Than I may ride again on half a morrwe,
It oughte lesse causen us to sorrwe.

"So as I shall not so been hid in mewe,°   *1310*
That day by day, mine owne herte deere,
Sin well ye wot that it is now a trewe,°
Ye shall full well all mine estate y-heere.°
And ere that trewe is done, I shall been here,
And then have ye both Antenor y-wonne,°   *1315*
And me also—beeth glad now if ye conne,

"And think right thus: 'Criseyde is now agon—
But what! She shall come hastily again.'
And when, alas? By God, lo, right anon,
Ere dayes ten—this dare I saufly sayn.   *1320*
And then at erste° shall we be so fain,
So as we shall togideres° ever dwelle,
That all this world ne might our blisse telle.

"I see that oft time, ther-as we been now,
That for the best, our counseil for to hide,   *1325*
Ye speke not with me, nor I with you,
In fourtenight,° ne see you go° ne ride.
May ye not ten dayes then abide,
For mine honour, in swich an aventure?
Ywis, ye mowen elles lite endure!°   *1330*

1301 **letten** prevent   1310 **mewe** cage (in the Greek camp)   1312
trewe truce   1313 **mine** . . . **y-heere** hear of my condition   1313
y-wonne retrieved   1321 **at erste** at last   1322 **togideres** together
1327 **In fourtenight** for a fortnight   1327 **go** walk   1330 **ye** . . .
endure you must endure little else

"Ye know eek how that all my kin is here,
But if that onlich it my fader be,°
And eek mine other thinges all yfere—
And namely, my deere herte, ye,
Whom that I nolde leeven for to see   *1335*
For all this world, as wide as it hath space—
Or elles see ich never Jove's face!

"Why trowe ye my fader in this wise
Coveiteth° so to see me, but for dreede
Lest in this town that folkes me despise,   *1340*
Because of him, for his unhappy deede?
What wot my fader what life that I leede?
For if he wist in Troy how well I fare,
Us needed for my wending nought to care.

"Ye seen that every day eek, more and more,   *1345*
Men treet of° peece, and it supposed is
That men the queen Heleine shall restore,°
And Greekes us restoren that is miss.
So though there nere comfort none but this—
That men purposen peece on every side—   *1350*
Ye may the better at eese of herte abide.

"For if that it be peece, mine herte deere,
The nature of the peece mot needes drive°
That men must entrecommunen° yfere,
And to and fro eek ride and goon as blive   *1355*
Alday as thick as been fleen° from an hive,
And every wight han libertee to bleve°
Wher-as him list the bet withouten leve.

"And though so be that peece there may be non,
Yet hider, though there never peece ne were,   *1360*
I muste come—for whider shold I goon,
Or how, mischance, shold I dwelle there,
Among tho men of armes ever in feere?
For which, as wisly God my soule reede,
I cannot seen whereof ye sholden dreede.   *1365*

1332 **But . . . be** unless it be my father   1339 **Coveiteth** desires
1346 **treet of** negotiate   1347 **restore** return (to the Greeks)   1353
mot . . . drive must needs compel   1354 **entrecommunen** inter-
mingle   1356 **as . . . fleen** as bees fly   1357 **bleve** remain

"Have here another way,° if it so be
That all this thing ne may you not suffise:
My fader, as ye knowen well, pardee,
Is old, and eld° is full of coveitise,°
And I right now have founden all the guise,° 1370
Withouten net, wherewith I shall him hente,
And herkeneth now if that ye will assente:

"Lo, Troilus, men sayn that hard it is
The wolf full and the wether hool° to have—
This is to sayn, that men full oft, ywis, 1375
Mot spenden part, the remnant for to save.
For ay with gold men may the herte grave
Of him that set is upon coveitise.°
And how I meen, I shall it you devise.

"The moeble,° which that I have in this town, 1380
Unto my fader shall I take, and saye
That right for trust and for salvacioun°
It sent is from a freend of his or twaye,
The whiche freendes ferventlich him praye
To senden after more, and that in hie, 1385
While that this town stant thus in jupartye,

"And that shall been an huge quantitee—
Thus shall I sayn; but lest it folk espide,
This may be sent by no wight but by me.
I shall eek shewen him, if peece betide, 1390
What freendes that I have on every side
Toward° the court, to doon the wrathe passe
Of Priamus, and doon him° stand in grace.

"So what for oo thing and for other, sweete,
I shall him so enchanten with my sawes° 1395

1366 way plan 1369 eld old age 1369 coveitise avarice 137◦
guise method 1374 wether hool ram whole (i.e., uneaten by the
wolf; the proverb means "you can't have it both ways") 1377–7◦
herte . . . coveitise impress the heart of him that is bent on avaric◦
1380 moeble personal possessions 1382 for . . . salvacioun for trus◦
(of Calkas) and for safekeeping 1392 Toward connected with
1393 him i.e., Calkas 1395 sawes speeches

That right in hevene his soul is, shall he mete.°
For all Apollo, or his clerkes' lawes,
Or calkuling, availeth not three hawes:°
Desire of gold shall so his soule blende°
That, as me list, I shall well make an ende.   1400

"And if he wold aught by this sort it preve,
If that I lie, in certain I shall fonde°
Disturben him, and pluck him by the sleeve,
Making his sort,° and beeren him on honde
He hath not well the goddes understonde—   1405
For goddes speken in amphibologies,°
And, for oo sooth, they tellen twenty lies.

"Eek dreede foond first goddes,° I suppose—
Thus shall I sayn—and that his coward herte
Made him amiss the goddes text to glose,°   1410
When he for-fered out of Delphos sterte.°
And but I make him soone to converte,°
And doon my reed within a day or twaye,
I will to you oblige me° to deye."

And trewelich, as written well I finde,   1415
That all this thing was said of good intente,
And that her herte trewe was and kinde
Towardes him, and spake right as she mente.
And that she starf for woe nigh when she wente,
And was in purpose ever to be trewe—   1420
Thus writen they that of her workes knewe.

This Troilus, with herte and eres spradde,°
Herde all this thing devisen to and fro,

1396 **right . . . mete** he shall dream his soul is right in heaven
1397 **For all** in spite of 1398 **Or . . . hawes** or divination (with
a pun on "Calkas"), aren't worth three hawthorn berries 1399
blende blind 1402 **fonde** try to 1404 **Making . . . sort** as he is
casting the lots 1406 **amphibologies** ambiguities 1408 **dreede . . .
goddes** fear first invented the gods. Medieval theologians explained
the pagan gods as inventions of superstition and fear; the idea went
back to late classical antiquity 1410 **glose** interpret 1411 **he
. . . sterte** he, terrified, bolted away from Delphi (where he first
learned of the fall of Troy from the god Apollo's oracle) 1412
converte change his mind 1414 **oblige me** pledge myself 1422
spradde open

And verraylich him seemed that he hadde
The selve wit.° But yet to let her go   1425
His herte misforyaf him° evermo.
But finally he gan his herte wreste°
To trusten her, and took it for the beste.

For which the greete fury of his penaunce
Was queint° with hope. And therewith hem betweene   1430
Began for joy the amorouse daunce;
And as the briddes,° when the sun is sheene,
Deliten in hir song in leeves greene,
Right so the wordes that they spake yfere
Delited hem and made hir hertes cleere.   1435

But natheless, the wending of Criseyde
For all this world may not out of his minde.
For which full oft he pitously her prayde
That of her hest he might her trewe finde,
And said her, "Certes, if ye be unkinde,   1440
And but ye come, at day set,° into Troye,
Ne shall I never have hele, honour, ne joye.

"For also sooth as sun uprist on morrwe—
And God so wisly thou me, woeful wrecche,
To reste bring out of this cruel sorrwe—   1445
I will myselven slee, if that ye drecche.°
But of my deeth, though litel be to recche,
Yet ere that ye me causen so to smerte,
Dwell° rather here, mine owne sweete herte.

"For trewely, mine owne lady deere,   1450
Tho sleightes yet that I have herde you steere°
Full shapely° been to failen all yfere.
For thus men saith, that 'One thinketh the beere,
But all another thinketh his leedere.'°

1424–25 he . . . wit he was of the same mind   1426 misforyaf him
had misgivings 1427 wreste compel 1430 queint quenched 1432
briddes birds 1441 at . . . set on the appointed day 1466 drecche
delay 1449 Dwell stay 1451 Tho . . . steere those stratagems
that I have heard you propose thus far 1452 shapely likely
1453–54 One . . . leedere "The bear thinks one thing, his leader
thinks something else entirely" (proverb)

Your sire° is wise, and said is, out of dreede, 1455
'Men may the wise at-ren and nought at-rede.'°

"It is full hard to halten unespied
Before a crepel, for he kan the craft.°
Your fader is in sleight as Argus eyed:°
For al be that his moeble is him beraft,° 1460
His olde sleighte° is yet with him laft.
Ye shall not blend° him for your womanheede,
Ne feign aright. And that is all my dreede.

"I noot if peece shall evermo betide,
But peece or no, for ernest ne for game, 1465
I wot, sin Calkas on the Greekes' side
Hath ones been, and lost so foule° his name,
He dare no more come here again for shame.
For which that way,° for aught I can espye,
To trusten on nis but a fantasye. 1470

"Ye shall eek seen your fader shall you glose°
To been a wife, and as he can well preeche,
He shall some Greek so praise and well alose°
That ravishen he shall you with his speeche,
Or do you doon by force as he shall teeche; 1475
And Troilus, of whom ye nill han routhe,
Shall causeless so sterven in his trouthe.

"And overal this, your fader shall despise
Us all, and sayn this citee nis but lorn,
And that the assege never shall arise, 1480
Forwhy the Greekes han it alle sworn,
Till we be slain and down our walles torn.
And thus he shall you with his wordes feere,
That ay dreed I that ye will bleven° there.

1455 **sire** father   1456 **Men ... at-rede** "Men may the wise outrun
but not outwit" (proverb)   1457–58 **to ... craft** (to pretend) to
limp before a cripple, for he knows the art   1459 **in ... eyed** in
tricks eyed like Argus (who had a hundred eyes)   1460 **moeble ...
beraft** possessions are taken away from him   1461 **sleighte** trickery
1462 **blend** deceive   1467 **foule** foully   1469 **way** proposal   1471
glose persuade deceitfully   1473 **alose** extoll   1484 **bleven** remain

"Ye shall eek seen so many a lusty knight   *1485*
Among the Greekes, full of worthinesse,
And eech of hem with herte, wit, and might
To pleesen you doon all his bisinesse,
That ye shall dullen° of the rudenesse
Of us sely Trojans—but if routhe   *1490*
Remorde you, or virtue of your trouthe.°

"And this to me so grevous is to thinke
That fro my breest it will my soule rende.
Ne dreedeless in me there may not sinke°
A good opinion if that ye wende,   *1495*
Forwhy your fader's sleighte will us shende.°
And if ye goon, as I have told you yore,°
So think I n'am but deed withoute more.

"For which with humble, trew, and pitous herte
A thousand times 'Mercy' I you praye.   *1500*
So reweth on mine aspre° paines smerte,
And doth somewhat as that I shall you saye,
And let us stele away betwix us twaye;°
And think that folly is when man may cheese
For accident his substance ay to lese.°   *1505*

"I meene thus: that sin we mow ere day
Well stele away, and been togider so,
What wit were it to putten in assay,°
In cas ye sholden to your fader go,
If that ye mighten come again or no?   *1510*
Thus meen I, that it were a greet follye
To put that sikerness in jupartye.

"And vulgarly to speken of substaunce,°
Of tresour may we bothe with us leede°

1489 **dullen** tire   1490–91 **but … trouthe** unless pity or the power of your fidelity cause remorse in you   1494 **sinke** take root   1496 **shende** destroy   1497 **yore** before   1501 **aspre** bitter   1503 **stele … twaye** steal away together alone   1504–05 **men … lese** men may choose to give up forever the essential in favor of appearances   1508 **What … assay** what sense would it be to put it to the test   1513 **vulgarly … substaunce** to speak of "substance" in the common sense (as opposed to the philosophical meaning in line 1505)—i.e., of money or means of livelihood   1514 **leede** lead away

Enough to live in honour and plesaunce,   *1515*
Till into time that we shall been deede.
And thus we may eschewen all this dreede.
For everich other way ye can recorde,°
Mine herte, ywis, may therewith nought accorde.°

"And hardily, ne dreedeth no poverte,   *1520*
For I have kin and freendes elleswhere
That, though we comen in our bare sherte,
Us sholde neither lacken gold ne gere,°
But been honoured while we dwelten there.
And go we anon, for as in mine intente   *1525*
This is the best, if that ye will assente."

Criseyde, with a sigh right in this wise,
Answered, "Ywis, my deere herte trewe,
We may well stele away, as ye devise,
And finden swich unthrifty wayes newe;   *1530*
But afterward full sore it will us rewe,
And help me God so at my moste neede,
As causeless ye sufferen all this dreede.

"For thilke day that I for cherishing,
Or dreed of fader, or for other wight,   *1535*
Or for estate, delit, or for wedding,
Be false to you, my Troilus, my knight,
Saturne's daughter, Juno, through her might,
As wood as Athamante do me dwelle°
Eternalich in Styx, the pit of helle!   *1540*

"And this on every god celestial
I swere it you, and eek on eech goddesse,
On every nymph and deitee infernal,
On satyry and fauny,° more and lesse,
That halve-goddes° been of wildernesse: *1545*
And Atropos my threed of life to-breste
If I be false—now trow me if you leste.

1518 **way . . . recorde** proposal you can suggest   1519 **accorde**
agree   1523 **gere** possessions   1539 **As . . . dwelle** cause me to
dwell as mad as Athamas (whom the Furies hounded to madness
at Juno's bidding)   1544 **satyry . . . fauny** satyrs and fauns   1545
halve-goddes demigods

"And thou, Simois, that as an arrow cleere
Through Troye runnest ay downward to the sea,
Bere witness of this word that said is here,   *1550*
That thilke day that ich untrewe be
To Troilus, mine owne herte free,
That thou returne backward to thy welle,
And I with body and soule sink in helle. ·

"But that ye speke away thus for to go   *1555*
And leten° all your freendes—God forbede
For any woman that ye sholden so,
And namely sin Troy hath now swich neede
Of help. And eek of oo thing taketh heede:
If this were wist, my life lay in balaunce,°   *1560*
And your honour—God sheeld us fro mischaunce!

"And if so be that peece hereafter take,°
As alday happeth after anger game°—
Why, lord!—the sorrow and woe ye wolden make,
That ye ne durste° come again° for shame;   *1565*
And ere that ye juparten so your name,
Beeth not too hastif in this hote fare,°
For hastif man ne wanteth never care.°

"What trowe ye the people eek all aboute
Wold of it say? It is full light t'areede:°   *1570*
They wolden say and swere it, out of doute,
That love ne drove you not to doon this deede,
But lust voluptuous and coward dreede.
Thus were all lost, ywis, mine herte deere,
Your honour, which that now shineth so cleere.   *1575*

"And also thinketh on mine honestee,°
That flowereth yet, how foul I shold it shende,°
And with what filth it spotted sholde be,
If in this form I sholde with you wende.

1556 **leten** abandon 1560 **lay . . . balaunce** would lie in the
balance 1562 **take** occurs 1563 **alday . . . game** fun always turns
up after anger 1565 **ne durste** wouldn't dare 1565 **again** back (to
Troy) 1567 **hote fare** rash conduct 1568 **hastif . . . care** "the
hasty man never lacks for sorrow" (proverb) 1570 **light t'areede**
easy to guess 1576 **honestee** good reputation 1577 **shende** ruin

Ne though I lived unto the worlde's ende,   *1580*
My name shold I never againward winne.°
Thus were I lost, and that were ruth and sinne,

"And forthy slee with reeson all this heete!°
Men sayn, 'The suffrant overcom'th,° pardee';
Eek, 'Whoso will han lief he lief mot lete.'°   *1585*
Thus maketh virtue of necessitee
By pacience, and think that lord is he
Of Fortune ay that nought will of her recche;
And she ne daunteth no wight but a wrecche.

"And trusteth this, that certes, herte sweete,   *1590*
Ere Phebus' suster, Lucina the sheene,
The Leoun pass out of this Ariete,°
I will been here, withouten any wene.°
I meen, as help me Juno, hevene's queene,
The tenthe day, but if that deeth m'assaile,   *1595*
I will you seen, withouten any faile."

"And now, so this be sooth," quod Troilus,
"I shall well suffer unto the tenthe day,
Sin that I see that need it mot be thus.
But for the love of God, if it be may,   *1600*
So let us stelen privilich away:
For ever in oon,° as for to live in reste,
Mine herte saith that it will be the beste."

"O mercy, God, what life is *this*?" quod she.
"Alas, ye slee me thus for verray teene!°   *1605*
I see well now that ye mistrusten me,
For by your wordes it is well y-seene.
Now for the love of Cynthia the sheene,°
Mistrust me nought thus causeless for routhe,
Sin to be trew I have you plight my trouthe,   *1610*

1581 **winne** win back 1583 **heete** passion 1584 **The ... overcom'th**
"he who is patient overcomes" 1585 **Whoso ... lete** "whoever
will have a dear thing must give up a dear thing" 1591–92 **Lucina
... Ariete** before the bright Lucina (the moon) passes out of the
House of the Ram and beyond the Lion. (About nine days) 1593
wene doubt 1602 **ever ... oon** constantly 1605 **teene** sorrow
1608 **Cynthia ... sheene** the bright moon, symbol of change

"And thinketh well that sometime it is wit
To spend a time, a time for to winne;°
Ne, pardee, lorn am I not fro you yit,
Though that we been a day or two atwinne.
Drive out tho fantasies you withinne,   *1615*
And trusteth me, and leeveth eek your sorrwe,
Or, here my trouth,° I will not live till morrwe.

"For if ye wist how sore it doth me smerte,
Ye wolde ceese of this; for God, thou wost
The pure spirit weepeth in mine herte   *1620*
To see you weepen that I love most,
And that I mot goon to the Greekes' host—
Yea, nere it that I wiste remedye
To come again, right here I wolde die!

"But certes, I am not so nice a wight   *1625*
That I ne can imaginen a way
To come again that day that I have hight—
For who may hold a thing that will away?
My fader nought, for all his quainte play!°
And by my thrift my wending out of Troye   *1630*
Another day shall turn us all to joye.

"Forthy with all mine herte I you beseeke,
If that you list doon aught for my prayere,
And for that love which that I love you eeke,
That ere that I departe fro you here,   *1635*
That of so good a comfort and a cheere
I may you seen, that ye may bring at reste
Mine herte, which that is on point to breste.

"And overal this, I pray you," quod she tho,
"Mine owne herte's soothfast suffisaunce,   *1640*
Sin I am thine all hool, withouten mo,
That while that I am absent, no plesaunce
Of other do me fro° your remembraunce.
For I am ever aghast, forwhy men reede
That love is thing ay full of bisy dreede.°   *1645*

1612 **To . . . winne** A variant of the proverb of line 1585: "lose time to gain time" 1617 **here . . . trouth** you have my promise 1629 **for . . . play** for all his cunning art 1643 **Of . . . fro** of another (love) put me out of 1645 **bisy dreede** anxiety

"For in this world there liveth lady noon,
If that ye were untrew—as God defende!—
That so betraised° were or woe-begon
As I, that alle trouth in you intende.°
And douteless, if that ich other wende, 1650
I nere but deed; and ere ye cause finde,
For Godde's love, so beeth me nought unkinde."

To this answered Troilus and saide,
"Now God, to whom there nis no cause y-wrye,°
Me glad, as wis I never unto Criseyde, 1655
Sin thilke day I saw her first with eye,
Was false, ne never shall till that I die.
At shorte wordes, well ye may me leve.
I can no more. It shall be found at preve."

"Graunt mercy, goode mine, ywis," quod she, 1660
"And blissful Venus let me never sterve
Ere I may stand of plesaunce in degree
To quit him well° that so well can deserve.
And while that God my wit will me conserve,
I shall so doon, so trew I have you founde, 1665
That ay honour to me-ward° shall rebounde.

"For trusteth well that your estate royal,
Ne vain delit, nor only worthinesse
Of you in wer or tourney marcial,°
Ne pomp, array, nobley,° or eek richesse, 1670
Ne made me to rew on your distresse,
But moral virtue grounded upon trouthe—
That was the cause I first had on you routhe.

"Eek gentil herte and manhood that ye hadde,
And that ye had, as me thought, in despit° 1675
Everything that souned into badde,°
As rudeness and peoplish° appetit,

1648 **betraised** betrayed 1649 **trouth . . . intende** assume faithfulness in you 1654 **y-wrye** hidden 1662–63 **of . . . well** in the fortunate position to repay him well 1666 **to me-ward** toward me 1669 **tourney marcial** martial tournament 1670 **nobley** nobility 1675 **despit** contempt 1676 **souned . . . badde** tended toward evil 1677 **peoplish** vulgar

And that your reeson bridled your delit°—
This made aboven every creature
That I was youre,° and shall, while I may dure.   *1680*

"And this may length of yeeres nought fordo,
Ne remuable° Fortune deface.
But Jupiter, that of his might may do
The sorrowful to be glad, so yive us grace
Ere nightes ten to meeten in this place,   *1685*
So that it may your herte and mine suffise.
And fareth now well, for time is that ye rise."

And after that they long y-plained° hadde,
And oft y-kissed, and strait° in armes folde,
The day gan rise, and Troilus him cladde,   *1690*
And rewfullich his lady gan beholde
As he that felte deethe's cares colde,
And to her grace he gan him recommaunde.°
Whe'r him was woe, this hold I no demaunde.°

For manne's heed imaginen ne can,   *1695*
N'intendement° consider, ne tongue telle
The cruel paines of this sorrowful man,
That passen every torment down in helle.
For when he saw that she ne mighte dwelle,
Which that his soul out of his herte rente,   *1700*
Withouten more, out of the chamber he wente.

1678 **delit** passions   1680 **youre** yours   1682 **remuable** changeable
1688 **y-plained** lamented   1689 **strait** closely   1693 **recommaunde**
commend   1694 **this . . . demaunde** i.e., there was no question of
this   1696 **N'intendement** nor (the) understanding

Book Five

Approchen gan the fatal destinee
That Joves hath in disposicioun,
And to you, angry Parcas, sustren three
Committeth to doon execucioun:°
For which Criseyde must out of the town,   5
And Troilus shall dwellen forth in pine,°
Till Lachesis his threed no longer twine.°

The golde-tressed Phebus high on lofte
Thries had alle with his beemes cleene
The snowes molte,° and Zephyrus° as ofte   10
Y-brought again the tender leeves greene,
Sin that the son of Hecuba° the queene
Began to love her first, for whom his sorrwe
Was all that she departe shold amorrwe.

Full redy was at prime° Diomede   15
Criseyde unto the Greekes' host to leede,
For sorrow of which she felt her herte bleede,
As she that niste what was best to reede.
And trewely, as men in bookes reede,

1–4 **Approchen . . . execucioun** the fated destiny approached that
Jove has disposed and (that he) commits to you three sisters, the
angry Parcae, to put in execution. Jove, the supreme deity, pre-
sides over the actions of the Fates: Clotho, who spins the thread
of human life; Lachesis, who determines the length of the thread
and hence the life span; and Atropos, who finally cuts the thread
6 **pine** pain   7 **twine** twist (on the spool of thread)   8–10 **The . . .
molte** the golden-tressed Apollo (the sun) high aloft three times
had melted the snow with his clear beams. The stanza is an
elegant way of indicating the passage of three years from the be-
ginning of the poem to the present   10 **Zephyrus** the fertile West
Wind, which arrives with spring   12 **son . . . Hecuba** Troilus
15 **prime** 9 a.m.

Men wiste never woman han the care,°   20
Ne was so looth out of a town to fare.

This Troilus, withouten reed or lore,
As man that hath his joyes eek forlore,
Was waiting on° his lady evermore,
As she that was the soothfast crop and more°   25
Of all his lust or joyes heretofore.
But Troilus, now farewell all thy joye—
For shalt thou never seen her eft in Troye.

Sooth is that while he bode in this mannere,
He gan his woe full manly for to hide,   30
That well unneth it seen was in his cheere.
But at the gate ther she shold out ride
With certain folk he hoved° her to abide,
So woe-begone, al wold he not him plaine,
That on his horse unneth he sat for paine.   35

For ire he quoke—so gan his herte gnawe—
When Diomede on horse gan him dresse,°
And saide to himself this ilke sawe:°
"Alas," quod he, "thus foul a wrecchednesse,
Why suffer ich it? Why nill ich it redresse?°   40
Were it not bet atones for to die
Than evermore in langour thus to drie?°

"Why nill I make atones rich and poore
To have enough to doon° ere that she go?
Why nill I bring all Troy upon a roore?°   45
Why nill I sleen this Diomede also?
Why nill I rather with a man or two
Stele her away? Why will I this endure?
Why nill I helpen to mine owne cure?"

But why he nolde doon so fell° a deede   50
That shall I sayn, and why him list it spare:°

20 **woman . . . care** a woman to have the sorrow   24 **on** for   25
crop . . . more branch and root   33 **hoved** lurked   37 **gan . . .**
dresse mounted   38 **sawe** speech   40 **redresse** correct   42 **in . . .**
drie to endure thus in distress   43–44 **Why . . . doon** i.e., why
don't I incite a riot   45 **bring . . . roore** cause an uproar all over
Troy   50 **fell** savage   51 **spare** refrain from it

He had in herte always a manner dreede
Lest that Criseyde, in rumor of this fare,°
Shold han been slain. Lo, this was all his care.
And elles, certain, as I saide yore,   55
He had it done withouten wordes more.

Criseyde, when she redy was to ride,
Full sorrowfully she sighed and said "alas!"
But forth she mot, for aught that may betide,
And forth she rit° full sorrowfully a pas.°   60
There is noon other remedy in this cas.
What wonder is though that her sore smerte,
When she forgoeth her owne sweete herte?

This Troilus, in wise of courteisye,
With hawk on hand and with an huge route°   65
Of knightes, rode and did her compaignye,
Passing all the valley far withoute,
And ferther wold han riden out of doute
Full fain, and woe was him to goon so soone.
But turn he must, and it was eek to doone.°   70

And right with that was Antenor y-come
Out of the Greekes' host, and every wight
Was of it glad and said he was welcome.
And Troilus, al nere his herte light,
He pained him with all his fulle might   75
Him to withold of weeping at the leeste,
And Antenor he kissed and made feste.°

And therewithal he must his leeve take,
And cast his eye upon her pitously,
And neer he rode, his cause for to make,°   80
To take her by the hand all soberly.
And Lord, so she gan weepen tenderly,
And he full soft and slyly gan her saye,
"Now hold your day,° and do me not to deye."

---

53 **in . . . fare** hearing about his behavior **60 rit** rides **60 a pas**
at a walk (amble) **65 route** company **70 it . . . doone** it had to
be done **77 made feste** greeted **80 his . . . make** to plead his
case **84 hold . . . day** keep to your appointed day

With that his courser turned he aboute   *85*
With face pale, and unto Diomede
No word he spake, ne none of all his route:
Of which the son of Tydeus° took heede,
As he that koude more than the creede
In swich a craft,° and by the rein her hente.   *90*
And Troilus to Troy homeward he wente.

This Diomede that led her by the bridel,
When that he saw the folk of Troy awaye,
Thought, "All my labour shall not been on idel,°
If that I may, for somewhat shall I saye.   *95*
For at the worst it may yet short° our waye;
I have herde said eek times twies twelve,
'He is a fool that will forget himselve.'°

But natheless, this thought he well enough,
That "Certainlich I am aboute nought°   *100*
If that I speke of love or make it tough.°
For douteless, if she have in her thought
Him that I guess, he may not been y-brought
So soon away.° But I shall find a meene
That she not wit as yet shall° what I meene."   *105*

This Diomede, as he that koud his good,°
When this was done, gan fallen forth in speeche
Of this and that, and asked why she stood
In swich diseese, and gan her eek beseeche
That if that he increese might or eche°   *110*
With anything her eese, that she sholde
Command it him, and said he doon it wolde.

For trewelich he swore her as a knight
That there nas thing with which he might her pleese,

That he nold doon his pain and all his might 115
To doon it, for to doon her herte an eese.
And prayed her she wold her sorrow appeese,°
And said, "Ywis, we Greekes can have joye,
To honouren you as well as folk of Troye."

He said eek thus: "I wot you thinketh straunge— 120
No wonder is, for it is to you newe—
The acquaintance of these Troyans to chaunge
For folk of Greece that ye never knewe.
But wolde never God but if as trewe
A Greek ye shold among us alle finde 125
As any Trojan is, and eek as kinde.

"And by the cause I swore you right, lo, now,
To been your freend, and helply, to my might°—
And for° that more acquaintance eek of you
Have ich had than another stranger wight— 130
So fro this forth I pray you day and night
Commandeth me, how sore that me smerte,
To doon all that may like unto your herte;

"And that ye me wold as your brother treete,
And taketh not my freendship in despit;° 135
And though your sorrows be for thinges greete—
Noot I not why—but out of more respit°
Mine herte hath for to amend it greet delit.
And if I may your harmes not redresse,
I am right sorry for your hevinesse. 140

"For though ye Trojans with us Greekes wrothe
Han many a day been, alway yet, pardee,
Oo god of Love in sooth we serven bothe.
And for the love of God, my lady free,
Whomso ye hate, as beeth not wroth with me: 145
For trewely, there can no wight you serve
That half so looth your wrathe wold deserve.°

---

117 appeese calm   128 helply . . . might helpful, as much as I
can   129 for because (parallel to "by . . . cause" of line 127)
135 taketh . . . despit disdain my friendship   137 out . . . respit
without further delay   147 That . . . deserve who would be half
so loath to gain your anger

"And nere it that we been so nigh the tente
Of Calkas, which that seen us bothe may,
I wold of this you tell all mine intente.   *150*
But this enseeled° till another day.
Yive me your hand: I am, and shall been ay—
God help me so—while that my life may dure,
Your own aboven every creature.

"Thus said I never ere now to woman born;   *155*
For God mine herte as wisly glade so,
I loved never woman herebeforn
As paramours,° ne never shall no mo.
And for the love of God, beeth not my foe,
Al can I not to you, my lady deere,   *160*
Complain aright, for I am yet to leere.

"And wondereth not, mine owne lady bright,
Though that I speke of love to you thus blive;
For I have herde ere this of many a wight
Hath loved thing he never saw his live.°   *165*
Eek I am not of° power for to strive
Agains the God of Love, but him obeye
I will alway, and mercy I you praye.

"There been so worthy knightes in this place,
And ye so fair, that everich of hem alle   *170*
Will painen him to standen in your grace.
But mighte me so fair a grace falle
That ye me for your servant wolde calle,
So lowly ne so trewely you serve
Nill none of hem, as I shall, till I sterve."   *175*

Criseyde unto that purpose lite answerde,
As she that was with sorrow oppressed so
That in effect she nought his tales° herde
But here and there, now here a word or two.
Her thought her sorrowful herte brust a-two,   *180*
For when she gan her fader far espye,
Well nigh down off her horse she gan to sie.°

---

151 **this enseeled** this is under wraps   158 **paramours** a lover (i.e.,
seriously)   165 **his live** in his life   166 **I . . of** I don't have the
178 **tales** words   182 **sie** sink (originally *sien* meant something like
"to fall in drops"; see OED, *sye*, v¹)

But natheless she thanked Diomede
Of all his travail and his goode cheere,
And that him list his freendship her to bede,°   *185*
And she accepteth it in good mannere,
And will do fain that is him lief and deere,°
And trusten him she wold, and well she mighte,
As saide she; and from her horse she alighte.

Her fader hath her in his armes nome,°   *190*
And twenty time he kissed his daughter sweete,
And said, "O deere daughter mine, welcome!"
She said eek she was fain with him to meete,
And stood forth muwet,° mild, and mansuete.°
But here I leeve her with her fader dwelle,   *195*
And forth I will of Troilus you telle.

* * *

To Troy is come this woeful Troilus
In sorrow aboven alle sorrows smerte,
With felon° look and face despitous.°
Tho suddenly down from his horse he sterte,   *200*
And through his palais, with a swollen herte,
To chamber he went—of nothing took he heede,
Ne none to him dare speke a word for dreede.

And there his sorrows that he spared hadde
He yaf an issue large,° and "Deeth!" he cride.   *205*
And in his throwes° frenetic and madde
He curseth Jove, Apollo, and eek Cupide,
He curseth Ceres, Bacchus, and Cypride,°
His birth, himself, his fate, and eek Nature,
And, save his lady, every creature.   *210*

To bed he goeth and walloweth there and turneth
In fury, as doth he Ixion° in helle,
And in this wise he nigh till day sojourneth.
But tho began his herte a lite unswelle
Through teeres which that gonnen up to welle,   *215*

185 **bede** offer   187 **him . . . deere** to him pleasing and agreeable
(cf. "near and dear") 190 **nome** taken   194 **muwet** mute   194
mansuete gentle 199 **felon** murderous 199 **despitous** cruel 205
yaf . . . large gave free vent to 206 **throwes** throes 208 **Cypride**
Venus 212 **Ixion** who was strapped to an ever-turning wheel in
Hades

And pitously he cried upon Criseyde,
And to himself right thus he spake and saide:

"Where is mine owne lady lief and deere?
Where is her white breest—where is it, where?
Where been her armes and her eyen cleere,   220
That yesternight this time with me were?
Now may I weep alone many a teere,
And grasp about I may, but in this place,
Save a pillow, I finde nought to embrace.

"How shall I do? When shall she come again?   225
I noot, alas! Why let ich her to go?
As wolde God ich had as tho been slain!
O herte mine, Criseyde, O sweete foe!
O lady mine that I love and no mo,
To whom for evermo mine herte I dowe,°   230
See how I die!—ye nill me not rescowe!

"Who seeth you now, my righte loode-sterre?°
Who sit right now, or stant in your presence?
Who can comforten now your herte's werre?
Now I am gone, whom yive ye audience?   235
Who speketh for me right now in mine absence?
Alas, no wight, and that is all my care,
For well wot I as evil as I ye fare.

"How shold I thus ten dayes full endure,
When I the firste night have all this teene?   240
How shall she doon eek, sorrowful creature?
For tenderness how shall she eek susteene
Swich woe for me? O pitous, pale, and greene
Shall been your freshe womanliche face
For langour,° ere ye turn° unto this place."   245

And when he fell in any slumberinges,
Anon begin he sholde for to groone,
And dremen of the dreedfulleste thinges
That mighte been: as mete he were° alone
In place horrible, making ay his mone,   250

230 **dowe** give (cf. "endow") 232 **righte loode-sterre** true loadstar
245 **langour** distress 245 **turn** return 249 **as . . . were** for ex-
ample, dream he was

Or meten that he was amonges alle
His enemies and in hir handes falle.

And therewithal his body sholde sterte,
And with the stert all suddenlich awake,
And swich a tremor feel about his herte   255
That of the feer his body sholde quake.
And therewithal he shold a noise make,
And seem as though he sholde falle deepe
From high on-loft—and then he wolde weepe,

And rewen on himself so pitously   260
That wonder was to heer his fantasye.
Another time he sholde mightily
Comfort himself, and sayn it was follye
So causeless swich dreede for to drie;°
And eft begin his aspre sorrows newe,   265
That every man might on his sorrows rewe.

Who coude tell aright or full descrive
His woe, his plaint, his langour, and his pine?
Not all the men that han or been on live.
Thou, reeder,° maist thyself full well divine   270
That swich a woe my wit cannot define.°
On idle for to write it shold I swinke,°
When that my wit is wery it to thinke.

On hevene yet the starres weren seene,
Although full pale y-woxen was° the moone,   275
And whiten gan the horisonte sheene°
All eestward, as it wont is to doone;
And Phebus with his rosy carte soone
Gan after that to dress him° up to fare,
When Troilus hath sent after Pandare.   280

This Pandar, that of all the day beforn
Ne might han comen Troilus to see,
Although he on his heed it hadde sworn,
For with the king Priam alday was he,

---

264 **drie** suffer 270 **reeder** reader 271 **define** describe 272 **swinke**
labor 275 **y-woxen was** had grown 276 **whiten . . . sheene** the
bright horizon whitened 279 **dress him** prepare

So that it lay not in his libertee   285
Nowhere to goon—but on the morrow he wente
To Troilus, when that he for him sente.

For in his herte he coude well divine
That Troilus all night for sorrow wok,
And that he wolde tell him of his pine.   290
This knew he well enough withoute book.
For which to chamber straight the way he took,
And Troilus tho soberlich he grette,°
And on the bed full soon he gan him sette.

"My Pandarus," quod Troilus, "the sorrwe   295
Which that I drie I may not long endure—
I trow I shall not liven till tomorrwe.
For which I wold always, on aventure,
To thee devisen of my sepulture
The form, and of my moeble thou dispone°   300
Right as thee seemeth best is for to doone.

"But of the fire and flaumbe funeral
In which my body brennen shall to gleede,°
And of the feste and playes palestral°
At my vigil, I pray thee take good heede   305
That that be well; and offer Mars my steede,
My sword, mine helm; and, leeve brother deere,
My sheeld to Pallas yive, that shineth cleere.

"The powder in which mine herte y-brend shall turne,
That pray I thee thou take and it conserve   310
In a vessel that men clepeth° an urn
Of gold; and to my lady that I serve,
For love of whom thus pitouslich I sterve,
So yive it her, and do me this plesaunce,
To pray her keep it for a remembraunce.   315

"For well I feele by my maladye,
And by my dreemes now and yore ago,
All certainly that I mot needes die:

293 **grette** greeted   300 **of . . . dispone** dispose of my personal
possessions   303 **to gleede** to coals   304 **playes palestral** athletic
games   311 **clepeth** call

The owl eek, which that hight Escaphilo,°
Hath after me shright° all these nightes two.   320
And god Mercury, of me now, woeful wrecche,
The soule guide, and when thee list it fecche."

Pandar answered and saide, "Troilus,
My deere freend, as I have told thee yore,
That it is folly for to sorrowen thus,
And causeless, for which I can no more.   325
But whoso will not trowen reed ne lore,
I cannot seen in him no remedye,
But let him worthen° with his fantasye.

"But Troilus, I pray thee, tell me now   330
If that thou trow ere this that any wight
Hath loved paramours° as well as thou?
Yea, God wot, and fro many a worthy knight
Hath his lady gone a fourtenight,°
And he not yet made halvendeel the fare.°   335
What need is *thee* to maken all this care?

"Sin day by day thou maist thyselven see
That from his love, or elles from his wif,
A man mot twinnen of necessitee—
Yea, though he love her as his owne lif.   340
Yet nill he with himself thus maken strif.
For well thou wost, my leeve brother deere,
That alway freendes may not been yfere.

"How doon this folk that seen her loves wedded
By freendes' might,° as it betit° full ofte,   345
And seen hem in hir spouses' bed y-bedded?
God wot, they take it wisely, fair and softe,
Forwhy good hope halt° up hir herte on lofte,
And for they can a time of sorrow endure:
As time hem hurt, a time doth hem cure.   350

319 **Escaphilo** Ascaphalus, whom Proserpina, queen of Hades,
changed into an owl (a bird of evil omen) 320 **shright** screeched
329 **worthen** dwell 332 **paramours** a woman (as a lover) 334
fourtenight fortnight 335 **halvendeel . . . fare** half the to-do
345 **By . . . might** i.e., because friends and relatives have arranged
the marriage 345 **betit** happens 348 **halt** holds

"So sholdest thou endure and leten slide
The time, and fonde° to been glad and light:
Ten dayes nis so longe not to abide.
And sin she thee to comen hath behight,
She nill her heste breeken for no wight.   355
For dreed thee not that she nill finden waye
To come again, my life that durst I laye.

"Thy swevens° eek and all swich fantasye
Drive out, and let hem faren to mischaunce;°
For they proceed of thy melancholye,°   360
That doth thee feel in sleep all this penaunce.
A straw for alle swevens' signifiaunce!
God help me so, I count hem not a beene—
There wot no man aright what dreemes meene.

"For preestes of the temple tellen this: 365
That dreemes been the revelaciouns
Of goddes, and as well they tell, ywis,
That they been infernals° illusiouns.
And leeches° sayn that of complexiouns°
Proceeden they, or fast, or gluttonye.   370
Who wot in sooth thus *what* they signifye?

"Eek other sayn that through impressiouns—
As if a wight hath fast a thing in minde—
That thereof comen swich avisiouns.°
And other sayn, as they in bookes finde,   375
That after times of the yeer, by kinde,°
Men dreem, and that the effect goeth by the moone.°
But leve no dreem, for it is nought to doone.

352 **fonde** try   358 **swevens** dreams   359 **faren . . . mischaunce**
go to confusion   360 **melancholye** melancholy humour (brought
on by an excess of black bile)   368 **infernals** hellish   369 **leeches**
physicians   369 **complexiouns** mixtures of humours. Pandarus pre-
sents two medieval theories of the origins and meaning of dreams:
the supernatural theory, favored by theologians, which claimed
that at least certain dreams are true visions of things present or to
come; the natural theory, favored by physicians and natural scien-
tists, which explained that dreams are caused by superfluity of
bodily fluids   374 **avisiouns** visions in dreams   376 **after . . . kinde**
according to the seasons of the year, naturally   377 **the . . . moone**
the significance depends upon the moon

"Well worth of dreemes ay these olde wives,°
And trewelich eek augury of these fowles,   380
For feer of which men weenen lose hir lives—
As ravens' qualm or shriking° of these owles.
To trowen on it bothe false and foul is!
Alas, alas, so noble a creature
As is a man shall dreeden swich ordure!°   385

"For which with all mine herte I thee beseeche
Unto thyself that all this thou foryive.
And rise now up withouten more speeche,
And let us cast how forth may best be drive°
This time, and eek how freshly° we may live,   390
When that she com'th, the which shall be right soone.
God help me so, the best is thus to doone.

"Rise! Let us speke of lusty life in Troye
That we han led, and forth the time drive;°
And eek of time coming us rejoye,   395
That bringen shall our blisse now so blive.
And langour of these twies dayes five
We shall therewith so forget our oppresse,
That well unneth it doon shall us duresse.°

"This town is full of lordes all aboute,   400
And trewes lasten all this meene while.
Go we play us in some lusty route
To Sarpedon, not hennes but a mile.
And thus thou shalt the time well beguile,
And drive it forth unto that blissful morrwe   405
That thou her see that cause is of thy sorrwe.

"Now rise, my deere brother Troilus,
For certes it noon honour is to thee
To weep and in thy bed to jouken° thus.
For trewelich, of oo thing trust to me: 410

379 **Well . . . wives** i.e., dreams are a proper subject for old wives
382 **qualm . . . shriking** croaking or screeching   385 **ordure** filth
389 **drive** spent   390 **freshly** eagerly   394 **drive** pass   397–99 **And
. . . duresse** and we shall thereby (by passing time together) so
forget our oppression and the languishing of these twice-five days
that it shall scarcely cause us hardship   409 **jouken** loll about (a
term from falconry)

If thou thus lie a day or two or three,
The folk will ween that thou for cowardise
Thee feignest sick, and that thou dar'st not rise."

This Troilus answered, "O brother deere,
This knowen folk that han y-suffered paine: *415*
That though he weep and make sorrowful cheere
That feeleth harm and smart in every veine,
No wonder is; and though ich ever plaine
Or alway weep, I am nothing to blame,
Sin I have lost the cause of all my game.°   *420*

"But sin of fine force° I mot arise,
I shall arise as soon as ever I may.
And God, to whom mine herte I sacrifice,
So send us hastily the tenthe day!
For was there never fowl so fain of May   *425*
As I shall been when that she cometh in Troye,
That cause is of my torment and my joye.

"But whider is thy reed," quod Troilus,
"That we may play us best in all this town?"
"By God, my counseil is," quod Pandarus,   *430*
"To ride and play us with king Sarpedoun."
So long of this they speken up and down,
Till Troilus gan at the last assente
To rise, and forth to Sarpedon they wente.

This Sarpedon, as he that honourable   *435*
Was ever his live, and full of high largesse,°
With all that might y-served been on table
That daintee was—al cost it greet richesse—
He fed hem day by day, that swich noblesse,
As saiden both the most and eek the leeste,   *440*
Was never ere that day wist at any feeste.

Nor in this world there is noon instrument
Delicious,° through wind or touch of corde,
As far as any wight hath ever y-went
That tongue tell or herte may recorde,°   *445*

---

420 **game** delight   421 **of . . . force** of sheer necessity   436 **largesse**
liberality   443 **Delicious** delightful   445 **recorde** remember

That at that feeste it nas well herde accorde;°
Ne of ladies eek so fair a compaignye
On daunce, ere tho, was never y-seen with eye.

But what availeth this to Troilus,
That for his sorrow nothing of it roughte?   *450*
For ever in oon his herte pietous
Full bisily Criseyde, his lady, soughte:
On her was ever all that his herte thoughte—
Now this, now that, so fast imagininge,
That gladde, ywis, can him no festeyinge.   *455*

These ladies eek that at the feeste been,
Sin that he saw his lady was awaye,
It was his sorrow upon hem for to seen,
Or for to heer on instruments to playe.
For she that of his herte beereth the keye   *460*
Was absent. Lo, this was his fantasye:
That no wight sholde maken melodye.

Nor there nas hour in all the day or nighte,
When he was ther-as no wight might him heere,
That he ne said, "O lufsome° lady bright,   *465*
How have ye faren sin that ye were here?
Welcome, ywis, mine owne lady deere."
But wailaway, all this nas but a maze.°
Fortune his howve intended bet to glaze.°

The letters eek that she of olde time   *470*
Had him y-sent, he wold alone reede
An hundred sithe° atwixen noon and prime,°
Refiguring° her shape, her womanheede,
Within his herte, and every word or deede
That passed was. And thus he drove to an ende   *475*
The fourthe day, and said he wolde wende,

And saide, "Leve brother Pandarus,
Intendest thou that we shall here bleve
Till Sarpedon will forth congeyen° us?

---

446 **accorde** to harmonize   465 **lufsome** lovely   468 **maze** delusion
469 **Fortune . . . glaze** Fortune intended better to glaze his hood
(i.e., to give him false hope; cf. *make one's hood*= delude)   472
sithe times   472 **prime** morning   473 **Refiguring** recalling   479
congeyen dismiss

Yet were it fairer that we took our leeve.   *480*
For Godde's love, let us now soon at eve
Our leeve take, and homeward let us turne,
For trewelich, I nill not thus sojourne."

Pandar answered: "Be we comen hider
To fecchen fire and runnen home again?°   *485*
God help me so, I cannot tellen whider
We mighte goon, if I shall soothly sayn,
Ther any wight is of us more fain
Than Sarpedon. And if we hennes hie°
Thus suddenly, I hold it villainye,°   *490*

"Sin that we saiden that we wolde bleve
With him a week—and now thus suddenly,
The fourthe day, to take of him our leeve!
He wolde wonderen on it, trewely.
Let us hold forth our purpose firmely,   *495*
And sin that ye behighten him to bide,
Hold forward° now, and after let us ride."

This Pandarus, with alle pain and woe,
Made him to dwell. And at the weeke's ende
Of Sarpedon they took hir leeve tho,   *500*
And on hir way they spedden hem to wende.
Quod Troilus: "Now Lord me grace sende,
That I may finden at mine home-cominge
Criseyde comen"—and therewith gan he singe.

"Yea, hazelwoode!"° thoughte this Pandare,   *505*
And to himself full softelich he saide,
"God wot, refraiden may this hote fare,°
Ere Calkas sende Troilus Criseyde!"
But natheless he japed thus and playde,
And swore, ywis, his herte him well behighte   *510*
She wolde come as soon as ever she mighte.

When they unto the palais were y-comen
Of Troilus, they down off horse alighte,

---

485 **To . . . again?** cf. "eat and run"   489 **hennes hie** hasten away
490 **villainye** rudeness 497 **forward** agreement 505 **hazelwoode** i.e.,
not very likely, "fat chance." Cf. III.890 507 **refraiden . . . fare**
this hot to-do may cool down

And to the chamber hir way then han they nomen.°
And into time that it gan to nighte,   *515*
They spaken of Criseyde the brighte;
And after this when that hem bothe leste,
They sped hem fro the supper unto reste.

On morrow, as soon as day began to cleere,
This Troilus gan of his sleep t'abraide,°   *520*
And to Pandar, his owne brother deere,
"For love of God," full pitously he saide,
"As go we seen the palais of Criseyde:
For sin we yet may have no more feste,
So let us seen her palais at the leeste."   *525*

And therewithal, his meinee° for to blende,
A cause he foond° in towne for to go,
And to Criseyde's house they gonnen wende.
But Lord, this sely Troilus was woe!
Him thought his sorrowful herte brust a-two,   *530*
For when he saw her doores spered° alle,
Well nigh for sorrow adown he gan to falle.

Therewith when he was ware, and gan beholde
How shet was every window of the place,
As frost, him thought, his herte gan to colde.   *535*
For which, with changed deedlich pale face,
Withouten word he forthby gan to passe.
And as God wold he gan so faste ride
That no wight of his countenance espide.

Then said he thus: "O palais desolat,   *540*
O house of houses, whilom best y-light,
O palais empty and disconsolat,
O thou lantern of which queint° is the light,
O palais, whilom day, that now art night—
Well oughtest thou to fall, and I to die,   *545*
Sin she is went that wont was us to gie.°

"O palais, whilom crown of houses alle,
Enlumined with sun of alle blisse,

514 **nomen** taken °520 **t'abraide** to awake 526 **meinee** retinue
527 **foond** concocted 531 **spered** barred 543 **queint** quenched
546 **gie** guide

O ring fro which the ruby is out falle,
O cause of woe, that cause hast been of lisse,°   550
Yet sin I may no bet, fain wold I kisse
Thy colde doores, durst I for this route:
And farewell, shrine, of which the saint is oute!"

Therewith he cast on Pandarus his eye
With changed face, and pitous to beholde.   555
And when he might his time aright espye,
Ay as he rode, to Pandarus he tolde
His newe sorrow, and eek his joyes olde,
So pitously, and with so deed an hewe,
That every wight might on his sorrow rewe.   560

Fro thennesforth he rideth up and down,
And everything came him to remembraunce,
As he rode foreby places of the town
In which he whilom had all his plesaunce:
"Lo, yonder saw ich last my lady daunce.   565
And in that temple, with her eyen cleere,
Me caughte° first my righte lady deere.

"And yonder have I herde full lustily
My deere herte laugh, and yonder playe
Saw ich her ones eek full blissfully.   570
And yonder ones to me gan she saye,
'Now goode sweete, love me well, I praye!'
And yond so goodly gan she me beholde,
That to the deeth mine herte is to her holde.°

"And at that corner, in the yonder hous,   575
Herde I mine alderlevest lady deere,
So womanly, with voice melodious,
Singen so well, so goodly, and so cleere,
That in my soule yet me thinketh ich heere
The blissful soun . . . And in that yonder place   580
My lady first me took unto her grace."

Then thought he thus: "O blissful lord Cupide,
When I the process have in my memorye

---

550 **lisse** joy   567 **Me caughte** caught my eye   574 **holde** beholden

How thou me hast wereyed° on every side,
Men might a book make of it like a storye.° 585
What need is thee to seek on me victorye,
Sin I am thine and hoolly at thy wille?
What joy hast thou thine owne folk to spille?°

"Well hast thou, Lord, y-wroke° on me thine ire,
Thou mighty God and dreedful for to greeve.° 590
Now mercy, Lord! Thou wost well I desire
Thy grace most of alle lustes leve.
And live and die I will in thy beleeve,°
For which I n'ask in guerdon but oo boone:°
That thou Criseyde again me sende soone. 595

"Distrain° her herte as faste to returne
As thou dost mine to longen her to see,
Then wot I well that she nill not sojourne.
Now blissful Lord, so cruel thou ne be
Unto the blood of Troy, I praye thee, 600
As Juno was unto the blood Thebane,
For which the folk of Thebes caught hir bane."°

And after this he to the gates wente,
Ther-as Criseyde out rode, a full good pas,°
And up and down there made he many a wente,° 605
And to himself full oft he said, "Alas!
From hennes rode my bliss and my solas.
As wolde blissful God now, for his joye,
I might her seen again come into Troye!

"And to the yonder hill I gan her guide, 610
Alas, and there I took of her my leeve.
And yond I saw her to her fader ride,
For sorrow of which mine herte shall to-cleeve.°
And hider home I came when it was eve,

584 **wereyed** made war on   585 **storye** history   588 **spille** destroy
589 **y-wroke** avenged   590 **greeve** offend   593 **beleeve** faith   594
I . . . boone I ask only a single favor as reward (for his faithful
service)   596 **Distrain** constrain   602 **caught . . . bane** came to
destruction. Juno helped bring about the ruin of Thebes because of
her anger at Jove's love affairs with various Theban women, in-
cluding Alcmena and Semele   604 **pas** distance   605 **wente** turn
613 **to-cleeve** split in two

And here I dwell, out cast from alle joye,　　　　　*615*
And shall, till I may seen her eft in Troye."

And of himself imagined he ofte
To been defeet,° and pale, and waxen lesse°
Than he was wont, and that men saiden softe,
"What may it be? Who can the soothe guesse　　*620*
Why Troilus hath all this hevinesse?"
And all this nas but his melancholye
That he had of himself swich fantasye.

Another time imaginen he wolde
That every wight that wente by the waye　　　　·*625*
Had of him ruth, and that they sayen sholde
"I am right sorry Troilus will deye."
And thus he drove a day yet forth or twaye,
As ye have herde. Swich life right gan he leede
As he that stood betwixen hope and dreede.　　*630*

For which him liked in his songes shewe
The enchesoun° of his woe, as he best mighte,
And made a song of wordes but a fewe,
Somewhat his woeful herte for to lighte;
And when he was from every manne's sighte,　　*635*
With softe voice he of his lady deere,
That absent was, gan singe as ye may heere:

Troilus's Song

"O star, of which I lost have all the light,
With herte sore well ought I to bewaile
That° ever dark in torment, night by night,　　*640*
Toward my deeth with wind in steer° I saile;
For which the tenthe night, if that I faile°
The guiding of thy beemes bright an houre,
My ship and me Charybdis° will devoure."

618 **defeet** disfigured　　618 **lesse** thinner　　632 **enchesoun** reason
640 **That** who　　641 **with . . . steer** with a following wind (driving
him toward his death)　　642 **faile** lack　　644 **Charybdis** a mythical
whirlpool which swallows up ships

This song, when he thus sungen hadde, soone 645
He fell again into his sighes olde.
And every night, as was his wone° to doone,
He stood the brighte moone to beholde,
And all his sorrow he to the moone tolde,
And said, "Ywis, when thou art horned newe,° 650
I shall be glad, if all the world be trewe.

"I saw thine hornes old° eek by the morrwe
When hennes rode my righte lady deere,
That cause is of my torment and my sorrwe;
For which, O brighte Latona° the cleere— 655
For love of God—run fast about thy sphere:
For when thine hornes newe ginnen springe,
Then shall she come that may my blisse bringe!"

The dayes more and longer every night,
Than they been wont to be, him thoughte tho, 660
And that the sunne went his course unright,
By longer way than it was wont to do;
And said, "Ywis, me dreedeth evermo
The sunne's son, Pheton,° be on live,
And that his fader cart amiss he drive." 665

Upon the walles° fast eek wold he walke,
And on the Greekes' host he wolde see.
And to himself right thus he wolde talke:
"Lo, yonder is mine owne lady free—
Or elles yonder ther tho tentes be. 670
And thennes cometh this air that is so soote°
That in my soul I feel it doth me boote.°

"And hardily, this wind that more and more
Thus stoundemele° increeseth in my face,
Is of my lady's deepe sighes sore. 675

647 wone custom   650 horned newe i.e., in its first quarter   652
hornes old i.e., the crescent of the moon's last quarter   655 Latona
doubtless a slip for Lucina, the moon   664 Pheton Phaeton, who
attempted to guide his father's sun-chariot across the skies but
found he could not manage the horses   666 walles i.e., of the city
671 soote sweet   672 boote good   674 stoundemele gradually (cf.
"piecemeal")

I preve it thus: for in noon other place
Of all this town—save only in this space—
Feel I no wind that souneth so like paine.
It saith, 'Alas, why twinned be we twaine?' "

This longe time he driveth forth right thus,   680
Till fully passed was the ninthe night.
And ay beside him was this Pandarus,
That bisily did all his fulle might
Him to comfort and make his herte light,
Yiving him hope alway the tenthe morrwe   685
That she shall come and stinten all his sorrwe.

* * *

Upon that other side eek was Criseyde,
With women few, among the Greekes stronge;
For which full oft a day, "Alas," she saide,
"That I was born! Well may mine herte longe   690
After my deeth, for now live I too longe.
Alas, and I ne may it not amende,°
For now is worse than ever yet I wende.

"My fader nill for nothing do me grace
To goon again. For nought I can him queme.°   695
And if so be that I my terme passe,
My Troilus shall in his herte deeme
That I am false—and so it may well seeme.
Thus shall I have unthank° on every side
That I was born. So wailaway the tide!°   700

"And if that I me put in jupartye
To stele away by night, and it befalle
That I be caught, I shall be hold° a spye—
Or elles, lo, this dreed I most of alle,
If in the handes of some wrecch I falle,   705
I n'am but lost, al be mine herte trewe.
Now mighty God, thou on my sorrow rewe!"

Full pale y-waxen was her brighte face,
Her limmes leen,° as she that all the day

692 **amende** improve 695 **queme** please 699 **unthank** blame 700
tide time 703 **hold** considered 709 **limmes leen** lean limbs

Stood, when she durst, and looked on the place   *710*
Ther she was born and she dwelt had ay.
And all the night weeping "alas" she lay.
And thus despaired out of alle cure
She led her life, this woeful creature.

Full oft a day she sighte° eek for distresse,   *715*
And in herself she went ay portrayinge°
Of Troilus the greete worthinesse,
And all his goodly wordes recordinge,
Sin first that day her love began to springe.
And thus she set her woeful herte afire   *720*
Through remembrance of that she gan desire.

In all this world there nis so cruel herte
That her had herde complainen in her sorrwe
That nold han weepen for her paines smerte:
So tenderly she wept both eve and morrwe,   *725*
Her needede no teeres for to borrwe.
And this was yet the worst of all her paine—
There was no wight to whom she durst her plaine.

Full rewfully she looked upon Troye,
Beheld the towers high and eek the halles.   *730*
"Alas," quod she, "the plesance and the joye—
The which that now all turned into gall° is—
Have ich had oft within tho yonder walles.
O Troilus, what dost thou now?" she saide.
"Lord, whether thou° yet think upon Criseyde!   *735*

"Alas, I ne hadde trowed on your lore,°
And went with you, as ye me redde ere this.
Then had I now not sighed half so sore!
Who might have said that I had done amiss
To stele away with swich one as he is?   *740*
But all too late cometh the letuarye
When men the corse unto the grave carrye.°

715 **sighte** sighed   716 **portrayinge** picturing   732 **gall** bitterness
735 **whether thou** do you   736 **I . . . lore** (that) I didn't follow
your plan   741–42 **all . . . carrye** "the medicine comes too late
when men carry the corpse to grave" (proverb)

"Too late is now to speke of that mattere.
Prudence, alas, one of thine eyen three°
Me lacked alway, ere that I came here!   745
On time y-passed well remembered me,
And present time eek coud ich well y-see,
But future time, ere I was in the snare,°
Coud I not seen: that causeth now my care.

"But natheless, betide what betide,   750
I shall tomorrow at night, by eest or west,
Out of this host stele on some manner side,
And goon with Troilus wher-as him lest.
This purpose will ich hold, and this is best.
No force of wicked tongues' janglerye,°   755
For ever on love han wrecches had envye.

"For whoso will of every word take heede
Or rulen him by every wighte's wit,
Ne shall he never thriven, out of dreede.
For that that some men blamen ever yit,   760
Lo, other manner folk commenden it.
And as for me, for all swich variaunce,
Felicitee clepe I my suffisaunce.°

"For which, withouten any wordes mo,
To Troy I will, as for conclusioun."   765
—But God it wot, ere fully monthes two,
She was full far fro that intencioun!
For bothe Troilus and Troye town
Shall knotteless° throughout her herte slide,
For she will take a purpose for to abide.   770

This Diomede, of whom you tell I gan,
Goeth now within himself ay arguinge—

744 **eyen three** In medieval iconography Prudence has three eyes
to view the past, present, and future   748 **snare** love's trap   755
No . . . janglerye never mind the babbling of wicked tongues
763 **Felicitee . . . suffisaunce** "I call it felicity when I have what
satisfies me" (Skeat)   769 **knotteless** i.e., smoothly, easily

With all the sleight° and all that ever he kan—
How he may best, with shortest tarryinge,
Into his net Criseyde's herte bringe.   775
To this intent he coude never fine:°
To fishen her, he laid out hook and line.

But natheless, well in his herte he thoughte,
That she nas not without a love in Troye,
For never sithen he her thennes broughte   780
Ne coud he seen her laugh or maken joye.
He nist how best her herte for to accoye.°
"But for to assay," he said, "it nought ne greeveth:°
For he that nought n'assayeth nought n'acheveth."°

Yet said he to himself upon a night: 785
"Now am I not a fool, that wot well how
Her woe for love is of another wight,
And hereupon to goon assay her now?
I may well wite—it nill not been my prow.°
For wise folk in bookes it expresse: 790
'Men shall not woo a wight in hevinesse.'

"But whoso mighte winnen swich a flow'r
From him for whom she mourneth night and day,
He mighte sayn he were a conquerour!"
And right anon, as he that bold was ay,   795
Thought in his herte: "Hap how happe may,°
Al shold I die, I will her herte seeche.
I shall no more lesen but my speeche."

This Diomede, as bookes us declare,
Was in his needes prest° and corageous,   800
With sterne voice and mighty limmes square—
Hardy, testif,° strong, and chivalrous
Of deedes, like his fader Tydeus.
And some men sayn he was of tongue large,°
And heir he was of Calidoine and Arge.°   805

773 **sleight** cunning 776 **fine** cease 782 **accoye** tame 783 **But . . .
greeveth** i.e., there's no harm in trying 784 **he . . . n'acheveth**
The modern form of the ancient proverb is "Nothing ventured,
nothing gained." Cf. II.807–08 (Criseyde) 789 **prow** profit 796
Hap . . . may come what may 800 **needes prest** actions quick
802 **testif** headstrong 804 **large** loose 805 **Calidoine . . . Arge**

Criseyde meene° was of her stature.
Thereto of shape, of face, and eek of cheere,
There mighte been no fairer creature.
And ofte time this was her mannere:
To goon y-tressed with her heeres cleere   810
Down by her collar at her back behinde,°
Which with a threed of gold she wolde binde.

And, save her browes joineden yfere,°
There nas no lack° in aught I can espyen.
But for to speken of her eyen cleere,   815
Lo, trewely they writen that her sien°
That Paradise stood formed in her eyen;
And with her riche beautee evermore
Strove Love in her ay which of hem was more.

She sober was, eek simple,° and wise withal,   820
The best y-nourished° eek that mighte be,
And goodly of her speech in general—
Charitable, estatlich,° lusty, free,
Ne nevermo ne lacked her pitee,
Tender herted, sliding of corage;°   825
But trewely I cannot tell her age.

And Troilus well waxen was in highte,
And compleet formed by proporcioun,°
So well that Kind it nought amenden° mighte—
Young, fresh, strong, and hardy as lioun,   830
Trew as steel in eech condicioun,
One of the best entecched° creature
That is, or shall, while that the world may dure.

And certainly in story it is y-founde,
That Troilus was never unto no wight,   835
As in his time, in no degree secounde

Calydon and Argos (cities in Greece) 806 **meene** average 810-
11 **To . . . behinde** to go around with her bright hair braided and
falling down behind over her collar 813 **save . . . yfere** except
that her eyebrows were joined together 814 **lack** blemish 816
that . . . sien who saw her 820 **simple** sincere 821 **y-nourished**
raised 823 **estatlich** dignified 825 **corage** heart, moral strength
828 **compleet . . . proporcioun** without defect in proportion 829
amenden improve 832 **entecched** endowed

In durring-doon that longeth° to a knight,
Al might a geant° passen him of might.
His herte ay with the first and with the beste
Stood paregal, to durr-doon° that him leste.   *840*

But for to tellen forth of Diomede:
It fell that after, on the tenthe day
Sin that Criseyde out of the citee yede,°
This Diomede, as fresh as branch in May,
Came to the tente ther-as Calkas lay,°   *845*
And feigned him with Calkas han to doone.°
But what he mente, I shall you tellen soone.

Criseyde, at shorte wordes for to telle,
Welcomed him and down him by her sette,
And he was ethe enough to maken dwelle.°   *850*
And after this, withouten longe lette,
The spices and the wine men forth hem fette,
And forth they speke of this and that yfere,
As freendes doon, of which some shall ye heere.

He gan first fallen of the war in speeche   *855*
Betwixen hem and the folk of Troye town,
And of the assege he gan her eek beseeche
To tell him what was her opinioun.
Fro that demand° he so descendeth down
To asken her if that her strange thoughte   *860*
The Greekes' guise° and workes that they wroughte;

And why her fader tarryeth so longe
To wedden her unto some worthy wight.
Criseyde, that was in her paines stronge°
For love of Troilus, her owne knight,   *865*
As ferforth as she konning had or might,
Answered him tho. But as of his intente,
It seemed not she wiste what he mente.

837 **In . . . longeth** in bravery that is proper   838 **geant** giant
840 **paregal . . . durr-doon** equal, to dare to do   843 **yede** went
845 **lay** lodged   846 **feigned . . . doone** pretended to have busi-
ness with Calkas   850 **ethe . . . dwelle** easy enough to persuade
to stay   859 **demand** question   861 **guise** ways   864 **in . . . stronge**
much in distress

But natheless, this ilke Diomede
Gan in himself assure,° and thus he saide: 870
"If ich aright have taken of you heede,
Me thinketh thus, O lady mine Criseyde:
That sin I first hand on your bridle laide,
When ye out came of Troye by the morrwe,
Ne could I never seen you but in sorrwe.   875

"Can I not sayn what may the cause be,
But if for love of some Trojan it were—
The which right sore wold a-thinken me,°
That ye for any wight that dwelleth there
Sholden spill a quarter of a teere,   880
Or pitously yourselven so beguile:
For dreedeless it is not worth the while.

"The folk of Troy, as who saith, all and some
In prison been, as ye yourselven see;
Fro thennes shall not one on live come   885
For all the gold atwixen sun and sea.
Trusteth well, and understandeth me:
There shall not one to mercy goon on live,°
Al were he lord of worldes twies five.

"Swich wrecch° on hem for fecching of Heleine   890
There shall been take, ere that we hennes wende,
That Manes,° which that goddes been of paine,
Shall been aghast that Greekes will hem shende.
And men shall dreed, unto the worldes ende,
From hennesforth to ravishen any queene,   895
So cruel shall our wrecch on hem be seene.

"And but if Calkas leed us with ambages°—
That is to sayn, with double wordes slye,
Swich as men clepe a word with two visages°—
Ye shall well knowen that I nought ne lie.   900
And all this thing right seen it with your eye,
And that anon, ye nill not trow° how soone.
Now taketh heed, for it is for to doone.

870 **assure** grow confident   878 **The . . . me** which I would deeply
regret   888 **to . . . live** escape alive with mercy   890 **wrecch** ven-
geance   892 **Manes** spirits of the dead; shades   897 **leed . . .
ambages** mislead us with ambiguities   899 **visages** meanings   902
ye . . . trow you won't believe

"What weene ye your wise fader wolde
Han yiven Antenor for you anon,   *905*
If he ne wiste that the citee sholde
Destroyed been? Why, nay, so mot I goon!
He knew full well there shall not scapen oon
That Trojan is. And for the greete feere
He durste not ye dwelte longer there.   *910*

"What will ye more, lufsome lady deere?
Let Troy and Trojan fro your herte passe.
Drive out that bitter hope, and make good cheere,
And clepe again° the beautee of your face,
That ye with salte teeres so deface.   *915*
For Troy is brought in swich a jupartye
That it to save is now no remedye.

"And thinketh well, ye shall in Greekes finde
A more parfit love, ere it be night,
Than any Trojan is, and more kinde,   *920*
And bet to serven you will doon his might.
And if ye vouchesauf, my lady bright,
I will been he to serven you myselve—
Yea, lever than be lord of Greeces twelve."

And with that word he gan to waxen red,   *925*
And in his speech a litel wight he quok,°
And cast aside a litel wight his heed,
And stint a while, and afterward he wok,°
And soberlich on her he threw his look,
And said, "I am, al be it you no joye,   *930*
As gentil man as any wight in Troye.

"For if my fader Tydeus," he saide,
"Y-lived had, ich hadde been ere this
Of Calidoine and Arge a king, Criseyde,
And so hope I that I shall yet, ywis.   *935*
But he was slain, alas, the more harm is,
Unhappily at Thebes all too rathe,
Polymite° and many a man to scathe.

914 **clepe again** recall   926 a . . . **quok** he shook a little   928 **wok**
stirred   938 **Polymite** Polynices. Tydeus fought with Polynices for
Thebes, so his early death did *scathe* (harm) Polynices's army

"But herte mine, sin that I am your man,
And been the first of whom I seeche grace,   940
To serve you as hertely° as I can—
And ever shall, while I to live have space—
So ere that I depart out of this place,
Ye will me grante that I may tomorrwe,
At better leiser, tellen you my sorrwe."   945

What shold I tell his wordes that he saide?
He spake enough for oo day at the meste.°
It preveth well, he spake so that Criseyde
Granted on the morrow, at his requeste,
For to speken with him at the leeste,   950
So that he nolde speke of swich mattere.°
And thus to him she said as ye may heere,

As she that had her herte on Troilus
So faste that there may it none arace;°
And strangely° she spake, and saide thus: 955
"O Diomede, I love that ilke place
Ther I was born—and Joves, for his grace,
Deliver it soon of all that doth it care!°
God, for thy might, so leeve it well to fare!

"That Greekes wold hir wrath on Troye wreke,°   960
If that they might—I know it well, ywis.
But it shall not befallen as ye speke,
And God toforn, and further over this,
I wot my fader wise and redy is;
And that he me hath bought, as ye me tolde,   965
So deer, I am the more unto him holde.

"That Greekes been of high condicioun
I wot eek well—but certain, men shall finde
As worthy folk withinne Troye town,
As konning° and as parfit and as kinde,   970
As been betwixen Orkades and Inde.°

941 hertely devotedly   947 meste most   951 swich mattere i.e., of
love   954 there . . . arace none could pluck it out   955 strangely
distantly   958 doth . . . care afflicts it   960 wreke wreak   970
konning able   971 Orkades . . . Inde the Orkney Islands and India
(the extremities of the known world)

And that ye coude well your lady serve,
I trow eek well, her thank for to deserve.

"But as to speke of love, ywis," she saide,
"I had a lord to whom I wedded was,   *975*
The whose mine herte all was, till that he deide;
And other love, as help me now Pallas,
There in mine herte nis, ne never was,
And that ye been of noble and high kinrede,
I have well herde it tellen, out of dreede—   *980*

"And that doth me to han so greet a wonder
That ye will scornen° any woman so.
Eek, God wot, love and I been far asunder.
I am disposed bet, so mot I go,
Unto my deeth to plain and maken woe.   *985*
What I shall after doon I cannot saye,
But trewelich, as yet me list not playe.

"Mine herte is now in tribulacioun,
And ye in armes bisy day by day.
Hereafter, when ye wonnen han the town,   *990*
Peraunter thenne so it happen may,
That when I see that I never ere say,°
Then will I worke that I never wroughte.°
This word to you enough suffisen oughte.

"Tomorrow eek will I speken with you fain—   *995*
So that ye touchen not of this mattere.
And when you list, ye may come here again,
And ere ye goon, thus much I say you here:
As help me Pallas with her heeres cleere,
If that I shold of any Greek han routhe,   *1000*
It sholde be yourselven, by my trouthe.

"I say not therefore that I will you love,
N'I say not nay . . . But in conclusioun,
I meene well, by God that sit above."
And therewithal she cast her eyen down,   *1005*

982 **scornen** mock. Criseyde feels that Diomede is offering love too
quickly   992 **that . . . say** what I never saw before   993 **worke
. . . wroughte** do what I never did

And gan to sigh, and said, "O Troye town,
Yet bid I God in quiet and in reste
I may you seen, or do mine herte breste."

But in effect, and shortly for to saye,
This Diomede all freshly new again   *1010*
Gan pressen on, and fast her mercy praye.
And after this, the soothe for to sayn,
Her glove he took, of which he was full fain.
And finally, when it was woxen eve
And all was well, he rose and took his leeve.   *1015*

The brighte Venus° followed and ay taughte
The way ther broode Phebus down alighte;°
And Cynthia her char-horse overraughte°
To whirl out of the Lion,° if she mighte;
And Signifer° his candles sheweth brighte,   *1020*
When that Criseyde unto her bedde wente,
Inwith° her fader's faire brighte tente,

Returning° in her soul ay up and down
The wordes of this sudden Diomede—
His greet estate, and peril of the town,   *1025*
And that she was alone, and hadde neede
Of freendes' help. And thus began to breede
The cause why, the soothe for to telle,
That she took fully purpose° for to dwelle.

The morrowen came, and ghostly° for to speke,   *1030*
This Diomede is come unto Criseyde.
And shortly, lest that ye my tale breeke,°
So well he for himselven spake and saide
That all her sighes sore adown he laide.°

1016 **Venus** the morning star   1016–17 **ay . . . alighte** indicated
where the broad sun set   1018 **Cynthia . . . overraughte** Cynthia,
the moon, urged on her chariot horses   1019 **out . . . Lion** out of
the sign of Leo. Criseyde promised she would return to Troy before
the moon left Leo   1020 **Signifer** the Zodiac ("sign-bearer")
1022 **Inwith** within   1023 **Returning** turning over   1029 **took . . .
purpose** finally made up her mind   1030 **ghostly** solemnly, truth-
fully   1032 **breeke** break off (stop reading)   1034 **adown . . .
laide** he dispelled

And finally, the soothe for to sayne,   *1035*
He reft her of the grete° of all her paine.

And after this the story telleth us
That she him yaf the faire baye steede,°
The which he ones won of Troilus;
And eek a brooch—and that was litel neede—   *1040*
That Troilus' was, she yaf this Diomede;
And eek, the bet from sorrow him to releeve,
She made him weer a pencel of° her sleeve.

I finde eek in stories elleswhere,
When through the body hurt was Diomede   *1045*
Of Troilus, tho wept she many a teere
When that she saw his wide woundes bleede;
And that she took, to keepen him, good heede,
And for to heel him of his sorrows smerte,
Men sayn—I not°—that she yaf him her herte.   *1050*

But trewely, the story telleth us.
There made never woman more woe
Than she, when that she falsed° Troilus.
She said, "Alas, for now is cleen ago°
My name of trouth in love for evermo!   *1055*
For I have falsed one the gentileste
That ever was, and one the worthieste.

"Alas, of me unto the worlde's ende
Shall neither been y-written nor y-songe
No good word—for these bookes will me shende.   *1060*
O, rolled shall I been on many a tongue!
Throughout the world my belle shall be ronge!
And women most will haten me of alle.
Alas, that swich a cas me sholde falle!

.

1036 **He . . . grete** he relieved her of the greater part   1038 **baye
steede** Chaucer summarizes his source rapidly here. Diomede cap-
tured a horse from Troilus and gave it to Criseyde. Later, Criseyde
returned it when Diomede needed a war horse   1043 **weer . . . of**
wear a token from   1050 **I not** I do not (say it); or, *I ne wot* (I
don't know). Possibly the phrase is meant to be taken either way
1053 **falsed** betrayed   1054 **cleen ago** entirely gone

"They will sayn, in as much as in me is,°   1065
I have hem done dishonour—wailaway!
Al be I not the first that did amiss,
What helpeth that to doon my blame away?
But sin I see there is no better way,
And that too late is now for me to rewe,   1070
To Diomede algate° I will be trewe.

"But Troilus, sin I no better may—
And sin that thus departen ye and I—
Yet pray I God, so yive you right good day,
As for the gentileste, trewely,   1075
That ever I saw to serven faithfully,
And best can ay his lady honour keepe"
—And with that word she brust anon to weepe.

"And certes, you ne haten shall I nevere,
And freende's love, *that* shall ye han of me,   1080
And my good word—al shold I liven evere.
And trewely, I wolde sorry be
For to seen you in adversitee,
And guilteless, I wot well, I you leve—
But all shall pass, and thus take I my leeve."   1085

But trewely, how long it was betweene
That she forsook him for this Diomede,
There is noon auctor telleth it, I weene.
Take every man now to his bookes heede:
He shall no terme° finden, out of dreede.   1090
For though that he began to woo her soone,
Ere he her won, yet was there more to doone.

Ne me ne list this sely woman chide°
Further than the story will devise.
Her name, alas, is punished so wide,   1095
That for her guilt it ought enough suffise.
And if I might excuse her any wise,
For she so sorry was for her untrouthe,
Ywis, I wold excuse her yet for routhe.

* * *

1065 **in . . . is** to my utmost   1071 **algate** anyway   1090 **terme**
specified length of time   1093 **Ne . . . chide** I don't care to take
this hapless woman to task

This Troilus, as I before have told,   *1100*
Thus driveth forth° as well as he hath might,
But often was his herte hot and cold—
And namely that ilke ninthe night,
Which on the morrow she had him behight
To come again. God wot, full litel reste   *1105*
Had he that night—nothing to sleep him leste.

The laurer-crowned Phebus, with his heete,
Gan in his course ay upward as he wente,
To warmen of the Eest Sea the wawes wete;°
And Nisus' daughter° sung with fresh intente,   *1110*
When Troilus his Pandar after sente,
And on the walles of the town they playde
To look if they can seen aught of Criseyde.

Till it was noon they stooden for to see
Who that there came. And every manner wight   *1115*
That came from far, they saiden it was she,
Till that they coude knowen him aright:
Now was his herte dull, now was it light.
And thus bejaped° standen for to stare—
Aboute nought°—this Troilus and Pandare.   *1120*

To Pandarus this Troilus tho saide:
"For aught I wot, before noon sikerly
Into this town ne com'th not here Criseyde.
She hath enough to doone, hardily,
To twinnen from her fader—so trow I.   *1125*
Her olde fader will yet make her dine
Ere that she go, God yive his herte pine!"°

Pandar answered: "It may well be, certain.
And forthy let us dine, I thee beseeche,
And after noon then maist thou come again."   *1130*
And home they go, withoute more speeche,
And come again. But longe may they seeche
Ere that they finde that they after gape:
Fortune hem bothe thinketh for to jape.

1101 **driveth forth** endures   1109 **of . . . wete** the wet waves of
the East Sea (possibly the Indian Ocean)   1110 **Nisus' daughter**
Scylla, who betrayed her father for love of Minos and was subse-
quently changed into a lark   1119 **bejaped** fooled   1120 **Aboute**
nought for nothing   1127 **pine** pain

Quod Troilus: "I see well now that she   *1135*
Is tarried with her olde fader so
That, ere she come, it will nigh even° be.
Come forth, I will unto the gate go.
These porters been unconning° evermo,
And I will doon hem holden up the gate,   *1140*
As nought ne were, although she come late."

The day goeth fast, and after that came eve—
And yet came not to Troilus Criseyde.
He looked forth by hedge, by tree, by greve,°
And far his heed over the wall he laide.   *1145*
And at the last he turned him and saide,
"By God, I wot her meening now, Pandare!
Almost, ywis, all newe was my care.

"Now douteless, this lady kan her good.°
I wot she meeneth riden prively.   *1150*
I commend her wisdom, by mine hood!
She will not maken people nicely
Gaure on° her when she com'th: but softely,
By night, into the town she thinketh ride.
And deere brother, think not long to abide.   *1155*

"We han nought elles for to doon, ywis.
And Pandarus, now wilt thou trowen me?
Have here my trouth—I see her! Yond she is!
Heeve up thine eyen, man! Maist thou not see?"
Pandar answered, "Nay, so mot I thee,   *1160*
All wrong! By God, what saist thou, man? Where arte?
That I see yond nis but a fare-carte."°

"Alas, thou saist right sooth," quod Troilus.
"But hardily, it is not all for nought
That in mine herte I now rejoice thus.   *1165*
It is·agains° some good I have a thought.
Noot I not how, but sin that I was wrought
Ne felt I swich a comfort, dare I saye:
She cometh tonight, my life that durst I laye."

1137 even evening   **1139 unconning** inept   **1144 greve** thicket
1149 kan . . . good knows what is good for her   **1153 Gaure on**
gawk at   **1162 fare-carte** wagon   **1166 agains** in expectation of

Pandar answered, "It may be well enough"
  —And held° with him of all that ever he saide.
But in his herte he thought, and softe lough,
And to himself full soberlich he saide,
"From hazelwood, ther jolly Robin playde,
Shall come all that that thou abidest here°—   *1175*
Yea, farewell all the snow of ferne yeere!"°

The warden of the gates gan to calle
The folk which that without the gates were,
And bade hem driven in hir beestes alle,
Or all the night they muste bleven there.   *1180*
And far within the night, with many a teere,
This Troilus gan homeward for to ride,
For well he seeth it helpeth nought to abide.

But natheless, he gladded him in this:
He thought he misaccounted had his day,   *1185*
And said, "I understand have all amiss.
For thilke night I last Criseyde say,°
She said, 'I shall been here, if that I may,
Ere that the moon, O deere herte sweete,
The Lion pass out of this Ariete.'°   *1190*

For which she may yet hold all her beheste."
And on the morrow unto the gate he wente,
And up and down, by west and eek by eeste,
Upon the walles made he many a wente°—
But all for nought. His hope alway him blente;   *1195*
For which at night, in sorrow and sighes sore,
He went him home withouten any more.

His hope all cleen out of his herte fledde:
He n'ath whereon now longer for to honge;°

1171 **held** agreed   1174–75 **From . . . here** i.e., Criseyde will
emerge only from the never-never land of Robin Hood. Chaucer
uses the word *hazelwood* to express profound doubt (cf. III.890
and V.505)   1176 **farewell . . . yeere** "farewell all the snows of
yesteryear." The sentiment is proverbial but is best known in
François Villon's phrase, as translated by Rossetti, "Where are
the snows of yester-year?"   1187 **say** saw   1190 **The . . . Ariete**
passes out of the Ram and beyond Leo (see IV.1592)   1194 **wente**
turn (i.e., he paced back and forth)   1199 **He . . . honge** he no
longer has anything to hang on to

But for the pain him thought his herte bledde—   *1200*
So were his throwes° sharp and wonder stronge.
For when he saw that she abode so longe,
He niste what he judgen of it mighte,
Sin she hath broken that she him behighte.

The thridde, fourthe, fifthe, sixthe day,   *1205*
After tho dayes ten of which I tolde,
Betwixen hope and dreed his herte lay,
Yet somewhat trusting on her hestes olde.
But when he saw she nold her terme holde,
He can now seen noon other remedye   *1210*
But for to shape him soone for to die.

Therewith the wicked spirit, God us blesse,
Which that men clepeth the woode Jelousye,
Gan in him creep in all this hevinesse;
For which, because he wolde soone die,   *1215*
He ne eet ne drank for his melancholye,
And eek from every compaigny he fledde.
This was the life that all the time he ledde.

He so defeet° was that no manner man
Unneth him mighte knowen ther he wente;   *1220*
So was he leen—and thereto pale and wan—
And feeble, that he walketh by potente.°
And with his ire he thus himselven shente;°
And whoso asked him whereof him smerte,
He said his harm was all about his herte.   *1225*

Priam full oft, and eek his moder deere,
His bretheren and his sustren gan him fraine°
Why he so sorrowful was in all his cheere,
And what thing was the cause of all his paine.
But all for nought. He nold his cause plaine,   *1230*
But said he felt a grevous maladye
About his herte, and fain he wolde die.

So on a day he laid him down to sleepe,
And so befell that in his sleep him thoughte

1201 **throwes** throes   1219 **defeet** disfigured   1222 **by potente** with
a crutch   1223 **shente** wasted   1227 **fraine** ask

That in a forest fast he welk° to weepe,   *1235*
For love of her that him these paines wroughte.
And up and down, as he the forest soughte,
He mette° he saw a boor° with tuskes greete,
That slept again° the brighte sunne's heete.

And by this boor, fast in his armes folde,°   *1240*
Lay kissing ay his lady bright, Criseyde.
For sorrow of which, when he it gan beholde—
And for despite—out of his sleep he braide,°
And loud he cried on Pandarus and saide,
"O Pandarus, now know I crop and roote!°   *1245*
I n'am but deed—there nis noon other boote.

"My lady bright, Criseyde, hath me betrayed,
In whom I trusted most of any wight.
She elleswhere hath now her herte apayed.°
The blissful goddes, through hir greete might,   *1250*
Han in my dreem y-shewed it full right.
Thus in my dreem Criseyde have I beholde . . ."
And all this thing to Pandarus he tolde.

"O my Criseyde, alas, what subtiltee,°
What newe lust, what beautee, what science,°   *1255*
What wrath of juste cause have ye to me?
What guilt of me, what fell° experience,
Hath fro me reft, alas, thine advertence?°
O trust, O faith, O deepe assuraunce,
Who hath me reft Criseyde, all my plesaunce?   *1260*

"Alas, why let I you from hennes go—
For which well nigh out of my wit I braide?
Who shall now trow on any oothes mo?
God wot, I wend, O lady bright, Criseyde,
That every word was gospel that ye saide.   *1265*
But who may bet beguile, if him liste,
Than he on whom men weeneth best to triste?

1235 **welk** walked   1238 **mette** dreamed   1238 **boor** boar   1239 **again** in   1240 **folde** folded, held. The image is of Criseyde held by and kissing the boar   1243 **braide** started   1245 **crop . . . roote** branch and root (i.e., everything)   1249 **apayed** satisfied   1254 **subtiltee** guile   1255 **science** knowledge   1257 **fell** dire   1258 **advertence** attentions

"What shall I doon, my Pandarus, alas?
I feele now so sharp, a newe paine,
Sin that there is no remedy in this cas,　　　　　　　　*1270*
That bet were it I with mine handes twaine
Myselven slew, alway than thus to plaine.
For through my deeth my woe shold have an ende,
Ther° every day with life myself I shende."

Pandar answered and said, "Alas, the while　　　　　　*1275*
That I was born! Have I not said ere this
That dreemes many a manner man beguile?
And why? For folk expounden° hem amiss.
How darest thou sayn that false thy lady is,
For any dreem right for thine owne dreede?　　　　　　*1280*
Let be this thought! Thou canst no dreemes reede.

"Peraunter, ther thou dremest of this boor,
It may so be that it may signifye
Her fader, which that old is and eek hoor,°
Again the sunne lieth on point to die,°　　　　　　　　*1285*
And she for sorrow ginneth weep and crye,
And kisseth him ther he lieth on the grounde.
Thus sholdest thou thy dreem aright expounde."

"How might I thenne doon," quod Troilus,
"To know of this—yea, were it never so lite?"　　　　*1290*
"Now saist thou wisly," quod this Pandarus.
"My reed is this: sin thou canst well endite,
That hastily a letter thou her write,
Through which thou shalt well bringen it aboute
To know a sooth of° that thou art in doute.　　　　　*1295*

"And see now why: for this I dare well sayn,
That if so is that she untrewe be,
I cannot trowen that she will write again.
And if she write thou shalt full soon y-see
As whether she hath any libertee　　　　　　　　　　*1300*
To come again; or elles, in some clause,
If she be let,° she will assign a cause.

1274 **Ther** whereas　　1278 **expounden** interpret　　1284 **hoor** hoar
1285 **on . . . die** on the brink of death　　1295 **a . . . of** the truth
concerning　　1302 **let** hindered

"Thou hast not written her sin that she wente—
Nor she to thee. And this I durste laye:
There may swich cause been in her intente   *1305*
That, hardily, thou wilt thyselven saye
That her abode° the best is for you twaye.
Now write her then, and thou shalt feele° soone
A sooth of all. There is no more to doone."

Accorded been to this conclusioun—   *1310*
And that anon—these ilke lordes two.
And hastily sit Troilus adown,
And rolleth in his herte to and fro
How he may best descriven her his woe;
And to Criseyde, his owne lady deere,   *1315*
He wrote right thus, and said as ye may heere:

"Right freshe flow'r, whose I been have° and shall,
Withouten part of ellesswhere service,°
With herte, body, life, lust, thought, and all—
I, woeful wight, in everich humble wise   *1320*
That tongue tell or herte may devise,
As oft as matter occupieth place,
Me recommend unto your noble grace.

"Liketh it you to witen,° sweete herte,
As ye well know, how longe time agon   *1325*
That ye me left in aspre paines smerte,
When that ye went, of which yet boote noon
Have I none had. But ever worse begon°
Fro day to day am I, and so mot dwelle—
While it you list—of wele and woe my welle.   *1330*

"Fro which to you with dreedful herte trewe
I write—as he that sorrow driveth to write—
My woe, that everich hour increeseth newe,
Complaining as I dare or can endite.

1307 **abode** staying (in the Greek camp) 1308 **feele** know 1317
been have have been. The awkwardness of this construction (sup-
ported by the best manuscripts), along with the cumbersome
syntax in the next line, may represent Troilus's attempt to embody
the high style 1318 **Withouten . . . service** without bestowing my
service elsewhere 1324 **Liketh . . . witen** may it please you to
know 1328 **worse begon** worse off

And that defaced is, that may ye wite° 1335
The teeres, which that fro mine eyen raine,
That wolden speke, if that they coud, and plaine.

"You first beseech I that your eyen cleere
To look on this defouled ye not holde;°
And overal this that ye, my lady deere, 1340
Will vouchesauf this letter to beholde.
And by the cause eek of my cares colde
That sleeth° my wit, if aught amiss me asterte,°
Foryive it me, mine owne sweete herte.

"If any servant durst or ought of right 1345
Upon his lady pitously complaine,
Then ween I that ich oughte be that wight,
Considered this, that ye these monthes twaine
Han tarried—ther ye saiden, sooth to sayne,
But dayes ten ye nold in host sojourne. 1350
But in two monthes yet ye not returne.

"But for as much as me mot needes like
All that you list, I dare not plaine more;
But humblely, with sorrowful sighes sike,°
You write ich mine unresty° sorrows sore, 1355
Fro day to day desiring evermore
To knowen fully, if your will it were,
How ye han ferde, and done, while ye be there—

"The whose welfare and hele eek God increese
In honour swich that upward in degree 1360
It grow alway, so that it never ceese.
Right as your herte ay can, my lady free,
Devise, I pray to God so mot it be,
And grant it that ye soon upon me rewe,
As wisly as in all I am you trewe. 1365

"And if you liketh knowen of the fare
Of me—whose woe there may no wight descrive—
I can no more but, chest° of every care,

1335 wite blame upon   1338–39 that . . . holde that you don't
consider your bright eyes to be defiled by looking on this letter
1343 sleeth slays   1343 me asterte escapes me   1354 sike sickly
1355 unresty unending   1368 chest i.e., repository

At writing of this letter I was on live,
All redy out my woeful ghost to drive;   *1370*
Which I delay, and hold him yet in honde,°
Upon the sight of matter of your sonde.°

"Mine eyen two, in vain with which I see,
Of sorrowful teeres salt aren woxen welles.°
My song in plaint of mine adversitee,   *1375*
My good in harm, mine eese eek woxen hell is,
My joy in woe—I can say you nought elles:
But turned is, for which my life I warye,°
Everich joy or eese in his contrarye.

"Which with your coming home again to Troye   *1380*
Ye may redress, and more a thousand sithe°
Than ever ich had, increesen in me joye.
For was there never herte yet so blithe
To han his life, as I shall been, as swithe°
As I you see. And though no manner routhe   *1385*
Commeve° you, yet thinketh on your trouthe.

"And if so be my guilt hath deeth deserved,
Or if you list no more upon me see,
In guerdon° yet of that I have you served,
Beseech I you, mine owne lady free,   *1390*
That hereupon ye wolden write me—
For love of God, my righte lode-sterre,
That deeth may make an end of all my werre;°

"If other cause aught doth you for to dwelle,
That with your letter ye me recomforte°—   *1395*
For though to me your absence is an helle,
With pacience I will my woe comporte,°
And with your letter of hope I will disporte.°
Now writeth, sweet, and let me thus not plaine:
With hope—or deeth—delivereth me fro paine.   *1400*

1371 **hold ... honde** i.e., delay (*him*= spirit)   1372 **matter ...
sonde** a message from you (*sonde*= sending)   1374 **aren ... welles**
have become fountains   1378 **warye** curse   1381 **sithe** times   1384
swithe soon   1386 **Commeve** move   1389 **guerdon** reward   1393
werre war   1395 **recomforte** comfort   1397 **comporte** endure
1398 **disporte** take heart

"Ywis, mine owne deere herte trewe,
I wot that when ye next upon me see,
So lost have I mine hele and eek mine hewe,
Criseyde shall not conne knowen me.
Ywis, mine herte's day, my lady free,   *1405*
So thirsteth ay mine herte to beholde
Your beautee, that my life unneth I holde.

"I say no more—al have I for to saye
To you well more than I telle may.
But whether that ye do me live or deye,   *1410*
Yet pray I God so yive you right good day!
And fareth well, goodly, faire, freshe may,°
As ye that life or deeth me may commande.
And to your trouth ay I me recommande,

"With hele swich that—but ye yiven me   *1415*
The same hele—I shall noon hele have.
In you lieth, when you list that it so be,
The day in which me clothen shall my grave;°
In you my life, in you might° for to save   *1420*
Me fro diseese of alle paines' smerte.
And fare now well, mine owne sweete herte,
                    Le vostre° T."

This letter forth was sent unto Criseyde,
Of which her answer in effect was this:
Full pitously she wrote again,° and saide
That also soon as that she might, ywis,   *1425*
She wolde come and mend all that was miss.
And finally she wrote, and said him thenne
She wolde come—yea, but she niste whenne.

But in her letter made she swich festes°·
That wonder was, and swer'th she loveth him best;   *1430*
Of which he found but bottomless behestes.°
But Troilus, thou maist now, eest or west,

1412 **may** maid   1418 **me . . . grave** my grave shall clothe me
1419 **in . . . might** in you is the power   1421 **Le vostre** your   1424
again back   1429 **festes** pleasantries   1431 **found . . . behestes**
experienced (later on) only empty promises

Pipe in an ivy leef,° if that thee lest.
Thus goeth the world—God sheeld us fro mischaunce!
And every wight that meeneth trouth avaunce!°   *1435*

Increesen gan the woe fro day to night
Of Troilus, for tarrying of Criseyde,
And lessen gan his hope and eek his might.°
For which all down he in his bed him laide:
He ne eet, ne drank, ne sleep, ne word saide,   *1440*
Imagining ay that she was unkinde,
For which well nigh he wex out of his minde.

This dreem, of which I told have eek beforn,
May never come out of his remembraunce.
He thought ay well he had his lady lorn,   *1445*
And that Joves, of his Purveyaunce,°
Him shewed had in sleep the signifiaunce
Of her untrouth, and his disaventure,
And that the boor was showed him in figure.

For which he for Sibylle° his suster sente,   *1450*
That called was Cassandre eek all aboute,
And all his dreem he told her ere he stente,
And her besought assoilen° him the doute
Of the stronge boor with tuskes stoute.
And finally, within a litel stounde,°   *1455*
Cassandre him gan right thus his dreem expounde:

She gan first smile, and said, "O brother deere,
If thou a sooth of this desirest knowe,
Thou must a few of olde stories heere,
To purpose° how that Fortune overthrowe   *1460*
Hath lordes old. Through which, within a throwe,°
Thou well this boor shalt know, and of what kinde°
He comen is, as men in bookes finde.

1433 **Pipe . . . leef** pipe to yourself, "go whistle"   1435 **And . . .
avaunce!** and aid every creature who intends fidelity!   1438 **might**
strength   1446 **of . . . Purveyaunce** in His foreknowledge   1450
Sibylle prophetess; but Chaucer uses this term as another name
for Cassandra, whose fate it was to be a soothsayer who always
was right but never believed   1453 **assoilen** to resolve   1455
stounde while   1460 **To purpose** concerning   1461 **throwe** little
while   1462 **kinde** family

"Diane°—which that wroth was and in ire,
For Greekes nolde doon her sacrifise,   1465
N'incense upon her auter° set afire—
She, for that Greekes gonne her so despise,
Wrake her° in a wonder cruel wise:
For with a boor, as greet as ox in stalle,
She made up frete hir corn and vines alle.°   1470

"To slee this boor was all the countree raised;°
Amonges which there came, this boor to see,
A maid—one of this world the best y-praised.
And Meleager, lord of that countree,
He loved so this freshe maiden free,   1475
That with his manhood, ere he wolde stente,
This boor he slew, and her the heed he sente;

"Of which, as olde bookes tellen us,
There rose a contek° and a greet envye.°
And of this lord descended Tydeus   1480
By line (or elles olde bookes lie).
But how this Meleager gan to die
Thorough his moder, will I you nought telle,
For all too long it were for to dwelle."

1464 **Diane** Diana, goddess of the hunt   1466 **auter** altar   1468
Wrake her avenged herself   1470 **She . . . alle** she caused their
(the Greeks') corn and grape vines to be eaten up   1471 **raised**
stirred up   1479 **contek** strife   1479 **envye** hostility. Meleager
killed his uncles in anger when they took offense at his presenting
the great boar's head to the maiden Atalanta. In the following lines
Cassandra summarizes important moments from the story of the
siege of Thebes—the same story that Criseyde and two ladies were
reading at II.100. Chaucer, through Cassandra's interpretation,
suggests that the quarrel between Troilus and the boar of his dream
(Diomede) has its roots in the Theban conflict. Troilus's personal
struggle is thus seen as part of a larger historical pattern of strife
and revenge which began when Meleager sent the boar's head to
the woman he loved. A dream about a boar conventionally boded
misfortune, usually connected with lust; see Beryl Rowland, *Animals with Human Faces* (Knoxville, Tenn.: University of Tennessee

She tolde eek how Tydeus, ere she stente,   *1485*
Unto the strange citee of Thebes,
To claimen kingdom of the citee, wente,
For his fellow, daun Polymites,°
Of which the brother, daun Ethiocles,
Full wrongfully of Thebes held the strengthe—   *1490*
This tolde she by process° all by lengthe.

She tolde eek how Hemonides asterte,°
When Tydeus slew fifty knightes stoute;
She tolde eek all the prophecies by herte,
And how that seven kinges, with hir route,°   *1495*
Besegeden the citee all aboute;
And of the holy serpent, and the welle,
And of the Furies—all she gan him telle:

Of Archimoris'° burying, and the playes,°
And how Amphiorax fell through the grounde;   *1500*
How Tydeus was slain, lord of Argeyes,
And how Ipomedon in litel stounde
Was dreint,° and deëde Parthonope of wounde;
And also how Capaneus° the proude
With thunder-dint° was slain, that cried loude.   *1505*

She gan eek tell him how that either brother,
Ethiocles and Polymite also,
At a scarmuch° eech of hem slew other,
And of Argives' weeping, and hir woe;
And how the town was brent she told eek tho—   *1510*

Press, 1973), p. 39   1488 **daun Polymites** lord Polynices. Polynices
and his brother, Eteocles, were supposed to take turns ruling Thebes.
Eteocles refused to give up his rule when the time came, so Poly-
nices enlisted the help of six other heroes and kings and launched
an attack on Thebes (the "Seven against Thebes")   1491 **by process**
in sequence   1492 **Hemonides asterte** When Tydeus was ambushed
by fifty Theban knights, he killed all but Haemonides, who got away
1495 **route** army   1499 **Archimoris** Archemorus was killed by a
serpent (line 1497) sent by Jupiter   1499 **playes** funeral games
1500–4 **Amphiorax . . . Capaneus** Amphiaraus, Tydeus, Hippome-
don, Parthenopaeus, and Capaneus were five of the Seven against
Thebes   1502–3 **in . . . dreint** in a brief time was drowned   1505
thunder-dint thunderbolt   1508 **scarmuch** skirmish

And so descendeth down fro gestes° olde
To Diomede, and thus she spake and tolde:

"This ilke boor betokeneth° Diomede,
Tydeus' son, that down descended is
Fro Meleager, that made the boor to bleede.   *1515*
And thy lady, whereso she be, ywis,
This Diomede her herte hath, and she his.
Weep if thou wilt, or leeve.° For out of doute,
This Diomede is in—and thou art oute."

"Thou saist not sooth!" quod he, "thou sorceresse,   *1520*
With all thy false ghost° of prophecye!
Thou weenest been a greet divineresse.°
Now seest thou° not this fool of fantasye
Paineth her on ladies for to lie?°
Away," quod he, "ther Joves yive thee sorrwe!   *1525*
Thou shalt be false, peraunter, yet tomorrwe!

"As well thou mightest lien on Alceste°—
That was of creatures, but men lie,
That ever weren, kindest and the beste—
For when her husband was in jupartye   *1530*
To die himself, but if she wolde die,
She chese for him to die, and goon to helle,
And starf anon, as us the bookes telle."

Cassandre goeth. And he with cruel herte
Forgot his woe for anger of her speeche.   *1535*
And from his bed all suddenly he sterte,
As though all hool him had y-made a leeche.°
And day by day he gan inquere and seeche
A sooth of this, with all his fulle cure.°
And thus he drieth forth his aventure.°   *1540*

1511 **gestes** stories   1513 **betokeneth** signifies   1518 **leeve** leave off, desist   1521 **ghost** spirit   1522 **Thou . . . divineresse** you think you're a great seeress   1523 **thou** a general audience (not Cassandra)   1524 **Paineth . . . lie** takes pains to lie about women   1527 **Alceste** Alcestis, paragon of wifely obedience and chief character of the Prologue to Chaucer's *Legend of Good Women*   1537 **leeche** physician   1539 **cure** care   1540 **he . . . aventure** he acts out his destiny. Cf. I.1092

Fortune—which that permutacioun
Of thinges hath, as it is her committed
Through purveyance and disposicioun
Of highe Jove, as regnes shall be flitted°
Fro folk in folk, or when they shall be smitted°—   *1545*
Gan pull away the fetheres bright of Troye
Fro day to day, till they° been bare of joye.

Among all this, the fin of the parodye°
Of Hector gan approchen wonder blive.
The Fate wold his soule shold unbodye,°   *1550*
And shapen had a meen it out to drive;°
Agains which Fate him helpeth not to strive,
But on a day to fighten gan he wende,
At which, alas, he caught his live's ende.

For which me thinketh every manner wight   *1555*
That haunteth° armes oughte to bewaille
The deeth of him that was so noble a knight,
For as he drew a king by th'aventaille,°
Unware° of this, Achilles through the maile
And through the body gan him for to rive:°   *1560*
And thus this worthy knight was brought of live,°

For whom, as olde bookes tellen us,
Was made swich woe that tongue it may not telle—
And namely, the sorrow of Troilus,
That next him was of worthinesse welle.   *1565*
And in this woe gan Troilus to dwelle,
That what for sorrow, and love, and for unreste,
Full oft a day he bade his herte breste.

But natheless, though he gan him despaire
And dradde ay that his lady was untrewe,   *1570*

1544 **regnes . . . flitted** kingdoms shall be shifted   1545 **smitted**
struck down   1547 **they** the Trojans   1548 **fin . . . parodye** end
of the lifespan   1550 **unbodye** leave the body   1551 **shapen . . .
drive** had devised a means for driving it out   1556 **haunteth** has
recourse to   1558 **drew . . . th'aventaille** dragged a king by the
chain mail chest and face cover   1559 **Unware** (Hector) being un-
aware   1560 **rive** pierce   1561 **of live** i.e., to his death

Yet ay on her his herte gan repaire,
And as these lovers doon, he sought ay newe
To get again Criseyde, bright of hewe,
And in his herte he went° her excusinge,
That Calkas caused all her tarryinge.   *1575*

And ofte time he was in purpose grete
Himselven like a pilgrim to disguise,
To seen her; but he may not countrefete
To been unknown of folk that weren wise,
Ne find excuse aright that may suffise,   *1580*
If he among the Greekes knowen were;
For which he weep full oft and many a teere.

To her he wrote yet ofte time all newe
Full pitously—he left° it not for slouthe—
Beseeching here, sin that he was trewe,   *1585*
That she will come again, and hold her trouthe.
For which Criseyde upon a day, for routhe—
I take it so—touching all this mattere,
Wrote him again, and said as ye may here:

"Cupide's son, ensample° of goodliheede,   *1590*
O sword of knighthood, source of gentilesse,
How might a wight in torment and in dreede,
And heleless,° you send as yet gladnesse?
I herteless, I sick, I in distresse—
Sin ye with me, nor I with you, may deele—   *1595*
You neither send ich herte may nor hele.

"Your letters full, the paper all y-plainted,°
Conceived hath mine herte's pietee.°
I have eek seen with teeres all depainted
Your letter, and how that ye requeren° me   *1600*
To come again, which yet ne may not be.
But why, lest that this letter founden were,
No mencioun ne make I now, for feere.

1574 **went** went on   1584 **left** neglected   1590 **ensample** pattern
1593 **heleless** without health   1597 **all y-plainted** filled with complaints   1598 **Conceived . . . pietee** my heart's pity has understood
1600 **requeren** importune

"Grevous to me, God wot, is your unreste,
Your haste, and that the goddes' ordinaunce°   *1605*
It seemeth not ye take it for the beste.
Nor other thing nis in your remembraunce,
As thinketh me, but only your plesaunce.
But beeth not wroth, and that I you beseeche,
For that I tarry is all for wicked° speeche.   *1610*

"For I have herde well more than I wende
Touching us two, how thinges han y-stonde,
Which I shall with dissimuling° amende;
And beeth not wroth, I have eek understonde
How ye ne do but holden me in honde.   *1615*
But now no force, I cannot in you guesse
But alle trouth and alle gentilesse.

"Come I will, but yet in swich disjointe°
I stand as now, that what yeer or what day
That this shall be, that can I not appointe.   *1620*
But in effect I pray you, as I may,
Of your good word and of your freendship ay,
For trewely, while that my life may dure,
As for a freend ye may in me assure.

"Yet pray ich you on evil° ye ne take   *1625*
That it is short which that I to you write.
I dare not, ther I am, well letters make,
Ne never yet ne could I well endite.
Eek greet effect men write in place lite°—
The intent is all, and not the letters' space.   *1630*
And fareth now well. God have you in his grace,
                    La vostre° C."

This Troilus this letter thought all straunge
When he it saw, and sorrowfullich he sighte:
Him thought it like a kalendes° of chaunge.

1605 **ordinaunce** decree   1610 **wicked** slanderous   1613 **dissimuling**
dissembling   1618 **disjointe** predicament   1625 **on evil** amiss   1629
Eek . . . lite also, in a short space men write things of great moment
1631 **La vostre** your   1634 **kalendes** beginning, point of départure

But finally, he full ne trowen mighte   *1635*
That she ne wold him holden that she highte.°
For with full evil will list him to leve
That loveth well, in swich case, though him greeve.°

But natheless, men sayn that at the laste,
For anything,° men shall the soothe see.   *1640*
And swich a case betidde, and that as faste,
That Troilus well understood that she
Nas not so kind as that her oughte be.
And finally he wot now, out of doute,
That all is lost that he hath been aboute.   *1645*

Stood on a day in his melancholye
This Troilus, and in suspecioun
Of her for whom he wende for to die.
And so befell that throughout Troye town,
As was the guise,° y-born was up and down   *1650*
A manner coot-armour,° as saith the storye,
Beforn Deiphebe, in sign of his victorye.

The whiche coot, as telleth Lollius,°
Deiphebe it hadde rent° fro Diomede
The same day. And when this Troilus   *1655*
It saw, he gan to taken of it heede,
Avising of° the length and of the brede,
And all the work. But as he gan beholde,
Full suddenly his herte gan to colde,

As he that on the collar found withinne   *1660*
A brooch, that he Criseyde yaf that morrwe

1635–36 **he . . . highte** he might not fully believe that she wouldn't
keep her promise to him   1637–38 **For . . . greeve** for he who loves
well is most reluctant to believe (the truth), in such a case, though
it grieve him   1640 **For anything** despite everything   1650 **guise**
custom   1651 **manner coot-armour** kind of tunic (worn over armor)
1653 **Lollius** Chaucer's supposed author. Cf. I.394   1654 **rent** torn
1657 **Avising of** studying. Troilus never liked Diomede. He con-
templated killing him when Criseyde was to be led off (V.45); he
spoke no word to him when he left Criseyde (V.86–87); and he
reacted violently when his sister identified him as his rival for
Criseyde's affections (V.1513f.). So he has more than a passing
interest in this war prize

That she from Troye muste needes twinne,
In remembrance of him and of his sorrwe—
And she him laid again her faith to borwe°
To keep it ay! But now full well he wiste,   *1665*
His lady nas no longer on to triste.

* * *

He goeth him home, and gan full soone sende
For Pandarus. And all this newe chaunce,°
And of this brooch, he told him word and ende,
Complaining of her herte's variaunce,°   *1670*
His longe love, his trouth, and his penaunce.
And after deeth, withouten wordes more,
Full fast he cried, his rest him to restore.

Then spake he thus: "O lady mine, Criseyde,
Where is your faith, and where is your beheste?   *1675*
Where is your love, where is your trouth?" he saide.
"Of Diomede have ye now all this feste?°
Alas, I wold han trowed at the leeste
That sin ye nold in trouthe to me stonde,
That ye thus nold han holden me in honde.°   *1680*

"Who shall now trow on any oothes mo?
Alas, I never wold han wend, ere this,
That ye, Criseyde, coud han changed so,
Ne but I had aguilt° and done amiss.
So cruel wend I not your herte, ywis,   *1685*
To slee me thus. Alas, your name of trouthe
Is now fordone,° and that is all my routhe.

"Was there noon other brooch you liste lete°
To feffe with° your newe love," quod he,
"But thilke brooch that I, with teeres wete,   *1690*
You yaf, as for a remembrance of me?
None other cause, alas, ne hadde ye,
But for despite, and eek for that ye mente
All outrely to shewen your intente.

1664 **laid . . . borwe** pledged her faith in return 1668 **chaunce**
happening 1670 **variaunce** fickleness 1677 **feste** pleasure 1680
nold . . . honde wouldn't have deceived me 1684 **aguilt** offended
1687 **fordone** destroyed 1688 **you . . . lete** it pleased you to part
with 1689 **feffe with** bestow upon

"Through which I see that cleen out of your minde   *1695*
Ye han me cast. And I ne can nor may,
For all this world, within mine herte finde
To unloven you a quarter of a day.
In cursed time I born was, wailaway!
That you, that doon me all this woe endure,   *1700*
Yet love I best of any creature.

"Now God," quod he, "me sende yet the grace
That I may meeten with this Diomede!
And trewely, if I have might and space,°
Yet shall I make, I hope, his sides bleede.   *1705*
O God," quod he, "that oughtest taken heede
To furtheren trouth and wronges to punice,
Why nilt thou doon a vengeance of this vice?

"O Pandarus, that in dreemes for to triste
Me blamed hast, and wont art oft upbraide,°   *1710*
Now maist thou see thyself, if that thee liste,
How trew is now thy neece, bright Criseyde!
In sundry formes, God it wot," he saide,
"The goddes shewen bothe joy and teene°
In sleep, and by my dreem it is now seene.   *1715*

"And certainly, withouten more speeche,
From hennesforth, as ferforth as I may,
Mine owne deeth in armes will I seeche.
I recche not how soone be the day.
But trewely, Criseyde, sweete may,°   *1720*
Whom I have ay with all my might y-served,
That ye thus doon, I have it not deserved."

This Pandarus, that all these thinges herde
And wiste well he said a sooth of this,
He not a word again to him answerde—   *1725*
For sorry of his freende's sorrow he is,
And shamed for his neece hath done amiss—
And stant astoned of° these causes twaye,
As still as stone: a word ne coud he saye.

1704 **space** opportunity   1710 **upbraide** to scold (me, for believing
dreams)   1714 **teene** sorrow   1720 **may** maid   1728 **stant . . . of**
stands stunned by

But at the laste thus he spake and saide: *1730*
"My brother deer, I may do thee no more.
What shold I sayn? I hate, ywis, Criseyde,
And God wot I will hate her evermore.
And that thou me besoughtest doon of yore°—
Having unto mine honour ne my reste   *1735*
Right no reward°—I did all that thee leste.

"If I did aught that mighte liken thee,
It is me lief. And of this treeson now,
God wot that it a sorrow is unto me;
And dreedeless, for herte's eese of you,   *1740*
Right fain I wold amend° it—wist I how.
And fro this world almighty God I praye
Deliver her soon. I can no more saye."

* * *

Greet was the sorrow and plaint of Troilus—
But forth her course Fortune ay gan to holde: *1745*
Criseyde loveth the son of Tydeus,
And Troilus mot weep in cares colde.
Swich is this world, whoso it can beholde:
In eech estate° is litel herte's reste.
God leeve us for to take it for the beste!   *1750*

In many cruel bataille, out of dreede,
Of Troilus, this ilke noble knight,
As men may in these olde bookes reede,
Was seen his knighthood and his greete might.
And dreedeless, his ire day and night   *1755*
Full cruelly the Greekes ay aboughte,°
And alway most this Diomede he soughte.

And ofte time I finde that they mette
With bloody strokes and with wordes greete,
Assaying how hir speeres weren whette;°   *1760*
And, God it wot, with many a cruel heete°
Gan Troilus upon his helm to beete.
But natheless, Fortune it nought ne wolde
Of other's hand that either dien sholde.

1734 **that . . . yore** what you asked me to do formerly   1736 **re-ward** regard   1741 **amend** correct   1749 **estate** rank   1756 **aboughte** paid for   1760 **Assaying . . . whette** testing how their spears were honed   1761 **heete** rage

And if I had y-taken° for to write   *1765*
The armes of this ilke worthy man,
Then wold ich of his batailles endite;
But for that I to writen first began
Of his love, I have saide as I can—
His worthy deedes, whoso list hem heere,   *1770*
Reed Dares,° *he* can tell hem all yfere—

Beseeching every lady bright of hewe,
And every gentil woman, what she be,
That, al be that Criseyde was untrewe,
That for that guilt she be not wroth with me.   *1775*
Ye may her guilt in other bookes see,
And gladlier I will write, if you leste,
Penelopeë's trouth° and good Alceste.

N'I say not this all only for° these men,
But most for women that betraised° be   *1780*
Through false folk—God yive hem sorrow, amen—
That with hir greete wit and subtiltee
Betraise you. And this commeveth° me
To speke, and in effect you all I praye,
Beeth ware of men, and herkeneth what I saye.   *1785*

Go, litel book: go, litel mine tragedye,
Ther God thy maker yet, ere that he die,
So sende might to make in some comedye.°
But litel book, no making thou n'envye,°
But subjet be to alle poesye,   *1790*
And kiss the steppes wher-as thou seest passe
Virgil, Ovid, Homer, Lucan, and Stace.°

And for there is so greet diversitee
In English, and in writing of our tongue,
So pray I God that none miswrite° thee,   *1795*

1765 **y-taken** undertaken   1771 **Dares** author of an account of the
Trojan War (cf. I.146)   1778 **Penelopeë's trouth** the fidelity of
Penelope, wife of Ulysses. This line is probably a reference to Chau-
cer's next work, *The Legend of Good Women*   1779 **for** of   1780
betraised betrayed   1783 **commeveth** moves   1787–88 **Ther . .°.
comedye** may God send to your composer the power to compose
in the manner of a kind of comedy. This line is probably a refer-
ence to *The Canterbury Tales*   1789 **no . . . n'envye** don't contend
with any poem   1792 **Stace** Statius   1795 **miswrite** miscopy

Ne thee mismetre for defaute of tongue;°
And red whereso thou be,° or elles songe,
That thou be understond, God I beseeche.
But yet to purpose of my rather° speeche:

The wrath, as I began you for to saye,   *1800*
Of Troilus the Greekes boughten deere,°
For thousandes his handes maden deye,
As he that was withouten any peere,
Save Hector, in his time, as I can heere.

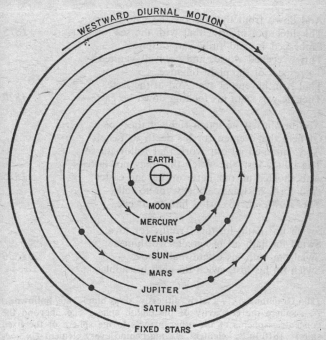

*The Ptolemaic or geocentric universe (Earth is represented as
a "T-O" map, which placed east at the top, diagrammed the
Danube, Mediterranean, and Nile as a T, and placed Jerusalem
at the center.)*

1796 **mismetre . . . tongue** get the meter wrong on account of
faulty speech   1797 **red . . . be** wherever you are read   1799
rather earlier   1801 **boughten deere** dearly paid for

But wailaway, save only Godde's wille,   *1805*
Despitously him slew° the fierce Achille.

And when that he was slain in this mannere,
His lighte ghost full blissfully is went
Up to the hollowness of the eighthe sphere,°
In converse leting everich element.°   *1810*
And there he saw, with full avisement,°
The erratic stars,° herkening harmonye,°
With sounes° full of hevenish melodye.

And down from thennes fast he gan avise
This litel spot of erth, that with the sea   *1815*
Embraced is, and fully gan despise°
This wrecched world, and held all vanitee
To respect of the plain felicitee°
That is in hevene above. And at the laste,
Ther he was slain his looking down he caste—   *1820*

And in himself he lough right at the woe
Of hem that wepten for his deeth so faste;
And dampned all our work that followeth so
The blinde lust, the which that may not laste—
And sholden all our herte on hevene caste;   *1825*
And forth he wente, shortly for to telle,
Ther-as Mercurye sorted him to dwelle.°

Swich fin° hath, lo, this Troilus for love;
Swich fin hath all his greete worthinesse;
Swich fin hath his estate real° above;   *1830*
Swich fin his lust, swich fin hath his noblesse;

1806 **Despitously . . . slew** pitilessly slew him   1809 **hollowness
. . . sphere** the concavity of the eighth sphere (i.e., beyond the
concentric spheres of the other planets to the sphere of the fixed
stars)   1810 **In . . element** leaving behind every element (*in con-
verse*= "on the other side")   1811 **with . . . avisement** with a full-
ness of vision   1812 **erratic stars** the seven planets (as opposed to
the "fixed" stars)   1812 **herkening harmonye** (he) listening to the
music of the spheres (created by the rubbing of the concentric
spheres against one another)   1813 **sounes** sounds   1816 **gan de-
spise** had contempt of   1818 **To . . . felicitee** in comparison with
the full bliss   1827 **Ther-as . . . dwelle** to where Mercury, con-
ductor of souls, determined he should reside   1828 **fin** ending
1830 **real** royal

Swich fin hath false worlde's brottlenesse.°
And thus began his loving of Criseyde,
As I have told, and in this wise he deide.

O younge freshe folkes, he or she,   *1835*
In which that love up groweth with your age,
Repaireth° home fro worldly vanitee,
And of your herte up casteth the visage
To thilke God that after his image
You made, and thinketh all nis but a faire,°   *1840*
This world, that passeth soon as flowers faire.

And loveth Him, the which that right for love
Upon a cross, our soules for to beye,°
First starf, and rose, and sit in hevene above:
For He nill falsen° no wight, dare I saye,   *1845*
That will his herte all hoolly on Him laye.
And sin He best to love is and most meeke,
What needeth feigned loves for to seeke?

Lo, here of payens'° cursed olde rites;
Lo, here what all hir goddes may availe;   *1850*
Lo, here these wrecched worlde's appetites;
Lo, here the fin and guerdon for travaille°
Of Jove, Apollo, of Mars, of swich rascaile;°
Lo, here the form of olde clerkes' speeche
In poetry, if ye hir bookes seeche.°   *1855*

O moral Gower,° this book I directe
To thee and to thee, philosophical Strode,°
To vouchensauf, ther need is, to correcte,
Of your benignitees and zeeles goode.
And to that soothfast Christ that starf on roode,°   *1860*

1832 **brottlenesse** brittleness   1837 **Repaireth** return   1840 **all . . .
faire** all the world is only a fair. The sentiment is proverbial. John
Gower, to whom Chaucer dedicates the *Troilus* (V.1856), writes:
"For all is but a cherry fair/ This worlde's good"   1843 **beye**
redeem   1845 **falsen** betray   1849 **here . . . payens'** here concern-
ing pagans'   1852 **the . . . travaille** the end and reward of service
1853 **rascaile** rascals   1855 **seeche** seek through, study   1856
Gower John Gower, Chaucer's friend and perhaps his teacher
1857 **Strode** Ralph Strode, Oxford philosopher   1860 **on roode** on
the cross

With all mine herte of mercy ever I praye.
And to the Lord right thus I speke and saye:

Thou one and two and three,° eterne on live,
That regnest ay in three and two and oon,
Uncircumscript, and all maist circumscrive,°   *1865*
Us from visible and invisible foon°
Defend; and to thy mercy everichoon
So make us, Jesus, for thy mercy digne,°
For love of Maid and Moder° thine benigne.° Amen

1863 **Thou . . . three** the Trinity: Father, Son, and Holy Ghost
1865 **Uncircumscript . . . circumscrive** uncircumscribed and (that)
can circumscribe all things   1866 **foon** foes   1868 **for . . . digne**
worthy of your mercy   1869 **Maid . . . Moder** the Virgin Mary
1869 **benigne** (make us) benign

CHAUCER'S WORDS UNTO ADAM,
HIS OWN SCRIVAIN

Adam scrivain,° if ever it thee befalle
Boece° or *Troilus* for to writen newe,
Under thy long lockes thou must have the scalle,°
But after my making thou write more trewe.°
So oft a day I mot° thy work renewe   5
It to correct, and eek to rub and scrape—
And all is through thy negligence and rape!°

1 **scrivain** scribe. Adam apparently transcribed Chaucer's works directly from the poet's own manuscripts. This poem has special importance as it indicates Chaucer's concern with the accurate transmission of his works. Cf. also *Troilus*, V.1786–98   2 **Boece** i.e., Chaucer's translation of Boethius   3 **thou . . . scalle** may you have scurf (an annoying skin ailment)   4 **But . . . trewe** unless you write faithfully what I've composed. A poet was called a "maker" in Middle English and his poetry was called his "making." The phrase "more trewe" has the sense of "with strict accuracy"   5 **mot** must   7 **rape** carelessness

THE COMPLAINT OF VENUS

1

There nis so high° comfort to my plesaunce,°
When that I am in any hevinesse,°
As for to have leiser° of remembraunce
Upon the manhood and the worthinesse,
Upon the trouth,° and on the stedfastnesse   5
Of him whose I am all, while I may dure.°
There oughte blame me no creature,°
For every wight praiseth his gentilesse.°

In him is bountee, wisdom, governaunce°
Well more than any manne's wit can guesse;   10
For grace hath wold so ferforth him avaunce°
That of knighthood he is parfit richesse.°
Honour honoureth him for his noblesse:°
Thereto so well hath formed him Nature
That I am his forever, I him assure,   15
For every wight praiseth his gentilesse.

0 **The Complaint of Venus** this poem is an adaptation of three ballades by Otes (or Oton) de Granson, a French poet killed in a duel in 1397. The title, *The Complaint of Venus*, is traditional, though it is unsuitable for the situation. According to another tradition, Chaucer wrote the poem for Isabel, Duchess of York—the "Princess" of the envoy (Isabel was daughter of Pedro, King of Castille). Skeat assigned titles to the three sections of the poem: (1) "The Lover's worthiness"; (2) "Disquietude caused by Jealousy"; (3) "Satisfaction in Constancy." The poem echoes common motifs like the lover's suffering (lines 25–32), the concern over jealous people, etc., which one finds in *Troilus and Criseyde* 1 **high** great 1 **plesaunce** pleasure 2 **hevinesse** sadness 3 **leiser** leisure, opportunity 5 **trouth** loyalty (one of the most important virtues for a lover) 6 **dure** endure 7 **There . . . creature** no creature ought to blame me 8 **gentilesse** nobility (cf. "gentility") 9 **governaunce** self-control 11 **grace . . . avaunce** favor has wished to aid him to such an extent 12 **parfit richesse** perfect richness (i.e., has a wealth of knightly qualities) 13 **noblesse** nobility

And notwithstanding all his suffisaunce,
His gentil herte is of so greet humblesse°
To me in word, in work, in countenaunce,°
And me to serve is all his bisinesse,°   20
That I am set in verray sikernesse.°
Thus ought I blesse well mine aventure,°
Sith that him list me serven° and honoure,
For every wight praiseth his gentilesse.

2

Now certes, Love, it is right covenable°   25
That men full deer aby° thy noble thing°—
As wake abed, and fasting at the table,°
Weeping to laugh, and sing in complaining,
And down to caste visage and looking,
Often to change hew and countenaunce,   30
Plain° in sleeping, and dreemen at the daunce,
All the reverse of any glad feeling.

Jelousy be hanged by a cable!
She wold all knowe through her espying.
There doth no wight nothing so reesonable,   35
That all nis harm in her imagining.°
Thus deer abought is Love in yiving,
Which oft he yiveth withouten ordinaunce,°
As sorrow enough, and litel of plesaunce,
All the reverse of any glad feeling.   40

18 **humblesse** humility   19 **in . . . countenaunce** in deeds, in (his)
manner   20 **bisinesse** diligence   21 **verray sikernesse** true security
22 **aventure** luck   23 **Sith . . . serven** since it pleases him to serve me
25 **covenable** fitting   26 **aby** pay for   26 **thing** i.e., the lover's situa-
tion, which the feminine narrator summarizes in the following
lines. Troilus, who embodies the courtly virtues which the narrator
describes in Part 1 of this poem, suffers from the lover's situation
(sleeplessness, loss of appetite, etc.)   27 **fasting . . . table** i.e., loss
of appetite   31 **Plain** complain   35–36 **There . . . imagining** i.e.,
Jealousy, in her imagination, turns every action that a person does
into an offense. Cf. Criseyde's attack on Jealousy in *Troilus*,
III.988ff., and the effects of jealousy on Troilus in V.1212ff.
38 **ordinaunce** order

A litel time his yift° is agreeable,
But full encumberous° is the using.°
For subtle Jelousy, the deceivable,
Full often time causeth disturbing.
Thus be we ever in dreed and suffering.   45
In non-certain° we languish in penaunce,°
And han full often many an hard mischaunce,°
All the reverse of any glad feeling.

3

But certes, Love, I say not in such wise
That for t'escape out of your laas I mente;°   50
For I so long have been in your service
That for to let of will I never assente.°
No force° though Jelousye me tormente!
Sufficeth me to seen him when I may.
And therefore, certes, to mine ending day   55
To love him best ne shall I never repente.

And certes, Love, when I me well avise°
On any estate° that man may represente,
Then have ye made me, through your fraunchise,°
Chese° the best that ever on erthe wente.   60
Now love well, herte, and look thou never stente,°
And let the jelous put it in assay°
That, for no paine, will I not say nay.
To love him best ne shall I never repente.

Herte, to thee it oughte enough suffise   65
That Love so high a grace to thee sente
To chese the worthiest in alle wise,°
And most agreeable unto mine intente.

41 **his yift** (Love's) gift   42 **encumberous** cumbersome, annoying
42 **the using** i.e., the practice of loving   46 **non-certain** uncertainty
46 **penaunce** suffering   47 **mischaunce** bad luck   50 **That . . .
mente** that I meant to escape from your leash   52 **for . . . assente**
I shall never assent of my will to stop   53 **No force** no matter   57
I . . . avise I consider well   58 **estate** social rank   59 **fraunchise**
generosity   60 **Chese** choose   61 **look . . . stente** see that you
never stop   62 **in assay** to the test   67 **in . . . wise** in all respects

Seek no further, neither way ne wente,°
Sith I have suffisaunce unto my pay.°   70
Thus will I end this complaint or this lay:°
To love him best ne shall I never repente.

Lenvoy

Princess, receiveth this complaint in gree°
Unto your excellent benignitee
Direct after° my litel suffisaunce.   75
For eld,° that in my spirit dulleth me,
Hath of enditing° all the subtiltee
Well nigh beraft out of my remembraunce.
And eek to me it is a greet penaunce,
Sith rime in English hath such scarcitee   80
To follow word by word the curiositee°
Of Graunson, flower of hem that make° in Fraunce.

69 **way ... wente** highway nor path 70 **unto ... pay** for my reward
71 **lay** song 73 **in gree** with good will 75 **Direct after** just ac-
cording to 76 **eld** old age 77 **enditing** composing 81 **curiositee**
i.e., the ingenious rhymes in French. There are fewer possibilities
for rhymes in English, and it is perhaps for this reason that Chau-
cer departs from his usual practice and rhymes *aventure* with
honoure (lines 22 and 23). *Curiositee* is probably trisyllabic, accents
on first and last syllables 82 **hem ... make** those who write
poetry

TO ROSEMOUNDE

A Ballade

Madame, ye been of alle beautee shrine
As far as circled is the mappemounde,°
For as the crystal glorious ye shine,
And like ruby been your cheekes rounde.
Therewith ye been so merry and so jocounde,   5
That at a revel, when that I see you daunce,
It is an oinement unto my wounde,
Though ye to me ne do no daliaunce.°

For though I weep of teeres full a tine,°
Yet may that woe mine herte not confounde;   10
Your semy° voice that ye so small out-twine°
Maketh my thought in joy and bliss abounde.
So courteisly I go, with love bounde,
That to myself I say, in my penaunce,
"Sufficeth me to love you, Rosemounde"—   15
Though ye to me ne do no daliaunce.

Nas never pike° wallowed in galauntine°
As I in love am wallowed and y-wounde;

0 **To Rosemounde** this humorous courtly lyric is a ballade, a
French song form whose characteristics are a refrain, three (or
sometimes four) rhymes, and an envoy. This poem has no envoy.
The rhyme scheme in each stanza is *ababbcbc*. It was not unusual
for poets to exaggerate and ridicule the extravagances of the lover's
weeping, woe, etc. One might compare Shakespeare's sonnet "My
mistress' eyes are nothing like the sun" 2 **mappemounde** world
map. Medieval world maps were often circular. The lady's name
suggests *Rosa mundi*, "rose of the world," i.e., perfection. The
details in the description of her contradict this extravagant implica-
tion 8 **do . . . daliaunce** pay no attention 9 **tine** tub 11 **semy**
tiny (a rich voice was standard for courtly ladies) 11 **out-twine**
bring out, perhaps "squeak" 17 **pike** a fish, one which has been
caught and is being cooked! 17 **galauntine** galantine sauce, made
with brown bread, vinegar, and cinnamon

For which full oft I of myself divine°
That I am trewe Tristam° the secounde. 20
My love may not refraide nor affounde;°
I bren° ay in an amorous plesaunce.
Do what you list, I will your thrall be founde,
Though ye to me ne do no daliaunce.

---

19 **divine** imagine 20 **Tristram** a faithful lover, who loved Isolde.
The love affair between Tristram and Isolde was heroic and tragic
21 **refraide . . . affounde** be cooled off or confounded (lit. "sub-
merged") 22 **bren** burn

AGAINST WOMAN UNCONSTANT

Ballade

Madame, for your newfanglenesse,°
Many a servant° have ye put out of grace.
I take my leeve of your unstedfastnesse,
For well I wot, while ye have live's space,°
Ye cannot love full half yeer in a place,°   5
To newe thing your lust° is ay so keene:
In stede of blew, thus may ye were all greene.°

Right as a mirror nothing may impresse,
But, lightly as it° com'th, so mot it passe,
So fareth your love, your works bereth witnesse.   10
There is no faith that may your herte embrace;
But, as a wedercock,° that turneth his face
With every wind, ye fare, and that is seene.°
In stede of blew, thus may ye were all greene.

Ye might be shrined, for your brottlenesse,°   15
Better than Dalida, Criseyde, or Candace;°
For ever in changing stant° your sikernesse.

0 **Against Woman Unconstant** though the authenticity of this love-song, a ballade in rhyme royal, has been doubted, it is almost certainly Chaucer's work   1 **newfanglenesse** fondness for new things (a word with the pejorative connotation of rapacity: related to *fang*)   2 **servant** i.e., suitor for love. Troilus sees his relationship with Criseyde as that of a servant to the lady who seeks her *grace* or favor   4 **have ... space** i.e., are alive   5 **in ... place** in one place   6 **To ... lust** for new things your desire   7 **blew ... greene** blue symbolized constancy, green inconstancy and jealousy   9 **it** i.e., the image which comes into the mirror   12 **wedercock** weathercock   13 **seene** evident   15 **shrined ... brottlenesse** enshrined, because of your brittleness (fickleness). Chaucer's antonym to *brottleness* is *sikerness* (cf. *Complaint of Venus*, 21)   16 **Dalida, Candace** Delilah, who betrayed Samson; Queen Candace, who tricked Alexander the Great   17 **stant** stands

That tacch° may no wight fro your herte arace.°
If ye lose one, ye can well twain purchase.
All light for summer,° ye wot well what I meene: *20*
In stede of blew, thus may ye were all greene.

---

18 **tacch** blemish, defect   18 **arace** uproot   20 **All . . . summer**
entirely in light clothes for summer (with a pun on *light* = wanton)

MERCILESS BEAUTEE

A Triple Roundel

1

Your eyen two will slee me suddenly:
I may the beautee of hem not sustene,°
So woundeth it throughout my herte keene.°

And but° your word will heelen hastily
My herte's wounde, while that it is greene,°   5
   Your eyen two will slee me suddenly:
   I may the beautee of hem not sustene.

Upon my trouth° I say you faithfully
That ye been of my life and deeth the queene,
For with my deeth the trouthe shall be seene.   10
   Your eyen two will slee me suddenly:
   I may the beautee of hem not sustene,
   So woundeth it throughout my herte keene.

2

So hath your beautee fro your herte chased
Pitee, that me ne availeth nought° to plaine,   15

0 **Merciless Beautee** here Chaucer demonstrates his skill in another
French courtly-love form, the triple roundel. A roundel typically
has thirteen or fourteen lines with but two rhymes and with several
lines repeated as a refrain. Like *To Rosemounde* this song strikes
an anti-romantic note. One might compare Chaucer's picture of
himself in the *Troilus* as one who is out of it in matters of love
2 **sustene** withstand 3 **So . . . keene** your beauty wounds (me) so
keenly 4 **but** unless 5 **greene** fresh 8 **trouth** word 15 **me . . .
nought** it avails me nothing

For Daunger halt° your mercy in his chaine.
Guiltless my deeth thus han ye me purchased°—
I say you sooth—me needeth not to feigne.
  So hath your beautee fro your herte chased
  Pitee, that me ne availeth nought to plaine.   20

Alas, that Nature hath in you compassed°
So greet beautee, that no man may attaine
To mercy, though he sterve° for the paine.
  So hath your beautee fro your herte chased
  Pitee, that me ne availeth nought to plaine,   25
  For Daunger halt your mercy in his chaine.

3

Sin I fro Love escaped am so fat,°
I never think to been in his prison leene.
Sin I am free, I count him not a beene.°

He may answer and saye this and that;   30
I do no force,° I speke right as I meene.
  Sin I fro Love escaped am so fat,
  I never think to been in his prison leene.

Love hath my name y-strike out of his sclat,°
And he is strike out of my bookes cleene   35
For evermo—there is noon other meene.°
  Sin I fro Love escaped am so fat,
  I never think to been in his prison leene.
  Sin I am free, I count him not a beene.

16 **Daunger halt** Disdain holds. *Daunger* is the aloofness or distance
that a courtly lady maintains from her ardent suitor. Here Daunger
is personified as a restraining influence on Chaucer's lady, as if she
were on a leash. (Cf. *Complaint of Venus*, 50) 17 **purchased**
brought about 21 **compassed** enclosed 23 **sterve** die 27 **fat** fully
(with a pun on *leene*, "lean," in line 28). Lovers were proverbially
thin from "fasting at the table" (*Complaint of Venus*, 27) 29 **count**
. . . **beene** don't give a bean for him 31 **do** . . . **force** don't care
34 **y-strike** . . . **sclat** struck out of his slate 36 **meene** course

WOMANLY NOBLESSE

Ballade that Chaucer Made

So hath mine herte caught in remembraunce
Your beautee hool, and stedfast governaunce,°
Your virtues alle, and your high noblesse,
That you to serve is set all my plesaunce.
So well me liketh your womanly countenaunce,   **5**
Your freshe feetures and your comelinesse
That, whiles I live, mine herte to his° maistresse
You hath full chose, in trew perseveraunce,
Never to change for no manner distresse.

And sith° I shall do you this observaunce   **10**
All my life, withouten displesaunce,
You for to serve with all my bisinesse,°

* * *

And have me somewhat in your souvenaunce.°
My woeful herte suffereth greet duresse;   **15**
And look how humblely, with all simplesse,
My will I conform to your ordinaunce,°
As you best list, my pains for to redresse.

Considering eek how I hang in balaunce
In your service, such, lo, is my chaunce,°   **20**

0 Womanly Noblesse like *To Rosemounde*, this poem is a ballade, but it has only two rhymes in three stanzas of nine lines each, and, instead of a refrain, it has an envoy. The final two lines of the envoy echo the opening lines. In this love-song Chaucer attempts to define his relationship with a lady who embodies "womanly noblesse" **2 Your . . . governaunce** your perfect beauty, and steadfast self-control **7 to his** for its **10 sith** since **12 bisinesse** diligence **14 souvenaunce** remembrance **17 ordinaunce** guidance **20 chaunce** luck or fortune

Abiding grace, when that your gentilesse
Of my greet woe listeth doon allegeaunce,°
And with your pitee me some wise avaunce
In full rebating° of mine hevinesse.°
And thinketh, by reeson,° that womanly noblesse   **25**
Shold not desire for to do thee outraunce
Ther-as she findeth noon unbuxomnesse.°

Lenvoye

Auctor of nurture, lady of plesaunce,
Sovereign of beautee, flower of womanheede,
Take ye noon heed unto° mine ignoraunce,   **30**
But this receiveth of your goodliheede,
Thinking that I have caught in remembraunce
Your beautee hool, your stedfast governaunce.

21–22 **Abiding . . . allegeaunce** awaiting favor, when it pleases your nobility to alleviate my great woe 24 **rebating** abatement 24 **hevinesse** sadness 25 **by reeson** with good reason 26–27 **Shold . . . unbuxomnesse** wouldn't want to desert you in whom she finds no disobedience. *Outraunce*= lit. an excessive thing, outrage 30 **Tak . . . unto** pay no attention to

LENVOY DE CHAUCER A SCOGAN

To-broken been the statutes high in hevene
That create were eternally to dure,°
Sith that I see the brighte goddes sevene°
Mow°.weep and wail and passion endure,
As may in erth a mortal creature.   5
Alas, fro whennes may this thing proceede,
Of which error° I die almost for dreede?

By word eterne whilom was it shape,°
That fro the fifthe circle,° in no mannere,
Ne might a drop of teeres down escape.   10
But now so weepeth Venus in her sphere
That with her teeres she will drench° us here.
Alas, Scogan, this is for thine offence!
Thou causest this deluge of pestilence.

Hast thou not said, in blaspheme of these goddes—   15
Through pride or through thy greete rakelnesse°—
Swich thing as in the law of Love forbode° is:
That, for° thy lady saw not thy distresse,
Therefore thou yave her up at Michelmesse?°
Alas, Scogan, of° olde folk ne younge   20
Was never erst° Scogan blamed for his tongue!

0 **Lenvoy de Chaucer a Scogan** this is a mock-serious verse letter
in which Chaucer·rebukes his friend Scogan for giving up his lady.
Scogan was a courtier and dabbler in writing verse   2 **create . . .
dure** were created to endure eternally   3 **goddes sevene** the plane-
tary gods   4 **Mow** may   7 **error** i.e., the abnormality of the broken
statutes and the gods' weeping   8 **whilom . . . shape** once it was
ordained   9 **fifthe circle** the circle of Venus (reckoning from the
outer circles in toward the earth). In the *Troilus*, III, Proem,
Chaucer identifies the sphere of Venus as the "thridde hevene,"
figuring from the earth outwards. (Cf. p. 279)   12 **drench** drown
16 **rakelnesse** recklessness   17 **forbode** forbidden   18 **for** because
19 **Michelmesse** Michaelmas, feast of St. Michael (one of the
English quarter days: Sept. 29)   20 **of** by   21 **erst** before

Thou drew in scorn Cupid eek to record°
Of thilke° rebel word that thou hast spoken,
For which he will no longer be thy lord;
And Scogan, though his bowe be not broken, 25
He will not with his arrows been y-wroken°
On thee, ne me—ne none of our figure:°
We shall of him have neither hurt ne cure.

Now certes, freend, I dreed of thine unhap,°
Lest for thy guilt the wrecch° of Love proceede 30
On all hem that been hoor° and round of shap,
That been so likely folk in love to speede.°
Then shall we for our labour have no meede;°
But well I wot thou wilt answer and saye,
"Lo, olde Grisel° list to rime and playe!" 35

Nay, Scogan, say not so, for I me excuse—
God help me so!—in no rime, douteless,
Ne think I never of° sleep to wake my muse,
That rusteth° in my sheethe still in pees.
While I was young, I put her forth in press;° 40
But all shall passe that men prose or rime:
Take every man his turn, as for his time.

Envoy

Scogan, that kneelest at the streeme's heed°
Of grace, of all honour and worthinesse,

22 **to record** as a witness 23 **thilke** that 26 **y-wroken** revenged
27 **our figure** Chaucer on a number of occasions alludes to his
portly shape and his unfitness for love affairs. In the *Troilus* he
speaks of his "unlikeliness" for love (I.16), and in line 31 of this
poem he implies that he is "round of shape" 29 **dreed . . . unhap**
fear your misfortune 30 **wrecch** revenge 31 **hoor** hoary-headed,
gray 32 **speede** succeed 33 **meede** reward 35 **olde Grisel** old
Grizzly (cf. "graybeard") 38 **of** from 39 **That rusteth . . .** Chau-
cer compares his flagging interest in writing love poetry to a sword
that rusts in its sheath, but he humorously mixes the metaphor by
saying that his "muse" rusts in his sheath (with a sexual innuendo)
40 **in press** among the crowd 43 **streeme's heed** stream's head
(probably the palace at Windsor, source of royal favor and
patronage)

In th'end of which streem I am dull as deed,°   *45*
Forgete° in solitarye wildernesse.°
Yet, Scogan, think on Tullius' Kindenesse:°
Minne° thy freend, ther it may fructifye.°
Farewell, and look thou never eft° Love defye!

45 **dull . . . deed** dull as a dead man   46 **Forgete** forgotten   46
wildernesse perhaps Chaucer's residence at Greenwich. Chaucer
explains that he and his sleeping, "rusty" muse have retired from
the theatre of love's warfare—the court—but that Scogan not only
continues in the fray but even breaks the rules by giving up his
lady. Chaucer goes on to offer Scogan his full friendship, for he
thinks Scogan will need a friend!   47 **Tullius' Kindenesse** Cicero's
famous treatise on friendship: *De Amicitia*   48 **Minne** remember
48 **fructifye** yield fruit   49 **eft** again

Textual Notes

Although Chaucer completed the *Troilus* about 1386–87, the earliest extant manuscripts of it date from the early fifteenth century. Some twenty manuscripts survive, along with three early printed editions including Thynne's edition of 1532, which is often accorded manuscript status. Scholars have determined that these manuscripts fall into three general groupings—*alpha*, *beta*, and *gamma*—but the authority of these groupings with respect to Chaucer's final intentions has been debated. It is generally agreed that the *beta* and *gamma* versions are later than *alpha*. And while the differences between the *beta* and *gamma* revisions sometimes pose difficulties for an editor, these differences are not, as Robinson notes, significant. The problems an editor of the *Troilus* encounters, that is, are not of the same order as those faced by an editor of the A,B, and C texts of *Piers Plowman*. R. K. Root, who provided much of the groundwork for textual study of the *Troilus* in *The Manuscripts of Chaucer's Troilus* (1914), *The Textual Tradition of Chaucer's Troilus* (1916), and his variorum edition of the poem (1926), judged that the *alpha* version is an early, unrevised text, the *beta* version constitutes the final revised text, while the *gamma* version descends from "a lost manuscript derived from Chaucer's original before the revision of the text was completed." Most authorities now agree, however, that the *gamma* version, consisting of seven manuscripts and Thynne's edition, constitutes the final, revised text of the *Troilus* as nearly as it can be determined. Recent editors—including Skeat (1894–97), Robinson (2nd ed., 1957), Donaldson (1958), and Baugh (1963)—base their texts for the most part upon the "best" and earliest *gamma* manuscripts.[1]

[1] Daniel Cook, in "The Revision of Chaucer's *Troilus*: the *Beta* Text," *Chaucer Review*, 9 (1974), 52, observes that recent editors who base their texts on the *gamma* manuscripts have never formally defended their method and choice. Cook believes that the unique *beta* readings in Books III and IV represent Chaucer's final intentions.

The present text is based upon a transcript of MS Corpus Christi College, Cambridge, 61 (abbreviated Cp), a *gamma* manuscript of the early fifteenth century, as published in *Three More Parallel Texts of Chaucer's Troilus and Criseyde*, F. J. Furnivall (ed.), Chaucer Society Pubs., First Ser. Nos. 87 and 88 (London and New York: Oxford University Press, 1894–95), and is corrected and emended by variant readings from six other manuscripts: St. John's College, Cambridge, L. 1 (abbreviated J), and Harleian 1239, British Museum (H_3), both published in *Three More Parallel Texts*; Campsall MS, Pierpont Morgan Library, New York (Cl), Harleian 2280, British Museum (H_1), and Cambridge University Library Gg. 4. 27 (Gg), as published in *A Parallel-Text Print of Chaucer's Troilus and Criseyde*, F. J. Furnivall (ed.), Chaucer Soc. Pubs., First Ser. Nos. 63 and 64 (London: N. Trübner & Co., 1881–82); and Harleian 3943, British Museum (H_2), as published in *Chaucer's Troylus and Cryseyde Compared with Boccaccio's Filostrato*, W. M. Rossetti (trans.), Chaucer Soc. Pubs., Second Ser. Nos. 44, 65 (London: N. Trübner, 1875). The readings of these transcribed manuscripts have been checked against Root's corrections in his Appendix to *The Textual Tradition of Chaucer's Troilus* (pp. 273–77), and against Bühler's supplement to Root's corrections for Cl.[2] I have also consulted the textual notes of Skeat, Root, and Robinson.

Cp, Cl, and H_1 are consistently *gamma* manuscripts; J is *beta* to IV.430–38, and *alpha* thereafter; H_2 is *alpha* through Books I–III, *beta* after IV.196; H_3 is a composite of *alpha*, *beta*, and *gamma*; Gg is *beta* and *alpha*, *alpha* from III.399. Cp and Cl are of the early fifteenth century, H_1 of the mid-fifteenth century. Cp, Cl, H_1, and J are usually described as the "most authoritative" manuscripts because they are early, well executed, orthographically consistent, and comparatively free of gross scribal blunders and corruptions.

While I usually follow the principle of *durior lectio* with respect to Cp and the *gamma* manuscripts, I have felt at liberty to consult other manuscripts when the meaning of a

---

[2] Curt F. Bühler, "Notes on the Campsall Manuscript of Chaucer's *Troilus and Criseyde* Now in the Pierpont Morgan Library," *Speculum*, 20 (1955), 457–60. Bühler offers 92 major corrections of the Chaucer Society transcript of Cl; yet of these only two (those at III. 623 and III. 917) affected the Textual Notes of this edition.

passage seemed unclear or when the prosody appeared defective. I agree with the sentiments of E. Talbot Donaldson, "The Psychology of Editors of Middle English Texts," who argues that editors should bring their judgment and experience to the editing of a text.[3]

Significant departures from Cp are listed below and sometimes explained. But spelling variants—including expanded spellings (e.g., our *wost thou* for *wostow* of Cp), elision (our *the assege* for *thassege*), metathesis (our *thirst* for *thrust*), syncopated forms (our *yelt* for *yeldeth*), tense (our *aileth* for *eyled*), or spellings which affect meter—are not recorded. The readings of the present text appear in italics preceded by line numbers; those of Cp follow in regular type. Present-text readings are given in normalized spelling; discarded and variant readings are retained in their original forms. When the best manuscripts—Cl, J, and H₁—concur in a variant against Cp, this variant appears in italics without manuscript attribution, followed by the Cp reading, so identified. When these manuscripts differ from one another, the several readings are listed with the manuscripts recorded in brackets following the variant.

[3] In *Speaking of Chaucer* (Athlone Press, England, 1970; rpt. New York: W. W. Norton, 1972), pp. 102–18.

Troilus and Criseyde

BOOK I

79 *full this* ful in this

87 *traitor fled was* [J, H₂, Gg] traitour fals fled was [Cp, Cl, H₁] traytowre was fledde [H₃]

91 *for to brennen* to be brent

92 *left* lost

143 *here* [J, H₃, Gg] [Cp, Cl, H₁, H₂ omit]

167 *both the most* [J] both moeste meyne [Cp, H₁] bothe meene meste [Cl] the moost [H₂] bothe tho moste [H₃] boþe meste [Gg]

170 *black* [Cp omits]

176 *said* [Cp omits]

193 *On* Or

198 *lewed* [J, H₂, H₃, Gg] [Cp, Cl, H₁ omit]

234 *that* [Cp omits]

256 *binde* blynde

257 *The* Tho

270 *or of withoute* [Cp omits of]

272 *His eye perced* [J, H₁, H₃] His sighte procede [Cp] His eye procede [Cl] his eye perceyvid [H₂] his eyȝen perseydyn [Gg]

315 *And eft on her, while that the service laste* [Cl; H₂ oft for eft; H₃ tho for the] And ofte on hire while that seruyse laste [Cp, H₁; J, Gg eft for ofte]

336 *ruled* piled

337 *non-certain* veyn certeyn

356 *he niste* hym nyst

358 *in chamber* in the chambre

363 *at temple* Only one MS, Rawlinson, reads *at temple*, though Cl has *a temple*. Cp, J, H₁, H₃, and Gg read *and temple*; H₂ has *in þe temple* which makes good sense but is hypermetrical

372 *grame* grace

436 *the wherefro* wherfro [H₁ ye wher-fro]

440 *brende* bringe
453 *is his breeste's* [Cp omits his]
458 *serve I and laboure* [Cl, H₃, Gg] [Cp, J, H₁, H₂ omit and]
466 *this* [Cl, H₁, H₂] his [Cp, J, H₃, Gg]
471 *bretheren* brother
506 *gan to plaine* [Cp omits to]
509 *hent, now gnaw* [Cp omits now]
517 *thanked be God* [Cl, H₂, H₃, Gg] [Cp, J, H₁ omit be]
532 *fool* folk
534 *yea, never* [H₁, H₂, Gg] the neuere [Cp, J] yet neuere [Cl] neuer [H₃]
539 *me behete* me heete
543 *in salte* in the salte
555 *some* [Cp omits]
565 *as far as* after as
582 *malt for woe* malt wo [Cl for sorwe]
583 *may* [Cp omits]
601 *deem* do me
606 *saileth* [H₁, H₂, Gg] failleth [Cp, Cl, J, H₃]
612 *colde* cole
614 *followen* fallen
634 *thing* [Cp omits]
645 *two* [Cp omits]
654 *Which* with
661 *he knew* [J, H₂, H₃] she knew [Cp, Cl, H₁] he knyt [Gg]
682 *final* [H₂] finaly [rest]
689 *the meen* [Cl, H₁, H₂, H₃] ʒe menen [Cp, J] þat [Gg]
727 *in frenesye* he in frenesie
728 *He* [Cp omits]
746 *governed* couered
755 *to* [Cp omits]
764 *that reeson* [Cl, H₂, H₃] that ther reson [Cp, H₁, Gg] yt ther resoun [J]
773 *this* [Cp omits]
776 *ever* [Cp omits]
788 *voltures* volturie
810 *many* may
812 *mouth he kiste* [J, H₁, H₂, H₃] mouth kiste [Cp] mouth yet kyste [Cl] mouth he ne kyst [Gg]
824 *and a sinne* [J, H₁, H₃] and synne [Cp, Cl, H₂] & a gret synne [Gg]
883 *Ne I* [J, H₁=Ny; H₂] Ne [rest]
890–96 Not in Cp, Cl, H₁, J, H₃, or Gg. The present text

for this stanza is based upon H_2 compared against Thynne's edition [Th]

894 *for nought but good* [Th] for good
909 *him* hem
918 *on hem* [Cl, J, H_2, Gg] on hym [Cp, H_1, H_3]
921 *when they sleepen* whan that thei slepen
928 *failing* fallyng
960 *parted* [J, H_2, Gg] deperted [rest]
962 *no* [Cp omits]
964 *or herb* of herbe
965 *up* [Cp omits]
978 *love's* lyues
980 *her to finde* [J, H_1, H_2, H_3] hire fynde [Cp, Cl, Gg]
983 *her not* it naught
1054 *by my trouth* is my trowthe
1074 *the leoun* [J, H_2] tho leoun [Cp, Cl, H_1, H_3] Gg lacks lines I.1037–II.85

BOOK II

4 *my conning* [H_1, H_3] my commyng [rest]
35 *no* [Cp omits]
61 *So shope it that* So shope it hym
86 *your book and all the compaignye* [J, H_2, H_3, Gg] with al ȝoure fayre book and al the faire compaignie [Cp; Cl, H_1 omit second faire]
168 *Is selde* In selde
188 *every wight* euen wight
194 *fro him* Cp and J read *for hym gonne fleen*, while Cl and Gg have *gonne fro hym flen*. H_2 offers *fro hym ded flene*. H_1 and H_3 read *fro hym gonne fleen*, which appears to be the sense of the MSS and so has been adopted
199 *him . . . him* [J, H_2, Gg] hem . . . hem [Cp, Cl, H_1, H_3]
239 *my uncle* [J, H_2, Gg] uncle [Cp, Cl, H_1, H_3]
281 *to* [Cp omits]
283 *that* [Cp omits]
309 *Now, my good* [J, H_2, H_3] And good [Cp] Now good [Cl, H_1] Now myn [Gg]
349 *in you there be* [Cl, H_1, H_3] in yow be [Cp, H_2] in yow ne be [J, Gg]
425 *this fin? O* this fy O
426 *for me* [Cp omits]
438 *harm or* [J, H_3, Gg] harm or any [Cp, Cl, H_1, H_2]

484 *But* [J, H₂, H₃, Gg] And [Cp, Cl, H₁]

487 *Of you, though* Of ʒoure thought

516 *afar* [J] therafter [Cp, Cl, H₁] yn a fere [H₂] aftur [H₃, Gg]. The full line in J—*And I afer gan for to romen to and fro*—is hypermetrical and awkward, a defect which can be emended by omitting the unnecessary *for to*

555 *It fell* It felte

588 *God yet grant* [Cl, Gg] god graunte [Cp, J, H₁] god us graunt [H₂, H₃]

597 *lord, so he* [J, H₃] lord he [Cp, Cl, H₁] lord she [H₂] lord how [Gg]

615 *lattice* [H₂= latis] All the other MSS read ʒates. Root, Robinson, Baugh, and Donaldson retain ʒates on the evidence of the MSS, though Root and Baugh express misgivings. Skeat adopts *latis* and comments: "The reading *yates*, gates, is wrong, as shewn by 1. 617." It is possible that ʒates is "Adam Scrivain's" anticipation of ʒate in line 617

621 *day* [Cp omits]

650 *And let it so* [Cl, H₃] And leet so [Cp, J, H₁] And lete it in her hert so softly synk [H₂] And let so soft it [Gg]

677 *her herte for* [H₂, H₃] hire for [rest]

704 *yet for* that for

713 *hate to purchase* hate purchace

735 *let hem leeve* [J, H₃] lat hem byleue [Cp, Cl, H₁]. For lines 734–35 H₂ reads: Men lovyn wymmen al þis toun about/ Be they þe wors nay wiþ-outyn dout [Gg whi nay]

737 *this noble town* [H₂, H₃, Gg] this ilk noble towne [Cp, Cl, H₁] Of women in this world [J]

780 *or* and

795 *when it is* [Cl, J, H₂, H₃] whan that it is [Cp, H₁, Gg]

801 *hem, that they* [J, H₂, H₃] hem they [Cp, Cl, H₁] hem þat [Gg]

815 *they made* [J, H₂, Gg] ther made [Cp, Cl, H₁] the made [H₃]

821 *blossomy* [Cl, J, H₁, H₂= blosmy] blosum [Cp] blosmed [H₃] blospened [Gg]

850 *love* lyue

855 *whoso* who

950 *But Troilus, that thought* [J, H₃] But Troilus thoughte [Cp, Cl, H₁] Troylus þat þought [H₂, Gg]

966 *before, all he* before and al he

968 *stalkes* [J, H₂] stalk [rest]

977 *Troyes* [J, H₂, H₃, Gg] Troyens [Cp, Cl, H₁]

996 *Been* But

997 *emforth* euenforth

1043 *nere* [H₁, H₂, Gg] were [Cl] uere [Cp, J] where [H₃]

1055 *Right* [J, H₂, Gg] [Cp, Cl, H₁, H₃ omit]

1081 *accused* excused

1099 *woe, a* wo and a

1109 *look alway that ye finde* [J, H₃] loke alwey ȝe fynde [Cp, Cl, H₂] loke þat ȝe alwey fynde [Gg]

1113 *For which I come to tell you new tidinges* This is a vexed line, and the MSS have a number of solutions to its problems: ffor which I come telle ȝow newe tydynges [Cp, H₁]; For whi come I to telle yow tidynges [J]; For which I am come to telle yow newe tidynges [Cl]; For which come y to telle ȝow tydynges [H₂, Gg]; For wyche I come. to bringe you tydinges [H₃]. The line in the present text is an attempt to reconcile these variant readings and preserve the meter

1119 *spake there no man* [J] spak. no man [Cp, Cl, H₁, H₃] wordis no man [H₂, Gg]

1154 *it* [Cp omits]

1181 *she took him by* [J, H₂, H₃, Gg] [Cp, Cl, H₁ omit him]

1185 *after anon* after Noon [all MSS]

1205 *Yea, for aught I kan* The MSS read *Ye, for I kan . . .* but this jars with her protestations, and with the next line: *And eek I noot . . .* One MS of no authority offers *Full febly can I write,* which seems a scribe's effort to rectify the apparent contradiction. Strangely, editors have overlooked the problem. A possible emendation would be *for I ne kan;* in such colloquial speech it would scan. Our emendation makes sense in the context, is idiomatic (cf. *LGW* 1611), and, with emphasis falling naturally on "I," scans *"Yéa, for aught I kan so wríten," quód she thó . . .*

1227 *into the streete* [H₁, H₂, H₃, Gg] into Strete [Cp, J] into a strete [Cl]

1231 *did a thing* dide thing

1240 *played the tyrant* [J, H₂, H₃, Gg] [Cp, Cl, H₁ omit the]

1245 *hardnesse* hardynesse

1259 *And up* A up

1327 *the* tho

1345 *his* [Cp omits]

1349 *gestes* [H₁, H₃, Gg] gostes [Cp] gistes [J, Cl] gyltes [H₂]. Recent editors have adopted *gistes* (chances) for *gestes* (deeds) on the strength of two good MSS; but *gistes*= either "casts of the dice" (a word not found in Old French or English), or "stopping places on a journey" (a sense not recorded in English until the sixteenth century). See Baugh's note

1361 *stinten all* stynten and **al**

1375 *ruth* [Cp omits]

1379 *What* [J, H₁, H₂, H₃, Gg] That [Cp, Cl]

1383 *doth it come* [H₃] doth it to come [Cp, Cl, H₁] makith it/come [J] doþ it þan fal [H₂] makiþ it to falle [Gg]

1400 *it* [Cp omits]

1424 *Yis* [Cl, J, H₂, Gg] this [Cp, H₁] sir yis [H₃]

1573 *therewithal he gan* therwith gan

1584 *yet* that

1585 *up with pris* [J, H₂, Gg] with pris [Cp, Cl, H₁, H₃]

1602 *If it your* [J, H₂, Gg] If ʒoure [Cp, Cl, H₁, H₃]

1614 *quod he* [Cp omits]

1663 *you tell* [J, H₂, H₃] me telle [Cp, Cl, H₁] it telle [Gg]

1690 *Or* [H₁, H₂, H₃, Gg] O [Cp, Cl, J]

1691 *that* [Cp omits]

1726 *Avising well* Although the best MSS and most recent editions read *Avysed-wel* [Cp, Cl, J, H₁], there is some MS support for the present rather than the past participle (e.g., H₂). The latter construction makes for difficult and unusual syntax, whereas the present participle would better suit the progression of Pandarus and Criseyde into the house: *inward with him she wente,/ Avising well* . . . Cf. III.155–57: "With that she gan her eyen on him caste/ Full eesily and full debonairly,/ Avising her . . ."

1749 *Less time y-lost* A vexed phrase. Cp, Cl, J, and H₁ read *Las tyme Iloste*, and a number of recent editors, on the authority of three MSS and Thynne's edition, have preferred *lest* to *las* ("less"). That is, they interpret the phrase to mean "Lest time be lost." There is no unanimity on *y-lost* either: two MSS have *is ylost*, two *is lost*, and two, along with Thynne, *be lost*. Such readings are unnecessary if the phrase *Less time y-lost* is understood as an elliptical construction—"(Let there be) less wasted time!"—reinforcing Pandarus's other injunctions to Criseyde: *Come off* (lines 1738, 1742, 1750)

BOOK III

11 *Thee feel* They fele [Cl feld]

17 *Commeveden* Comended

17 *him* Though the MSS read *hem* (suggesting that Venus made amorous "all things that live and be"), it makes better sense to understand Jove as the direct object of both *commeveden* and *made*; that is, Venus first incited Jove and then made

him amorous. Boccaccio's Italian óriginal supports *him* rather
than *hem*: "Tu Giove prima . . ./ Movesti, o bella dea; e man-
sueto/ Sovente il rende all' opere noiose/ Di noi mortali"

28 *him* The MSS (with the exception of H₂) read *it*, but as
with the *him* of line 17, most recent editors emend *it* to *him*.
If we understand *it* as the direct object of *sendeth* (and in
apposition to *joyes*), the plural, *hem*, would be appropriate

30 *Ye* The

49 *To which gladness, who* [J, H₂] [Cp, Cl, H₁, H₃ omit glad-
ness]. Gg lacks lines 1–56 of Book III

62 *See* So

65 *Aaah* The MSS render this blissful ejaculation in several
ways: Ha a [Cp, H₁] ha.a.a [J, Gg] Aha [Cl, H₂, H₃]

73 *do* de

83 *And sire* And fro

104 *you* [Cp omits]

119 *ere ye wende* [H₃, Gg] er that ȝe wende [Cp, Cl, H₁] or
we wende [J, H₂]

136 *And I to han* [J, H₂, H₃, Gg] [Cp, Cl, H₁ omit I]

173 *N'I nill* [J, H₁=Ny] Ne I nyl [Cl, Gg] Ne nyl [Cp] Ne
I wyl [H₂] Nyl [H₃]

183 *his* [Cp omits]

193 *and oon* an oon

194 *And two* And to

217 *Commended, that it joye* The scribes tried to resolve
the problems posed by this line in a number of ways: Comen-
dede Ioye [Cp] Commendeden/ it Ioye [J, Cl, H₁, H₃] Comen-
did it was joy [H₂] Comendenyt joye [Gg]. The present read-
ing occurs in a single MS [S₁]

234 *in short withouten wordes mo* on short withouten
wordes no

258 *gentilesse* [Cl, J] gentileste [Cp, H₁] gentylnesse [H₃,
Gg] gentilnes to [H₂]

295 *all shall been* [Cl, J, H₂, H₃, Gg] al ben shal [Cp, H₁]

299 *enough* [Cp omits]

445 *he missed* [J, H₁, H₂, H₃] hym missed [Cp, Cl, Gg]

450 *That in this while* [Cl, H₂, H₃] That in this which [Cp,
H₁] This mene while [J]

468 *she thought* [Cl, H₁, H₂, H₃, Gg] he thought [Cp] hir
thoght [J]

470 *this process* his processe

510 *fulfille* Thynne emends *fulfille* to *fulfelle* to rhyme with
telle in line 511. Skeat observes that *fulfelle* is a Kentish form;

and a number of recent editors follow Thynne and Skeat in adopting *fulfelle*. Perhaps the pronunciation of *fulfille* was close to *fulfelle*, in which case the issue is merely an eye rhyme

525 *an* [Cl, H₁, H₂, H₃] and [Cp, J, Gg]

527 *every pie* euere pie

535 *hereupon eek made greet* [Cl, H₁, H₃] here vp made grete [Cp] here vpon eke/ maad his [J, H₂] vp on here mad his [Gg]

557 *him* [Cp omits]

561 *which* swich

576 *when he* [J, H₁, H₃, Gg] whan that he [Cp, Cl, H₂]

586 *avise him* This is the reading of Cp, Cl, H₁, and recent editions, referring to what Criseyde beseeched Pandarus to do; i.e., "to be ware . . . and [to] well *avise him*." J has *wel auyse hem*, which could be the correct reading, referring to what the "goosish people" do; i.e., they "dream things which never were, and well *avise hem* whom he brought there"

605 *alle joy* a Ioie

617 *O Fortune* .of. fortune

623 *At the goddes' will* So Cp, H₁, and the *gamma* MSS (according to Root). Cl, J, H₂, H₃, Gg, and most recent editions read *The goddes wil*, which is interpreted as the subject of *execut* (line 622); *all* thus becomes an adverb. But the more authoritative reading makes the best sense: "But all was executed, irrespective of her desires, at the gods' will"

715 *And if* [H₁, H₂, H₃, Gg] As if [Cp] An if [Cl, J]

716 *of Mars* O Mars

722 *O Jove* [J, H₁, H₂, H₃, Gg] Ioue [Cp, Cl]

743 *gan to route* [Cl, H₂, H₃] kan to route [Cp, H₁] gan it route [J] be-gan to route [Gg]

758 *how thus unwist* [J, H₂, Gg] [Cp, Cl, H₁, H₃ omit thus]

765 *cause to divine* cause for to deuyne

775 *an houve* [Cl, H₁, H₃] in howue [Cp] at howue [J] a howe [H₂] a houe [Gg]

827 *he wot* [Cl, J, H₂, H₃, Gg] ȝe wot [Cp, H₁]

876 *if ye that been* [Cl, J, Gg] if ȝe ben [Cp, H₁, H₂] ye that bene [H₃]

892 *might a dede man* [Cl] myht dede men [rest]

894 *heed is* hedes

917 *all* [Cp omits]

928 *I hadde grace for to* [Cl, H₃] ich a grace hadde for to [Cp] ich hadde a grace to [J] ich grace had for to [H₁] y had grace to [H₂] I hadde to [Gg]

931 *At dulcarnon* [J, H₃, Gg] A dulcarnoun [Cp, Cl, H₁] At Bulcarnon [H₂]

936 *This said* This is seyde

941 *for the love* [Cp omits the]

944 *I honour may have* I may haue honour

977 *other* [Cp omits]

1018 *hir injure* So Cp, H₁, and H₃. Cl, J, and Gg read *here injure*, which could mean "their injury," "injury to them," or "injury here" (i.e., in the world, here on earth). H₂ has the corrupt *her hure*

1024–25 Cp has gaps in the MS. Cl provides the copy-text for these lines

1037 *some* seme

1054 *Troilus was* Troilus I was

1081 *might he sayn* [Cp omits he]

1131 *herte's* [Cl, J, H₂, H₃, Gg] herte [Cp, H₁]

1136 *This light nor I* [Cl, H₁] This light ner I [Cp] I nor this candel [J] þis liȝt nece I [H₂] This lyght and I [H₃] þis liȝt ne I [Gg]

1142 *it* [Cp omits]

1157 *He must* [Cl, J, H₂, H₃, Gg] Hym most [Cp, H₁]

1165 *wrought* [J, H₂, Gg] bought [Cp, Cl, H₁, H₃]. Cf. III. 1503

1192 *it* [Cl, J, H₂, H₃, Gg] hym [Cp, H₁]

1193 *but* [Cp omits]

1208 *boot is noon* bote is ther non

1211 *ywis* I was

1228 This line is missing in Cp. Cl is the copy-text

1252 *thousand times* [H₂, H₃] thousand tyme [Cp, Cl, H₁, J] þousent siþis [Gg]

1286 *So thinketh, though that* [J, H₂] So thynk that though that [Cp, H₁] So þenk þowgh þat [Cl] So thinketh. though [H₃] So þynkiþ þat [Gg]

1291 *As thus I meen, he will* This is the emendation favored by Skeat and most recent editors. The MSS read: As thus I mene ȝe wol [Cp; H₁ þis for thus] As thus/ he wol þat [J] As þus I mene þat ye [Cl] As thus he wyll. how that [H₂, H₃] As þus I mene wil ȝe [Gg]. Cp's reading, while preserving the meter, does not make good sense since Troilus explains why God has created him; namely, to serve Criseyde and to act according to her guidance

1294 *so that I through* [J, H₁] so that thorugh [Cp, Gg] so þurgh [Cl] This line is defective in H₂ and H₃

1299 *N'I will not* [J, H₂, H₃, Gg=Ne I] Ny wol [Cp, H₁; Cl Ne I wole]

1357 *is, sooth, to* is soth is to

1375 *crecche* Root's emendation (Gg gives *crache* but rhymes it with *wreche*). Cp, H₁, H₂, and H₃ read *tecche* (= "find fault"), J has *kechche* and Cl has *kecche*

1380 *so that they* [Cl, J, Gg] [Cp, H₁, H₂, H₃ omit that]

1385 *ther God* that god

1404 *in a newe joy* [Cp omits a]

1436 *too* so

1438 *and thine unkinde vice* [Cl, H₁, H₂, Gg] and vnkynde vice [Cp]. For lines 1438–39 J and H₃ read: ffor thow so downward hasteth of malice./ The corse/ and to oure emyspye bynde [H₃ emysperie]

1473 *mine* [Cp omits]

1474 *shall I go* [Cl] shall I so [Cp, H₁, H₂, H₃] schal I so go [Gg]

1486 *Yet* [J, H₂, H₃, Gg] [Cp, Cl, H₁ omit]

1552 *he* [Cl, J, H₂, H₃, Gg] she [Cp, H₁]

1553 *eft* ofte

1576–82 Cp omits. Cl is the copy-text for these lines

1578 *gan to* [J, H₁, H₂, H₃, Gg] gan for to [Cl]

1593 *wold of* [J, H₁, H₂, H₃, Gg] wold out of [Cp, Cl]

1595 *and gan* [Cl, J, H₂, H₃, Gg] he gan [Cp, H₁]

1608 *And that I thus am heres* [Cl, H₁] And that I Troilus am hires [Cp] And þat I thus am hyrs [J, H₂] Than that I am heers [H₃] And þat I am þus ȝouris [Gg]

1612 *For which* [Cl, J, H₂, H₃, Gg] ffor whi [Cp, H₁]

1643 *stere* Root's choice, based upon three MSS (including H₃) and Caxton's edition. Recent editors adopt this reading. All MSS except H₃ have *tere* or *teere*

1675 *and eek of his* [J, H₂; Gg here for his] and of his [Cp, Cl, H₁] & his [H₃]

1681 *it to you* [Cp omits to]

1702 *Troilus: "Alas, now* [J, H₂, H₃, Gg] Troilus now [Cp, Cl, H₁]

1708 *him* [J, H₂, H₃, Gg] hire [Cp, H₁] here [Cl]

1718 *jousteth* Iolteth

1765 *is of* [Cl, J, H₂, H₃, Gg] of his [Cp, H₁]

1770 *him list* The MSS read *hem liste*, but the construction seems to be: *wolde I that he twiste . . . and that him list*

1771 *On hertes* [Cl, H₁, H₂, H₃] Or hertes [Cp] And hertes [J, Gg]

BOOK IV

57 *at Greeks' requeste* [Cl, H₂] a greke requeste [Cp, H₁]
But natheles a trewe was ther take./ At gret requeste [J] at his
Requeste [H₃]. Gg lacks lines III.1807–IV.112

69 *to doon* so don

72 *as it* and it

87 *I left* [J, H₃] I leeste [Cp, H₁] I loste [Cl, H₂]

127 *his tale* his olde tale

128 *Humble in speech* [Cl] Humble in his speche [Cp, H₁,
J, H₃, Gg] humblely his speche [H₂]

159 *First, how to* [Cl, H₁, H₃] ffor how to [Cp] ffirst to [J,
Gg] Ferst for to [H₂]

165 *ne do not so* [J, H₁, Gg] no nat so [Cp] do not so [Cl,
H₂, H₃]

191 *of folk* [J, H₂, Gg; H₃ folkis] to folk [Cp, Cl] tolk [H₁]

200 *let hem not discerne* [Cl, J, Gg] lat hem discerne [Cp,
H₂] ne lat hem disterne [H₁] let hem to dyscerne [H₃]

210 *here and howne* here howne

286 *gerful* serful

291 *that I so deer* [Cp omits I]

295 *shall I doon* [J, H₂, H₃, Gg] I may don [Cp, Cl, H₁]

299 *will I seen* wol seen

438 *traisen her* [Cl, J, H₃; Gg trostyn] traysen a wight [Cp,
H₁; H₂ truste]

462 *her for thy woe that care* [H₂] The scribes propose a
number of solutions to the problems of this line. Cp and H₁
make no sense: Now foul falle hire for thi wo and care. J's
reading is syntactically cumbersome: Now fowle falle hir þat
for thy wo þat care. The Cl scribe emends a similar variant to:
Now fowle falle here þat for þi wo hath [in a "corrector's
hand"] care. H₃ reads the same as Cl but offers *has* rather than
hath. Gg has: Now foule falle hire for þyn wo þat care; and
this reading, as expressed in H₂, best represents, I think,
Chaucer's intentions. I believe Chaucer originally meant, "Now
[let] evil fall on her who cares for thy woe," but the *gamma*
scribes misconstrued the syntax of the last part of the line to
be "on account of thy woe and care." Cf. IV.630: "The devil
speede him that recche!"

469 *lightly* wightly

470 *my* [Cp omits]

478 *shold a lesse paine* [Cl, J, H₃] sholde lasse peyne [Cp,
H₁] shulde/ Allas peyne [H₂] schulde allas pleyne [Gg]

491–532 Missing in Cp. Cl, checked against J and H₁, is the copy-text for these lines

510 *in teeres* [J, H₁] yn þis teris [Cl]

520 *licour out of a lambik* [J, H₁] [Cl omits out]

525 *unto him saye* [J, H₁] vn-to it seye [Cl]

527 *thee list mine arguments to blame* [J, H₁] ȝow list myn argumentȝ blame [Cl]

530 *Go* [H₁, H₃, Gg] To [Cl, J, H₂]

535 *been* [Cp omits]

596 *It is no shame unto you, ne no vice* [H₁; Cl to for unto] It is no shame vnto ȝow no vice [Cp] It is no rape in my dom ne no vice [J, H₃] HIt is no shame to you more þan vise [H₂] It is no iape/ in myn dom ne vice [Gg]

668 *whe'r* The MSS and editions read *whan*, but since Calkas is alive in V.190ff., Criseyde's not caring *when* her father died makes no sense

670 *Yive* ȝe

708–14 Missing in Cp, Cl, and H₁. J is the copy-text for these lines

750 *from* [Cp omits]

751 *Down fell as shower in Aperil swithe* So Cp, Cl, H₁, H₂. In J, H₃, and Gg lines 750–52 read: The salte teeris from hir eyne tweyne./ Out ronne/ as shoure in april swithe./ Hire white breste she bet/ and for the peyne. The entire stanza (lines 750–56) in these MSS occurs after line 735. Gg and two MSS have *aprille ful swyþe*, and most recent editors insert *ful*; but the line is decasyllabic without the insertion

776 *out* [Cp omits]

854 *This that by me* [J, H₃, Gg] This message which by me [Cp, H₁] This/ which by me [Cl] The whiche by me [H₂]

858 *What* Than

867 *In her, and eek her* [Cl, H₂] On hire an ek hire [Cp; H₁ and] In hir and other [J, H₃, Gg]

869 *two a purpre* [Cl, J, H₂, H₃] two purpre [Cp, H₁, Gg]

910 *herte beeteth* [H₃, Gg] herte he beteth [rest]

931 *Bet* But

957 *lorn, so wailaway* [J] [rest omit so]. Gg lacks lines 953–1078

997 *thus* this

1044 *this* the

1080 *of all this thing the soothfastnesse* [H₁, H₃, Gg] of al thyng the sothefastnesse [Cp] of al this thing sothfastnesse [J] of alle þinge þe sothfastnesse [Cl, H₂]

1107 *of that I shall thee saye* [H₂] of that I shal seye [Cp]

what þat I shal the seye [J] of þat þat I shal seye [Cl] of al þat
I shall seye [H₁] what I shal the sey [H₃] what I schal þe say
[Gg]

1120 *thy* [Cl, J, H₂, H₃] this [Cp, H₁, Gg]

1137 *as is* [Cl, H₁, H₂, H₃, Gg] as in [Cp, J]·

1165 *none find in nothing on* [Cl, H₁, H₂] non fynde noth-
yng of [Cp] non fynde in no cas on [J] not fynde/ in no cas
on [H₃; Gg of for on]

1205 *I leeve* [Cl, Gg leue] I lyue [Cp, J, H₁, H₂, H₃]

1216 *Cypride* [J, H₂] Cupide [rest]

1223 *that* [Cp omits]

1240 *which* [Cp omits]

1268 *Sooth is, the woe the which that* [H₁, H₂] Swich is the
wo that [Cp] Soth is that wo the which þat [J, Gg] Soth is þe
wo whiche þat [Cl] Swych is woo/ that [H₃]

1303 *The sooth is this: that twinning* [J] The soth is the
twynnyng [Cp] The soþe is þat þe twynnynge [Cl] The sothe
þe twynynge [H₁] Such is þis þe twinnyng [H₂] To sothe is
that/ the [t]wynnyng [H₃] þe soþe þis is þat twynnyng [Gg]

1319 *By God, lo, right anon* [J, over erasure; Cl, H₁] lo
right anon [Cp] be god riȝt A noon [H₂, H₃] lo hasteliche
a-non [Gg]

1339 *so* [Cp omits]

1344 *Us needed for my wending nought to care* [Cl, H₂; J
going for wending] Us nedeth for my wendyng nought care
[Cp; H₁ neded for nedeth] Vs nedyth not for my wendyng for
to care [H₃] Vs nedith not for myn goinge to care [Gg]

1360 *there never peece* ther pees neuere

1373 *that hard it is* [J, H₂, H₃, Gg] that ful harde it is [Cp,
Cl, H₁]

1374 *and the wether* [Cp omits the]

1388–1409 Missing in Cp. Cl, checked against J and H₁, is
the copy-text for these lines

1391 *freendes that I have* [J, H₁] frendes ich haue [Cl]

1394 *So what for oo thing and for other* [J, H₁] So þat for
oþer þing and for oþer [Cl]

1397 *Apollo, or his* [H₁, H₂, H₃, Gg] Apollo and or [Cl, J]

1399 *blende* [J, H₃] blynde [Cl, H₁, H₂, Gg]. The rhyme is
with *ende* (line 1400)

1447 *deeth* [Cp omits]

1511 *it* [Cl, J, H₂, H₃, Gg] [Cp, H₁ omit]

1535 *for other* [J, H₂] for any other [Cp] of oþer [Cl] of
any other [H₁, Gg] or other [H₃]

1541 *this* thus
1697 *The* [J, H₁, H₂, H₃] This [Cp, Cl]. IV.1667–V.35 are lacking in Gg

BOOK V

9 *beemes cleene* [J] bemes clere [Cp, Cl, H₁, H₃] bemes shene [H₂]

12 *the son of Hecuba* the sone I Troilus of Ecuba

16 *host to leede* [J, H₁, H₂, H₃] oost for to lede [Cp, Cl]

25 *was the soothfast crop* [Cl, J, H₂] was sothefast crop [Cp, H₁; H₃ Rote for crop]

42 *drie* [Cl, J, H₂, H₃, Gg] crye [Cp, H₁]

82 *she* he

88 *son of Tydeus* sone Diomede of Tideus

115 *pain and all* [Cl, H₁] peyne al [Cp] herte and al [J, H₂, H₃, Gg]

211 *walloweth* [Gg= walwith] weyleth [Cp, Cl, H₁, H₂, H₃] whieleth [J]

212 *as doth he Ixion in helle* [Cl, H₁] as dothe he in helle [Cp] as dostow Ixion in helle [J] as doth þe Ixion in hell [H₂] as dothe/ the Tucius in helle [H₃] as thow he laye in helle [Gg "by corrector"]

242 *she eek susteene* [J, H₂, Gg; H₃ ye for she] she this ustene [Cp, Cl, H₁]

243 *pale, and greene* [Cl, J, H₂, H₃, Gg] pale grene [Cp, H₁]

268 *his pine* in pyne

289 *all night for sorrow* for sorwe al nyght

319 *eek* [Cp omits]

436 *largesse* [J, H₂, H₃, Gg] prowesse [Cp, Cl, H₁]

446 *herde* [Cp omits]

464 *no wight* [Cl, J] nought [Cp, H₁] no man [H₂, H₃, Gg]

466 *here* [J, H₁, H₂, H₃, Gg] there [Cp, Cl]

468 *nas* nat

480 *that* [Cp omits]

509 *japed thus and playde* Iaped thus and seyde [Cp, Cl, H₁, J, Gg] Iaped he þus & pleyde [H₂] Iapith forthe And pleyde [H₃]. Though the *gamma* form with *seyde* could be correct, referring to what Pandarus says to himself (lines 507–08), the variant *pleyde* makes better sense together with *japed*. It is

possible that the *seyde* of line 509 is an early, erroneous scribal
repetition of the *seyde* of line 506

513 *off horse* [Cp omits]

514 *han* [Cp omits]

532 *gan to falle* [Cp omits to]

541 *y-light* [H₃] ihight [rest]

547 *of houses* of paleis

552 *Thy* [Cl, J, H₂, H₃] The [Cp, H₁] þese [Gg]

565 *last* [J, H₂, H₃, Gg] myn owene [Cp, Cl, H₁]

583 *in my memorye* [J, H₂, H₃, Gg] [Cp, Cl, H₁ omit my]

626 *that* [Cp omits; H₁ at for that]

733 *tho yonder* the yonder

739 *Who might* we myghte

742 *unto the grave* to graue

780 *never* euere

783 *it nought ne greeveth* [Cl, J, H₂, H₃] naught it ne gre-
ueth [Cp, H₁] ʒiftys he ʒeuyth [Gg]

836 *his time* this tyme

867 *him tho* hym so

885 *Fro thennes* [Cl] ffor thennes [Cp, H₁] Ne thennes [J]
Neuyr thens [H₂] Nor thennes [H₃, Gg]

885 *one on live* oon lyue

932 *if* of

991 *thenne* [Cp omits]

1060 *word* [H₁, H₂, H₃, Gg] wood [Cp, Cl, J]

1125 *twinnen* [Cl, J] winnen [Cp, H₁, H₂, H₃] wyndyn [Gg]

1140 *I* [Cp omits]

1153 *when she com'th* [J, H₂, H₃, Gg] whan that she comth
[Cp, Cl, H₁]

1175 *all that that thou* [Cl, J] al that thou [rest]

1215 *die* dyne

1228 *so* [Cp omits]

1233–74 Missing in Cp. Cl, checked against J and H₁, is the
copy-text for these lines

1272 *to plaine* [J, H₁] compleyne [Cl]

1275 *while* whiles

1277 *beguile* bigiles [H₁ rhymes bigiles with while of line
1275]

1324 *Liketh it you* [Cl, Gg] Liketh you [Cp, H₁, J, H₂] And
like it you [H₃]

1327 *of which yet boote* [Cl, J, H₂, H₃; Gg but for boote] of
which boot [Cp, H₁]

1367 *wight* [Cl, H₂, H₃, Gg] wit [Cp, J]. H₁ lacks V.1345–
1428

1393 *That deeth* [J, H₃, Gg] There deth [Cp, Cl] The deth [H₂]

1413 *me may* [Cl, J, H₂, H₃, Gg] may me [Cp]

1414 *I* [Cp omits]

1483 *you* [Cp omits]

1484 *for* [Cp omits]

1502–3 *And how Ipomedon in litel stounde/ Was dreint, and deede Parthonope of wounde* This is the reading of recent editions, for it was Hippomedon who drowned. H₁ perhaps comes closest to this reading: And how ypomedon in litel stounde/ was dreint/ and ded parthonopo of wounde [H₂ omits of] And how ypomedoun a litel stounde/ was dreynt and dede Parthonope of wownde [Cp] And how ypomedon with blody wownde./ And ek Parthonope in litel stownde./ Ben slayn [J; Gg omits ek] And ypomedon y lytel stounde./ was dreynt and ded Parthonope of wounde [Cl] And how ypomedon/ in litel stounde/ was dede And dreynt/ parthenope of wounde [H₃]

1567 *for unreste* [Cp omits for]

1588 *touching all this* [J, H₁, H₂, H₃, Gg] touchyng this [Cp, Cl]

1628 *Ne never yet ne coud I* [Cl, H₁] Ne neuere ȝet koude I [Cp, H₃] Ny neuere yit koude ek [J] Ne neuer I coude I [H₂] Ne neuere ȝit ne couþe [Gg]

1630 *not the letters'* [Cl, H₂, Gg; J lettre for letters] nat lettres [Cp, H₁, H₃]

1641 *that* [Cp omits]

1726 *freende's* frende

1779 *N'I* [= Ny or Ne I] Ne

1782 *wit* [Cp omits]

1791 *passe* [Cl] space [Cp, J, H₁, H₂, H₃]. Gg lacks lines V.1702–869

1795 *So pray I God* [Cl] So prey I to god [Cp, H₁, H₂] So prey to god [J, H₃]

1796 *Ne thee mismetre* Ne the this mysmetre

1798 *God I beseeche* [H₁, H₃] god biseche [Cp, Cl, J] god I þe beseche [H₂]

1809 *eighthe sphere* [J= viij speere] seuenthe spere [Cp, Cl, H₁, H₃]. H₂ omits lines 1807–22

1857 *to thee, philosophical Strode* [J] to Philosophical strode [Cp] and the Philosophical Strode [Cl, H₁] to þi sophistical stroode [H₂] to thy Philosofical Strode [H₃]

Short Poems

Adam Scrivain

There is only one MS: Shirley's R. 3. 20, Trinity College, Cambridge. The text here is based on a transcription of this MS by F.J. Furnivall for the Chaucer Society in *A Parallel-Text Edition of Chaucer's Minor Poems*, Chaucer Soc. Pubs., First Ser. Nos. 21, 57, 58 (London: N. Trübner, 1871–87), p. 177. The poem is printed without emendation. Skeat omits *for* in line 2, *long* in line 3, and *more* in line 4 because he finds them superfluous and damaging to the prosody, but those lines can be scanned as endecasyllabic without the omissions.

The Complaint of Venus

There are eight MSS and one edition with MS status. The Chaucer Society has divided the MSS into three groups: *alpha*, *beta*, and *gamma*, with *beta* yielding the best text. The MSS are as follows: *alpha*—Shirley's MS R. 3. 20, Trinity College Cambridge (R); Shirley's Ashmole MS 59, Bodleian Library Oxford (A); *beta*—Tanner MS 346, Bodleian (T); Fairfax MS 16, Bodleian (F); *gamma*—MS Ff. 1. 6, University Library, Cambridge (Ff); Archbishop Selden B. 24, Bodleian (S); edition of Julian Notary, 1499–1501 (N); Pepys 2006 (Hand B), Magdalene College, Cambridge, Cambridge (Pb); and Pepys 2006 (Hand E), Magdalene College (Pe). F is here the copy-text as transcribed by Furnivall in *A Parallel-Text Print of Chaucer's Minor Poems*, pp. 412–17, and in his *A Supplementary Parallel-Text Edition of Chaucer's Minor Poems*, Chaucer Soc. Pubs. No. 59 (London: N. Trübner, 1880), pp. 158–60. Variants from F are noted below.

9 *bountee, wisdom, governaunce* [T] bounte/ wysdom and gournaunce [F, R, A, N] wisdoom bounte gouernaunce [Ff, S] beaute wysdam and gouernaunce [Pb]. Pe lacks lines 1–44

26 *aby thy* [T, R, A, N] bye the [F] abye the [Ff, Pb] aby a [S]

27 *fasting* [R, A, Ff, S, N, Pb] fasten [F, T]

30 *hew* [R, A, S, Pb] visage [F, T, Ff, N]. The latter reading is probably an early scribal repetition of *visage* in the previous line

31 *Plain* The MSS read *Pley(e)* uniformly but, as Skeat and Robinson both note, the corresponding word in the French poem is "*plaindre*," to complain. *Pley* makes little sense in this context

33 *be hanged* [Ff, S, N, Pb] he hanged [F] y-hanged [T]. For line 33 R reads: þaughe Ialousye wer hanged by a Kable. A omits lines 33–40

56 *ne shall I never* [R, A, Pb] shal I neuer [F, Ff, N, Pe] shall I me neuyr [T] that schall I neuer [S]. F reads *ne shall* in line 64 but not in line 72

64 *him* [T, R, A, S, Pe] yow [F, Ff, N, Pb]. F reads *him* in lines 56 and 72

66 *thee* [R, A, Ff, S] yow [F, T]. For line 66 N reads: That loue to the/ soo byghe a grace hath sente. Pe has: That loue to þe so hy A grace sent. Pb lacks lines 65–72

70 *I* [A, R, Ff, S, N, Pe] ye [F, T]

73 *Princess* All but R and A read *Princes*. The reading *Princess* supports the hypothesis that Chaucer wrote this poem for Isabel, Duchess of York

To Rosemounde

MS Rawlinson Poet. 163, Bodleian Library, Oxford, is unique. The text printed here is based upon the revisions of Skeat offered by Helge Kökeritz in "Chaucer's *Rosemounde*," *MLN*, 63(1948), 310–18. Kökeritz observes that in line 21—printed, normalized, and emended by Skeat to "My love may not refreyd be nor afounde"—the word *be*, which is above the line and before *refreyde* in the MS, is in a different and later hand from that of the rest of the text.

Against Woman Unconstant

There are three MSS: Fairfax 16, Bodleian (F); Harley 7578, British Museum (H); and Cotton Cleopatra D. vii, British Museum (C). Furnivall transcribes C for the Chaucer

Society in *Odd Texts of Chaucer's Minor Poems*, Part 2, Chaucer Soc. Pubs., First Ser. No. 60 (London: N. Trübner, 1880), Appendix, p. xiii. The present text is based upon Furnivall's transcription of C and is checked against the editions and Textual Notes of Skeat and Robinson. Departures from C are noted below.

4 *have live's* [F] to lyve haue [C]
6 *thing your lust is ay* [F] thinges your lust is Euer [C]
8 *mirrour nothing* [F] Mirrour, that nothing [C]

Merciless Beautee

MS Pepys 2006, Magdalene College, Cambridge, is unique. The present text is based upon Furnivall's transcription for the Chaucer Society in *More Odd Texts of Chaucer's Minor Poems*, First Ser. No. 77 (London: Kegan Paul, Trench, Trübner & Co., 1886), pp. 51–52.

1 *Your eyen two* The MS reads *Yowre two yen*, but lines 6 and 11 have *Your eyen two*, which is metrically superior

36 *there* MS *this*. *Ther* is Skeat's emendation (from Percy), and Robinson adopts it

Womanly Noblesse

MS Additional 34360, British Museum, is unique. The present text is based upon Skeat.

10 *do you this* The MS has *do this*. The emendation is Skeat's, and Robinson adopts it

13 This line is missing in the MS. Skeat suggests: "I pray yow, do to me som daliaunce"; Furnivall: "Taketh me, lady, in your obeisaunce"; MacCracken: "Take my service in gre, and nat grevaunce."

16 *And look how humblely* The MS has *And how humbly*. Both *look* and *humblely* are Skeat's emendations. The expansion of *humbly* to *humblely* for metrical purposes is in accordance with Chaucer's regular practice

22 *doon* Skeat's emendation; MS= *do*

30 *mine* Skeat's emendation; MS= *my*. As with *doon* (line

22), *mine* before a vowel accords with Chaucer's regular practice

Scogan

There are three MSS: Gg. 4. 27, Cambridge University Library (Gg); Fairfax 16, Bodleian (F); Pepys 2006, Magdalene College, Cambridge (P). The Chaucer Society prints all three versions, transcribed by Furnivall, in *A Parallel-Text Edition of Chaucer's Minor Poems*, pp. 421–22. The present text is based upon Furnivall's transcription of F; departures from F are noted below.

8 *it shape* [Gg, P] yshape [F]
27 *our* [Gg, P] youre [F]
28 *ne* [Gg, P] nor [F]
35 *olde* [Gg, P] tholde [F]

Glossary of Basic Words

Accorden *v* agree

Al *conj* although; even if

Alday *adv* constantly, everyday

Algate(s) *adv* at least

Als *adv* also

Also . . . as as . . . as

An, and *conj* if

Anon *adv* immediately

Apaid *pp* pleased; *evil apaid* displeased

Atones *adv* at once; once and for all

Avis *subst* advice, counsel; *avisement* deliberation

Avisen *v* consider; *aviseth you* think it over; *unavised* unaware

Ay *adv* ever; always

Been *v* to be; *sg* am, art, is; *pl* are, been; *pt* was, were(n); *imp sg* be; *imp pl* beeth; *pp* been, y-be(en); *neg* nis; *pt neg* nas, nere

Behest *subst* promise, vow (also *heste*)

Behete *v* to promise; *pt* behight(e)

Bet *adj & adv* better

Bisiness *subst* task; diligence; *doon . . . bisiness* to exert oneself, take pains

Blende *v* to deceive, blind; *pt s* blente; *pp* blent, y-blent

Blive *adv* quickly; *as* (or, *also*) *blive* as soon as possible

Brennen *v* to burn; *pp* brend, brent, y-brent

But *adv & conj* but; only, unless, except; *but as* except that; *but if* unless

Buxom *adj* obedient, gracious

Cas *subst* event, happening; circumstance; accident; *par cas, upon cas* by chance

Casten *v* to decide, determine, plan

Certes *adv* certainly

Cheer *subst* face, look; manner; gladness

Clepen *v* to call, name; recall; *pp* cleped, clept, y-cleped

Devise (n) *v* to decide; relate, set forth, talk; imagine

Digne *adj* worthy; proud, haughty

322